Praise for **HUNTER'S RUN**

"A remarkably smooth adventure with
intriguing psychological underpinnings
. . . suspenseful and unpretentious."
San Francisco Chronicle Book Review

"[A] tense interspecies battle of wits with
tangy atmospherics and a bleak lesson
on the meaning of freedom. A."
Entertainment Weekly

"This novel provides solid escapism for those who love
adventures on strange planets; the detailed descriptions
of assorted aliens are especially fascinating."
Lansing State Journal

"This is smashing SF—a great manhunt story."
The Express

"This tightly written novel, with its
memorable protagonist and intriguing
extrapolation, delivers on all levels."
Publishers Weekly

"Suspenseful and absorbing."
Romantic Times BOOKreviews, 4 stars

Also by Daniel Abraham

The Long Price Quartet

A Shadow in Summer: Book One

A Betrayal in Winter: Book Two

An Autumn War: Book Three (forthcoming)

The Price of Spring: Book Four (forthcoming)

HUNTER'S RUN

GEORGE R. R. MARTIN
GARDNER DOZOIS
DANIEL ABRAHAM

An Imprint of HarperCollins*Publishers*

This book is a work of fiction. The characters, incidents, and dialogue are drawn from the author's imagination and are not to be construed as real. Any resemblance to actual events or persons, living or dead, is entirely coincidental.

A portion of this story was previously published on scifi.com as "Shadow Twin," copyright © 2004 by George R. R. Martin, Gardner Dozois, and Daniel Abraham.

EOS
An Imprint of HarperCollins*Publishers*
10 East 53rd Street
New York, New York 10022–5299

Copyright © 2008 by George R. R. Martin, Gardner Dozois, and Daniel Abraham
Afterword and Author Q & A copyright © 2007 by George R. R. Martin, Gardner Dozois, and Daniel Abraham
Map copyright © 2008 by HarperCollins Publishers
Map created by Andrew Ashton
Cover art by Stephen Martiniere
ISBN 978-0-06-137330-5
www.eosbooks.com

First Eos paperback printing: February 2009
First Eos hardcover printing: January 2008

HarperCollins® and Eos® are registered trademarks of Harper-Collins Publishers.

Printed in the U.S.A.

10 9 8 7 6 5 4 3 2

To Connie Willis,
who learned everything she knows
from Gardner and George and
taught it all to Daniel

Contents

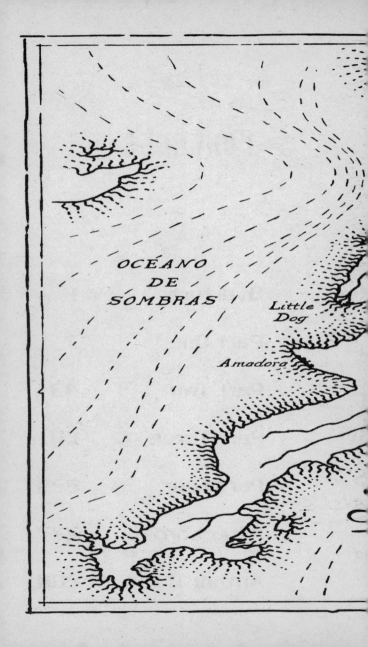

Sierra Hueso Mt.

Sawtooth Mt.

Fiddlers Jump

OCÉANO TÉTRICO

Diegotown

Nuevo Janeiro

SÃO PAULO

N

HUNTER'S
RUN

◄ Overture ►

Ramón Espejo awoke floating in a sea of darkness. For a moment, he was relaxed and mindless, drifting peacefully, and then his identity returned to him lazily, like an unwanted afterthought.

After the deep, warm nothingness, there was no pleasure in recalling who he was. Without coming fully awake, he nonetheless felt the weight of his own being settling on his heart. Despair and anger and the constant gnawing worry sounded in his mind like a man in the next room clearing his throat. For some blissful time, he had been no one, and now he was himself again. His first truly conscious thought was to deny the disappointment he felt at being.

He was Ramón Espejo. He was working a prospecting contract out of Nuevo Janeiro. He was . . . he was . . . Ramón Espejo.

Where he had expected the details of his life to rush in—what he had done last night, what he was to do today, what grudges he was nursing, what resentments had pricked him recently—the next thought simply failed him. He knew he was Ramón Espejo—but he did not know where he was. Or how he had got there.

Disturbed, he tried to open his eyes, and found that they were open already. Wherever he was, it was a totally lightless place, darker than the jungle night, darker than the deep caves in the sandstone cliffs near Swan's Neck.

Or perhaps he was blind.

That thought started a tiny spring of panic within him. There were stories of men who'd got drunk on cheap synthetic muscat or Sweet Mary and woke up blind. Had he done that? Had he lost that much control of himself? A tiny rivulet of fear traced a cold channel down his spine. But his head didn't hurt, and his belly didn't burn. He closed his eyes, blinking them hard several times, irrationally hoping to jar his vision back into existence; the only result was an explosion of bright pastel blobs across his retinas, scurrying colors that were somehow more disturbing than the darkness.

His initial sense of drowsy lethargy slid away from him, and he tried to call out. He felt his mouth moving slowly, but he heard nothing. Was he deaf, too? He tried to roll over and sit up, but could not. He lay back against nothing, floating again, not fighting, but his mind racing. He was fully awake now, but he still couldn't remember where he was, or how he had got there. Perhaps he was in danger: his immobility was both suggestive and ominous. Had he been in a mine cave-in? Perhaps a rockfall had pinned him down. He tried to concentrate on the feel of his body, sharpening his sensitivity to it, and finally decided that he could feel no weight or pressure, nothing actually pinioning him. *You might not feel anything if your spinal cord has been cut,* he thought with a flash of cold horror. But a moment's further consideration convinced him that it could not be so: he *could* move his body a little, although when he tried to sit up, something stopped him, pulled his spine straight, pulled his arms and shoulders back down from where he'd raised them. It was like moving through syrup, only the syrup pushed back, holding him gently, firmly, implacably in place.

He could feel no moisture against his skin, no air, no breeze, no heat or cold. Nor did he seem to be resting on anything solid. Apparently, his first impression had been correct. He was floating, trapped in darkness, held in place. He imagined himself like an insect in amber, caught fast in the gooey syrup that surrounded him, in which he seemed to be totally submerged. But how was he breathing?

He wasn't, he realized. *He wasn't breathing.*

Panic shattered him like glass. All vestiges of thought blinked out, and he fought like an animal for his life. He clawed the enfolding nothingness, trying to pull his way up toward some imagined air. He tried to scream. Time stopped meaning anything, the struggle consuming him entirely, so that he couldn't say how long it was before he fell back, exhausted. The syrup around him gently, firmly pulled him back precisely as he had been—back into place. He felt as if he should have been panting, expected to hear his blood pounding in his ears, feel his heart hammering at his chest—but there was nothing. No breath, and no heart-beat. No burning for air.

He was dead.

He was dead and floating on a vast dry sea that stretched away to eternity in all directions. Even blind and deaf, he could sense the immensity of it, of that measureless mid-night ocean.

He was dead and in Limbo, that Limbo that the Pope at San Esteban kept repudiating, waiting in darkness for the Day of Judgment.

He almost laughed at the thought—it was better than what the Catholic priest in the tiny adobe church in his little village in the mountains of northern Mexico had promised him; Father Ortega had often assured him that he'd go right to the flames and torments of Hell as soon as he died un-shriven—but he could not push the thought away. He had died, and this emptiness—infinite darkness, infinite still-ness, trapped alone with only his own mind—was what had always waited for him all his life, in spite of the blessings and benedictions of the Church, in spite of his sins and occa-sional semi-sincere repentance. None of it had made any dif-ference. Numberless years stretched before him with noth-ing but his own sins and failures to dwell upon. He had died, and his punishment was to be always and forever himself under the implacable, unseen eye of God.

But *how* had it happened? How had he died? His memory

seemed sluggish, unresponsive as a tractor's engine on a cold winter morning—hard to start and hard to keep in motion without sputtering and stalling.

He began by picturing what was most familiar. Elena's room in Diegotown with the small window over the bed, the thick pounded-earth walls. The faucets in the sink, already rusting and ancient though humanity had hardly been on the planet for more than forty years. The tiny scarlet skitterlings that scurried across the ceiling, multiple rows of legs flailing like oars. The sharp smells of iceroot and ganja, spilled tequila and roasting peppers. The sounds of the transports flying overhead, grinding their way up through the air and into orbit.

Slowly, the recent events of his life took shape, still as fuzzy as a badly aligned projection. He had been in Diegotown for the Blessing of the Fleet. There had been a parade. He had eaten roasted fish and saffron rice bought from a street vendor, and watched the fireworks. The smoke had smelled like a strip mine, and the spent fireworks had hissed like serpents as they plunged into the sea. A giant wreathed in flames, waving its arms in agony. Was that real? The smell of lemon and sugar. Old Manuel Griego had been talking about all his plans for when the Enye ships finally emerged from the jump to the colony planet São Paulo. He flushed with the sudden, powerful recollection of the scent of Elena's body. But that was before . . .

There had been a fight. He'd fought with Elena, yes. The sound of her voice—high and accusing and mean as a pit bull. He'd hit her. He remembered that. She'd screamed and clawed at his eyes and tried to kick him in the balls. And they'd made up afterward like they always did. Later, she had run her fingers along the machete scars on his arm as he fell into a sated sleep. Or was that another night? So many of their nights together ended like that . . .

There *had* been another fight, earlier still, with someone else . . . But his thoughts shied away from that like a mule might shy away from a snake on a path.

He'd left her before first light, sneaking out of her room heavy with the smell of sweat and sex while she was still asleep so he wouldn't have to talk to her, feeling the morning breeze cool against his skin. Flatfurs had scurried away from him as he walked down the muddy street, their alarm cries sounding like panicked oboes. He'd flown his van to the outfitter's station, because he was going . . . before they caught him . . .

His mind balked again. It was not the nauseating forgetfulness that seemed to have consumed his world, but something else. There was something his mind didn't want to recall. Slowly, gritting his teeth, he forced his memory to bend to his will.

He'd spent the day realigning two lift tubes in the van. Someone had been there with him. Griego, bitching about parts. And then he had flown off into the wastelands, the outback, *terreno cimarrón* . . .

But his van had exploded! Hadn't it? He suddenly remembered the van exploding, but he remembered seeing it from a distance. He hadn't been caught in the blast; nonetheless, the memory was thick with despair. The van's destruction was part of it, then, whatever *it* was. He tried to bring his focus to that moment—the brightness of the flame; the hot, sudden wind of the concussion . . .

Had his heart been beating, it would have stopped then in terror as memory returned.

He remembered now. And maybe dying and being in Hell would have been better.

Part One

Chapter 1

Ramón Espejo lifted his chin, daring his opponent to strike. The crowd that filled the alleyway behind the ramshackle bar called the El Rey formed a ring, bodies pressing against each other in the tension between coming close enough to see and retreating to a safe distance. Their voices were a mixture of shouts urging the two men to fight and weak, insincere exhortations to make peace. The big man bobbing and weaving across the narrow circle from him was a pale European, his cheeks flushed red from liquor, his wide, soft hands balled into fists. He was taller than Ramón, with a greater reach. Ramón could see the man's eyes shifting, as wary of the crowd as of Ramón.

"Come on, *pendejo*," Ramón said, grinning. His arms were raised and spread, as if he were ready to embrace the fighter. "You wanted power. Come have a taste of it."

The shifting LEDs of the bar's signs turned the night blue and red and amber in turn. Far above them all, the night sky shone with countless stars too bright and close for the lights of Diegotown to drown.

The constellation of the Stone Man stared down at them as they circled, a single star smoldering balefully like a red eye, as if it was watching, as if it was urging them on.

"I ought to do it, you ugly little greaser!" the European spat. "I ought to go ahead and kick your skinny ass!"

Ramón only bared his teeth and motioned the man nearer. The European wanted this to be a *talking* fight again, but it was too late for that. The voices of the crowd merged into a single waterfall roar. The European made his move, graceless as a falling tree; the great left fist made its slow way through the air, moving as though through molasses. Ramón stepped inside the swing, letting the gravity knife slip from his sleeve into his hand. He flicked the blade open in the same motion that brought his fist against the larger man's belly.

A look of almost comical surprise crossed the European's face. His breath went out of him with a *whoof.*

Ramón stabbed twice more, fast and hard, twisting the knife just to be sure. He was close enough to smell the nose-tingling reek of the flowery cologne the man wore, to feel his licorice-scented breath panting against his face. The crowd went silent as the European slipped to his knees and then sat, legs spread, in the filthy muck of the alley. The big, soft hands opened and closed aimlessly, slick with blood that turned pale when the LEDs were red, black when the light shifted blue.

The European's mouth gaped open, and blood gushed out over his teeth. Slowly, very slowly, seeming to move in slow motion, he toppled sideways to the ground. Kicked his feet, heels drumming the ground. Was still.

Someone in the crowd uttered an awed obscenity.

Ramón's shrill, self-satisfied pleasure faded. He looked at the faces of the crowd—wide eyes, mouths open in little surprised O's. The alcohol in his blood seemed to thin, sobriety floating to the top of his mind. A sinking sense of betrayal possessed him—these people had been pushing him on, *encouraging* the fight. And now they were abandoning him for winning it!

"What?" Ramón shouted to the other patrons of the El Rey. "You heard what he was saying! You saw what he did!"

But the alley was emptying. Even the woman who'd been with the European, the one who had started it all, was gone. Mikel Ibrahim, the manager of the El Rey, lumbered toward

him, his great bear-like face the image of patient, saintly
suffering. He held out his wide hand. Ramón lifted his chin
again, thrust out his chest, as if Mikel's gesture was an
insult. The manager only sighed and shook his head slowly
back and forth, and made a pulling gesture with his fingers.
Ramón curled his lip, half turned away, then slapped the
handle of the knife into the waiting palm.

"Police are coming," the manager warned. "You should
go home, Ramón."

"You saw what happened," Ramón said.

"No, I wasn't here when it happened," Mikel said. "And
neither were *you,* eh? Now go home. And keep your mouth
shut."

Ramón spat on the ground and stalked into the night. It
wasn't until he began to walk that he understood how drunk
he was. At the canal by the plaza, he squatted down, leaned
back against a tree, and waited until he was sure he could
walk without listing. Around him, Diegotown spent its
week's wages on alcohol and kaafa kyit and sex. Music tumbled in from the rough gypsy houseboats on the canal; fast,
festive accordion mixing with trumpets and steel drums and
the shouts of the dancers.

Somewhere in the darkness, a tenfin was calling mourn-
fully, a "bird" that was really a flying lizard, and sounded
uncannily like a woman sobbing in misery and despair,
something that had led the superstitious Mexican peasants
who made up a large percentage of the colony's population
to say that *La Llorona,* the Crying Woman, had crossed the
stars with them from Mexico and now wandered the night
of this new planet, crying not only for all the children who'd
been lost and left behind on Earth, but for all the ones who
would die on this hard new world.

He, of course, didn't believe in such crap. But as the
ghostly crying accelerated to a heartbreaking crescendo, he
couldn't help but shiver.

Alone, Ramón could regret stabbing the European;
surely it would have been enough just to punch him around,
humiliate him, slap him like a bitch? But when Ramón was
drunk and angry, he always went too far. Ramón knew that

he shouldn't have drunk so much, and that whenever he got around people, it always seemed to end like this. He'd begun his evening with the sick knot in his belly, which being in the city seemed to bring, and then by the time he'd drunk enough to untie that knot, as usual someone had said or done something to enrage him. It didn't always end with a knife, but it rarely ended well. Ramón didn't like it, but he wasn't ashamed of it either. He was a man—an independent prospector on a tough frontier colony world less than a generation removed from its founding. By God, he was a man! He drank hard, he fought hard, and anyone who had a problem with that would be wise to keep their *pinche* opinions to themselves!

A family of *tapanos*—small, raccoonlike amphibians with scales like a hedgehog's spikes—lumbered up from the water, considered Ramón with dark, shining eyes, and made their way toward the plaza, where they would scavenge for the dropped food and trash of the day. Ramón watched them pass, slick dark paths of canal water trailing behind them, then sighed and hauled himself to his feet.

Elena's apartment was in the maze of streets around the Palace of the Governors. It perched above a butcher's shop, and the air that came in the back window was often fetid with old gore. He considered sleeping in his van, but he felt sticky and exhausted. He wanted a shower and a beer and a plate of something warm to keep his belly from growling. He climbed the stairs slowly, trying to be quiet, but the lights were burning in her windows. A shuttle was lifting from the spaceport far to the north, tracking lights glowing blue and red as the vessel rose toward the stars. Ramón tried to cover the click and hiss of the door with the throbbing rumble of the shuttle's lift drive. But it was no use.

"Where the *fuck* have you been?" Elena yelled as he stepped inside. She wore a thin cotton dress with a stain on the sleeve. Her hair was tied back into a knot of black darker than the sky. Her teeth were bared in rage, her mouth almost square with it. Ramón closed the door behind him, and heard her gasp. In an instant, the anger had left her. He followed her gaze to where the European's blood had soaked the side of his shirt, the leg of his pants. He shrugged.

"We'll have to burn these," he said.

"Are you okay, *mi hijo*? What happened?"

He hated it when she called him that. He was no one's little boy. But it was better than fighting, so he smiled, pulling at the tongue of his belt.

"I'm fine," he said. "It was the other *cabrón* who took the worst of it."

"The police . . . will the police . . . ?"

"Probably not," Ramón said, dropping his pants around his knees. He pulled his shirt up over his head. "Still, we should burn these."

She asked no more questions, only took his clothes out to the incinerator that the apartments on the block all shared, while Ramón took a shower. The time readout in the mirror told him that dawn was still three or four hours away. He stood under the flow of warm water, considering his scars— the wide white band on his belly where Martín Casaus had slashed him with a sheet-metal hook, the disfiguring lump below his elbow where some drunken bastard had almost sheared through his bones with a machete. Old scars. Some older than others. They didn't bother him; in fact, he liked them. They made him look strong.

When he came out, Elena was standing at her back window, arms crossed below her breasts. When she turned to him, he was ready for the blast furnace of her rage. But instead, her mouth was a tiny rosebud, her eyes wide and round. When she spoke, she sounded like a child; worse, like a woman trying to be a child.

"I was scared for you," she said.

"You never have to be," he said. "I'm tough as leather."

"But you're just one man," she said. "When Tomás Martinez got killed, there were eight men. They came right up to him when he came out of his girlfriend's house, and . . ."

"Tomás was a little whore," Ramón said and waved a hand dismissively, as if to say that any *real* man ought to be able to stand up against eight thugs sent to even a score. Elena's lips relaxed into a smile, and she walked toward him, her hips shifting forward with each step, as if her pussy were coming to him, the rest of her trailing behind reluctantly. It could have gone the other way, he knew. They could as easily have passed the night as they had so many others, shouting at each other, throwing things, coming to blows. But even that might have ended in sex, and he was tired enough that he was genuinely grateful they could simply fuck and then sleep, and forget about the wasted, empty day that had just gone by. Elena lifted off her dress. Ramón took her familiar flesh in his arms. The scent of old blood rose from the butcher's shop below like an ugly perfume of Earth and humanity that had followed them across the void.

Afterward, Ramón lay spent in the bed. Another shuttle was lifting off. Usually there was hardly more than one a month. But the Enye were coming soon, earlier than expected, and the platform above Diegotown needed to be fitted out to receive the great ships with their alien cargoes.

It was generations ago that mankind had raised itself up from the gravity wells of Earth and Mars and Europa and taken to the stars with dreams of conquest. Humanity had planned to spread its seed through the universe like a high councilor's son at a port-town brothel, but it had been disappointed. The universe was already taken. Other star-faring races had been there before them.

Dreams of empire faded into dreams of wealth. Dreams of wealth decayed into shamed wonder. More than the great and enigmatic technologies of the Silver Enye and Turu, it was the nature of space itself that defeated them, as it had defeated every other star-faring race. The vast dark was too great. Too *big*. Communication at the speed of light was so slow as to barely be communication at all. Governance was impossible. Law beyond what could be imposed locally was farcical. The outposts of the Commercial Alliance that humanity had been "persuaded" to join by the Silver Enye (much as Admiral Perry's gunships had "persuaded" Japan to open itself up for trade in a much earlier generation) were wide-flung, some outposts falling out of contact for generations, some lost and forgotten or else put on a bureaucrat's schedule of concerns to be addressed another generation hence by another bureaucrat as yet unborn.

Establishing dominance—or even much continuity—across that gaping infinity of Night was something that seemed possible only from the provincially narrow view-point imposed by looking up from the bottom of a gravity well. Once you got out among the stars, you learned better.

No race had been able to overcome such vast distance, and so they had striven to overcome time. And it was in this that humanity at last found some small niche in the crowded, chaotic darkness of the universe. Enye and Turu saw the damage done by humanity to its own environment, the deeply human propensity for change and control and the profoundly limited ability to see ahead to consequences, and they had found it more virtue than vice. The vast institutional minds, human and alien both, entered into a glacially slow generational agreement. Where empty planets were, intractable and inconvenient and dangerous, with wild flora and unknown fauna, there humans would be put. For the slow decades or centuries that it required to tame, to break, to pave over whatever marvels and threats evolution had put there, the Silver Enye and Cian and Turu and whatever other great races happened by would act as trade ships once had in the ancient days when mankind had displaced itself from the small islands and insignificant hills of Earth.

The São Paulo colony was barely in its second generation. There were women still alive who could recall the initial descent onto an untouched world. Diegotown, Nuevo Janeiro, San Esteban. Amadora. Little Dog. Fiddler's Jump. All the cities of the south had bloomed since then, like mold on a Petri dish. Men had died from the subtle toxins of the native foods. Men had discovered the great cat-lizards—soon nicknamed *chupacabras,* after the mythical goat-suckers of Old Earth—that had stood proud and dumb at the peak of the planet's food chain, and men had died for their discovery. The oyster-eyed Silver Enye had not. The insect-and-glass Turu had not. The enigmatic Cian with their penchant for weightlessness had not.

And now the great ships were coming ahead of schedule; each half-living ship heavy, they all assumed, with new equipment and people from other colonies hoping to make a place for themselves here on São Paulo. And also rich with the chance of escape for those to whom the colony had become a prison. More than one person had asked Ramón if he'd thought of going up, out, into the darkness, but they had misunderstood him. He had *been* in space; he had come *here*. The only attraction that leaving could hold was the chance to be someplace with even fewer people, which was unlikely. However ill he fit in São Paulo, he could imagine no situation less odious.

He didn't recall falling asleep, but woke when the late morning sun streaming through Elena's window shone in his face. He could hear her humming in the next room, going about the business of her morning. *Shut up, you evil bitch,* he thought, wincing at the flash of a lingering hangover. She had no talent for song—every note she made was flat and grating. Ramón lay silent, willing himself back to sleep, away from this city, this irritating noise, this woman, this moment in time. Then the humming was drowned by an angry sizzling sound, and, a moment later, the scent of garlic and chili sausage and frying onions wafted into the room. Ramón was suddenly aware of the emptiness in his belly. With a sigh, he raised himself to his elbow, swung his sleep-sodden legs around, and, stumbling awkwardly, made his way to the doorway.

"You look like shit," Elena said. "I don't know why I even let you in my house. Don't touch that! That's *my* breakfast. You can go earn your own!"

Ramón tossed the sausage from hand to hand, grinning, until it cooled enough to take a bite.

"I work fifty hours a week to make the credit. And what do *you* do?" Elena demanded. "Loaf around in the *terreno cimarrón,* come into town to drink whatever you earn. You don't even have a bed of your own!"

"Is there coffee?" Ramón asked. Elena gestured with her chin toward the worn plastic-and-chitin thermos on the kitchen counter. Ramón rinsed a tin cup and filled it with yesterday's coffee. "I'll make my big find," he said. "Uranium or tantalum. I'll make enough money that I won't have to work again for the rest of my life."

"And then you'll throw me out and get some young *puta* from the docks to follow you around. I know what men are like."

Ramón filched another sausage from her plate. She slapped the back of his hand hard enough to sting.

"There's a parade today," Elena said. "After the Blessing of the Fleet. The governor's making a big show to beam out to the Enye. Make them think we're all so happy that they came early. There's going to be dancing and free rum."

"The Enye think we're trained dogs," Ramón said around a mouthful of sausage.

Hard lines appeared at the corners of Elena's mouth, her eyes went cold.

"I think it would be fun," she said, thin venom in her tone. Ramón shrugged. It was her bed he was sleeping in. He'd always known there was a price for its use.

"I'll get dressed," he said and swilled down the last of the coffee. "I've got a little money. It can be my treat."

They skipped the Blessing of the Fleet—Ramón had no interest in hearing priests droning mumbo-jumbo bullshit while pouring dippers of holy water on beaten-up fishing boats— but they'd arrived in time for the parade that followed. The main street that ran past the Palace of the Governors was wide enough for five hauling trucks to drive abreast, if they stopped traffic coming the other way. Great floats moved slowly, often stopping for minutes at a time, with secular subjects—a "Turu spacecraft" studded with lights, being pulled by a team of horses; a plastic *chupacabra* with red-glowing eyes and a jaw that opened and closed to show the great teeth made from old pipes—mixing with oversized displays of Jesus, Bob Marley, and the Virgin of Despegando Station. Here came a twice-life-sized satirical (recognizable but very unflattering) caricature of the governor, huge lips pursed as if ready to kiss the Silver Enyes' asses, and a ripple of laughter went down the street. The first wave of colonists, the ones who had named the planet São Paulo, had been from Brazil, and although few if any of them had ever been to Portugal, they were universally referred to as "the Portuguese" by the Spanish-speaking colonists, mostly Mexicans, who had arrived with the second and third waves. "The Portuguese" still dominated the upper-level positions in local government and administration, and the highest-paying jobs, and were widely resented and disliked by the Spanish-speaking majority, who felt they'd been made into second-class citizens in their own new home. A chorus of boos and jeers followed the huge float of the governor down the street.

Musicians followed the great lumbering floats: steel bands, string bands, mariachi bands, tuk bands, marching units of Zouaves, strolling guitarists playing *fado* music. Stilt-walkers and tumbling acrobats. Young women in half-finished carnival costumes danced along like birds. With Elena at his side, Ramón was careful not to look at their half-exposed breasts (or to get caught doing so).

The maze of side streets was packed full. Coffee stands and rum sellers; bakers offering frosted pastry redjackets and *chupacabras;* food carts selling fried fish and tacos, satay and jug-jug; sideshow buskers; street artists; fire-eaters; three-card monte dealers—all were making the most of the improvised festival. For the first hour, it was almost enjoyable. After that, the constant noise and press and scent of humanity all around him made Ramón edgy. Elena was her infant-girl self, squealing in delight like a child and dragging him from one place to another, spending his money on candy rope and sugar skulls. He managed to slow her slightly by buying real food—a waxed paper cone of saffron rice, hot peppers, and strips of roasted butterfin flesh, and a tall, thin glass of flavored rum—and by picking a hill in the park nearest the palace where they could sit on the grass and watch the great, slow river of people slide past them.

Elena was sucking the last of the spice from her fingertips and leaning against him, her arm around him like a chain, when Patricio Gallegos caught sight of them and came walking slowly up the rise. His gait had a hitch in it from when he'd broken his hip in a rockslide; prospecting wasn't a safe job. Ramón watched him approach.

"Hey," Patricio said. "How's it going, eh?"

Ramón shrugged as best he could with Elena clinging to him like ivy on brick.

"You?" Ramón asked.

Patricio wagged a hand—not good, not bad. "I've been surveying mineral salts on the south coast for one of the corporations. It's a pain in the ass, but they pay regular. Not like being an independent."

"You do what you got to do," Ramón said, and Patricio nodded as if he'd said something particularly wise. On the street, the *chupacabra* float was turning slowly, the great idiot mouth champing at the air. Patricio didn't leave. Ramón shielded his eyes from the sun and looked up at him.

"What?" Ramón said.

"You hear about the ambassador from Europa?" Patricio said. "He got in a fight last night at the El Rey. Some crazy *pendejo* stabbed him with a bottle neck or something."

"Yeah?"

"Yeah. He died before they could get him to the hospital. The governor's real pissed off about it."

"So what are you telling *me* for?" Ramón asked. "I'm not the governor."

Elena was still as stone beside him, her eyes narrow in an expression of low cunning. Ramón quietly willed Patricio to go away, or at least to shut up. But the man didn't pick up on it.

"The governor's all busy with the Enye ships coming in. Now he has to track down the guy that killed the ambassador, and show how the colony is able to keep the law and all. I've got a cousin who works for the chief constable. It's ugly over there."

"Okay," Ramón said.

"I was just thinking, you know. You hang out at the El Rey sometimes."

"Not last night," Ramón said, glowering. "You can ask Mikel if you want. I wasn't there all night."

Patricio smiled and took an awkward step back. The *chupacabra* made a weak, synthesized roar and the crowd around it shrilled with laughter and applause.

"Yeah, okay," Patricio said. "I was just thinking. You know . . ."

And with the conversation trailing away, Patricio smiled, nodded, and limped back down the hill.

"It wasn't *you*, was it?" Elena half whispered, half hissed. "You didn't kill the fucking *ambassador*?"

"I didn't kill anyone, and sure as hell not a European. I'm

not stupid," Ramón said. "Why don't you watch your fucking parade, eh?"

Night came on as the parade wound down. At the bottom of the hill, in a field near the palace, they were putting a torch to the pile of wood surrounding Old Man Gloom— Mr. Harding, some of the colonists from Barbados called him—a hastily cobbled-together effigy, almost twenty feet tall, with a face like a grotesque caricature of a European or a *norteamericano*, green-painted cheeks, and an enormous Pinocchio nose. The bonfire blazed, and, wreathed in flames, the giant effigy began to swing its arms and groan in seeming agony, a somehow eerie sight that sent a chill up Ramón's spine, as if he had been given the dubious privilege of watching a soul being tormented in the fires of Hell.

All the bad luck that dogged people throughout the year was supposed to be burning up with Old Man Gloom, but watching the giant twist and writhe in slow motion in the flames, its deep, electronically amplified moans echoing off the walls of the Palace of the Governors, Ramón had a glum presentiment that it was his *good* luck that was burning instead, that from here on in he was headed for nothing but misery and misfortune.

And one glance at Elena—who had been sitting silently with her jaw set tight and white lines of anger etched around her mouth ever since he had snapped at her—was enough to tell him that it wasn't going to be very long before that prophecy started to come true.

Chapter 2

He hadn't intended to go back out for another month. Even though they'd fucked passionately the night before, after one of their most vicious arguments ever, tearing at each other's bodies like crazed things, he'd decided to leave before she could wake up. If he'd waited, they'd only have had another fight, and she probably would have kicked him out anyway; he'd taken a swing at her with a bottle the night before, and she would be outraged at that once she'd sobered up. Still, if it wasn't for the killing at the El Rey, he might have tried staying in town. Elena'd probably calm down in a day or two, at least enough that they could speak to each other without shouting, but the news of the European's death and the governor's wrath made Diegotown feel close and claustrophobic. When he went to the outfitter's station to buy rations and water filters, he felt like he was being watched. How many people had been in that crowd? How many of those would know him by sight—or name? The outfitter didn't have everything on Ramón's list, but he had bought what was immediately available, and then had flown his van to Manuel Griego's salvage yard in Nuevo Janeiro. The van needed some work before it could head out into the world, and Ramón wanted it done *now*.

Griego's yard squatted at the edge of the city. The hulking frames of old vans and canopy fliers and personal shuttles littered the wide acres. In the hangar, it was equal parts junk shop and clean room. Power cells hung from the rafters, glowing with the eerie light that all Turu technology seemed to carry with it. A nuclear generator the size of a small apartment ran along one wall, humming to itself. Storage units were stacked floor to ceiling; tanks of rare gas and undifferentiated nanoslurry mixed in with half-bald tires and oily drive trains. Half the things in the shop would cost more than a year's wages just to make use of; half were hardly worth the effort to throw out. Old Griego himself was hammering away on a lift tube as Ramón set his van down on the pad.

"Hey, *ese*," Griego called out when Ramón popped the doors and came down to the working floor. "Long time. Where you been keeping yourself?"

Ramón shrugged.

"I got a power drop in my back lift tubes," he said.

Griego frowned, put down his hammer, and wiped greasy hands on greasy pants.

"Put on the diagnostic," he said. "Let's take a look."

Of all the men in Diegotown and Nuevo Janeiro—or possibly on this world—Ramón liked old Griego best, which was to say he only hated him a little. Griego was an expert on all things vehicular, a post-contact Marxist, and, so far as Ramón could make out, totally free of moral judgments. It took them little more than an hour to find where the lift tube's chipset had lost coherence, replace the card, and start the system's extensive self-check. As the van stuttered and chuffed to itself, Griego lumbered to one of the gray storage tanks, keyed in a security code, and opened a refrigeration panel to reveal a case of local black beer. He hauled out two bottles, snapping the caps free with a flick of his thick, callused fingers. Ramón took the one that was held out to him, squatted with his back against a drum of spent lubricant, and drank. The beer was thick and yeasty, sediment in the bottom like a spoonful of mud.

"Pretty good, eh?" Griego said and drank a quarter of his own at a pull.

"Not bad," Ramón said.

"So you're heading out?"

"This is going to be the big one," Ramón said. "This time I'm coming back a rich man. You wait. You'll see."

"You better hope not," Griego said. "Too much money kills men like you and me. God meant us to be poor, or He wouldn't have made us so mean."

Ramón grinned. "God meant *you* to be mean, Manuel. He just didn't want me taking any shit from anybody." A quick vision of the European, mouth gaping open, blood gushing out over tombstone teeth, came to him, and he frowned.

Griego was shaking his head. "The same thing again, eh? *This* time's the one, just like every other time you been out." He grinned. "You know how many times I heard you say that?"

"Yep," Ramón said. "This time's different, just like always."

"Go with God, then," Griego said. His grin faded. "Everyone's been scrambling. Trying to get things finished. Aliens caught everyone with their pants around their knees, coming early like this. Funny, though. I don't see a whole lot of people heading out right now. Pretty much everyone's coming in for the ships—except you."

Ramón sneered, but he felt the constant fear in his breast tighten a notch.

"What? They're going to give half a shit about a prospector like me? What's there for me if I stay?"

"Didn't say you should," Griego said. "Just said there's not many people going out right now."

I look suspicious, Ramón thought. *I look like I'm running from something. He'll tell the police, and then I'm fucked.* He clamped his hand around the bottle so hard his knuckles ached.

"It's Elena," Ramón said, hoping the half lie would be convincing enough.

"Ah," Griego said, nodding sagely. "I thought it must be something like that."

"She kicked me out again," Ramón said, trying to sound hangdog despite the relief washing through him. "We had a fight about the parade. It got a little out of hand is all."

"She know you're taking off?"

"I don't think she cares," Ramón said.

"Right now, maybe she doesn't. But you fly out of here and three weeks later she decides that all is forgiven, she's going to come around tearing up my place."

Ramón chuckled, remembering the incident that Griego was talking about. He was wrong, though. That hadn't been about making peace; Elena had convinced herself that Ramón had taken a woman with him when he went out in the field. She hadn't stopped raging and ranting until she found the girl on whom her paranoia had fixed still in town and involved with one of the magistrates, and even then she still seemed to hold a grudge. Ramón had had to spend almost half the money he'd gotten from his survey work just buying beer and kaafa kyit for all his business contacts whom she'd alienated.

Griego didn't laugh with him.

"You know she's crazy, don't you?" he asked instead.

"She does get pretty wild," Ramón said with a half smile, trying the expression on like it was a new shirt.

"No, I know wild girls. Elena is fucking *loca*. I know you like that girl down at the exchange. What's her name?"

"Lianna?" Ramón asked, disbelief in his voice.

"Yeah that's the one. Lives over on the north side. Used to be you had a thing with her, didn't you?"

Ramón remembered those days, when he'd been a younger man, new to the colony. Yes, there had been a woman with coffee-and-milk skin and a laugh that made a man happy just listening to it. Maybe he had even dreamed about her a few times since. But that had carried its own slice of hell with it. Ramón scratched at the scar that striped his belly. Griego raised an eyebrow and Ramón coughed out a laugh.

"She's . . . No. No, she's not like that. There couldn't be anything between someone like her and someone like me. And don't ever let Elena hear you say different."

Griego gestured his discretion with a wave of his bottle. Ramón took another pull. The thick, earthy taste of the beer was growing on him. He wondered how much alcohol the brew carried.

"Lianna was a good woman," Ramón said. "Elena's like me, though. We understand each other, you know?" His voice filled with a sudden bitterness that surprised him. "We deserve each other."

"If you say so," Griego said, and the van chimed, its self-test complete. Ramón levered himself up and followed Griego to where the results floated in the air. The power and variance checked at each level, just edging down below optimal on the highest range. Griego waved a crooked finger at the drop.

"That's a little weird," he said. "Maybe we should take another look at—"

"It's the cable," Ramón said. "Salt rats ate through the old one. I had to get gold for the replacement. Couldn't afford the carbon mesh."

"Ah," Griego said and clicked his tongue in something between sympathy and disapproval. "Yeah, that would do it. Too bad about the rats. That's the problem with scaring away all the predators, eh? We wind up protecting all the things they used to eat, like salt rats and flatfurs, and then they're everywhere."

"I'll take a few rats if I don't have to worry that there's *chupacabras* and redjackets in the street every time I go out for a piss," Ramón said. "Besides, if we didn't have vermin, how would we know we'd made a real city, right?"

Griego snapped off the display and shrugged. They settled the account; half from Ramón's available credit, half into an interest-bearing tab that the salvage yard's system kept track of automatically. The sun was setting; the sky pink and gold and blue the color of lapis. Stars glimmered shyly from behind daylight's veil. And Diegotown spread below them, its lights like a permanent fire. Ramón finished the last of his beer, then spat out the sediment. It left grit between his teeth.

"The last mouthful's not the best one," Griego said. "Still. Beats water."

"Amen," Ramón said.

"How long you going out for?"

"A month," Ramón said. "Maybe two."

"Miss the whole festival."

"That's the idea," Ramón agreed.

"You got enough food for that?"

"I got hunting gear," Ramón said. "I could live out there forever if I wanted." He was surprised at the wistful, even yearning, tone that he could hear in his own voice.

There was a moment's silence before Griego spoke again; words that made Ramón's nerves shrill with sudden fear.

"You hear about the European that got killed?"

Ramón looked up, startled, but Griego was sucking at his teeth, his expression placid.

"What about him?" Ramón asked warily.

"Governor's all pissed off about it, from what I hear."

"Too bad for the governor, then."

"The police came by. Two constables looking real serious. Asked if anyone had been in, getting a van in shape to head out fast. You know, someone who was maybe trying not to be found."

Ramón nodded, staring at the van. His throat felt tight and the thick beer in his belly seemed to have turned to stone.

"What did you tell them?"

"Told them no," Griego said with a shrug.

"There wasn't anyone?"

"A couple," Griego said. "Orlando Wasserman's kid. And that crazy gringa from Swan's Neck. But I figured, what the hell, you know? The police don't pay me, these other people do. So where do my loyalties lie?"

"Man got killed," Ramón said.

"Yeah," Griego agreed, pleasantly. "A gringo." He spit sideways, then shrugged, as if the death of a gringo or any other kind of European was of no great consequence. "I'm just saying it because I'm not the only one they're asking. You taking off, they may take that the wrong way, give you a hard time about it. Just keep that in mind when you supply up."

Ramón nodded.

"They gonna catch him, you think?" Ramón asked.

"Oh yeah," Griego said. "They'll have to. Bust a gut to do it, if they got to. Show the Enye that we're a justice-loving people. Not that *they* care. Shit, fucking Enye *lick* each other hello. Probably lick the governor and get pissed off if he doesn't lick them back. Anyway, he'll make a big show out of the trial, do everything to prove how they got the right guy, then put him down like a fucking dog. You know, whoever it is they decide did it. No one else, there's always Johnny Joe Cardenas. They've been looking for something to hang on him for years."

"Maybe it'll be good that I get out of the city for a while, then," Ramón said. He tried a weak smile that felt as obvious as a confession. "You know. Just to avoid misunderstandings."

"Yeah," Griego said. "Besides, this is the big one, right?"

"Lucky strike," Ramón agreed.

When he started up the van, he could feel the difference. The lift tubes seemed to chime as he lifted up into the sky, all of Diegotown, with its unplanned maze of narrow streets and red-roofed buildings, below him. Elena was down there somewhere. The police too. The body of the European. Mikel Ibrahim and the gravity knife Ramón had handed to him, just handed to him. The murder weapon! And slumped in a bar or a basement opium den—or maybe breaking into someone's house—Johnny Joe Cardenas, just waiting to hang.

And Lianna, maybe, somewhere in the good section by the port, who didn't think of Ramón anymore and probably never would.

Ramón's thoughts were interrupted by the pulsing hum of a shuttle rising up into the thin and distant air. Another load of metal or plastic or fuel or chitin for the welcoming platform. Ramón spun the van north, set it for proximity avoidance, and headed out alone, leaving all the hell and shit and sorrow of Diegotown behind.

Chapter 3

It was a warm day in the Second June. He flew his beat-up old van north across the Fingerlands, the Greenglass country, the river marshes, the Océano Tétrico, heading deep into unknown territory. North of Fiddler's Jump, the northernmost outpost of the metastasizing human presence on the planet, were thousands of hectares that no one had ever explored, or even thought of exploring, land so far only glimpsed from orbit during the first colony surveys.

The human colony on the planet of São Paulo was only a little more than forty years old, and the majority of its towns were situated in the subtropic zone of the snaky eastern continent that stretched almost from pole to pole. The colonists were mostly from Brazil and Mexico, with a smattering from Jamaica, Barbados, Puerto Rico, and other Caribbean nations, and their natural inclination was to expand south, into the steamy lands near the equator—they were not effete *norteamericanos,* after all; they were used to such climates, they knew how to live with the heat, they knew how to farm the jungles, their skins did not sear in the sun. So they looked to the south, and tended to ignore the cold northern territories, perhaps because of an unvocalized common conviction—one anticipated centuries before by the first Spanish settlers in the New World of the Americas—that life was not worth living any place where there was even a remote possibility of snow.

Ramón, however, was part Yaqui, and had grown up in the rugged plateau country of northern Mexico. He liked the hills and white water, and he didn't mind the cold. He also knew that the Sierra Hueso mountain chain in the northern hemisphere of São Paulo was a more likely place to find rich ore than the flatter country around the Hand or Nuevo Janeiro or Little Dog. The peaks around the Sierra Hueso had been piled up many millions of years before by a collision between continental plates squeezing an ocean out of existence between them; the former sea-bottom would have been pinched and pushed high into the air along the collision line, and it would be rich in copper and other metals.

Few if any of the mule-back prospectors like himself had as yet bothered with the northern lands; pickings were still rich enough down south that the travel time seemed unnecessary to most people. The Sierra Hueso had been mapped from orbit, but no one Ramón knew had ever actually been there, and the territory was still so unexplored that the peaks of the range had not even been individually named. That meant that there were no human settlements within hundreds of miles, and no satellite to relay his network signals this far north; if he got into trouble he would be on his own. He would be one of the first to prospect there, but years would pass, the economic pressure in the south would get higher, and more people would come north, following the charts Ramón had made and sold, interpreting the data he rented out to the corporations and governing bodies. They would follow him like the native scorpion ants—first one, and then a handful, and then countless thousands of small insectoid bodies in the consuming river. Ramón was that first ant, the one driven to risk, to explore. He was a leader not because he chose to be, but because it was his nature to seek distance.

It was better that way, to be the first ant. Although he was reluctant to admit it, he'd finally come to realize that it was better if he worked someplace away from other prospectors. Away from other people. The bigger prospecting cooperatives might have better contracts, better equipment, but they also had more rum and more women. And between those two, Ramón knew, more fighting. He couldn't trust his own volatile temper, never had been able to. It had held him back for years, the fighting, and the trouble it got him into. Now it had gotten him into trouble that might cost him his life, if they caught him. No, it *was* better this way—mule-back prospecting, just himself and his van.

Besides, he was finding that he liked to be out on his own like this, on a clear day with São Paulo's big, soft sun blinking dimly back at him from rivers and lakes and leaves. He found that he was whistling tunelessly as the endless forests beneath the van slowly changed from blackwort and devilwood to the local conifer-equivalents: iceroot, creeping willow, *hierba*. At last, there was no one around to bother him. For the first time that day, his stomach had almost stopped aching.

Almost.

With every hour that passed, every forest and lake that appeared, drew near, and slipped away, the thought of the European he'd killed grew in Ramón's mind, his presence sharpening pixel by pixel, becoming more real, until he could almost, almost, see him sitting in the copilot's seat, that stupid look of dumb surprise at his own mortality still stamped on his big, pale face—and the more real his ghostly presence became, the deeper Ramón's hatred for him grew.

He hadn't hated him back at the El Rey; the man had just been another bastard looking for trouble and finding Ramón. It had happened before more times than he could recall. It was part of how things worked. He came to town, he drank, he and some rabid asshole found each other, and one of them walked away. Maybe it was Ramón, maybe it was the other guy. Rage, yes, rage had something to do with it, but not hatred. Hatred meant you knew a man, you cared about him. Rage lifted you up above everything—morality, fear, yourself. Hatred meant that someone had control over you.

This was the place that usually brought him peace, the outback, the remote territory, the unpeopled places. The tension that came with being around people loosened. In the city—Diegotown or Nuevo Janeiro or any place where too many people came together—Ramón had always felt the press of people against him. The voices just out of earshot, the laughter that might or might not have been directed at him, the impersonal stares of men and women, Elena's lush body and her uncertain mind; they were why Ramón drank when he was in the city and stayed sober in the field. In the field there was no reason to drink.

But here, where that peace should have been, the European was with him. Ramón would look out into the limitless bowl of the sky, and his mind would turn back to that night at the El Rey, the sudden awed silence of the crowd. The blood pouring from the European's mouth. His heels drumming against the ground. He checked his maps, and instead of letting his mind run freely across the fissures and plates of the planetary surface, he thought of where the police might go to search for him. He could not let go of what had happened, and the frustration of that was almost as enraging as the guilt itself.

But guilt was for weaklings and fools. Everything would be all right. He would spend his time in the field, communing with the stone and the sky, and when he returned to the city, the European would be last season's news. Something half remembered and retold in a thousand different versions, none of them true. It was one little death among all the hundreds of millions—natural and otherwise—that happened every year throughout the known universe. The dead man's absence would be like taking a finger out of water; it wouldn't leave a hole.

Mountains made a line across the world before him: ice and iron, iron and ice.

Those would be the Sawtooths, which meant that he'd already overflown Fiddler's Jump. When he checked the navigation transponders, there was no signal. He was gone, out of human contact, off the incomplete communication network of the colony. On his own. He made the adjustments he'd planned, altering his flight path to throw off any human hounds that the law might set after him, but even as he did so, the gesture seemed pointless. He wouldn't be followed. No one would care.

He set the autopilot, tilted his chair back until it was

almost as flat as his cot, and, in spite of the reproachful almost-presence of the European, let the miles rolling by beneath him lull him to sleep.

When he woke, the even-grander peaks of the Sierra Hueso range were thrusting above the horizon, and the sun was getting low in the sky, casting shadows across the mountain faces. He switched off the autopilot and brought the van to rest in a rugged upland meadow along the southern slopes of the range. After the bubbletent had been set up, the last perimeter alarm had been placed, and a fire pit dug and dry wood scavenged to fill it, Ramón walked to the edge of a small nearby lake. This far north, it was cold even in summer, and the water was chill and clear; the biochip on his canteen reported nothing more alarming than trace arsenic. He gathered a double-handful of sug beetles and took them back to his camp. Boiled, they tasted of something midway between crab and lobster, and the gray stone-textured shells took on an unpredictable rainbow of iridescent colors when the occupying flesh was sucked free. It was easy to live off this country, if you knew how. In addition to sug beetles and other scavengeable foodstuffs, there was water to hand and there would be easy game nearby if he chose to stay longer than the month or two his van's supplies would support. He might stay until the equinox, depending on the weather. Ramón even found himself wondering how difficult it would be to winter over here in the north. If he dropped south to Fiddler's Jump for fuel and slept in the van for the coldest months . . .

After he'd eaten, he lit a cigarette, lay back, and watched the mountains darken with the sky. A flapjack moved against the high clouds, and Ramón rose up on one elbow to watch it. It rippled its huge, flat, leathery body, sculling with its wing tips, seeking a thermal. Its ridiculous squeaky cry came clearly to him across the gulfs of air. They were almost level; it would be evaluating him now, deciding that he was much too big to eat. The flapjack tilted and slid away and down, as though riding a long, invisible slope of air, off to hunt squeakers and grasshoppers in the valley below. Ramón watched the flapjack until it dwindled to the size of a coin, glowing bronze in the failing light.

"Good hunting!" he called after it, and then smiled. Good hunting for both of them, eh? As the last of the daylight touched the top of the ridgeline on the valley's eastern rise, Ramón caught sight of something. A discontinuity in the stone. It wasn't the color or the epochal striations, but something more subtle. Something in the way the face of the mountain sat. It wasn't alarming as much as interesting. Ramón put a mental flag there; something strange, worth investigating in the morning.

He lounged by the fire for a few moments while the night gathered completely around him and the alien stars came out in their chill, blazing armies. He named the strange constellations the people of São Paulo had drawn in the sky to replace the old constellations of Earth—the Mule, the Stone Man, the Cactus Flower, the Sick Gringo—and wondered (he'd been told, but had forgotten) which of them had Earth's own sun twinkling in it as a star? Then he went to bed and to sleep, dreaming that he was a boy again in the cold stone streets of his hilltop pueblo, sitting on the roof of his father's house in the dark, a scratchy wool blanket wrapped around him, trying to ignore the loud, angry voices of his parents in the room below, searching for São Paulo's star in the winter sky.

Chapter 4

In the morning, Ramón poured water over the remains of the fire, then pissed on it just to be sure it was out. He ate a small breakfast of cold tortillas and beans, and disconnected his pistol from the van's power cells and tucked it into his holster, where it was a warm, comforting weight on his hip; out here, you could never be sure when you were going to run into a *chupacabra* or a snatchergrabber. He exchanged the soft flatfur slippers he wore in the van for his sturdy old hiking boots, and set out to hike to the discontinuity he'd spotted the night before; as always, his boots somehow seemed more comfortable crunching over the uneven ground than they had been on the city streets. Dew soaked the grasses and the leaves of the shrubs. Small monkeylike lizards leaped from branch to branch before him, calling to each other with high, frightened voices. There were millions of uncataloged species on São Paulo. In the twenty minutes it took him to make his way to a promising site at the base of a stone cliff, Ramón might have climbed past a hundred plants and animals never before seen by human eyes.

Before long, he found the discontinuity, and surveyed it almost with regret; he'd been relishing the effort for its own sake, pausing frequently to enjoy the view or to rest in the watery sunlight. Now he'd have to get to work.

The lichen that clung to the rock of the mountainside was

dark green and grew in wide spirals that reminded Ramón of cave paintings. Up close, the discontinuity was less apparent. He could trace the striations from one face to the next without sign of a break or level change. Whatever Ramón had caught in the failing light of the day before, it was invisible now.

He took the field pack from his shoulders, lit a cigarette, and considered the mountain face before him. The stones around him appeared to be largely metamorphic—their elongated grain speaking to Ramón of the unthinkable pressure and heat near São Paulo's mantle. The glaciers, when they passed, would have carved this ground, strewing parts of any given field far from their origin. Still, the underlying stone was certainly igneous or metamorphic. The sedimentary layers, if there were any, would be higher up, where the ground was newest. It was the sort of place where a man might find the strike he'd hoped for. Uranium ore, possibly. Tungsten or tantalum, if he was lucky. And even if he only found gold or silver or copper, there were places he could still sell the data. The information would be worth more than the metals themselves.

The sad irony of his profession had not escaped Ramón. He would never willingly move off São Paulo. Its emptiness was the thing that made it a haven for him. In a more developed colony, the global satellites and ground-level networked particulates would have made solitude impossible. São Paulo still had frontiers, limits beyond which little or nothing was known. He and the others like him were the hands and eyes of the colony's industry; his love of the unknown corners and niches of the world was unimportant. His experience of them, the data and surveys and knowledge—those had value. And so he made his money by destroying the things that gave him solace. It was an evil scheme, but typical, Ramón thought, of humanity's genetic destiny of contradiction. He stubbed out his cigarette, took a hand pick from the field pack, and began the long, slow process of scouting out a good place for a coring charge.

The sun shone down benevolently, and Ramón stripped off his shirt, tucking it into the back of his pistol belt. Between the hand pick and his small field shovel, he cleared away the thin covering of plants and soil, finding hard, solid rock not more than a foot and a half below the surface. If it had been much more, he'd have gone back for the tools in the van—powered for minor excavations, but expensive, prone to breaking down, and with the whining electrical sound of civilization to argue against their use. Looking along the mountainside, he thought there would likely be other places that would require the more extensive labor. All the better, then, that he begin here.

The coring charge was designed to carve a sample out of the living rock the length of an arm. Longer, if it was a particularly soft stone. In the next week, Ramón would gather a dozen or so such cores from sites up and down the valley. After that, there would be three or four days while the equipment in the van sifted through the debris for trace elements and ores too slight to identify simply by looking. Once Ramón had that in hand, he could devise a strategy for garnering the most useful information in the cheapest possible way. Even as he set the first charge, he found himself fantasizing about those long, slow, lazy days while the tests ran. He could go hunting. Or explore the lakes. Or find a warm place in the sun and sleep while the breeze set the grasses to singing. His fingers danced across the explosives, tugging at wires and timing chips with the ease and autonomous grace of long practice. Many prospectors lost careers and hands—sometimes lives—by being too careless with their tools. Ramón was careful, but he was also practiced. Once the site was chosen and cleared, placing the charge took less than an hour.

He found himself, strangely, procrastinating about setting it off. It was so quiet here, so still, so peaceful! From up here, the forested slopes fell away in swaths of black and dead-blue and orange, the trees rippling like a carpet of moss as the wind blew across them. Except for the white egg of his bubbletent on the mountain shoulder below, it was a scene that might not have changed since the beginning of time. For a moment, he was almost tempted to forget about prospecting and just relax and unwind on this trip, as long as he was being forced to hide out in the hills anyway, but he shrugged the temptation away: once the fuss over the European had blown over, once he went back, he would still need money, the van wouldn't hold together forever, and he wasn't anxious to face Elena's scorn if he returned empty-handed again. Perhaps there will be no ore here anyway, he told himself, almost wishing it, and then wondered at the tenor of his thoughts. Surely it could not be a bad thing to be rich? His stomach was beginning to ache again.

He looked up at the mountain face. It was beautiful; rugged and untouched. Once he was done with it, it would never be the same.

"All apologies," he said to the view he was about to mar. "But a man has to make his money somehow. Hills don't have to eat."

Ramón took one last cigarette from its silver case and smoked it like a man at an execution. He walked down to the boulders he'd chosen for shelter stringing the powder-primed fuse cord, hunkered down behind the rocks, and lit the fuse with the last ember.

There was the expected blast; but while the sound should have been a single report echoing against the mountains and then fading, it grew louder and longer instead. The hillside shifted greasily under him, like a giant shrugging in uneasy sleep, and he heard the express-train rumble of sliding rock. He could tell from the sound alone that something had gone very wrong.

A great cloud of dust enveloped him, white as fog and tasting like plaster and stone. A landslide. Somehow Ramón's little coring charge had set off a landslide. Coughing, he cursed himself, thinking back to what he'd seen. How could he have missed a rock face that unstable? It was the kind of mistake that killed prospectors. If he had chosen shelter a little nearer than he had, he could have been crushed to death. Or worse, crippled and buried here where no man would ever find him—trapped until the redjackets came and stripped the flesh off his bones.

The angry, thundering roar quieted, faded. Ramón rose from behind the boulders, waving his hand before his face as if stirring the air would somehow put more oxygen in it or lessen the thick coating of stone dust that was no doubt forming in his nose and lungs. He walked slowly forward, his footing uncertain on the newly made scree. The stones smelled curiously hot.

A metal wall stood where the façade of stone had fallen away; half a mountain high and something between twenty and twenty-five meters wide.

It was, of course, impossible. It had to be some bizarre natural formation. He stepped forward, and his own reflection—pale as the ghost of a ghost—moved toward him. When he reached out, his blurred twin reached out as well, pausing when he paused. He stopped the motion before hand and ghostly hand could touch, noticing the stunned and bewildered expression on the face of his reflection in the metal, one no doubt matched by the expression on his own face. Then, gingerly, he touched the wall.

The metal was cool against his fingertips. The blast had not even scarred it. And though his mind rebelled at the thought, it was clearly unnatural. It was a *made* thing. Made by somebody and *hidden* by somebody, behind the rock of the mountain, though he couldn't imagine by whom.

It took another moment for the full implication to register. Something was buried here under the hill, something big, perhaps a building of some sort, a bunker. Perhaps the whole mountain was hollow.

This *was* the big one, just the way he'd told Manuel it would be. But the find wasn't ore; it was this massive artifact. It couldn't be a human artifact, the human colony here wasn't old enough to have left ruins behind. It had to be alien. Maybe it was millions of years old. Scientists and archaeologists would go insane over this find; perhaps even the Enye would be interested in it. If he couldn't parlay this discovery into an immense fortune, he wasn't anywhere near as smart as he thought he was. . . .

He flattened his palm against the metal, matching hands with his reflection. The cool metal vibrated under his hand, and, even as he waited, a deeper vibration went through the wall—boom, *boom*—low and rhythmic, like the beating of some great hidden heart, like the heart of the mountain itself, vast and stony and old.

A warning bell began to sound in the back of Ramón's mind, and he looked uneasily around him. Another man might not have reacted to this strange discovery with suspicion, but Ramón's people had been persecuted for hundreds of years, and he himself well remembered living on the grudging sufferance of the *mejicanos,* never knowing when they would find some pretext to wipe out his village.

Whatever this wall was, whatever reason it had for existing here in the twice-forsaken ass-end of a half-known planet, it was no dead ruin—something was at work beneath this mountain. If this was hidden, it was because someone didn't want it to be *found.* And might not be happy that it *had* been. Someone unimaginably powerful, to judge from the scale of this artifact—and probably dangerous.

Suddenly, the sunlight seemed cold on his shoulders. Again, he looked nervously around him, feeling much too exposed on the bare mountain slope. Another flapjack called, away across the air, but now its cries sounded to him like the shrill and batlike wailing of the damned.

It was time to get *out* of here. Get back to the van—maybe take a short video recording of the wall, and then find someplace else to be. Anywhere else. Even back in Diegotown, where the threats were at least knowable.

He couldn't *run* back to his camp—the terrain was too rough. But he scrambled down the mountainside as recklessly as he dared, sliding on his buttocks down bluffs in a cloud of dust and scree when he could, jumping from rock to rock, bulling his way through bushes and tangles of scrub *hierba,* scattering grasshoppers and paddlefoots before him.

He moved so quickly that he was more than a third of the way to his camp before the mountain opened behind him and the alien came out.

High above him, a hole opened in the mountain's side—a cave in the metal that a moment ago had not been there and now simply was. There was a high-pitched whine, like a centrifuge spinning up, and then, a breath later, *something* flew out of the hole.

It was square-shaped and built awkwardly for flight, like something designed to move in vacuum. Bone-white and silent, it reminded Ramón of a ghost, or a great floating skull. Against the great empty blue of the sky—atmosphere thin enough at the top that stars shone through the blue—it could have been any size at any distance. The strange boxy thing hung in the sky, rotating slowly. Looking, Ramón thought. Looking for him.

Sick dread squeezed his chest. His camp. The thing was clearly searching for something, and Ramón hadn't done anything to conceal the white dome of the bubbletent or the van beside it. There had been no reason to. The thing might not see him down here in the underbrush, but it *would* see his camp. He had to get there—get back to the van and into the air—before the thing from the mountain discovered it. His mind was already racing ahead—would his van outpace the flying white box? Just let him get it in the air. He could fly it low, make it hard to spot or attack. He was a good pilot. He could dodge between treetops from here to Fiddler's Jump if he had to . . .

But he had to get there first.

He fled, raw panic pushing away the last shreds of caution. The demonic white box was lost from sight as he reached the edge of the scree and dove into the underbrush. The bushes and low scrub that had seemed thin and easily navigable when he'd been walking were now an obstacle course. Branches grabbed at him, raking his face and ripping his clothes. He had the feeling that the flying thing from the mountain was right on top of him, at his back, ready to strike. His breath burned as he sprinted, legs churning, back toward the van.

"I didn't see anything," he gasped. "Please. I wasn't doing anything! I don't know anything. Please. I dreamed it!"

When halfway back to the van he paused, leaning against a tree to catch his breath, the sky was empty. No ghostly box hung in the air, searching for him. He was surprised to find that his pistol was already in his hand. He didn't recall drawing it. Still, now that he did think of it, the weight and solidity of it were reassuring. He wasn't defenseless. Whatever that fucking thing was, he could shoot it. He spat, anger taking the place of fear. Maybe he didn't know what he was facing, but it didn't know *him* either. He was Ramón Espejo! He'd tear the alien a new asshole if it messed with him.

Buoyed by his bravado and rage, Ramón started again for the van, one eye to the skies. He had cleared more ground than he thought; the van was only a few more minutes away. Just let him get it in the air! He wasn't going to stop to video anything, not with that thing out there sniffing for him. But he'd bring back a force from Diegotown—the governor's private guard maybe. The police. The army. Whatever was in the hill, he'd drag it out into the light and crack its shell. He wasn't afraid of it or anyone. He wasn't afraid of *God*. His litany of denial—*Please! I didn't see anything!*—was already forgotten.

He reached the meadow that contained his camp just as the alien reappeared overhead. He hesitated, torn between dashing for the van and diving back into the brush.

It was close enough that Ramón could size it now; it was smaller than he'd thought—perhaps half the size of his van. It was ropey; long white strands like the dripping of a candle making up its walls. Or its face. As it swooped nearer, Ramón felt a knot in his throat. It was too close. He would never be able to reach the van before it came between them.

Perhaps it's friendly, Ramón thought. Madre de Dios, *it had* better *be friendly!*

The van exploded. A geyser of fire and smoke shot up out of the meadow with a waterfall roar, and tenfin birds rose screaming all along the mountain flank. The shockwave buffeted Ramón, splattering him with dirt and pebbles and shredded vegetation. He staggered, fighting to maintain his balance. Pieces of fused metal thumped down around him, burning holes in the moss of the meadow floor. It was shooting at him! Through the plume of smoke, Ramón saw the thing turn, flying five meters above the ground, swooping toward him again. The bubbletent went up in a ball of expanding gas, pieces of torn plastic tumbling and swooping like frightened white birds in the hot turbulence of the explosion.

Ramón caught only a glimpse of that. He was already in frantic motion, running, swerving, tearing through the brush. He could hear his own gasping breath, and his heart slammed against his ribs like a fist. Faster!

He felt the alien craft coming up behind him more than he saw it. With a despairing cry, Ramón whirled, fired three times at the looming thing as fast as he could, then turned and fled again. A tree detonated as he passed it, splinters biting into his face and legs. He heard a high whine coming close, getting louder, dopplering up the frequencies. A shockwave knocked the air from him, and he lost his footing. He fired the pistol again as he fell, without knowing where he'd aimed or if he'd hit anything.

Something hit him. Hard. His consciousness blinked out, like a suddenly snuffed candle.

When he woke, he woke in darkness. . . .

Part Two

Chapter 5

In the darkness—immobile, unbreathing—Ramón found his memory growing clearer and clearer. The way Griego had shrugged. The rattling mechanical roar of the *chupacabra* float. The European's blood; pale in the red light and black in the blue. The taste of the stone dust. The taste of Elena's mouth. Details that had been vague grew clearer until, by concentrating, he could hear the voices, feel the cloth of the shirt he'd worn. All of it. The thing from the mountain had taken him and had done something to him. Imprisoned him in this vast, empty blackness through a process he could not imagine and for reasons he couldn't guess. The silence and the emptiness changed the nature of time. There was no longer a sense of duration. He couldn't say how long he had been there or whether he had slept. He could no more judge his own sanity than point north; without context, ideas like madness and direction were meaningless.

The movement, when it came, was so slight that Ramón could believe he had imagined it. Something nudged him. A current moved against his skin; an invisible current in an invisible sea. He had the feeling of being turned in slow circles. Something solid bumped his shoulder, and then rose up against his back, or else he sank down upon it. The syrupy liquid streamed past him, flowing past his face and his body. He thought of it as draining away, though he could as easily imagine being lifted up through it. The flow grew faster and more turbulent. A deep vibration shook him: *boom*. Then again, beating through flesh and bone: *boom, boom*. A blurred, watery light appeared above him, very dim and immensely far away, like a star in a distant constellation. It grew brighter. The liquid in which he floated drained, the surface coming nearer, like he was rising from the bottom of a lake, until he finally breached it, and the last of the liquid was gone.

Air and light and sound hit him like a fist.

His body convulsed like a live fish on a frying pan, every muscle knotting. He arched up like an epileptic—head and heels bearing his weight, his spine bent like a bow. Something he couldn't see flipped him onto his belly, and he felt a needle slide in at the base of his spine. He vomited with wrenching violence—thick amber syrup gouting from his mouth and nose. And then again, sick, racking spasms that expelled even more, as if his lungs had been filled with the stuff.

I will live, Ramón told himself. *It's no worse than being sick from too much muscat. I can live through this. . . .*

Another long needle dug into his neck. A cold fire sprang to life where the thing had pierced him; he felt the saliva-like secretion running down his sides, then heat, like boiling water pouring into him.

What have you done to me? Ramón tried to scream. *What did you put in me?*

Suddenly, violently, his heart came to life—and, with a terrible shudder, he began to breathe.

The air he gulped cut like glass, and his heart thundered in his chest. The world went red. Pain drove away all thought, all sense of self, and then slowly abated.

Another wave of the sickness shook him. He voided his bowels, weeping with pain and shame when he wasn't coughing. It seemed to go on for hours, but the moments of peace between spasms gradually grew longer, and it seemed as if some of the strength was beginning to come back to his arms and legs. His heart ceased to race like a bird trying to free itself from a net. Tentatively, he sat up.

He was sprawled naked on the bottom of a metal tank not more than ten feet square. So much for his measureless midnight ocean! The walls were too high to see over, and the lights—blue-white and bitter—were too bright to see past and make out the ceiling beyond. He tried to stand up, but his muscles were putty. It was bitingly cold. He settled against the metal floor and shivered, feeling his teeth start to chatter. He tried lifting an arm, but the impulse was slow to reach his flesh, and the limb swayed drunkenly when it rose. Strong smells that he couldn't identify burned his nostrils.

A thing like a snake reared up above the rim of the tank—thick as a strong man's arm, it was a dead gray color, like old meat, and segmented like a worm's body. Pulsations seemed to travel along its length. Ramón saw it hesitate, as if considering him, and then stretch down toward him. Three long, thin tendrils split off where the head should have been. The gray snake brushed aside Ramón's clumsy parry and seized him by the shoulder. Ramón struggled weakly. But his strength was gone, and the snake's grip was as cold and pitiless as death. Another snake stretched down and wrapped itself around his waist.

The snakes lifted him smoothly out of the tank. He tried to scream, but the sound he made was more like a cough. He was high in the air now, above what seemed to be a vast, high-domed cavern full of noise and lights and motion and alien shapes. The cavern swarmed with activity that Ramón could not resolve into recognizable patterns, having no referents for it. His nose and mouth were filled with a biting, acrid odor, something like formaldehyde.

The two snakes set him down on a platform near one wall of the cavern, the surface solid but spongy, like a great dark tongue. He collapsed as soon as they released him, his legs too weak to bear his weight. He waited on his hands and knees, staring into the terrible bright lights, panting like a trapped animal, suddenly longing for the timeless darkness he'd left behind.

It was dimmer here, in the angle of the wall and the cavern floor. Inchoate shapes moved ponderously in the shadows; as they came forward, they were finished and fleshed by the light, but Ramón still could not make them out. His mind kept fighting to resolve them into the familiar aspects of humanity, and—terribly, terrifyingly—they would not. They were too big, and shaped wrong, and their eyes were a bright, glowing orange.

A needle slid out of the end of a hovering gray tentacle, thrust quickly into Ramón's arm, too quickly for him to move or protest. Another prickly wave of heat passed through him, and he suddenly felt much stronger. What kind of injection had it given him? Glucose? Vitamins? Perhaps there'd been a tranquilizer in it as well; his head was clear now, and he felt more alert, less frightened. He drew himself up to his knees, one hand instinctively covering his crotch.

The shapes had stopped a few feet away. There were three of them, all bipedal, one bigger than the others. Ramón could see them more clearly now. His mind accepted them by treating them as frauds; he thought of them now as men wearing grotesque costumes, and kept looking for some unconvincing detail that would betray the disguise.

Intellectually, he knew better, of course. They were not men in costume. They were not men at all. They were aliens, and not of any race he knew. Ramón had sailed among the stars on one of the great galley ships of the Silver Enye, and once he had glimpsed three of the furred, six-legged H'zhei on the back streets of Acapulco, exotic creatures that looked like a cross between a cat and a caterpillar. The Turu he had seen only on video, and even there they made his skin crawl. These aliens were not Turu, not Enye, not Cian, not members of any of the Great Races. They were not part of the universe as he knew it. They did not belong. A hundred questions, accusations, and pleas fought in his mind. *Who are you? What do you want? Please don't kill me.*

At least they were humanoid bipeds, not spiders or octopi or big-eyed blobs, although something about the articulation of their limbs was disturbingly odd. The smaller two were perhaps six and a half feet tall, the larger one seven feet, which made even the shortest of them far taller than Ramón. Their torsos were columnar, seemingly of uniform breadth at hip and waist and shoulder, and surely they must weigh

more than three hundred pounds apiece, although somehow
the dominant impression they created was one of grace and
suppleness. Their skins were glossy, shining, but each had
its own distinctive coloration: one was a mottled blue and
gold, the second a pale amber, while the largest one had yellowish flesh covered with strange, swirling patterns in silver
and black.

All wore broad belts hung with unknown objects of metal
and glass, and nondescript halters of some ash-gray and lusterless material. Their arms were disproportionately long,
the hands huge, the fingers—three fingers, two thumbs—
incongruously slender and delicate. Their heads were set
low in a hollow between the shoulders, and thrust a little
forward on thick, stumpy necks, giving them a belligerent
and aggressive look, like snapping turtles. Crests of hair or
feathers slanted back from the tops of their heads at rakish
angles. Quills protruded from their shoulders, the napes
of their necks, and the tops of their spinal ridges, forming
bristly ruffs. Their heads were roughly triangular, flattened
on top but bulging out at the base of the skull, the faces
tapering sharply to a point. And the faces were faces out of
nightmare: large, rubbery, black snouts streaked with blue
and orange, trembling and sniffing, mouths like raw, wet
wounds, too wide and lipless, and small, staring eyes set too
low on either side of the snout. Orange eyes, hot and feature-
less as molten marbles.

Staring at him.

They were staring at him as though he was a bug, and that
fanned a spark of anger inside him. He got to his feet and
glared back at them, still shaky but determined not to show
it. Ramón Espejo knelt to nobody! Especially not to ugly,
unnatural monsters like these!

"Which one," he croaked, coughed, and began again.
"Which one of you *pinche* motherfuckers is paying for my
van?"

The aliens didn't react to his words. The large one reached
out a strangely articulated arm—a motion that reminded
Ramón of seaweed stirred by some gentle oceanic current.
Ramón frowned as the alien curled what he had to think of

as its fingers back toward itself once, twice, three times. The thing paused and then repeated the movement. There was something studied about the motion, as though it had been learned by rote, as though its natural equivalent might be without meaning for humans. A low, thudding boom came from deep below them; a mountainous heart that beat twice and went silent. Ramón glanced around him. The alien repeated the curling gesture.

"You want me to come close to you?" Ramón demanded. The great thing's snout twitched, and the quills on its head rose and fell. Again, the strange curling motion. Ramón suddenly recalled a journalist who had come to São Paulo from Kigiake whose only word of Spanish had been *gracias*. The alien was the same—a single gesture repeated for every occasion; employed ubiquitously.

The alien turned away, took a few inhumanly graceful strides, then shifted its torso back toward Ramón and gestured again. *Follow me.* The other two aliens were still as stone except for the restless twitching of their snouts.

"I get taken captive by aliens, and they're too stupid to talk," Ramón said, bravado and anger filling him. "Hey, you. *Pendejo.* Why the fuck would I follow you, eh? Give me a good fucking reason."

The alien stood motionless. Ramón spat, the sputum vanishing as soon as it struck the black tongue-like platform, which seemed to absorb it with a slurping noise. Ramón shook his head in disgust; in fact, there didn't seem to be anything else for him to do but follow. He came forward slowly, his footing unreliable on the disturbingly wet, velvety ground, which gave under him with every step, looking warily all around him, wondering if he should try to run. Run to where, though? And some of the objects suspended from the alien's belt were almost certainly weapons . . .

Ahead was a door cut through the naked rock of the cavern wall, into which the alien disappeared, looking back once again to make its favorite gesture.

Trying to wear his nakedness like a suit of clothes, Ramón followed the alien into the darkness. The other two beasts fell in close behind.

Chapter 6

Afterward, Ramón could not clearly remember that trip. He was led through tunnels barely wide and tall enough to allow the alien to pass. The tunnels slanted steeply up and down, and doubled back on themselves, seemingly at random. The rock was slightly phosphorescent, providing just enough light to let him see his footing. He refused to look behind at the following shapes, although his nerves were crawling like worms.

The silence was heavy here in the belly of the hill, although occasionally a faraway hooting could be heard through many thicknesses of rock. It sounded to Ramón like the noise damned souls might make crying unheeded to a cold and distant God. Sometimes they passed through pockets of light and activity, rooms full of chattering noise and rich, rotten smells, rooms drenched in glaring red or blue or green illumination, rooms dark as ink but for the faint silver line of the path they followed. Once, they stood motionless for long moments in such a room, while Ramón's stomach dropped and he wondered if they could be in an elevator.

Each chamber they passed through seemed more surreal than the last. In one, things that looked like oversize spiders lay in a clump in the center of what looked like a sluggishly moving pool of glowing blue oil. Another high-ceilinged chamber teemed with aliens, swarming over terraced layers of strange objects on the cavern floor. Equipment, perhaps, machines, computers, although most things here were so unfamiliar that they registered only as indecipherable blurs, weird amalgams of shape and shadow and winking light. Far across the cave, two giant aliens—similar to his three companions but fifteen or twenty feet tall—labored in gloom, lifting and stacking what looked like huge sections of honeycomb, moving with ponderous grace, as unreal and hallucinatorily beautiful as stop-motion dinosaurs in old horror movies. To one side, a smaller alien was herding a flow of what looked like spongy molasses down a stairstep fall of boulders, touching the flowing mass occasionally with a long, black rod, as if to urge it along.

It was too much to take in. Ramón's conscious mind was spinning too fast in desperate attempts to make sense of what he saw. The nightmare walk became an interminable series of incomprehensibilities. A great gray tentacle reached out from one wall, caressing the alien before him, and then dropped to the ground and slithered away like a snake. A scent like cardamom and fried onions and rubbing alcohol filled the air and vanished. The deep throbbing booms that he had heard earlier filled the air at intervals that seemed to have no pattern, though Ramón found himself slowly learning to anticipate them.

Away from the chambers, in the tunnels, it was close and dark and silent. The lead alien's back gleamed pale and faint in the phosphorescent glow of the rock, like a fish in dark water, and, for a moment, it seemed to Ramón as if the markings on its flesh were moving, writhing and changing like living things. He stumbled, and instinctively clutched the alien's arm to keep from falling. Its skin was warm and dry, like snakeskin. In the enclosed space of the tunnel, he could smell the alien; it had a heavy, musky odor, like olive oil, like cloves, strange rather than unpleasant. It neither looked behind nor paused nor made a sound. The three aliens continued to walk on imperturbably, at the same steady pace, and Ramón had no choice but to follow after them or be left alone in the chilly darkness of this black alien maze.

At last, they came to a stop in another garishly lit chamber, Ramón almost walking into the wide back of the alien

in front of him. To the human eye, there was something
subtly wrong about the proportions and dimensions of the
chamber: it was more a rhombus than a rectangle, the floor
was slightly tilted, the ceiling tilted at another angle and not
of uniform height, everything subliminally disorienting, everything *off,* making Ramón feel sick and dizzy. The light
was too bright and too blue, and the chamber was filled with
a whispering susurrus that hovered right at the threshold of
hearing.

 This place had not been made by human beings, nor was
it meant for them. As he entered the chamber, he saw that
the walls streamed with tiny crawling pictures, as though a
film of oil was continuously flowing from ceiling to floor
and carrying with it a thin scum of ever-changing images:
swirls of vivid color, geometric shapes, mazy impression-
istic designs, vast surrealistic landscapes. Occasionally,
something recognizable would stream by: representations of
trees, mountains, stars, tiny alien faces that would seem to
stare malignly at Ramón out of the feverdream chaos as they
poured down to be swallowed by the floor.

The alien who'd escorted him gestured him forward.
Gingerly, Ramón crossed the chamber, feeling uneasy and
disconcerted, unconsciously leaning to one side to correct
the tilt of the floor and putting his feet down cautiously, as
though he expected the chamber to pitch or yaw.

In the center of the chamber was a deep, circular pit, lined
by metal, and at the bottom of the pit was another alien.

It was even taller than Ramón's guides, and much fatter,
the lower part of its body bloated to four or five times the cir-
cumference of the other aliens, and its crest and quills were
much longer. Its skin was maggot-white, and completely free
of markings. White with age? Dyed white as an indication
of rank? Or was it of a different race? Impossible to say, but
as the alien's eyes turned upward, toward Ramón, he was
seized and shaken by the force behind its gaze, by the harsh
authority it exuded. He noticed, with another little shock,
that the creature was physically connected to the pit—things
that might have been wires or rods or cables emerged from
its body and disappeared into the smooth metal walls, forming an intricate cat's cradle around it. Some of the cables

were black and dull, some were luminescent, and some, glossy red and gray and brown, pulsed slowly and rhythmically, as if with an obscene life of their own.

The hot orange eyes considered him. Ramón felt his nakedness acutely, but refused to bend to this alien's will even to cover himself. The great pale head shifted.

"Noun," the alien said. "Verb form. Identifier. Semantic placeholder. Sense of identity."

Ramón stared at the alien, fighting to keep surprise from his face. It had spoken in Spanish (Ramón also spoke some English and Portuguese and French, as well as, of course, Portuglish, the bastard lingua franca of the colony), and quite clearly, though its voice was disturbingly rusty and metallic, as though it was a machine. How in hell had it learned a human language? "What the fuck are you saying?" Ramón said. "By Holy Jesus, what do you want?"

"Idiomatic vulgarity. Religious fear," the alien said, and then, with something that sounded like disappointment, "Unflowing." The great beast shifted in its web of wires and cables, its swollen abdomen rippling as if with a life of its own.

Ramón felt his gorge rise. "What do you want from me?"

"You are man," the beast intoned.

"Yes, I'm a fucking man. What did you *think* I was?"

"You lack *tatecreude*. You are a flawed thing. Your nature is dangerous and tends to *aubre*."

Ramón spat on the ground. The arrogance of the harsh, unused voice and the steady gaze of those orange, unblinking eyes made him angry. In times of stress—when he had lost his first van in a drunken bet, when Lianna had finally left him, when Elena threatened to throw him out—Ramón's rage had never deserted him. Now it returned, flushing him with heat and certainty. "What *are* you, you creatures?" he said. "Where do you come from? From this planet? Somewhere else? What do you think you're doing, attacking me, keeping me here against my will? And what about my van, eh? Who's going to get me a new *van*?"

Suddenly, the absurdity of the situation struck him. Here he was, in an alien hive, locked away in the middle of a mountain, surrounded by demons. And he was bitching about his van! He had to fight down the urge to laugh, fearing that once he started he would be unable to stop.

The alien was staring at him wordlessly. "If you want to talk, talk sense," Ramón rasped. Anger gave him a sense of power and control that he knew was at odds with the truth. Any small thing that kept his mind his own, however, was precious. "You don't like what I am, you can show me the way out of this shithole."

The great pale alien seemed to take a moment to consider Ramón's words. Its snout lifted as if it was tasting the air. "Those are sounds, not words," the alien said after a long pause. "Discordances outside proper flow. You must not speak in meaningless sounds, or you will be corrected."

Ramón shivered and looked away; his rage had ebbed as quickly as it had flared, and now he felt tired, chilled by the alien's imperturbability. "What do you want from me?" he asked wearily.

"We do not 'want' anything," the alien said. "Again, you speak outside the way of reality. You have a function: therefore, you exist. You will exercise that function because it is your purpose to do so, your *tatecreude*. No 'wanting' is involved: all is inevitable flow. You are man. You will flow in the pathways in which a man would flow. As he is of you, our path to him will be carved clean. You will fulfill your function."

The creature's voice seemed to be growing clearer as it spoke, as if every word brought it a greater understanding of Ramón's language. He wondered how long he'd have to talk to the thing before it took on a Mexican accent and started cussing. "And if I do not function as you wish?" Ramón asked.

The alien paused, as though briefly puzzled. "You live," it said finally. "Therefore, you exercise your function. Nonfunctioning, you could not exist. To exist and yet not exist— you would be a contradiction, *aubre*, a disruption in the flow. *Aubre* cannot be tolerated. To restore balanced flow, it would be necessary to deny the illusion that you exist."

That at least was clear enough, Ramón thought, feeling gooseflesh sweep across his skin. He chose his words carefully when he spoke again. "And what function am I to fulfill?"

The hot orange eyes fixed on him again. "Take care," the alien warned. "That we must interpret your *tatecreude* for you is a sign that you incline toward *aubre*. But we will grant you a dispensation, as you are not a proper creature. Listen: a man has escaped from us. Three days ago he fled from us, and we have not been able to find him. By this act, he has shown himself to be *aubre,* and so proved that he does not exist. The illusion of his existence must therefore be negated. The man must not be allowed to reach a human settlement, to tell other humans about us. Should he do so, that would interfere with our own *tatecreude.* Such interference is *gaesu,* prime contradiction. Therefore you will find him, negate him, in order to restore balanced flow."

"How am *I* supposed to find him if you could not?"

"You are man. You are the same. You will find him."

"He could be anywhere by now!" Ramón protested.

"Where you would go and where he would go—they are the same. You will go where he has gone, and you will find him."

Ramón considered that.

"So you mean there's a man out there who found you and got away, and now you want me to help you catch him before he can get back to civilization? You want me to hunt for you? Is that what you're saying?"

The thing in the cables considered this.

"Yes," it said.

"And why the *fuck* would I do that?"

The deep, awesome, booming sound rose from the depths of the planet below. Ramón was reminded again where he was, and to what sort of creature he was speaking. Vertigo washed through him. The great alien didn't seem to notice his distress.

"You are imbued with purpose," it said, almost patiently. "Your heart beats. You exchange gases. You do so for a purpose. To be and yet be without purpose is contradictory. Your language is flawed in that it can express illusory states. Your purpose is to aid in locating the man. If you are without purpose, the illusion of your existence must be rectified."

Well, Ramón thought, that was clear enough. Hunt or die. The answer was simple. He would lie. He had no intention of

playing Judas goat for these demons, but likewise he would
never be able to break away from them as long as he was ass-
deep in their mountain. If he could make his way to the open
air, there was at least hope. A chilling thought struck him.

"How long did you keep me here?" he asked. "Is it still
summer out there? Because tracking some mad fucker in
winter isn't going to work."

The beast was silent. Ramón grew impatient. If the time
he had spent in darkness had been long enough for the seasons to change, escape from the aliens would be suicide. The
weather would kill him as effectively as a knife in the ribs.

"How long was I in that fucking vat?"

"Three days," the thing said without hesitation.

Ramón felt a stab of fear, sharper for being unexpected.

"The man you want tracked down. That's how long he's
been running? All the time I've been here?"

The alien paused for a long moment, before its deep,
hoarse voice answered.

"Yes."

This far to the north, there was no way it could be coincidence; Ramón had been followed. Some poor fucker from
the constabulary had come north after him, searching for
the European's killer, and instead had walked into this scene
from Hell. Ramón couldn't help imagining it—a Diegotown
cop, or maybe one of the governor's own security agents,
making his stealthy way toward Ramón's camp only to find
scorched ground, twisted plastic, and these monsters flying
from the great metal wall he had uncovered. Had the bastard had time to call for help? No satellites reached this far
north, but the police had radio they could bounce off the
atmosphere. Had the aliens destroyed the policeman's van
as they had Ramón's?

Ramón had been poor all his life, and, like most poor
people, the instinct to be afraid of the police had been
burned into his soul. The thought that they had been close
enough to him to fall into the same alien snare brought the
coppery taste of panic to Ramón's mouth. And yet, his logi-
cal mind told him that the constabulary was his best hope
now. Usually the last thing he'd want to see were the police,
but there were situations dire enough, like this one, when

even somebody like him, who had frequently run afoul of the law, would be damn glad to see the cops coming over the hill. If word could get as far as Fiddler's Jump, aid would come. The military forces of the colony. Ramón had to hope that the man who had been set to follow him was as good at fleeing as he'd been at shadowing him.

And if the cavalry came, and Ramón was freed, what then? He had killed the European. Would the governor still be hot to have Ramón hanged for it? Or would his part in discovering the alien nest win him amnesty? He was trapped between the Devil and the deep blue sea.

"All right," Ramón said. "You want the guy found, I'll find him for you. He's no friend of mine." He rubbed his chin shrewdly. It wouldn't do to give in too easily, though. Even things as strange as these might recognize that as subterfuge. "If I do this thing for you," he asked slyly, "what do I get out of it?"

The alien stared at him for several long moments, long enough that Ramón began to fear that he had overplayed his hand. "You are an improper and contradictory creature. *Aubre* may manifest in you. We will ensure against such manifestations by accompanying you."

"You? All of you?"

"We. Not-we. Your language is flawed, it admits contradiction where none exists. We will separate part of the whole. Maneck will sacrifice himself to maintain the flow. Maneck is we, and not-we. Maneck will accompany you and watch over you. Through him, your *tatecreude* will be protected."

Well, the thought that the aliens would send him out alone into the bush, trusting him to keep to the task they had assigned, was one that had always been too good to be true. But the fact that there would be only a single guard was a blessing. Two or three of the things would have been difficult to evade. More than that, impossible. Only one, however . . .

The alien who had led him here moved silently to Ramón's side. It was eerie—nothing so big should be so quiet.

"Maneck, eh?" Ramón said to the thing. "Your name's Maneck? I'm Ramón Espejo."

While Ramón was still wondering if he should attempt to shake hands with it, Maneck abruptly reached out and took him by the shoulders, lifted him like a doll, and held him immobile in the air. Ramón fought instinctively—nights at the bar and in the street coming back to his arms and legs in a rage. He might as well have punched the ocean. Maneck didn't budge.

Up from the pit rose a pale white snake.

Ramón watched in horrified fascination. It was obviously a cable of some sort—two bare wires protruded from the visible end—but its movements were so supple and lifelike that he could not help but think of it as a pale and sinister cobra. It reared almost to eye level, swayed slowly from side to side, and aimed its blind pallid head at Ramón. The head quivered slightly, as though the snake was testing the air in search of its prey. Then it stretched out toward him.

Again Ramón tried desperately to break free, but Maneck wrenched him effortlessly back into position. As the cable-snake came closer, he saw that it was pulsating rhythmically, and that the two naked wires in its head were vibrating like a serpent's flickering tongue. His flesh crawled and he felt his testicles retract. He felt his nakedness vividly now—he was unprotected, helpless, all of the soft, vulnerable parts of his body exposed to the hostile air.

"I'll do it!" Ramón shrieked. "I said I'd do it! You don't have to do this to me! I'll help you!"

The cable touched the hollow of his throat.

Ramón felt a sensation like the touch of dead lips, a double pinprick of pain, a flash of intense cold. An odd, quivering shock ran up and down his body, as though someone were tracing his nervous system with feather fingers. His vision dimmed for a heartbeat, then came back. Maneck lowered him to the ground.

The cable was now embedded in his neck. Fighting nausea, he reached up and took hold of it, feeling it pulse in his hands. It was warm to the touch, like human flesh. He pulled at it tentatively, then tugged harder. He felt the flesh of his throat move when he tugged. To rip it free would obviously be as difficult as tearing off his own nose. The cable pulsed again, and Ramón realized that it was pulsing in time to the beating of his heart. As he watched, it seemed to darken slowly, as if it were filling with his blood.

He saw with horror that the opposite end of the cable had somehow linked itself to the alien that had held him, blending into its right wrist. Maneck. He was on a leash. A hunting dog for demons.

"The *sahael* will not injure you, but it will help to resolve your contradictions," the thing in the pit said, as if sensing his distress but failing to understand it. "You should welcome it. It will help to protect you from *aubre*. Should you manifest *aubre,* you will be corrected. Like this."

Ramón found himself on the floor, though he did not remember falling. Only now that the pain had passed could he look back at it and realize that it had been the worst pain he had ever experienced, as a swimmer turns to look back at a wave that has passed over his head. He didn't remember screaming, but his throat was raw, and it almost seemed as if the echo of his shriek was still reverberating from the chamber walls. He caught his breath, and then retched. He knew that he would do whatever was required to prevent that from happening again, anything at all, and for the first time since he woke in darkness, Ramón Espejo felt truly ashamed.

I will kill you all, Ramón thought. *Somehow, I will cut this thing out of my throat, and then I will come and kill you all.*

"School yourself," the pale alien said. "Correct *aubre,* and even such a flawed thing as yourself may achieve cohesion or even coordinate level."

It took Ramón some time to realize that this gibberish had been a dismissal: a stern but kindly admonition, hellfire threatened, the prospect of redemption dangled, and *go forth and sin no more.* The sonofabitch was a missionary!

Maneck lifted Ramón back to his feet and nudged him toward a tunnel. The fleshy leash—the *sahael*—shrank to match whatever distance was between them. Maneck made a sound that he couldn't interpret and apparently gave up gentle coaxing. The alien moved briskly forward, the *sahael* tugging now at Ramón's throat. He had no choice but to follow, like a dog trotting at its master's heel.

And you, mi amigo, Ramón thought, staring at Maneck's indifferent back, *will be the very first to die.*

Chapter 7

Back through the tunnels they went, through cavern after cavern, through rhythmic noise, billowing shadow, and glaring blue light. Ramón walked leadenly, like an automaton, pulled along by Maneck, the tether in his neck feeling heavy and awkward. The chill air leached the heat from his body, and even the work of walking wasn't enough to keep him warm.

As he stumbled along, in the privacy of his mind, Ramón searched for hope.

How long would it be before Elena noticed his absence? Months, at least. Or she might think he'd gone off again, down to Nuevo Janeiro without her, to file his reports and collect his fees and keep his money for himself. Or run off on a drunken spree with some other woman. Rather than start a search for him, she was more likely to work herself into a blind rage and go fuck some hairy prospector from a bush bar or rum shack in revenge. Likewise, Manuel Griego would expect him to be in the field for three or four weeks at the least. Ramón silently berated himself for talking about hunting and his fantasy of disappearing into the Sierra Hueso to live off the land. Manuel might assume he wasn't coming back at all, especially if he suspected (as he probably did) that Ramón knew that the cops were after him.

The only ones who would look for him were the law, and

the law would have followed him with public execution in mind.

There was no one. That was the truth. He had lived his life on his own terms—always on his own terms—and here was the price of it. He was on his own, hundreds of miles from the nearest human settlement, captured and enslaved.

If he was going to get out of this, he would have to find his own way out.

Maneck tugged at the *sahael* and Ramón looked up, aware for the first time that they had stopped. The alien thing pushed a bundle into his arms. Clothes.

The clothes were a sleeveless one-piece garment, something like pajamas, a large cloak, and hard-soled slipper-boots, all made from a curious, lusterless material. He pulled them on with fingers stiff from cold. The aliens were obviously not used to tailoring for humans; the clothes were clumsily made and ill-fitting, but at least they afforded him some protection against the numbing cold. It wasn't until his nakedness was covered and warmth began to return to his limbs that his teeth began to chatter.

Maneck led him down a bright white passageway to another great, high-vaulted chamber. Things the color and size of aphids swarmed across the floor, bumping into each other and into his legs, singing incomprehensible gibberish in high, sweet voices. In the center of the room squatted a bone-colored box like the one that had destroyed his van. As they drew near, Ramón saw that the thing was not solid. Instead, a million tiny strands of dripping white and cream made a webwork of slats that shifted to create an opening and then close it behind them.

The interior of the box was likewise only half-solid—a wide, low bench that appeared intended for Maneck's barrel-like form and also a smaller area set into the wall where Ramón himself might sit, legs pulled up to his chest.

Ramón waited leadenly while Maneck examined the box, leaning in to run its long, slender fingers carefully over the controls. He could feel himself becoming dazed and passive, numbed by weariness and shock—he'd been through too much, too fast. And he was tired, more tired than he could remember being before; perhaps the shot they'd given him, glucose or adrenaline or whatever it had been, was wearing off. He was almost asleep on his feet when Maneck seized him, lifted him into the air as if he was a little child, and stuffed him into the box. He struggled to sit up, but Maneck seized his arms, drew them behind his back, and bound them with a thin length of wirelike substance, then hobbled his legs, before turning and sitting down in front of the controls. Maneck touched a pushplate, and the box rose smoothly into the air.

Acceleration shoved Ramón's head sideways, pinning it at an uncomfortable angle. In spite of the terror of his situation, he realized that he was unable to stay awake any longer. Even as they rose toward the high-domed cavern roof, his eyes were squeezing shut, as though the mild g-forces that pulled with mossy inevitability on his bones were also drawing him inexorably into sleep.

Above them, the rock opened.

As Ramón's consciousness faded, drowning him in hissing white snow, he saw, beyond the hole in the stone, a single pale and isolate star.

A freezing wind lashed him awake. He struggled to sit up. The box lurched to the left, and he found himself looking through the spaces between the woven slats straight down through an ocean of air at the tiny tops of the trees. The box canted over the other way, violently, and the darkening evening sky swirled around his head, momentarily turning the faint, newly emerged stars into tight little squiggles of light.

They leveled off. Maneck sat behind the box's control panel unshakably, firm and cold as a statue, quills rippling in the bitter wind. Banking again, they fell at a slant through the air. He couldn't have been insensible for more than a minute or two, Ramón realized; that was the aliens' mountain just behind them, the exit hole now irised shut again, and that was the mountain slope where he'd been captured, just below. Even as they coasted down toward the slope, the sky was growing significantly darker. The sun had sunk beneath the horizon some moments before, leaving only the

thinnest sliver of glazed red along the junction line of land
and air. The rest of the sky was the color of plum and egg-
plant and ash, dying rapidly to an inky blackness overhead
and to the west. Armed and bristling with trees, the mountain slope rushed up to meet them. Too fast! Surely they
would crash . . .

They touched down lightly in the middle of an alpine
valley, settling out of the sky as silently as a feather. Maneck
killed the box's engine. Darkness swallowed them, and they
were surrounded by the sly and predatory noises of evening.
Maneck seized Ramón, and, lifting him like a rag doll,
dragged him from the box, carried him a few feet away, and
dropped him to the ground.

Ramón groaned involuntarily, startled and ashamed by
the loudness of his voice. His arms were still bound behind
him, and to lie upon them was excruciatingly painful. He
rolled over onto his stomach. The ground under him was
so cold that it was comfortable, and even in his sick and
confused condition, Ramón realized that meant death. He
thrashed and squirmed, and managed to roll himself up in
the long cloak he'd been given; it was surprisingly warm.
He would have fallen asleep then, in spite of his pain and
discomfort, but light beat against his eyelids where there had
been no light, and he opened his eyes.

The light seemed blinding at first, but it dimmed as his
eyes adjusted. Maneck had brought something from the box,
a small globe attached to a long metal rod, and jammed
the sharp end of the rod into the soil; now the globe was
alight, burning from within with a dim bluish light, emit-
ting rhythmic waves of heat. As Ramón watched, Maneck
walked around the globe—the *sahael* shortening visibly
with each step—and came slowly toward him with seeming deliberation. Only then, watching Maneck prowl toward
him, seeing the wet gleam in the corner of its orange eyes as
it looked from side to side, seeing the way its nose crinkled
and twitched, the way its head swiveled and swayed restlessly on the stubby neck, the shrugging of its shoulders at
each step, hearing the iron rasp of its breath, smelling its
thick, musky odor—only then did some last part of Ramón's

mind fully accept the fact that he was its captive, alone and at its mercy in the wilderness.

That simple knowledge hit Ramón with such force that he felt the blood begin to drain from his face, and even as he was worming and scrambling backward in a futile attempt to get away from his captor, he was losing his grip on the world, losing consciousness, slipping down into darkness.

The alien stood over him, seen again through the hazy white snow of faintness, seeming to loom up endlessly into the sky like some horrid and impossible beanstalk, with eyes like blazing orange suns. That was the last thing Ramón saw before the snow piled up over his face and buried him, and everything was gone.

Morning was a blaze of pain. He had fallen asleep on his back, and he could no longer feel his arms. The rest of his body ached as though it had been beaten with clubs. The alien was standing over him again—or perhaps it had never moved, perhaps it had stood there all night, looming and remote, terrible, tireless, and unsleeping. The first thing Ramón saw that morning, through a bloodshot haze of pain, was the alien's face; the long, twitching black snout with its blue and orange markings, the quills stirring in the wind and moving like the feelers of some huge insect.

I will kill you, Ramón thought once again. There was very little anger in it. Only a deep, animal certainty. *Somehow, I will kill you.*

Maneck hauled Ramón to his feet and set him loose, but his legs would not hold him, and he crashed back to the ground as soon as he was released. Again Maneck pulled him up, and again Ramón fell.

As Maneck reached for him the third time, Ramón screamed, "Kill me! Why don't you just kill me?" He wormed backward, away from Maneck's reaching hand. "You might as well just kill me now!"

Maneck stopped. Its head tilted to one side to regard Ramón curiously in an oddly birdlike manner. The hot orange eyes peered at him closely, unblinking.

"I need food," Ramón went on, in a more reasonable tone.

"I need water. I need rest. I can't use my arms and legs if they're tied like this. I can't even stand, let alone walk!" He heard his voice rising again, but couldn't stop it. "Listen, *puto,* I need to *piss*! I'm a man, not a machine!" With a supreme effort, he heaved himself to his knees and knelt there in the dirt, swaying. "Is this *aubre*? Eh? Good! Kill me, then! I can't go on like this!"

Man and alien stared at each other for a silent moment. Ramón, exhausted by his outburst, breathed in rattling gasps. Maneck studied him carefully, snout quivering. At last, it said, "You possess *retehue*?"

"How the shit would *I* know?" Ramón croaked, his voice rasping in his dry throat. "What the fuck is it?" He drew himself up as much as he could, and glared back at the alien.

"You possess *retehue*," the alien repeated, but it was not a question this time. It took a quick step forward, and Ramón flinched, afraid that the death he'd demanded was on its way. But instead, Maneck cut him free.

At first, he could feel nothing in his arms and legs; they were as dead as old wood. Then sensation flooded back into them, burning like ice, and they began to spasm convulsively. Ramón set his face stoically and said nothing, but Maneck must have noticed and correctly interpreted the sudden pallor of his skin, for it reached down and began to massage Ramón's arms and legs. Ramón shrunk away from its touch—again he was reminded of snakeskin, dry, firm, warm—but the alien's powerful fingers were surprisingly deft and gentle, loosening knotted muscles, and Ramón found that he didn't mind the contact as much as he would have thought that he would; it was making the pain go away, after all, which was what really counted.

"Your limbs have insufficient joints," Maneck commented. "That position would not be uncomfortable for me." It bent its arms backward and forward at impossible angles to demonstrate. With his eyes closed, Ramón could almost believe that he was listening to a human being—Maneck's Spanish was much more fluent than that of the alien in the pit, and its voice had less of the rusty timbre of the machine.

But then Ramón would open his eyes and see that terrible alien face, ugly and bestial, only inches from his own, and his stomach would turn over, and he would have to adjust all over again to the fact that he was chatting with a monster.

"Stand up now," Maneck said. It helped Ramón up, and supported him while he limped and stomped in a slow semi-circle to work out cramps and restore circulation, looking as if he was performing some arthritic tribal dance. At last, he was able to stand unsupported, although his legs wobbled and quivered with the strain.

"We have lost time this morning," Maneck said. "This is all time we might have employed in exercising our functions." Ramón could almost imagine that it sighed. "I have not previously performed this type of function. I did not realize that you possessed *retehue,* and therefore failed to take all factors into account. Now we must suffer delays accordingly."

Suddenly, Ramón understood what *retehue* must be. He was more baffled than outraged. "How could you not realize that I was sentient? You were there all the while I talked to the white thing in the pit!"

"We were present, but I had not integrated yet," Maneck said simply. It did not elaborate further, and Ramón had to be content with that. "Now that I am, I will observe you closely. You are to demonstrate the limitations to the human flow. Once we are informed, the man's path is better predicted." It gestured around them. "Here is the last of places the man was known," it said. Its voice was deep and resonant. Ramón could almost think that the thing sounded sorrowful. "We will begin here."

Ramón looked around. Indeed, there were signs of a small, improvised camp. A tiny lean-to hardly big enough to sleep in had been constructed with fresh boughs and tied together with lengths of bark. A fire pit ringed by stone showed ashes where the lawman had cooked something at the end of a fire-hardened stick. Whoever they'd sent after Ramón had spent enough time in the field to know how to survive with what came to hand. Good for him.

Maneck stood silent by the bone-colored box, the thick,

fleshy *sahael* attached to its arm. Ramón looked at it, waiting to see what strategy the thing would adopt. The alien, however, did nothing. After a few minutes of uncomfortable silence, Ramón cleared his throat.

"Monster. Hey. Now we're here, what is it you want me to do, eh?"

"You are a man," Maneck said. "Behave as he would behave."

"He's got tools and clothes, and he doesn't have a leash on," Ramón said.

"Your confluence will be approximate at the beginning," Maneck said. "This is expected. You will not be punished for it. Your needs will lead you to a matched flow. That is sufficient."

"Speaking of needs and flowing," Ramón said, "I got to piss."

"That will do," Maneck said. "Begin by achieving piss."

Ramón smiled.

"You stay here, then, I'll go achieve piss."

"I will observe," Maneck said.

"You want to watch me piss?"

"We are to explore the banks which bound the man's possible channels. If this task is a necessity of his being, then I will understand it."

Ramón shrugged.

"You're just lucky I'm not shy about this kind of thing," he said, walking to the nearest tree. "There's some men couldn't get a drop out, not with you watching them, eh?"

The ground was rough, and Ramón's feet were tender. The long bath in the alien gel seemed to have softened away all his calluses. As he relieved himself against the tree trunk, he tried to make sense of the alien's behavior. The limitations of human flow, it had said. For a being so impatiently concentrated on pragmatic results, Maneck was strangely interested in Ramón's need to urinate, which ought to have struck it as irrelevant. It wasn't an activity that seemed important to hunting the fugitive. But it had not known that binding his arms behind him would discomfort him, either. Perhaps the aliens needed him to understand what the habits of a man were. He was more than a hound. Merely by *being human,* he was a guide for them.

Ramón stood for a long moment after his bladder was empty, taking the opportunity to turn his mind to strategy. He could not refuse the aliens. The demonstration of the pain his leash could deliver had convinced him of that. But there was a long history of labor protests in which things simply took a longer time and more materials than expected. Slowdowns. Ramón might have to be on the job for these devils, but he didn't have to be a good worker. He would move slowly, explain the fine points of pissing and shitting and hunting and trapping for as long as Maneck would allow it. Every hour Ramón could waste was another one that the lawman had to make his return to civilization and send help back. How things would unfold once that had happened, Ramón didn't know.

He shook his penis twice as long as was truly required, then let the robe drop back down to cover his knees. Maneck's great head shifted, but whether this was a sign of approval or disgust, Ramón had no way to tell.

"You are complete?" Maneck asked.

"Sure," Ramón said. "Complete enough for the moment."

"You have other needs?"

"I'll need to find fresh water to drink," Ramón said. "And some food to eat."

"Complex chemical compounds which can be harvested of their potential to facilitate flow and prevent pooling," Maneck said. "This is *mehiban.* How will you manufacture this?"

"Manufacture? I'm not going to make it. I'm going to *catch* it. Hunt for it. What is it you devils do?"

"We consume complex chemical compounds. These are *ae euth'eloi.* Made things. But the *oekh* I have would not nourish you. How do you obtain food? I will allow you to procure it for yourself."

Ramón scratched his arm and shrugged.

"Well, I'm going to kill something. I'd try making a sling, maybe killing a flatfur or dragonjay, but I've got this fucking thing in my neck. You wouldn't want to take it out of me, just long enough I can show you how this is done?"

Maneck stood unresponsive as a tree.

"Didn't think so, monster. It's trapping, then. It might take a little longer, but it will do. Come on."

In fact, the fastest and easiest thing would have been to gather up sug beetles as he had the other night. He had seen a few even this deep under the forest canopy. Or a half hour of gathering would have gotten him enough mianberry to make a small meal; this far north, you could pick them off the trees by the handful. Feeding off the land wasn't hard. The amino acids that had built up the biosphere of São Paulo were almost all identical to those on Earth. But that would have been simple, and would have allowed them to move quickly on to whatever the next phase of their hunt would be. So, instead, Ramón taught the alien how to trap.

His equipment had, of course, been destroyed with his van. If the thought had truly been that he should catch his dinner easily and well, that would have enraged him. Since his intention now was to stall, it only made him peevish. The bastard things had destroyed his van, after all.

Ramón scrounged through the underbrush for the raw material of a snare: whipvine, a few longish sticks seasoned enough to break but green enough to bend first, a handful of São Paulo's nut equivalent—a sticky bole that smelled of honey and resin—to act as bait. He was annoyed to find that all this hurt his fingers, which had been as tough as old leather; the syrup bath in which the aliens had soaked him must have melted away the calluses on his hands as well, leaving his fingers ill-prepared for real work. Through it all, Maneck watched in silence. Ramón found himself explaining the process as he went. The pressure of the thing's unspeaking regard made him jumpy.

When at last Ramón had the snares in place, he led Maneck back into the underbrush to wait for some unsuspecting animal to happen by. It was unlikely to take long; the animals this far north were naive, unfamiliar with traps, never having been hunted by humans before, and so were easy to catch. Still, he would stall for as long as he could before checking the traps.

They sat well in among the branches, Maneck watching

him with what seemed sometimes like profound curiosity, sometimes like impatience, but was likely an emotion Ramón had never felt or heard named.

"The food-thing comes to you to be ended?" Maneck said in its sad, sonorous voice.

"Not if you keep making a fucking racket," Ramón whispered. "It isn't as if we're getting its consent first."

"It is unknowing? This is *niedutoi*?"

"I don't know what that means," Ramón said.

"Interesting," Maneck said. "You understand purpose, and killing, but not *niedutoi*. You are a disturbing creature."

"That's what they tell me," Ramón said.

"Under what circumstances do you kill?"

"Me?"

Maneck was silent. Ramón felt a stab of annoyance at the thing for spoiling the hunt, even as he reminded himself that it was all a play for time. He sighed.

"Men kill for all sorts of reasons. If someone's going to kill you, you kill them first. Or if they're fucking your wife. Or sometimes men will be so poor they have to rob someone for money. That can go too far. Or if someone declares war, then soldiers go and kill each other. Or sometimes . . . sometimes you just walk into the wrong bar and start acting like a *cabrón* where the wrong bastard can hear you, and he kills you for it."

For a moment, he was back in the El Rey. He couldn't recall anymore what precisely it was the European had said that started things. The details were all misty and uncertain, like a half-remembered dream. There had been a pachinko machine, its tiny steel balls bouncing crazily against the network of pins. And a woman with straight, black hair. It hadn't been anything the man had said to Ramón. No one had liked the *pendejo*. Everyone had wanted to crack the man's ass the other way, but Ramón had been the one to do it.

Why did you kill him?

Ramón shivered. Maneck's steady gaze seemed to peer into his soul, as if every truth and lie in Ramón's long, sorry life were written on his face. A sudden rush of shame possessed him.

"You have declared war on the food-thing," Maneck intoned and Ramón's sudden guilt vanished. Maneck no more understood him than a dog could read a news feed. With an act of will, he refrained from laughing.

"No," Ramón said. "It's just an animal. I need food. It *is* food. It's not killing, only hunting."

"The food-thing is not killed?"

"Yes, okay. Fine. You kill animals to eat them if you need food," Ramón said. Then, a moment later: "And also if they're fucking your wife."

"I understand," the alien said and lapsed into silence.

They waited as the sun rose higher in the perfect blue sky. Maneck ate some of his *oekh,* which turned out to be a brown paste the consistency of molasses with a thick, vinegary scent. Ramón scratched at the place in his neck where the *sahael* anchored in his flesh, and tried to ignore the emptiness of his belly. The hunger grew quickly, though, and, in spite of his good intentions about stalling as long as he could, it was less than two hours later that he rose and walked out to check his catch—two grasshoppers (almost identical to the locusts of Earth, but warm-blooded and able to nurse their young from tiny, fleshy nipples at the joints of their carapace), and a *gordita,* one of the fuzzy round marsupials that the colonists called "the little fat ones of the Virgin." The *gordita* had died badly, biting itself in its frenzy. Its spiky fur was already black with thick, tarry blood. Maneck looked on with interest as Ramón removed the animals from the snares.

"It is difficult to think of this as having anything to do with food," it said. "Why do the creatures strangle themselves for you? Is it their *tatecreude*?"

"No," Ramón said as he strung the bodies on the length of carrying twine. "It's not their *tatecreude*. It's just something that happened to them." He found himself staring at his hands as he worked, and, for some reason, his hands made him uneasy. He shrugged the feeling away. "Don't your people hunt for food?"

"The hunt is not for food," Maneck said flatly. "The hunt is wasted on creatures such as these. How can they appreciate it? Their brains are much too small."

"My stomach is also too small, but it will appreciate *them*." He stood up, swinging the dead animals over his shoulder.

"Do you swallow the creatures now?" Maneck asked.

"First they must be cooked."

"Cooked?"

"Burned, over a fire."

"Fire," Maneck repeated. "Uncontrolled combustion. Proper food does not require such preparation. You are a primitive creature. These steps waste time, time which might be better used to fulfill your *tatecreude*. *Ae euth'eloi* does not interfere with the flow."

Ramón shrugged. "I cannot eat your food, monster, and I cannot eat these raw." He held the carcasses up for inspection. "If we are to get on with me exercising my function, I need to make a fire. Help me gather sticks."

Back at the clearing, Ramón improvised a bow-starter and started a small cook fire. When the flames were crackling well, the alien turned to look at Ramón. "Combustion is proceeding," it said. "What will you do now? I wish to observe this function 'cooking.'"

Was that an edge of distaste in the alien's voice? He suddenly had a flash of how odd the process must seem to Maneck: catching and killing an animal, cutting its pelt off and pulling out its internal organs, dismembering it, toasting the dead carcass over a fire, and then eating it. For a moment, it seemed a grotesque and ghoulish thing to do, and it had never seemed like that before. He stared down at the *gordita* in his hand, and then at his hand itself, sticky with dark blood, and the subtle feeling of wrongness he'd been fighting off all morning intensified once again. "First I must skin them," he said resolutely, pushing down the uneasiness, "before I can cook them."

"They have skin already, do they not?" Maneck said.

Ramón surprised himself by smiling. "I must take their skin off. And their fur. Cut it off, with a knife, you see? Way out here, I'll just throw the pelts away, eh? Waste of money, but then grasshopper pelts aren't worth much anyway."

Maneck's snout twitched, and it prodded at the grasshoppers with a foot. "This seems inefficient. Does it not waste a large portion of the food, cutting it off and throwing it away? All of the rind."

"I don't eat fur."

"Ah," Maneck said. It moved up close behind Ramón and sank to the ground, its legs bending backward grotesquely. "It will be interesting to observe this function. Proceed."

"I need a knife," Ramón said. When Maneck said nothing, he added, "The man would have a knife."

"You will require one also?"

"Well, I can't do this with my teeth," Ramón said.

Wordlessly, the alien plucked a cylinder from its belt and handed it to Ramón. When Ramón turned it over in bafflement, Maneck reached across and did something to the cylinder, and a six-inch silver wire sprang out stiffly. Ramón took the strange knife and began gutting the *gordita*. The wire slid easily through the flesh. Perhaps it was the hunger that focused Ramón so intently on his task, because it wasn't until he had set the *gordita* on a spit and begun on the first grasshopper that he realized what the alien had done.

It had handed him a weapon.

The thing had made its mistake. Now it would die for it.

He fought the sudden rush of adrenaline, struggling to keep the blade from wobbling in his hands, to keep his hands from shaking. Bent over the careful task of digging out the grasshopper's rear gills, he glanced at Maneck. The alien seemed to have noticed nothing. The problem was, where to strike it? Stabbing it in the body was too great a risk; he didn't know where the vital organs were, and he couldn't be sure of striking a killing blow. Maneck was larger and stronger than he was. In a protracted fight, Ramón knew, he would lose. It had to be done swiftly. The throat, he decided, with a rush of exhilaration that was almost like flying. He would slash the knife as deep across the alien's throat as he could. The thing had a mouth and it breathed, after all, so there had to be an air passage in the neck somewhere. If he could sever that, it would only be a matter of remaining alive long enough for the alien to choke to death on its own blood. It was a thin chance, but he would take it.

"Look here," he said, picking up the body of the *gordita*.

With its legs and scales cut away, its flesh was soft and pink as raw tuna. Maneck leaned closer, as Ramón had hoped, its eyes trained on the dead flesh in his left hand, ignoring the blade in his right. The heady elation of violence filled him, as if he was in the street outside a bar in Diegotown. The monsters didn't know that this thing they'd captured knew how to be a monster too! He waited until Maneck turned its head a little to the side to better squint at the *gordita,* exposing the mottled black-and-yellow flesh of its throat, and then he struck—

Abruptly, he was sprawled on his back on the ground, staring up into the violet sky. His stomach muscles were knotted, and he was breathing in harsh little gasps. The pain had hit him like a stone giant's fist, crumpled him and thrown him aside. It had been over in an eyeblink, too quick to be remembered, but his body still ached and twitched with the shock. He had dropped the knife.

You fool, he thought.

"Interesting," Maneck said. "Why did you do that? I pose you no danger, and so you need not defend yourself. I am not food for you, and so you need not kill me to eat. You have not declared war upon me. I have not gone to a bar, nor do I have money. I have not fucked your wife. And still you experience a drive to kill. What is the nature of that drive?"

Ramón would have laughed if he could; it was comic and tragic and deserving of his despairing rage. He levered himself up to sitting. Blood was smeared on his hands and chest from writhing on the corpse of the *gordita.*

"You . . ." Ramón began. "You *knew.*"

Maneck's quills rose and fell. The evil, implacable orange of its eyes seemed to glow in the soft light that filtered through the forest canopy.

"The *sahael* participates in your flow," it said. "It will not permit actions on your part that would interfere with your *tatecreude.* You cannot harm me in any fashion."

"You can read my mind, then."

"The *sahael* can prevent action that is *aubre* before the action takes place. I do not understand 'read my mind.'"

"You know what I am thinking! You know what I'm going to do before I do it."

"No. To drink from first intentions would disturb the flow and affect your function. It is only when your intention expresses *aubre* that you are corrected."

Ramón wiped his eyes with the back of his hand.

"So you can't tell what I'm thinking, but you can tell what I'm going to do?"

Maneck considered him in silence, and then said, "Every movement is a cascade from intent to action. The *sahael* drinks from far up the cascade. The intention to act precedes the action, so you cannot act before I am aware of the action you are taking. Attempts to harm me cannot be completed, and will be punished. You are a primitive being not to know this." It tilted its head to stare more closely at him. "Please return to the issue at hand. What is the nature of that drive? Why do you wish to kill me?"

"Because a man is supposed to be free," Ramón said, pushing ineffectually at the thick, fleshy leash at his throat. "You're holding me prisoner!"

The alien shifted its head from one side to the other, as if the words meant nothing to it and were literally falling from its ears. Maneck lifted him easily and set him on his feet. To Ramón's shame and humiliation, the alien gently placed the wire knife back in his hand.

"Continue the function," Maneck said. "You were flaying the corpse of the small animal."

Ramón turned the silver cylinder slowly, shaking his head. He was unmanned. He could no more defeat this thing than an infant child could best his father. He was so little threat to it that it would hand him a weapon with total unconcern. He felt the urge to drive the knife into his own chest and end this humiliation, but he pushed the thoughts away before the *sahael* could exact its punishment.

He sharpened another small stick, using the alien knife, impaled the small bodies upon it, and held the raw meat over the flame. In the beginning, he kept the *gordita* and the grasshoppers far enough back that the cooking went slowly, but as the scent of grease and cooked meat woke his own belly, he let the branch dip.

The thin, stringy meat tasted better than Ramón had remembered—it was salty and had a rich, earthy taste. When he had stripped the small corpses to their thin, yellow bones, he wiped his hands on his robe and stood up.

"Let's go. I have to find fresh water."

"The seared flesh is not sufficient?"

Ramón spat.

"I can live for weeks without food," he said. "No water, and I'll die in days."

It rose and let Ramón lead the way through the forest to a cold rushing stream, foaming white as it broke over streambed rocks. This far north, the glaciers fed the streams and eventually the great river, the Río Embudo, that passed through Fiddler's Jump. As he squatted, cupping the numbing cold water to his lips, he imagined setting a message in a bottle to bob its way down to civilization. *Trapped by monsters! Send help!* He might as well plan to make a flock of flapjacks fly him back to Diegotown. Dreaming was no better than dreaming.

He wiped his mouth with the back of his hand and sat back.

"This is all then?" Maneck said. "Consume dead flesh and water. Emit piss. These are the channels that constrain the man?"

"Well, he'll have to take a dump sometimes. Like pissing, sort of. And he'll sleep."

"You will do these things," Maneck said.

Ramón stood, turning back toward the camp and the flying box. The alien followed him.

"You can't just command those things," Ramón said. "It's not like I'm some kind of *pinche* machine that you can press a button and I fall asleep. Things come in their own time."

"And the dumping?"

Ramón felt a surge of rage. The thing was an idiot; he was enslaved by a race of morons.

"It comes in its own time too," Ramón said.

"Then we will observe the time," Maneck said.

"Fine."

"While we observe, you will explain 'free.'"

Ramón paused, looking back over his shoulder. Light

dappled the alien's swirling skin, an effect like camouflage.

"You will kill to be free," Maneck said. "What is 'free'?"

"Free is not with a fucking thing sticking into my neck," Ramón said. "Free is able to do what I want when I want without having to dance to anyone's fucking tune."

"Is this dance customary?"

"Christ!" Ramón yelled, wheeling on his captor. "Free is being your own goddamn man! Free is not answering to anybody for anything! Not your boss, not your woman, not the *pinche* governor and his *pinche* little army! A man who's free makes his own path where he wants to make it, and no one can stand in the way. No one! Are you too fucking stupid to understand that?"

Ramón was breathing hard as if he'd been running, his cheeks hot with blood. The hot orange eyes shifted over him. The *sahael* pulsed once, and a shudder of fear ran through Ramón—the presentiment of pain that never came.

"Free is to be without constraint?"

"Yes," Ramón said, mincing the words as if he were speaking to a child he disliked. "Free is to be without constraint."

"And this is possible?" it asked.

Thoughts and memories flickered through Ramón's mind. Elena. The times he'd had to scrape by without liquor in order to make the payment on his van. The police. The European.

"No," Ramón said. "It's not. But you aren't a real man if you don't try. Come on. You're holding me back. If you're going to keep this fucking thing in me, the least you can do is keep up when I walk."

At the camp, Ramón lapsed into silence, and the alien allowed him that. It seemed thoughtful and introspective itself, as far as one could judge that in a creature that looked the way it did. As the day shifted toward night, Ramón did indeed feel the call to relieve himself, and was humiliated as the alien looked on.

"How about dinner, eh?" Ramón said briskly afterward, trying to shake off his shame. "More food? It's too late to go on today anyway."

"You've just emptied your bowels," Maneck said. "Now you will fill them up again?"

"That's what it is to be alive," Ramón said. "Eating and shitting, they never stop until you're dead. Dead men don't shit, or eat, but living men have to, or they soon stop living." A thought struck him, and he glanced slyly at the alien. "The *man* will have to eat too. The man you're chasing. You may as well learn how he'll do it. I'll show you how to fish."

"He will not set snares? As you did earlier?"

"He will," Ramón said. "But he'll set them in the water. Here. I'll show you."

Once the alien understood what Ramón needed, it co-operated. They rigged a crude fishing pole from a thin, dry limb snapped off a nearby iceroot and—after a tedious consultation with Maneck, who took a long time to understand what Ramón wanted—a length of pale, soft, malleable wire supplied by the alien. A stiffer sort of wire was shaped into a hook, and Ramón stamped along the shore, turning over rocks until he found a fat orange gret beetle to use for bait. Maneck's snout twitched with sudden interest as Ramón impaled the insect.

Ramón led the alien to a likely-looking spot on the side of the stream and dropped the line. As he fished, Ramón stole glances at Maneck from time to time. The alien stood and watched the water. For all the impatience it sometimes showed about getting on with their task, it seemed perfectly content to stand there, immobile and untiring, for as long as it might take. Halfway across the stream, Ramón glimpsed a flash of blue as a fish leaped from the water, but nothing took his bait. Never the most patient of men, he began to grow restive. To occupy the time, he began to whistle a silly little tune that Elena had taught him early in their time together, before the fighting had grown so bad. He could not remember the words that went with it, but that didn't matter. The song made him think of Elena, her long, dark hair and her quick hands, callused by endless hours in her little vegetable garden. She was a small, dark woman, very pretty, though her face was dotted with the craters left by some childhood disease. Sometimes Ramón would trace the marks with his fingertips, unconsciously, and then Elena would look away. "Stop," she would say, "stop, you remind me of how ugly I am." And then, if he hadn't had too much to drink, he would say, "No, no, they're not so bad, you are very beautiful." But Elena would never believe him.

"What is that sound you are making?" Maneck demanded, shattering Ramón's reverie.

He frowned. "I was whistling, monster. A little song."

"'Whistling,'" the alien repeated. "Is this another language? I do not understand, although I hear a structure, an ordering. Explain the meaning of what you were saying."

"I wasn't *saying* anything," Ramón said. "It was *music*. Your people, they don't have music?"

"Music," Maneck said. "Ah. Ordered sound. I comprehend. You derive pleasure from the sequencing of certain patterns. We don't have music, but it is an interesting mathematical function. To order that which is random enhances the flow. You may resume whistling music, man."

Ramón did not accept the alien's invitation. He pulled in his line and threw it in again. The first cast brought up something Ramón had never seen. That wasn't odd—there were new creatures caught in the nets at Diegotown and Swan's Neck every week, so little yet was known about São Paulo. This was a bloated, gray bottom dweller whose scales were dotted by white, vaguely pustulant nodules. It hissed at him as he pulled the hook free, and, with a sense of disgust, he threw it back into the water. It vanished with a plop.

"Why did you throw the food away?" Maneck asked.

"It was monstrous," Ramón said. "Like you."

He found another beetle, and they resumed their watch on the river as night slowly gathered around them. The sky above the forest canopy shifted toward the startling violet of the São Paulo sunset. Auroras danced green and blue and gold. Watching them, Ramón felt for an instant the profound peace that the open wilderness always gave him. Even captive and enslaved, even with his flesh pierced by the *sahael,* the immense, dancing sky was beautiful and a thing of comfort.

A few minutes later, Ramón finally caught a fat, white

bladefish with vivid scarlet fins. As he hauled it out of the water, he caught sight of Maneck's curiously watching face, and shook his head. "You don't have music and you don't eat real food," he mused. "I think you are a very sad sort of creature. What about sex? Do you have that much, at least? Do you fuck, what about that? Are you a boy or a girl?"

"Boy," the alien said, "girl. These concepts do not apply to us. Sexual reproduction is primitive and inefficient. We have transcended this."

"Too bad," Ramón said. "That's taking transcendence too far! Still, at least I suppose that means I don't have to worry about you sneaking into the lean-to with me tonight, eh?" He grinned at the look of incomprehension on the alien's face, and walked back to camp, Maneck pacing silently at his side. There, he quickly rebuilt the cook fire, and roasted the fish gently, briefly wishing he had some garlic or habanero powder to rub on it. Still, the flesh was warm and succulent, and when he had eaten his fill, and smoked some strips of the fish and wrapped them in *hierba* leaves for the next day, he sat back on his heels and yawned. He felt very full and oddly contented despite his perilous situation and inhuman companion.

There were no more questions, no more obscure demands. When at last his body began to feel heavy, he pulled himself into the rough lean-to that the policeman had made, cradled his head on his arms, and let himself drift, always half aware that the thing was nearby and watching.

Let it watch him. Every hour it spent here with him was another chance for the stranger who had been Ramón's pursuer and was now his prey. The man who the aliens hadn't made into a puppet. Who hadn't killed the European.

The one who was still free.

Chapter 8

The next day dawned cold and clear. Ramón woke slowly, drifting into consciousness so gradually that he was never quite sure when he passed the dividing line between sleep and wakefulness. Even when he had come fully awake, he remained very still, wrapped in his cloak, savoring the sounds and smells of morning. It was snug and warm within the folds of his alien garment, but the outside air was crisp and chilly on his face, and fragrant with the distinctive cinnamon-tang scent of the iceroot forest. Ramón could hear the rush and gurgle of the nearby stream, the whistling calls of small "birds" up with the sun, and, off in the distance, the odd, booming cry of a *descamisado* returning to its lair in the trees after a long night of hunting.

Although his body ached from sleeping on the hard, stony ground and his bladder was full enough to be painful, Ramón was reluctant to stir. It was peaceful lying there; peaceful and familiar. The discomforts were old friends. How many times had he woken alone in the forest like this, after a hard day of prospecting? Many, he thought. Too many to count, too many to recall.

It was almost possible to pretend that this was just another morning like all those others, that nothing had changed, that it had all been a bad dream. He held that thought closely for a while, reluctant to release it. It was a lie, but it was a comforting lie, so he took his time in waking. He opened his eyes carefully, and found himself staring off through the opening of the lean-to toward the west. The tall iceroots seemed to have an azure glow playing about their tops, where dawn had broached them. Beyond them, to the far southwest, he saw a handful of bright stars, fading now as the sun came up: Fiddler's Bow, the distinctive northern constellation from which Fiddler's Jump took its name, since that was the southernmost point from which the Bow could be seen. He watched until the last bright star had been swallowed by the sky, then he stirred, and the illusion of safety and normality died as he felt the *sahael* pull against the soft flesh of his throat. Ramón pushed himself reluctantly to a sitting position. Maneck still stood outside the lean-to, beads of dew on its swirling, oil-sheen skin. Its quills were stirring in the morning wind; seemingly, it hadn't moved since he had gone to sleep, standing still as a stone, watching him throughout the night. Ramón suppressed a shiver at the thought.

As Ramón groaned and climbed to his feet, he saw that the alien's eyes were open, and said, "What, monster? You waiting for something?"

"Yes," it said. "You have returned to a functional state. Sleep is now complete?"

Ramón scratched his belly under the robe and yawned until he felt his jaw might dislocate. Twigs and scraps of leaf had found their way into the lean-to and knotted themselves in his hair. He combed them out with his fingers. Other than that, the shelter had been solid—well-crafted, dry, and just the right size. The policeman had even left a layer of iceroot fronds under the bedding to reflect up the heat of his body in the night. He'd spent some time in the wild.

"The sleep is now complete?" the alien repeated.

"I heard you the first time," Ramón said. "Yes, the sleep is fucking complete. Your kind, they do not sleep either, eh?"

"Sleep is a dangerous state. It takes you outside the flow. It is an unnecessary cessation of function. The need for sleep is a flaw in your nature. Only inefficient creatures need to be unconscious half their lives."

"Yeah?" Ramón said, yawning. "Well, you should try it sometime."

"The sleep is complete," Maneck said. "It is time to start fulfilling your function."

"Not so fast. I've got to piss."

"You made piss before."

"Well, I'm an ongoing fucking process," Ramón said, misquoting a priest he'd heard once preaching in the plaza at Diegotown. The sermon had been about the changing nature of the soul, the man who was delivering it red-faced and sweaty. Ramón and Pauel Dominguez had thrown sugared almonds at him. It wasn't something he'd thought of in years, and yet he could recall it now as clearly as if it had happened moments before. He wondered whether the alien goo in which he'd been incarcerated might have done something to his memory. He had heard that men waking from stasis sometimes suffered episodes of amnesia or powerful dislocation.

Now, standing before a mesh-barked pseudo-pine and pissing at its base, Ramón found more strange rushes of memory returning to him. Martín Casaus, his first friend when he'd come to Diegotown, had lived by the port, in a two-room apartment with butter-yellow bamboo flooring that peeled up at the corners. They'd gotten drunk there every night for a month, singing and sucking down beer. Martín had told him stories about being out in the forest working as a trapper, tricking a *chupacabra* into a spear pit with fresh meat, and Ramón had made up sexual exploits from his time in Mexico, each one more lurid and improbable than the last. Martín's landlady had come once and threatened to have them both arrested, and Ramón had exposed himself. He remembered the old woman's shocked expression, the way her hands had fluttered, unsure whether his penis was an insult to her or a threat. It was like seeing a recording of it: a flashback as powerful as the experience, and then gone again and only a memory.

Ramón scratched his belly idly, fingertips moving over the smooth curve of his skin. Poor old Martín. He wondered what had happened to the bastard. Nothing, he had to imagine, worse than what he himself was going through now.

"You don't piss either, do you?" Ramón said, shaking the last drops from his penis.

"The voiding of waste is necessary only because you ingest improper foods," Maneck replied. "*Oekh* provides nourishment without waste. It is so designed, in order to increase efficiency. Your food is full of poisons and inert substances that your body cannot absorb. This is why you must make piss and dump. This is primitive and unnatural."

Ramón chuckled. "Primitive, maybe," he said, "but *you* are the one who goes against nature! We are animals, both of us. Animals sleep, and eat other animals, and shit, and fuck. You do none of those things. So who is the unnatural one, eh?"

Maneck looked down on him. "A being possessed of *retehue* has the capacity to be more than an animal," it said. "If an ability exists, it must be used. Therefore *you* are unnatural, because you cling to the primitive although you possess the ability to transcend that state."

"Clinging to the primitive can be a lot of fun," Ramón started to say, but Maneck, who seemed to be growing impatient, cut him off. "We have begun with making piss," it said, "and we have returned to this place in the cycle. We are now prepared. You will enter the *yunea*. We will proceed."

"*Yunea?*"

Maneck paused.

"The flying box," it said.

"Oh. But I need to eat still. You can't have a man go without breakfast."

"You can continue for weeks without food. This is what you reported in the night."

"Doesn't mean I'd want to," Ramón said. "You want me working at my best, I've got to eat. Even machines need to be refueled to work."

"No more delays," Maneck said, fingering the *sahael* ominously. "We go now."

Ramón considered objecting, claiming that there was some further biological function that humanity required— he could spit for an hour or two, just to take more time. But

Maneck seemed resolute, and he didn't want it to resort to the *sahael* in order to get him to obey.

"Okay, okay, I'm coming. Just wait a second."

Ramón had done what he could for the policeman. Any bastard who'd come out to arrest him should be fucking grateful for what he'd done so far! Ramón snatched up the leaf-wrapped strips of smoked fish he'd prepared the night before and followed the alien back to its bone-white box. A cold breakfast in transit would have to do.

His belly lurched as the strange ship took to the air. They flew south and west. Behind them, to the north, were the tall peaks of the Sierra Hueso, their upper slopes now obscured by wet, churning gray cloud—it was snowing back there, behind, above. South, the world flattened into forested low-land, then tilted down toward the southern horizon, steaming and slopping like a soup plate, puddled with marshes on the edge of sight. Also on the edge of sight, from up here only a thin silver ribbon in a world of green and blue and orange trees and black stone, was the Río Embudo, the main channel of the great river system that drained the Sierra Hueso and all the north lands. Hundreds of kilometers to the southwest, Fiddler's Jump sat high on its rocky, red-veined bluffs above the same river, its ramshackle wooden hotels and houses full of miners and trappers and lumberjacks, its docks crowded with ore barges and vast log floats soon to be launched downstream to Swan's Neck. It was there, to the safety and lights and raucous humanity of Fiddler's Jump, that the policeman was almost surely headed.

How would he do it? Anybody who could construct a lean-to as well as the policeman had would have no trouble constructing a raft out of the materials ready to hand. Once he reached the Río Embudo and built his raft, he'd be off down the river to Fiddler's Jump; much easier and faster than walking through the thick, tangled forest. It was where *he* would have gone and what *he* would have done had he been stranded out here without a van, desperate and alone. And he was sure that the policeman would do the same. The aliens had been smart to use him as their hunting dog after all—he *did* know what the policeman would do, where he would go. He *could* find him.

How long would he have to stall to give the policeman time to get away? Could he have reached the river yet? From the foothills of the Sierra Hueso, it was a long way on foot through rough terrain. On the other hand, a number of days had gone by . . . It would be close.

Below them now was another thick forest of iceroot—tall, gaunt trees with translucent blue-white needles like a million tiny icicles. They flew on. Here a great tower-of-Babel hive had pushed up through the trees, the strange, metallic-looking insects, like living jewelry, swarming up to menace them in defense of their queen as they passed. A clearing empty but for the wide, six-legged carcass of a *vaquero*—the horselike body half eaten by a *chupacabra* and left to rot. The iceroots again. They were circling. How *did* Maneck intend to find the policeman?

"What are we looking for?" Ramón called over the sound of the wind rushing past them. "You can't see anything from up here. You got sensors on this thing?"

"We are aware of much," Maneck said.

"We? I'm not aware of a fucking thing."

"The *yunea* participates in my flow, the *sahael* participates. It is your nature that you must fail to participate. That is why you are an occasion of great sorrow. But it is your *tatecreude,* and therefore it is to be accepted."

"I don't want to participate in your goddamn flow," Ramón said. "I just asked if you had some kind of sensors on this thing. I wasn't asking if you put out on the first date."

"Are these noises needed?" Maneck asked. If Ramón had had any faith that the aliens experienced emotions a human being might comprehend, he would have said that the thing sounded annoyed. "The search is the expression—"

"Of your *tatecreude,* whatever the fuck that is," Ramón said. "Whatever you say. Since I'm not able to do this flow thing, maybe this is the best thing I can do, eh? Make some friendly conversation?"

The quills on Maneck's head rose and fell rapidly. Its thick head jounced from one side to another. It turned to him, and the slats of the bone-pale box thickened, the sound of wind lessening. "You are correct," Maneck said. "This spitting of air is the primary communication available to you. It is right that I should attempt to engage your higher functions to aid you in avoiding *aubre*. And if I better understand the mechanism of an uncoordinated self, the nature of the man will also become clearer."

"That half sounded like an apology, monster," Ramón said.

"This is a strange term. I have not fallen into *aubre*. I have no reason to express regret."

"Yeah, fine. Be like that."

"But if you wish to speak, I will participate in this fashion. I do indeed have sensors. They are of the nature of the *yunea* as the drinking of your flow is of the nature of the *sahael* or the management and direction of this form," and the alien gestured at itself, "is mine. The man, however, is much like the other creatures, and discovering the channels which he has been bound into is subtle."

Ramón shrugged.

Their best bet of catching the policeman was to head west for the Río Embudo, get well south of where he could have reached on foot, and then wait there by the riverside until the bastard came floating by on his raft, but if the alien didn't see it that way, Ramón felt no particular impulse to enlighten his captor. If the alien wanted to swing uselessly back and forth all day like a missionary's balls, Ramón was fine with that.

"What are you going to do with the poor fucker when you catch him?"

"Correct the illusion of his existence," Maneck said. "To be observed *cannot happen*. The illusion that it *has* happened is prime contradiction, *gaesu*, the negation of reality. If we were to be seen, we would not be what we are, we would *never have been* what we are. That which cannot be found cannot *be* found. This is contradiction. It must be resolved."

"That doesn't make sense. The man, he's *already* seen you."

"He is still within illusion. If he is prevented from reaching his kind, the information cannot diffuse. He will have been corrected. The illusion of his existence will have been denied. If *he* is real, however, *we* cannot be."

Ramón unwrapped the *hierba* leaf, sucked the meat from his strip of smoked fish, then dropped the empty bone on the slats at his feet.

"You know, monster, to make as little sense as you, I have to drink for half a night."

"I do not understand."

"That's the point, *cabrón*."

"Your consumption of liquid affects your communication? Was your time at the camp insufficient to express this?"

"That was river water," Ramón said impatiently. "Liquor. I mean, drink *liquor*. I've got the only devil in hell that's never heard of hard drink!"

"Explain to me 'hard drink.'"

Ramón scratched his belly. The smooth skin under his fingertips seemed momentarily odd. How could he explain drinking—really drinking—to a thing with a half-crazed devil's mind?

"There's a thing. It's a liquid," Ramón said. "It's called alcohol. You get it from things fermenting. Fermenting. Breaking down. Potatoes make vodka, and grapes make wine, and grain makes beer. And when you drink it, when a man drinks it . . . it lifts him up out of himself. You understand? All the things he's supposed to be, they don't bother him so much anymore. All the petty fucking shit that ties him up, it lets loose a little. Piss. I don't know. This is like telling a virgin what it's like to fuck."

"It loosens bindings," Maneck said. "It makes you free."

Memory assaulted Ramón again; the world vanished.

He was fourteen, two long years stretching out before him until he would elect to join a job gang and get off Earth. August brought thunderstorms to the mountains of Mexico, great white clouds that went gray-black at the base. Having come down from his tiny cliff-top pueblo, Ramón was living in an older boy's shack in a squatters' village on the north slope of a mesa near Mexico City.

The day of his memory, he'd been sitting on the misshapen mass of rotten wood and worn plastic that he and the older boy jokingly called their front porch, watching the clouds form and rise toward the sky. The storm would reach them by night, Ramón had guessed. He was trying to judge whether the shack could withstand another hard storm or if it would collapse under wind and water when the older boy appeared, sauntering down the thin street of mud and rocks that separated one line of hovels from the next. He had a girl with him, his arm around her waist. He had a bottle in the other.

Ramón didn't ask where he'd found either of them. He remembered the astringent fire of the gin, the fascination and repulsion of listening to the older boy and the girl fuck while he sat outside drinking and counting the seconds between lightning flashes and thunder. By the time the rain came, the older boy had passed out, and Ramón, drunk, had split the last of the gin with the girl and she'd let him fuck her too. The wind had rattled the walls. Rain leaked in, running down the windows in rivulets while he bent over her, thrusting, and she looked away.

It was the best night Ramón remembered having on Earth. Possibly the best night he'd had since. He couldn't remember the older boy's name now, but he could see the mole on the girl's neck, just above her collarbone, the scar on her lip where it had split badly once and healed strangely. He only ever thought of her when he was drinking gin, and he preferred whiskey.

Maneck's arm touched his shoulder, steadying him. Ramón batted it away without thinking. "There was turbulence," Maneck said. "You gained focus, but its reference was obscure."

"I remembered something," Ramón said. "That's all. One time when I was drinking. When it made me free."

"Ah. Fidelity continues to increase. This is an excellent thing. Your *tatecreude* gains focus. But you are still unflowing."

"Yeah, well, and you're still fucking ugly. You wanted to know about drinking hard liquor. Here. Hard liquor makes a man able to stand the things he can't stand. It makes him free the way nothing else can. When a man's drunk, it's like being alone. Everything's possible. Everything's good. It's like having lightning in your hands. There's nothing that makes a man feel so complete."

"So hard drink is good. It increases flow pathways and focuses intention. It makes freedom, and this is among the man's central desires. To drink is to express virtue."

In the alleyway, the European sat down, hand to his belly. The crowd drew back. Ramón felt again the cold sense of having been betrayed by them.

"It's got its good points," he said. "Why are you asking me all these damn questions? Aren't you supposed to be hunting someone down?"

"I wish to participate in you," the alien said. "You cannot sense flow. These words are your only channel." The thing sounded like the ship psychiatrist from Ramón's jump out. Ramón lifted his hands, palms-out, pushing the thing's attention away.

"I'm tired of talking," Ramón said. "Leave me the fuck alone."

"You may require a period of assimilation," Maneck agreed, as if they were talking about a lift tube that needed tuning. The alien turned away. Ramón leaned against the thin white slats of the box, peering out over the shimmering orange-and-black sea of leaves below them. If he hadn't been drunk, he probably wouldn't have killed the European. He would never have come out so far, the constabulary silently on his heels.

But to be in Diegotown and not be drunk was unthinkable. As well tell him to fly a van without fuel or dig a mine by hand. It was how he could stand people. Ramón was a drinker, and a good one, but the bottle didn't control him. When he was here, out in the world, alone and away from the press of humanity, he didn't need the whiskey, so he didn't drink it. A single bottle could last him a month in the field, and half a night in the city. He wasn't a drunk. That was his proof of it.

The first sign he had that something had changed came when the flying box stopped suddenly, hovering silently in the air as if they'd been hung there by a rope from heaven. Ramón looked down, squinting against the early evening sun, but the trees below them seemed no different from any of the other hundred thousand trees they'd flown over.

"There's something?" Ramón demanded.

"Yes," Maneck answered, but said nothing more. The flying box descended.

This new camp was larger than the one they'd left. The lean-to was larger—big enough to sit up in—and a fire pit made of stones and sand held the remains of several fires. The fugitive might have remained here for a day if he'd kept the fire going the whole time, or several if he'd only used it to cook. Maneck led the way, moving slowly across the small clearing, its head swaying back and forth, keeping time to some slow internal music. Ramón trotted behind, led by his neck. A pile of sug beetle shells glittered in the dapples of sunlight. A pile of flatfur pelts lay abandoned, one of them gnawed at and then ignored by some small, toothy scavenger. The gray-blue butt of a cigarette lay withered beside the lean-to.

How far, Ramón wondered, had the policeman traveled? Three days the man had been running before Maneck had led Ramón into the hunt. Another day since. If the man had spent a single night at the first campsite and two here, that meant he now had only one day's lead on them. Ramón silently cursed the cop for dawdling. Everything depended on the bastard getting to the river, floating away to the south, and bringing back help. The governor, the police, maybe even the Enye and some alien security force from the Enye ships that would be arriving any day now. That would be best—humanity's great alien patron species rolling through like moss-covered boulders and licking Maneck to death.

Ramón chuckled, but the alien ignored him, continuing its inspection.

There were several places, Ramón saw, where the policeman had ventured out into the forest, and several where he had returned. Broken branches and scuffed, turned litter showed it as clearly as if he'd left signs. This was a base of operations, then. The man had some plan or thought deeper than simple flight. Perhaps something he was searching for.

Could the constabulary have an emergency beacon hidden somewhere nearby? It seemed too great a coincidence, but the thought alone was enough to make Ramón's heart beat faster. Or perhaps the man was an idiot, and still thought himself the hunter and Ramón the game. In which case, Maneck would surely find him, kill him, and return Ramón to the sickening darkness and noise of the alien hive, never to be heard from again.

Maneck stopped at the lean-to and reached down, stirring the leaves the man had used as bedding. Something among the green and blue leaves tumbled—dirty white and the black-red of old blood. Maneck leaned forward and made a rapid clicking sound that Ramón interpreted as pleasure. Ramón scratched his elbow, vaguely uneased by the sense that something had gone wrong.

"Qué es?" he asked.

The alien lifted a scrap of cloth—a shirt sleeve soaked in blood. The cloth was wrinkled and bunched where it had been tied as a bandage or tourniquet and then hardened as the blood dried.

"Looks like you hit the poor *pendejo* pretty good," Ramón said, trying to sound pleased.

Maneck didn't reply, only dropped the bandage back into the disturbed litter. It paced off toward the fire pit, the *sahael* extending and narrowing, but still pulling Ramón to follow. Something glittered in the dirt beside the rough, gathered stones of the pit. Silver and blue. The alien paused, considering it. Ramón walked up to the thing's side, and then, divided between wonder and fear, he knelt and put the tips of his fingers on the cigarette case that Elena had given him.

"This is mine," he said softly.

"It is the artifact of the man," Maneck said, as if agreeing.

"No," Ramón said. "No, this is *mine*. This belongs to me. The police, they couldn't have got this unless they found . . ."

He half scrambled back to the lean-to, scooping up the blood-soaked sleeve. The cloth was rough canvas, designed to last for months in the field. The button at the sleeve's end was half shattered.

"This is my shirt. The *pendejo*'s wearing my shirt!"

Ramón turned to Maneck, a sudden towering rage roaring in his ears. He waved the bloody cloth in his clenched fist.

"Why does that fucking sonofabitch have *my shirt*?"

The quills rose and fell on the huge alien's crest; its oil-sheened skin swirled. Only the knowledge that the *sahael* would visit him with unimaginable pain kept Ramón from attacking it.

"Answer me!"

"I do not understand. The garment with which you were provided—"

"Is *your* shirt," Ramón shouted, plucking at the alien robe. "*You* fucking devils made this. You make me wear it. This is *my* shirt. Mine. I wore it from Diegotown. I bought it. I wore it. It's *mine,* and some . . . some . . ."

Martín Casaus appeared suddenly before his mind's eye, a memory as powerful and transporting as a drug flashback. Her name had been Lianna, the one he'd told Griego about. She'd been a cook at the Los Rancheros Grill down by the river. Martín had thought he was in love with her, and for a week he'd made up poems that started by comparing her eyes to the stars and ended near dawn and after a bottle of cheap whiskey, talking about what it would be like to fuck her. Ramón had seen her in the sleazy all-night bar they all called Rick's Café Americain even though there was some other name on the alcohol license.

Ramón had been drunk. He saw her again, black hair pulled back from an oval face. The lines at the corners of her mouth. The deep, saturated red of the wallpaper behind her. He'd seen her, and he'd remembered all the images he'd endured, all the fantasies Martín had spun of her body. When she'd looked up, caught his eye, it was like water flowing downhill. He hadn't had a choice. He'd just gone to her.

Martín, before him now, had the sheet metal hook in his hand. Ramón dropped the bloody rag at Maneck's feet, his hand going to his belly. Martín's hand had looked flayed and skinless, but the blood had been Ramón's. The pain had been hideous, the bleeding so bad Ramón had felt it in his crotch and thought he'd pissed himself. He opened the alien robe, half expecting the Martín of his memory to swing again, to cut him further, though when it had actually happened, the man had broken down weeping.

Ramón's fingers touched a smooth, almost unblemished belly. The thick, knobby scar was gone, only a hairline of white in its place. He realized now that he'd known it, his fingers had kept straying to the missing wound, his body knowing better than his mind that something was missing. The roughness of the alien cloth against his skin, the calluses gone from his fingertips and feet. Slowly, he pulled back his sleeve. The scar he'd gotten in the machete fight with Chulo Lopez at the bar outside Little Dog, the trails of puckered white flesh that Elena's fingertips opened and reopened when they tore at each other during half-crazed sex were gone. There were no cigarette stains on his fingers. None of the small nicks and discolorations and calluses that were the legacy of a lifetime working with one's hands. Over the years, his arms had been burned almost black by the sun, but now his skin was smooth and unblemished and pale brown as an eggshell. An awareness half-buried rose in him, and he went cold.

He had not been breathing in that tank. His heart had not been beating.

"What did you do to me?" Ramón whispered, horror-struck. "What the fuck did you *do* to me? To my *body*?"

"Ah! Interesting," Maneck said. "You are capable of *kahtenae*. This may not serve us well. I doubt the man is capable of multiple integration, and even if he were, it would not produce this disorientation. You must take care not to diverge. It will not focus your *tatecreude* if you become too much unlike the man."

"What are you talking about, monster?"

"Your distress," Maneck said. "You are becoming aware of who you are."

"I am Ramón Espejo!"

"No," the alien said, "you are not."

Chapter 9

Ramón—if he *was* Ramón—squatted, his elbows resting on his knees, hands wrapped around his bowed head. Maneck, looming beside him, explained in its deep, sorrowful voice. The man who had discovered the alien hive had been Ramón Espejo. There had been no one following him; no constable, no other van from the south. The discovery of the nest in itself had constituted contradiction, and in order to correct the illusion that the man existed, he had been attacked. He had escaped, but not uninjured. An appendage—a finger—had been torn from him in the attack. That flesh had acted as the seed for the creation of a made thing—*ae euth'eloi*—that had participated in the original being's flow, and woken with Ramón's memory and knowledge. Maneck had to explain twice before Ramón truly understood that it meant *him*.

"You participate in his flow," Maneck said. "All of the whole is present in the fragment, and the fragment may express the whole. There was some loss of fidelity, and the decision was made to favor functional knowledge and immediate recall over precise physical approximation. As you progress, you collapse into the form that shaped the fragment."

"I *am* Ramón Espejo," Ramón said. "And you are a lying whore with breath like a Russian's asshole."

"Both of these things are incorrect," Maneck said patiently.

"You're lying!"

"The language you use is not a proper thing. The function of communication is to transmit knowledge. To lie would fail to transmit knowledge. That is not possible."

Ramón's face went hot, then cold. "You're lying," he whispered.

"No," the alien said sadly. "You are a made thing."

Ramón surged to his feet, but Maneck didn't step back. The great orange eyes flickered.

"I am Ramón Espejo!" Ramón shouted. "I flew that van out here. I set the charges. Me! I am the one that did that! I'm not some fucking finger grown in a fucking vat!"

"You are becoming agitated," Maneck said. "Contain your anger, or I will use the pain."

"Use it!" Ramón shouted. "Go on, you coward! Are you afraid of me?" He gathered saliva in his mouth and spit full into Maneck's face.

The glob of spittle struck the alien beneath one eye and ran slowly down the side of its face. Maneck seemed more puzzled than offended, displaying none of the normal human revulsion. It wiped the spit away carefully and stared at the wetness of its fingers. "What is the meaning of this action?" it asked. "I sense that this substance is not venomous. Does it have a function?"

All the fight went out of Ramón, like air rushing from a pricked balloon. "Wipe your face, *pendejo*," he whispered, and then sank to a crouch, wrapping his arms around his knees. It was true. He was an abomination. Cold sweat broke out on his forehead, his armpits, the back of his knees. He was coming to believe what Maneck had said: he was not the real Ramón Espejo, he wasn't even really human, he was some monster born in a vat, an unnatural thing only three days old. Everything he remembered was false, had happened to some *other* man, not to him. *He'd* never been out of the mountain before, never broken heads in a bar fight, never fucked a woman. He'd never even met a real human being, in spite of his memories of all the people he thought he knew.

How he wished he had never come here, never set that fateful charge! And then he realized that he had *not* done any of those things. It had been *the other* who had done them. All of the past belonged to the other. He had nothing but the present, nothing but Maneck and surrounding forest. He was nothing. He was nobody. He was a stranger to the world.

The thought was vertiginous, almost unthinkable, and deliberately, with an enormous effort of will, he put it aside. To think deeply about it would lead to madness. Instead, he concentrated on the physical world around him, the cold wind in his face, the clouds scuttling through an ominous indigo sky. Whoever or whatever he was, he was alive, out in the world, reacting to it with animal intensity. The ice-root smelled as good as his false memories said it should, the wind felt as cool and refreshing as it swept across the meadow; the immense vista of the Sierra Hueso on the far horizon, sun flashing off the snowcaps on the highest peaks, was as beautiful as it ever was, and the beauty of it lifted his heart, as it always did. *The body keeps on living,* he thought bitterly, *even when we do not wish it to.*

He forced the thought from his mind. He couldn't afford despair, if he was going to survive. Nothing had changed, regardless of his origin, whether he'd been grown in a pot like a chili pepper or popped bloody and screaming out of his mother's womb. He *was* Ramón Espejo, no matter what the alien said, no matter what his hands looked like. He had to be, because there was no one else to *be.* What difference did it make if there was another man out there that also thought that he was him? Or a hundred such? He was alive, right here and now, in this instant, whether he was three days old or thirty years, and that was what mattered. He was alive— and he intended to stay that way.

He looked up at the alien, who was waiting with surprising patience. "How can what you say be true?" Ramón said through tight lips. "I'm not an ignorant peasant—I know what a clone is. It's just a baby that has to grow up, like every baby. It wouldn't have my memories. It doesn't work like that."

"You know nothing of what we can and cannot do," Maneck chided, "and yet you assert otherwise. You refer to the creation of a novel individual from a similar gross molecular template. That process would be development. You are the expression of recapitulation. The two are dissimilar." Maneck paused. "The thought fits poorly in your language, but if you were to gain enough *atakka* to understand it fully, you would diverge further from the model. It interferes with our *tatecreude*."

"My belly. My arm. The scars I had . . ."

"Perfect fidelity was sacrificed. As time progresses, they will tend toward the forms that express the whole."

"I'll get my scars back?"

"All of your physical systems will continue to approximate the source form. The information retrieval is similarly progressing."

"My memory? You're saying that all this is fucking with my memory too?"

"To better approximate is to better approximate," it said. "This is self-evident."

Ramón stared at Maneck. All at once, he realized why the aliens didn't have sex. They were grown in vats too, just like he had been. Maybe they'd been created in the same one! He and this ugly sonofabitch were brothers, more alike than either of them were like the *real* Ramón Espejo.

"You've made me a monster, just like you," he said bitterly, feeling himself beginning to shake again. "I'm not even human anymore!"

The *sahael* pulsed once, as if in warning, and Ramón's belly went cold and tight with fear, but the pain didn't come. Instead, to Ramón's great surprise, Maneck extended one long, oddly jointed arm and placed its hand awkwardly on Ramón's shoulder, like a gesture of comfort copied from a bad description. "You are a living creature possessed of *retehue*," it said. "Your origin is of no consequence, and you should not concern yourself with it. You may still fulfill your *tatecreude* by exercising your function. No living being can aspire to more than that."

This was close enough to his earlier thoughts to give

him pause. He pushed the thing's arm away and stood up. The *sahael* thinned and extended, letting him walk some distance away. Surprising Ramón again, Maneck made no attempt to follow. At the fire pit, Ramón sat, taking the cigarette case from the ground, flipping it open. It was the nearest thing he'd had to a mirror since he'd been lifted from the vat. His face was smoother than the one he was accustomed to, fewer lines at the corners of his eyes. The moles and scars were gone. His hair was finer and lighter. He looked different, unformed. He looked young. He looked like himself, but also *not*.

The world threatened to whirl around him again, and he steadied himself with his hands, his palms against the solid ground of São Paulo, anchoring himself in reality, anchoring himself in the present. If what Maneck had revealed was true, if there was another Ramón Espejo out there, that changed everything. There was no advantage to stalling anymore. If the other Ramón returned to Fiddler's Jump, there might be a reaction to his story of a secret alien base, sure, but neither that other Ramón nor anyone else would have any idea that *he* existed. An armed party might come to follow up, or even attack the aliens, but they wouldn't be looking for *him*. Maybe if he could actually *find* that other Ramón, though, together they could somehow turn the tables on the alien. He knew what he himself would have done if he knew he were being hunted. *He* would have found a way to kill his hunters. And that now was Ramón's only chance. If he could alert the other Ramón that he was being pursued and trust him to take the right action, together they might destroy the alien that held his leash. For a moment, he hoped deeply that what Maneck had said was the truth, that there was another mind like his own out free in the wilderness. He felt an odd surge of pride in that other Ramón—in spite of these monsters and all the powers at their command, he had gotten away from them, fooled them, showed them what a *man* could do.

But would the other Ramón help him, or would he be as horrified by him as he was by the alien? If he helped the other Ramón escape from his pursuers, surely the other Ramón would be grateful. Ramón tried to imagine himself turning away someone who had come to his aid when he was most in need. He didn't believe it was a thing he would do. He would embrace this new man like a brother, hide him, help him. Set him up in business, maybe go into business with him . . .

Ramón spat.

That was bullshit. No, instead he'd put a knife between the other Ramón's—*his*—ribs, and laugh while the alien abomination died. And yet, what other choice did he have? The other Ramón was Maneck's enemy too. It was a common ground for now, and if there was a way to kill Maneck and free himself from the *sahael,* then he could handle the rest later. The questions of who and what he was, how he'd fit into a world with another Ramón in it, they'd have to wait. Survival came first. Freedom from this slavery came first. And the first thing to do was to earn Maneck's trust, make it think that he was wholeheartedly cooperating, lull it into a sense of false security until he could find the chance to put a blade in the alien's throat.

The plan, amorphous as it was, steadied him. If he had a scheme, there was at least a way to move forward. . . .

"You have calmed yourself," Maneck said. Ramón hadn't heard it approach.

"Yes, demon," Ramón said. "I suppose I have."

He flipped open the cigarette case. It was empty, save for the engraved *Mi Corazón* that Elena had had etched in the silver. My heart. Here, my heart, smoke yourself to death. Ramón chuckled.

"I do not understand your reaction," the alien said. "You will explain it."

"I just wanted a cigarette," Ramón said, keeping his tone friendly. *See how safe I am? See how ready I am to cooperate with you?* "Looks like that greedy fuck out there smoked them all. Too bad, eh? Ah! I would enjoy a good smoke." He thought wistfully of the cigarette he'd used to light the fuse all that time ago. Or that the other had used. The cigarette he had smoked with other lungs, in another lifetime.

"What is a 'smoke'?" Maneck said.

Ramón sighed. When it wasn't like speaking to a foreigner, it was like speaking to a child.

He tried to describe a cigarette to the creature. Maneck's

snout began to twitch in revulsion before Ramón had half finished.

"I do not comprehend the function of smoking," Maneck said. "The function of the lungs is to oxygenate the body. Does not filling the lungs with the fumes of burning plants and the waste products of their incomplete combustion interfere with this function? What is the purpose of smoking?"

"Smoking gives us cancer," he said, repressing a grin. The alien seemed so solemn, and puzzled, that he could not resist the impulse to have a little fun with it.

"Ah! And what is 'cancer'?"

Ramón explained.

"That is *aubre*!" Maneck said, its voice harsh and grating in its alarm. "Your function is to find the man, and you will not be permitted to interfere with this purpose. Do not attempt to thwart me by contracting cancer!"

Ramón chuckled, then laughed. One wave of hilarity seemed to overrush the next, and soon he was holding his side and coughing with the strength of the laughter shaking him. Maneck moved nearer, its crest rising and falling in a way that made Ramón think it was questioning—like a child who has to ask her parents what she has said to amuse them.

"Are you having a seizure?" Maneck demanded.

It was too much. Ramón howled and kicked his feet, pointing at the alien in derision. He couldn't speak. The absurdity of his situation and the powerful strain his mind had been under amplified the humor of Maneck's confusion until he was helpless before it. The alien moved forward and then back, agitated and uncertain. Slowly, the fit faded, and Ramón found himself spent, lying on the ground.

"You are unwell?" Maneck asked.

"I'm fine," Ramón said. "I'm fine. You, though, are very funny."

"I do not understand."

"No. No, you don't! That's what makes you funny. You are a funny, funny, sad little devil."

Maneck stared solemnly at him. "You are fortunate that I am not in cohesion," it said. "If I were, we would destroy you at once and start again with another duplicate, as such fits indicate that you are a defective organism. Why did you undergo this seizure? Is it a symptom of cancer?"

"Stupid *cabrón*," Ramón said. "I was *laughing*."

"Explain 'laughing.' I do not comprehend this function."

He groped for an explanation the alien would understand. "Laughter is a good thing," he said weakly. "Pleasurable. A man who cannot laugh is nothing. It is part of our function."

"This is not so," Maneck replied. "Laughing halts the flow. It interferes with proper function."

"Laughing makes me feel good," Ramón said. "When I feel good, I function better. It's like food, you see."

"That is an incorrect statement. Food provides energy for your body. Laughing does not."

"A different kind of energy. When something is funny, I laugh."

"Explain 'funny.'"

He thought for a minute, then recalled a joke he had heard the last time he was in Little Dog. Eloy Chavez had told it to him when they went drinking together. "Listen, then, monster," he said, "and I will tell you a funny story."

The telling did not go very well. Maneck kept interrupting with questions, asking for definitions and explanations, until Ramón finally said irritably, "Son of a whore, the story will not be funny if you do not shut up and let me tell it to you! You are ruining it with all your questions!"

"Why does this make the incident less funny?" Maneck asked.

"Never mind!" Ramón snapped. "Just listen."

The alien said nothing more, and this time Ramón told it straight through without interruption, but when he was finished, Maneck twitched its snout and stared at him from expressionless orange eyes.

"Now you are supposed to laugh," Ramón told it. "That was a very funny story."

"Why is this incident *funny*?" it said. "The man you spoke of was instructed to mate with a female of his species and kill a large carnivore. If this was his *tatecreude,* he did not fulfill it. Why did he mate with the carnivore instead? Was he *aubre*? The creature injured him, and might have killed him. Did he not understand that this might be the result of his actions? He behaved in a contradictory manner."

"That's *why* the story is funny! Don't you understand? He fucked the *chupacabra*!"

"Yes, I comprehend that," said Maneck. "Would the story not be more 'funny' if the man had performed his function properly?"

"No, no, *no*! It would not be funny at *all* then!" He glanced sidelong at the alien, sitting there like a great, solemn lump, its face grave, and couldn't help but start to laugh again.

And then the pain came—world-rending, humiliating, abasing. It lasted longer than he had remembered; hellish and total and complex as nausea. When at last it ended, Ramón found himself curled tight in a ball, his fingers scrabbling at the *sahael,* which pulsed with his own heartbeat. To his shame, he was weeping, betrayed as a dog kicked without cause. Maneck stood over him, silent and implacable, and, in that moment, to Ramón, a figure of perfect evil.

"Why?" Ramón shouted, ashamed to hear the break in his voice. "*Why?* I didn't *do* anything!"

"You threaten to contract cancer to avoid our purpose. You engage in a seizure that impairs your functioning. You take pleasure in contradictions. You take pleasure in the failure to integrate. This is *aubre*. Any sign of *aubre* will be punished thus."

"I laughed," Ramón whispered. "I only laughed!"

"Any laughter will be punished thus."

Ramón felt something like vertigo. He had forgotten. He had forgotten again that this thing on the far end of his tether was not a strangely shaped man. The mind behind the opaque orange eyes was not a human mind. It had been easy to forget. And it had been dangerous.

If he was to live—if he was to escape this and return to the company of human beings—he had to remember that this thing was not like him. He was a man, however he had been created. And Maneck was a monster. He had been a fool to treat it otherwise.

"I will not laugh again," Ramón said. "Or get cancer."

Maneck said nothing more, but sat down next to him. Silence stretched between them, a gulf as strange and dark as the void between stars. Many times Ramón had felt estranged from the people he was forced to deal with— *norteamericanos,* Brazilians, or even the full-blooded *mejicanos* to whom he was related courtesy of rape; they thought differently, those strangers, felt things differently, could not wholly be trusted because they could not wholly be understood. Often women, even Elena, made him feel that way too. Perhaps that was why he had spent so much of his life by himself, why he was more at home alone in the wilderness than he had ever been with the others of his kind. But all of them had more in common with him than Maneck ever could. He was separated from a *norteamericano* by history, culture, ánd language—but even a gringo knew how to laugh, and got mad when you spat on him. No such common ground united Ramón and Maneck; between them lay lightyears, and a million centuries of evolution. He could take nothing for granted about the thing at the other end of the *sahael.* The thought made him colder than the breeze from the mountains.

It was something Mikel Ibrahim, the manager of the El Rey, had said more than once: If lions could speak, we still wouldn't understand them. His only chance was to never let himself forget that he was tethered to a lion.

Maneck nudged him. "Time to resume our functioning."

"Give me a minute," Ramón said. "I don't think I can walk yet."

Maneck was silent for a time, then turned and began pacing between the abandoned lean-to and the trees. The *sahael* tugged and stretched as the alien moved. Ramón tried to ignore it. Somewhere in the blindness that was the *sahael*'s punishment, Ramón had bit his tongue. His mouth tasted of blood. Not alien ichor: coppery human blood. When he spat, it was red. If he had harbored any doubt or fears that he might have been something inhuman after Maneck and his fellow demons had done whatever it was they had done to him, they were gone now. Maneck had shown how far removed it was from humanity, and so it had also shown how much Ramón was indeed a man.

"There's something," Ramón said. "The plan you have—watching me and then searching. If I'm really the same as the *pendejo* that's out there now, I can tell you some things that he'd do. Specific things. Not just something any man might think of."

Maneck strode back to Ramón's side as he stood and brushed ashes and litter from his alien robes.

"You have insight into the man's probable flow," Maneck said. "You will express this insight."

"The river," Ramón said. "He'll head toward the river. If he can make it there and build a raft, he can ride it down to Fiddler's Jump. There are fish to eat, and the water's safe to drink. He could travel day and night both and he wouldn't have to rest. It would be the best thing for him to do."

Maneck was silent, its snout moving as if tasting the idea. And why not, Ramón thought. Tasting ideas was no stranger than anything else about the creature that controlled him.

"The man was here," Maneck said at last. "If it is his function to approach the river, it becomes a better expression of our *tatecreude*. You have functioned well. To avoid *aubre* is better than funny."

"If you say so."

"We will proceed," Maneck said and led Ramón back to the flying box.

As they swooped over the forest, he began to think more carefully about the campsite they had left behind. Small things tugged at his attention. Why had the other Ramón left the camp and returned to it so many times? Why had he gone to the trouble of catching and skinning animals when there were perfectly good sug beetles to eat? Where was the spit he'd used to roast the little animals? Slowly it occurred to Ramón that his double out there in the bush was up to something. There was a plan forming besides his own, and he couldn't quite make out its shape.

And if *he* was Ramón Espejo remade from a bit of flesh by unthinkable alien technology, if he was truly identical to the man out there, the man he remembered being, shouldn't he already *know* what it was? Perhaps his simple acceptance of his identity wasn't as straightforward as he'd thought. He found himself wondering whether the *sahael* could do more than humiliate him with pain. Perhaps it could slide some sort of drug into his blood that made him calmer, more accepting, more likely to ignore the questions that arose from his curious situation. Now that he considered it, this was not how he would have expected himself to react.

The alien had instructed him not to diverge from his identity as Ramón Espejo, and he had followed that order. Was that really how a man would react? Was that how *he* would have reacted, if his route to this moment hadn't been through the vat?

There was no way to know. All he could do was dismiss these doubts from his mind and pin his hopes on that other Ramón Espejo, who was lurking somewhere out there in the forest. He was probably close. Three days, Maneck had said, the other had been running. It was almost five now. He guessed that he could cover thirty kilometers in a day, especially with all the demons of Hell on his heels. That would put his twin almost to the river by day's end. Unless his wounds had slowed him. Unless he had become septic and died alone in the woods, far from help. Ramón shuddered at the thought, but then dismissed it. That was *Ramón Espejo* out there. A tough-ass bastard like that wasn't going to die easy!

Jesus God, he better not!

Chapter 10

Ramón had never intended to leave Earth. It was one of those accidents of circumstance, and little more. At fifteen, he'd taken work in the open pit mines of southern Mexico. One of the operators had fallen sick—too much dust in his lungs—and Ramón had taken his place. The overseer had shown him how to drive the old lift, warned him that the three-story-tall earthmovers weren't going to slow down if he got in the way, and his career had begun. Sixteen-hour days in sun hot enough to melt and crack the plastic seals around his pitted windshield, moving and smoothing slag and gravel according to the shouted orders. The rags he tied over his mouth began the morning in any number of bright colors—blue and red and orange—and ended the gray of dirt. After one of the older workers had kicked the shit out of him, he joined a work gang under Palenki—old Palenki who was queer and crazed, mean as a rat and ruthless as the cancer that finally killed him. But he made sure no one fucked with his team. He was the one who'd shown Ramón how to stick a woman's sanitary pad in his hard hat to keep the sweat out of his eyes.

Those had been terrible days, working the mines. He'd slept on a company cot in a wood shack hardly better than the squatters' holes he'd grown up in. The food had tasted of grit. It was a grinding, endless exhaustion, and the money he made was hardly enough to get drunk with on Saturday night. And still, it was work.

Palenki had been his ticket. The old bastard had made his crew learn. In the nights, when no one wanted anything more than to sleep and try to forget the day, Palenki made them all watch tutorials on mining technology and industrial geology. Ramón had hated it, but he didn't want to get cut from the work gang. So, half against his will, he'd learned. And though he would never have said it, he found himself enjoying it. Stone made sense to him, the way that land formed, folding ancient histories into itself until someone like him came along and cracked it open. The half-hour tutorial sessions were the best part of his day, almost worth losing the sleep for.

And perhaps Palenki had seen it in him. Because the time came when the Silver Enye ships arrived at the platforms above Mexico City. Huge beyond imagining, they hung in the sky like hawks riding an updraft. There was a contract. A colony planet. The first wave had left thirty years before, and now the Enye wanted to sling a ship after them to bring the industrial infrastructure that the planet would need. The first colonists wouldn't reach the planet for another several centuries, according to the clocks sitting on Earth, but with the effects of relativity and the stuttering reality of the Enye drive engines, Ramón could be there in little more than a year of ship's time. Anyone who took a contract to go out into the black carrying the questionable fruits of human industry would by definition outlive everyone who stayed behind. That alone seemed enough to convince Palenki. He accepted a contract and signed his whole work gang up with him.

Ramón remembered taking the orbital shuttle up to the platform, gliding twice around Earth and ending practically right above where he'd started. He was sixteen, and leaving his world behind. The only regret he'd felt at the prospect was when he'd looked down from the Enye ship. The blue of the ocean, the white of the clouds, the industrialized land masses glittering in the crescent nighttime like a permanent fire; Earth was prettier when you were away from it. If you backed up far enough, it was even beautiful.

Palenki had died on the trip. The tumor had been pressing on his heart for months. Ramón and the others of the work gang had scrambled to reorganize themselves, fearing that the Enye wouldn't honor the contract without Palenki, and they were right. The agreement was voided, and when the great ships reached the São Paulo colony, the excess boys were sent out into the strange world as generalized laborers. He'd gone from being nothing on Earth to being nothing on a colony world. There was no way to return to Earth; everyone he'd known there was already dead. But he knew what Palenki had taught him, he found more tutorials, apprenticed himself to a prospecting outfit that went bankrupt after a few years. He'd bought one of the old vans just before the foreclosure and set himself up as an independent.

That first run out into the *terreno cimarrón* had been like winning the lottery, like coming back to a place he'd forgotten. The great, empty sky, the forests and the ocean, the great fissures in the south, the towering mountains in the north. Empty. It was the first time in his memory that he'd been truly alone, and he'd wept. He remembered now how he'd sat in the driver's seat, letting the autopilot carry him, and wept like a man who'd seen Jesus.

"You are suffering the effects of recapitulation," Maneck said. "As the structures of your brain complete their formation, the memories will become less intrusive."

Ramón looked over at the thing, wondering if it was trying to reassure him or scold him or if its agenda in speaking was comprehensible in human terms.

"What the fuck are you talking about?"

"As your neural paths conform to their proper flow, older patterns will command temporary inappropriate prominence."

"Thanks," he said. "I wasn't worried about it." And then, a moment later, "So if I try real hard, I can make a memory grow back?"

"No," Maneck said. "The process would be impeded by will. You are not to try to remember specific events. To do so will decrease your function. You will refrain."

"Kind of like picking at scabs means they won't heal," Ramón said, then shrugged and changed the subject. "Hey. How was it you got here, anyway?"

"We participate in flow. Our presence is inevitable."

"Yeah, whatever. But you monstrosities, you don't come from here, right? You can't. There aren't any cities or factories or those bug-tower things like the Turu use. You don't eat the animals or plants here the way you would if you fuckers had evolved here with them. This isn't your planet. So how was it you got here?"

"Our presence was inevitable," Maneck said again. "Given the constraints upon the flow of what your flawed language would call my people, this outcome was required."

"You hide inside a mountain," Ramón said, looking out between the thinned slats of the flying box to the green-and-orange smudge of the treetops three meters below. "You're all hot and bothered to stop this other version of me so no one finds out about you. You know what I think?"

Maneck didn't respond. A thin, transparent membrane slipped over its eyes, dulling the orange color. Ramón thought there were birds who did something like that—had eyelids they could see through. Or perhaps it was fish. Ramón grinned and leaned back.

"I think you were out there for the same reason I was. I think you're hiding from something."

"From what was the man hiding?" Maneck asked. Ramón felt a stab of unease; he hadn't meant to tell the thing about the European. But how could it matter now?

"I killed someone. He was with a woman and he didn't treat her so good. I was drunk and he was being loud and stupid. He said some shit, I said some shit. It ended up in the alley, you know? Turned out he was the ambassador from Europa. And I put a knife in him. Anyway, I wanted to get the fuck away. Get someplace they wouldn't find me and wait for the thing to blow over. And then I find you *pendejos*."

"You killed one of your own kind?"

"Sort of," Ramón said. "He was from Europa."

"Had he restricted your freedom?"

"No, and he didn't fuck my wife or any of that other shit. It wasn't like that."

"Then why was it you killed him?"

"It doesn't bother me," Ramón said. "It was just one of those things. They happen sometimes. Like an accident. We were both drunk."

"Hard drink," the alien said. "It removed your constraints."

"Yes."

"You kill to be free, and freedom causes you to kill," the alien said. "This cycle is *aubre*."

"It's got drawbacks," Ramón said.

What had the *cabrón* said? Ramón tried to remember how it had happened. The European must have said something or done something; made some joke or crack or comment that had driven them out to the alley. Had it been over the woman? It seemed like perhaps it had. He remembered the alley, the knife, the blood changing colors under the shifting light, but before that, things were missing and out of focus. He didn't know how to tell if that was a result of being drunk or the unformed nature of his new alien-built brain.

Why did you kill him?

The question seemed better and better all the time.

In the northern sky, great clouds gathered, piling up white and gray and yellow. Green balloons—the hydrogen-bladdered plants they called sky-lilies—dotted the clouds, moving in slow, lazy whorls where the high, thin winds caught them and made them tumble like jellyfish in the sea. They were a sure sign of coming weather. Ramón saw flashes of lightning beneath the cloudbank's belly, but it was too far to hear the thunder. It would rain, but not here. Wherever the other Ramón was now, at least he wouldn't need to worry about getting soaked. How strange it must be for the other Ramón—hurt, alone, unaware that there was someone else now who knew about the aliens and was plotting to keep him alive and free. Ramón imagined his twin out there, hiding under the leaves, possibly even watching the bone-white box make its wide arcing path through the air.

Frightened. The other Ramón would be frightened. And pissed off. Frightened not only because of what he'd found and the hunt in which he was now the prey, but also from being so alone—so isolated. There was a difference between isolation and solitude. With the van and his supplies, he'd enjoyed solitude. Thinking he was the only man north of Fiddler's Jump with no way to call for help, sleeping in improvised shelters, and fleeing an inscrutable alien civilization—that was different. He tried to imagine himself in that place. He tried to think how he would feel.

He'd want to kill the *pinche* alien. And he knew that was right, because sitting here next to the thing, that was exactly what *he* wanted. Ramón sighed. At least the other Ramón didn't have this thing stuck in his neck.

Maneck shuddered, the *yunea* coming to a sudden halt in midair. Ramón's attention snapped to the alien. Its quills were as agitated as grass in a high wind; its arms seemed to fidget with each other and with nothing. Ramón felt a deep sense of dread bloom in his belly. Something had happened.

"You got something?" he asked.

"The man has been nearby. Recently. You were correct in your interpretation of his flow. You are an apt tool."

"Where is he?"

Maneck didn't answer. The *yunea* began to sway slowly back and forth as if hung from the sky by a rope. Ramón stood up, the slats of the floor biting into the soft, uncalloused soles of his feet. His heart was racing, though he couldn't say what it was he hoped or feared would happen. The *sahael* pulsed once and went quiet again.

"Where is he?" Ramón repeated, and this time, Maneck turned to him.

"He is not present," the alien rumbled. "You will interpret this."

The *yunea* shifted, sloping down through the air. Ramón stumbled and sat back down. The leafy canopy parted, and a long, wide meadow came into view. Great flat stones—granite, from the look of them—lay among the grasses and wildflowers. And at the side of one of them, something fluttered. Ramón squinted, fighting to make it out. A branch or a stick had been driven into the soil at the great stone's edge, and a rag had been tied to the top, like a banner. The cloth was dirty and pale, with darker stains. His shirt. It was the rest of Ramón's shirt, tied by its one remaining sleeve.

"What is the significance of this object?" Maneck asked.

"Fuck if I know," Ramón said. "Maybe it's a flag of surrender? Could be that he wants to talk."

"If he wishes to converse, why would he not be present?"

"You shot his finger off!"

Maneck went silent. The *yunea* made a slow circuit of the strange flag. Ramón sucked at his teeth. It had to have been put there to get their attention. And yet the idea of surrender fit poorly with Ramón's intuition. Ramón Espejo would not want to surrender. The *yunea* hovered over the stone, lowering itself slowly toward the ground. Ramón imagined his twin out in the forest, maybe watching them. Had he had binoculars in his pack when the aliens found him, or had they been left in the van and got incinerated? No, they wouldn't have been. There wouldn't have been room in his pack for the field glasses and coring charges both.

Ramón's unease sprang to full panic. The coring charges! The branch set just at the edge of the stone where it could amplify any vibration within the granite slab. It wasn't a flag. It was a trigger.

"Stop!" he shouted, a half second too late. The *yunea* touched down. Ramón thought he could see the branch shudder in the immeasurably brief moment before the explosion came.

Chapter II

Ramón struggled to move. There was something, something urgent, but he couldn't quite remember what it was. The earth beneath him felt unstable, like when he'd drunk until it was hard to walk. Only there was something bad, something important. And he couldn't remember what it was.

It was the shell of the *yunea* that first brought a glimmer of recognition. The bone-white slats and dripping strands of the thing's walls and floor had been broken and ripped apart. They lay on the ground, scattered on the granite stone like a child's game of pick-up sticks. Only one wall and a corner remained standing, and it was slumped like an old man's spine. The air smelled hot and acid—the scent, familiar to prospectors, of spent explosives. Across the stone, a great spray of fresh earth and new gravel showed where the charges had gone off, angled up toward anyone on the surface instead of down into the ground. He had an impression—likely more his own imagination than the truth—of the slats clicking closed and opaque at the moment of the blast. Shielding him. Him and the alien. Maneck.

Ramón tried to sit up and failed, slipping back down onto the ground. His arms were weak; his right leg was bleeding freely from a gash just above his knee. He forced himself to roll over. His head was beginning to clear, memories of the immediate past fitting themselves together.

The fucker had tried to kill them. The other Ramón, wherever he was, had known he was being followed, and he'd laid a trap to kill the alien. Outrage bloomed in his heart, followed almost instantly by respect and a strange pride. Let aliens everywhere know it: Ramón Espejo was a tough little fucker, and dangerous to cross. Ramón laughed, hooted, slapped ineffectually at the ground, his mouth aching with a grin. That had been a fucking ride. It occurred to him that he was laughing and not being punished for it.

The *sahael* was still trailing from his neck. Its pale flesh had gone dark as a bruise. Ramón swallowed. He wondered for the first time what would happen if the evil thing died while it was inside of him.

"Monster!" he called, and his voice seemed deep and far away. The high register of his hearing had been blown out by the explosion, leaving him only the low bass tones of his voice. "Monster! Are you okay?"

There was no answer. Ramón finally levered himself up to sitting, and, one hand on the dark, injured *sahael,* followed its line to the massive bulk of the alien. Maneck was standing, but its stance seemed lower and squat, as if it needed a wider base of support to keep its balance. One of its strangely jointed arms hung limp at its side. Its left eye had gone from hot orange to a deep ruby red and swollen to half again its previous size. The most dramatic change, though, was its skin. Where the silver had swirled on the black like oil over water, half of the alien's body had turned ashy and gray. Its flesh looked tighter as well, like a sausage cooked almost to the point of bursting. Pale mucus dribbled from its snout, spattering to the ground at its feet. Ramón couldn't guess what it was, but nothing about the alien spoke well of its condition.

"Monster?" Ramón said again.

"You failed to foresee this," the alien intoned.

"No shit," Ramón said.

"It is your purpose to mirror the man's flow," the alien said.

"Well, I'm only so good a tool," Ramón said, and spat. "I forgot that the fucker had those coring charges in his pack. It was a mistake."

"What other devices does he have?"

Ramón shrugged, trying to recall the layout of his field pack.

"Some food, but he's probably already eaten that. There's an emergency beacon, but it's short-range. It's designed to trigger a bigger beacon in the van, and you motherfuckers already took care of that. A pistol. I had a pistol."

"That is the device that accelerated metal using magnetic fields?" Maneck asked. Its voice seemed flatter and more mechanical. Ramón didn't know if the change was in the alien's voice or his own ears.

"That's the one."

"It was removed from him," Maneck said. "It was this that separated the man's appendage."

"The pistol guard ripped his finger off?" Ramón asked. "You mean that *pendejo*'s done all this without his *trigger* finger?"

Maneck blinked, the red eye's lid not entirely closing.

"Is this significant?" Maneck asked.

"No. It's just kind of impressive."

A low wheeze came from the alien that, in another context, Ramón might have mistaken for laughter. Instead, he wondered if the thing was suffering a seizure or choking on something. The mucus flowing from its snout became a violent blue for a moment, then turned pale again.

"How many more charges of this kind does the man possess?" Maneck asked.

"I don't know," Ramón said. "I had four in the pack. That's standard. I used one finding you bastards, so that's three, but I don't know if he just used one charge on this or all of them."

"Can this be determined?"

"Sure, probably," Ramón said. "I can take a look. I should probably do something about my leg first, though. And you look like shit."

"You will determine the number of charges used," Maneck said, its voice becoming strident and tinny. Ramón decided that his high-register hearing was starting to come back. "You will do so immediately."

"Fine," Ramón said. "I have to go over and look at the

crater. You think this fucking leash stretches that far?"

The alien was still for a moment, and then began to haul itself across the wreckage of the flying box toward the new scar in the landscape. Its steps were pained and awkward. Ramón could hear its breath; the low wheeze again. It had clearly been seriously hurt.

The crater was wide but shallow. Ramón considered the stone where the blast had sheared away the corners of the granite. If the charge had been shaped to burrow into or even under the slab, the damage to stone would have been much more extensive. The other Ramón had angled the blast up, toward whatever set it off. The triggering branch was currently nothing more than a handful of toothpicks scattered from the meadow up toward low orbit. He had a momentary image of a flapjack somewhere high in the air, surprised at being impaled by a length of branch, but he suppressed a chuckle.

If the edge of the stone had been more intact, he could have gotten a better idea of how the trigger had been set. It would have been tricky to isolate the movement of the stone from the vibrations of the branch and its flapping banner. He could think offhand of three ways that might have done the trick, depending on the formation of the rock.

But that wasn't the critical issue. The important thing was that the blast had been pointing upward. He paced the crater's perimeter, limping when the wound in his leg sent an unexpected pain shooting through him. The blast pattern was lobed and roughly triangular. He could almost see how it had been done. The branch had been set as a trigger particularly sensitive to the relatively stable stone, but anyone taking the shirt off or shifting the branch itself would have set off the charges as well. His twin hadn't known what direction the hunters would approach from, and he'd set the blasts meant to make a rough circle. He'd bet everything on the one trap, and it hadn't been a bad wager at all.

Ramón squatted, his fingers brushing the dirt more for the simple pleasure of feeling fresh soil than for anything he expected to learn. The ground smelled strongly of the explosives. He wondered what it had been like, setting the trap.

Joyous or nerve-wracking? Or both? Fumbling with coring charges and an improvised trigger, and working with a mutilated right hand besides. And it had worked. The *yunea* was wrecked, Maneck badly injured. The score was even now—blow for blow, van for flying box. Ramón had a feeling bordering on presentiment that his other self out there in the trees was going to win.

"Hey, monster!" Ramón called. Maneck had not moved from its place at the crater's edge. Its stillness, so eerie before, now seemed like an indication of weakness. Ramón limped back toward it. "Are you dead? Can you hear me?"

"I hear you," Maneck said.

"I'm pretty sure he used all three charges. There aren't going to be any more like this."

Maneck didn't reply. Ramón spat and scratched himself. The alien shuddered once and lowered its head. The quills lay as limp as wilted ivy.

"I have failed to fulfill my *tatecreude*," the alien said. "I am damaged. The man has progressed. We will return to the others and confer."

"We can't do that!" Ramón said, fearful images of the alien hive filling his mind. He couldn't return to *that*, to be trapped in that smothering darkness for the rest of his life; the hunt had to continue, or he had no hope of getting free of this thing. "He's got to be close. He's got nothing now. What, he's going to stop us with a hunting knife and a pair of dirty pants?"

"I am weakened," Maneck said.

"So's he! You shot his *pinche* finger off! It's been festering for days. He's been *running* for days. He's got to be ready to collapse!"

Maneck went silent. Ramón tried to will the alien on, tried to push something—anger, bloody-minded resolve, duty, thirst for revenge, anything—send it up the bruised *sahael* and into the thing's flesh. They couldn't turn back now.

"Is it your fucking *tatecreude* to give up and run back to your fucking mother? Like a coward? Is that it? The man is still out there, still heading for Fiddler's Jump, only now we know where he's going. We can get to him. If we limp back, it's going to take days. By then, he could have gotten anywhere. It'll be too late to stop him from telling everybody about you!"

Maneck didn't reply, so Ramón pressed on.

"This trap he set? It can't have been set for very long. Something would have triggered it by accident. No, he's close. He probably stayed to watch and see if it worked. Even if he was in a treetop someplace, he can't be more than two or three klicks from here. You can still get to him."

Maneck's head shifted slowly from side to side as if the alien were shaking its head no. A cold dread shook Ramón. It couldn't end like this. They had to go after the other Ramón. They *had* to. There had to be something—some way to make the injured alien keep going rather than folding up and running. Ramón's hands were trembling, his mind whirling like a storm. He had to struggle not to lash out at the thing, kick it, punch it, *make* it do the right thing. He didn't consider what he was going to say, and when he spoke, his own words surprised him.

"What will they think of you? The other ones back under that mountain, your brothers? They know you're out here. They know why, and you can't fucking tell me they don't admire you for it. You want to go back in shame as a *failure* and see how they look at you then? Fine. You want to know what it's like to have your own people turn their backs on you? Fine. Let's go, then. Come on, you great fucking bitch!"

Ramón did swing a foot then, kicking the alien where its ankle would have been if it had one. The impact was soft and hard at the same time, like kicking a tree wrapped in a layer of rubber. Maneck didn't react.

"Go back, then, you sad little devil!" Ramón shouted, his rising blood making his face warm with rage. "Turn around, and let's march back home and let them see that you're *nothing*. That you're connected to nothing. You aren't a part of them. Let's see how you like it that they don't want shit to do with you anymore. Or keep moving forward, do what they want you to do, and finish this thing! *They* don't have the balls to do it. Show them that *you* do! What's the worst that can happen? That shit-crazy ratfuck out there could kill us. Is that what you're worried about? Is going back as a failure better than dying in a fight? Have some balls! Be a *man*!"

The alien bowed its head, the quills stirring slightly.

"I must rest," it said, its voice low. "But you are correct. To cease to function is *aubre*. To express my *tatecreude* is paramount."

"Fucking right it is!"

"I will focus on my own repair for a time. When proceeding will cause no further damage, we will locate the man."

"Well," Ramón said, nodding, relief and pleasure flushing through him. "All right, then! Good you grew some fucking *huevos*. We'll track him down on foot. We can do that."

"Is *he* like this as well?" the alien asked.

"Like what?"

"You are not coordinated in your thoughts," the alien said. "Your *tatecreude* is unfocused, and your nature is prone to *aubre*. You comprehend killing and will, but not *niedutoi*. You are flawed at your core, and if you were a *kii* hatchling, you would be reabsorbed. You attempt to separate and also to rejoin. Your flow is always in conflict with itself, and the violence of this confuses your proper function but also overcomes boundaries that would otherwise restrict you. Is this what the man is like, or are you continuing to deviate?"

Ramón looked into the alien's uninjured eye, trying to make sense of what it had said. Flow and conflict, violence and restriction. Belonging and not belonging. Or maybe he was the one who'd brought that up.

"No, monster," he said at last. "It's not deviation. I've always been like this."

Chapter 12

After an hour, the alien heaved itself to its feet, with a ratcheting sigh that sounded like a length of chain being dropped through a hole. "We proceed," it said grimly, and gestured to Ramón to take the lead.

It took a little more than an hour of pacing slowly around the meadow's edge to find the other man's trail. Through the long hours of the morning and into the afternoon, Ramón took point, the *sahael* trailing behind him to Maneck's slow, steady plodding. It would have been a harder thing if Ramón hadn't known the kind of tricks he himself would have employed to create a false trail. Twice they came upon what looked like a mistake on the other man's part—a muddy footprint leading up onto a stony ridge, a length of roughened ground where he might have lost control as he went down a slope. Ramón guided them past the red herrings easily.

The nature of the forest changed as they walked. On the higher ground near the mountains, the trees were all iceroot and pine analogs. The farther they moved toward the river, the more exotic the foliage became. Wide-branched *perdida* willows with black trunks shaped like half-melted women; towering *pescados blancos,* named for the paleness of their leaves and the oceanic scent of their sap; half-mobile colonies of coral moss with bright pink skeletons peeking out from beneath the rich green flesh. The weariness and the throbbing of his knee seemed to fall away from Ramón as he caught his stride. It felt almost as if he knew beforehand where he was going, where the other Ramón had gone before him. He almost forgot Maneck's lumbering form walking behind him, matching his path perfectly to avoid catching the *sahael* on two different sides of the same tree.

A flatfoot blatted at him as he passed, scolding him with a noise like an annoyed oboe. The thin, gnawed bones of a kyi-kyi lay scattered at the base of a small cliff, pale as the slats of the *yunea*. The other Ramón was roughly following the creek that had run by the meadow where he'd set his trap. The water was an infallible guide, and though there was no trail beside it, Ramón found they were rarely out of earshot of its chuckling flow. A sense of peace infused him, and he found himself smiling. The sun rose, the temperature inched up. If he'd been wearing a shirt, Ramón would have been tempted to take it off and tuck it into his belt, not because he was overheated but only because the air would feel good against his skin. At last, untypically, Maneck called for a halt. Its skin was ashen gray, and it seemed almost unsteady on its feet.

"We will rest here," it said. "It is necessary to recuperate."

"For a little while," Ramón said. "We can't let him get too far ahead. If he gets to the river . . . well, if he gets to the river, he'll have to take the time to build some kind of raft. And with a fucked-up hand, so I guess that could take him a while. But if he does get out on the river, we'll never catch him. We should have just used your flying box to get downstream. We could have just waited for him to drift by."

"This suggestion is of no effect. We did not, therefore there can be no previous shall. Your language violates the nature of time. We must rest, here."

It was a good site. The brook pooled here into a tiny lake. The afternoon sun glittered silver on its surface. A low, gray-green ground cover made a wide, soft place to rest. When Ramón lay back, the bruised leaves smelled like basil, like nutmeg, like nothing he had a name for. Maneck trundled to the water's edge and looked out before closing its eyes. The red, wounded one still had a bright slit where the lid no longer entirely closed.

From where he lay, Ramón could turn his head and put one eye level with top of the ground cover and see how the patterns of sun and wind on the lake mirrored the waving of the tiny silver leaves. It took him a few minutes to spot the hidden grave.

It was at the edge of the clearing, near a small waterfall where the lake once again became a brook. A swath of the ground cover stood higher than the surrounding plants. It was no longer than Ramón's forearm, no wider than his spread hand. He walked to the anomaly, the *sahael* tugging at his throat. The ground, he saw, had been dug up, the plants removed and then laid back on top of the tiny excavation when it was done. Ramón felt a moment's unease. It seemed like the thing a man would do—the other Ramón. As if there was something buried here he wanted to hide, but what would that be? There hadn't been anything in his field pack precious enough to preserve. Maybe a note? Some written record that would expose the aliens? But who would ever find it here?

With only a moment's hesitation—might he have forgotten how many coring charges had been in the pack or might the trap in the meadow have only used two?—Ramón dug his fingers into the soft soil. Hardly an inch beneath the surface, he touched flesh. When he pulled his hand back in disgust, his fingertips were red with blood. A flatfur, skinned and raw and buried hardly deep enough to make any difference from leaving the little body openly on the ground. He considered the corpse, and remembered the skins at the other Ramón's first camp. Whatever the man was doing, it was intentional, and he'd planned it back that long ago, when traps were on his mind. Ramón lifted the thing with a branch broken from the nearest tree. There seemed to be no mechanism associated with it—no sharpened sticks or knives. He might have poisoned the meat, but it seemed unreasonable that he might expect the alien to eat it. What was the man—his other self—thinking?

Ramón took the dead animal by its thin legs, walked it to the lake, and flung it out into the water. The body sank like a stone. Maneck's eyes remained closed, its stance still as a statue and as unresponsive. Ramón debated for a moment. He could wake the thing and tell it what he had found, or else keep the other Ramón's secret. The strange animal offering made him uncomfortable; his first impulse was to talk about it. But if it was part of his twin's plot to defeat the aliens, perhaps it would be better to hold back.

Maneck's eyes flickered open. "I can go on no more today," it said. It actually sounded apologetic, perhaps even ashamed. "I am too weak. I must recuperate further."

"That's okay," Ramón said. He felt almost sorry for it. How badly injured was it? Was it dying? "It'll be dark soon anyway. We might as well camp for the night."

Maneck remained quiescent through the rest of the day and into the night. Ramón broke branches and fronds to make himself a lean-to, the *sahael* stretching to accommodate his movements. When night fell, he roused Maneck long enough to scoop water from a tiny creek and find a double handful of sug beetles. The alien didn't ask about his change in diet, and Ramón didn't volunteer any information.

When the beetles were reduced to their empty, colorful shells, Ramón lay back on the soft ground, looking up into the vast starscape of night. The small fire he'd made to boil water for washing out his wound and cooking had fallen to coals and ashes. In other circumstances, it would have been a perfect night. In the distance, something called—an animal or bird or insect that might never have been seen by human eyes. The sound was high and fluting, and a moment after it came, two more answered it. Another memory filled his awareness. Elena in her apartment. They had had one of their first fights over his habit of camping outside the van. She had been certain that a wild animal would find him and kill him in the darkness. She'd had a friend taken by redjackets, and she claimed to suffer nightmares. He'd been sleeping with her for a month and hadn't seen evidence of it, but when he said so, she only got angrier.

The argument had ended with her throwing a kitchen

knife at him. He'd slapped her. Afterward they'd screwed.

Far above him, a meteor streaked across the sky, burning and vanishing in the space of a heartbeat. The Sick Gringo peered down on them from the stars, and, on the horizon, the Stone Man was beginning to rise.

He knew she was crazy. Elena was the kind of woman who wound up killing herself or her lover or her children, and he didn't love her any more than she loved him. It was all perfectly clear to him, and also totally unimportant. People, he decided, didn't come together from love or hatred. They came together because they were the kind of people who fit. She was a crazed bitch. He was a drunk and a killer. They deserved each other.

Except he wasn't a drunk when he was here. In the field, he was sober as a priest. He was a better man out here. His mind was growing muzzy and losing itself in sleep when the alien jerked to attention. Ramón sat up.

"What is it?" he whispered.

"Something is observing us," Maneck said.

A chill went up Ramón's spine. There were enough *real* monsters waiting out here in the bush that São Paulo featured relatively few myths about duppies and mothmen and mysterious unknown creatures. Ghosts were a different story, though. There were plenty of ghosts here—from the ghost of Ugly Pete, a prospector who wandered the night looking for a replacement for the head he'd lost in a mine accident, to Black Maria, who appeared to men at the moment of their deaths. One cult in Little Dog believed that São Paulo was where the dead of Earth went when they died. So the night here swarmed with ghosts, like moths around a light, and out here in the dark wilderness, that was not a good thing to think about—although, of course, *he* didn't believe in such things. Whatever was out there in the dark, it was more likely to be a real physical creature than a ghost.

With that thought, Elena's terror of redjackets and *chupacabras* abruptly returned to Ramón, and he rose, moving closer to the huge alien. He closed his eyes for the space of twenty breaths, adapting them to darkness, then scanned the meadow's edge. It was dark enough that he couldn't see anything directly. Only his peripheral vision would pick out movement from the gloom beneath the trees.

"There," he whispered. "Just to the right of the white-barked tree. In that bush."

Maneck did something complex with its arm. A flash of light extended from its hand, and the bush exploded in a ball of fire. Ramón jumped back.

"Come," Maneck said, and began moving forward. Ramón hung back half a pace, struggling between curiosity, fear of whatever was in the trees, and unease at his alien captor's weapon. He had thought the thing was unarmed after the *yunea*'s crash. It was the sort of mistake that would get him killed if he wasn't more careful.

The corpse at the foot of the tree, twisted in sudden agony and scorched black on its spine, was a *jabali rojo,* something like a boar that had decided to be a fox instead halfway through its evolution; the ornate tusks at the sides of its open, lifeless mouth were better suited for impressing female *jabali* than attacking men or aliens.

"It's nothing," Ramón said. "It was no danger to us."

"It might have been the man," Maneck said. Was there regret in its tone? Relief? Fear? Who could say?

When they returned to the modest camp, Ramón lay back down, but found it hard to sleep. His mind worked variation after variation on his new circumstances. Maneck was still well-armed. The other Ramón didn't have a pistol or any more coring charges. He tried to imagine ways in which he might be able to give his other self an edge—some chance that would make his own freedom possible.

And what then?

He found himself staring at Maneck, his strange alien shape silhouetted against the cold stars like some pagan idol dedicated to unimaginable gods. Before long, he found himself beginning to drift. In his torpor, he realized that the *alien* had been the one learning all this time—how a man ate, how he pissed, how he slept. *Ramón* had learned nothing. For all his strategy and subterfuge, he knew hardly more about the alien than when he'd first woken in darkness.

He would learn. If he had been created as the thing said,

then, in a way, Ramón was part alien himself—the product of an alien technology. He was a new man. He could learn new ways. He would come to understand the aliens, what they believed, how they thought. He would leave no tool unused.

Sleep stole into him, taking him gently down below consciousness, his determination to *know* still locked in his mind like a rat in a pit terrier's teeth. Ramón Espejo felt dreams lapping at his mind like water at the bank of a river, and at last let them come. They were strange, dreams such as Ramón Espejo had never dreamed before.

But, after all, he was not Ramón Espejo.

Chapter 13

In his dream, he was within the river. He had no need to breathe, and moving through the water was as simple as thinking. Weightless, he inhabited the currents like a fish, like the water itself. His consciousness shifted throughout the river as if it were his body. He could feel the stones of the riverbed where the water smoothed them, and the shift, far ahead, where the banks turned the flow one way and then another. And farther, past that, to the sea.

The sea. Vast as a night sky, but *full*. The flow shifting throughout, alive and aware. Ramón floated down through the waters until he came near the dappled bottom and it swam away, the back of a leviathan larger than a city and still insignificant in the living abyss.

And then he was also the abyss.

Ramón dreamed of flow. Meaningless syllables took on significance and passed back into nonsense. Insights as profound as love and sleep moved through him, and left him filled with a terrible awe. The sky was an ocean, and the flow filled the space between stars. He followed the flow for hundreds or thousands of years, swimming between the stars, his belly heavy with generations yet unborn, searching for refuge, for someplace *safe*, away from pursuit, where he could hide and fulfill his destiny. And behind him, relentlessly pursuing, was something black and ominous, calling

out to him in a voice at once terrible and seductive. Ramón
tried not to listen to that terrible voice, tried not to let it pull
him back. The beauty of the flow, the power of it, the deep
and wordless promise; he fought to fill his mind with this
and not think of the thing behind him, the thing that was
reaching out toward him, dead tendrils still stinking with
blood. Only the act of thinking itself gave the thing power;
awareness of it, even in the act of repudiation, gave it reality.

Then, while he was still dreaming, something caught
him. A powerful eddy threw him in a direction he could
not name, back to the dim, hellish place from which he had
struggled to escape.

Abruptly, there was a dead sun above him, hanging gray
in an ashen sky. This was his home, the place of his hatch-
ing, his source, as rivers sprang from a glacier. His heart
was tight with dread; he knew what was coming and also
did not.

Around him were alien forms, as familiar as lovers. The
great pale beast in the pit that had counseled him before this
desperate hunt began. The small, bluish forms of *kait* eggs,
now destined never to hatch. Yellow-fringed *mahadya* and
half-grown *ataruae* still bent at the spine. (These were not
words that Ramón knew, and yet he knew them.) All of the
young beyond redemption, crushed, lifeless. He was Maneck,
athanai of his cohort, and these dead that touched him, that
polluted the flow, were *his* failing. His *tatecreude* was un-
fulfilled, and each of these beautiful things had fallen into
illusion because he had failed to bear the weight of truth.

With a sorrow as profound as any Ramón had ever felt—
more than the loss of his mother and his Yaqui father, more
than the heartbreak of first love—he began to eat the dead,
and with every corpse that he took into himself, he became
less real, more lost in *aubre* and sin, more fully damned.

But there was no end of them. With every tiny body he
consumed, *they* killed a thousand more. The screaming
blackness that had followed him in flight began here, opened
here like a box whose lid lifted forever, continually reveal-
ing the horror that would never end. The eaters, the flowless

ones, the enemy. They saw the great boulder-shaped bodies, heard the strange, piping voices raised in praise of the slaughter, saw the hatchlings lifeless and crushed beneath the vast machines. Ships hung in the air like birds of prey.

I know that ship, Ramón thought. Ramón only, and not Maneck. *I've been* on *that ship.*

With a shriek that was both his and Maneck's, Ramón awoke.

Maneck crouched beside him, its long arms lifting him with something between tenderness and anger.

"What have you done?" the alien whispered, and, as it did, it seemed somehow less alien, lost and frightened and alone.

"Yes, *gaesu,*" Ramón mumbled, hardly knowing what he was saying. "Prime contradiction! Very bad."

"You should not have been able to use the *sahael* this way," Maneck said fretfully. "You should not have been able to drink of *my* flow. You are diverging from the man. It threatens our function. You will not do this again, or I will punish you!"

"Hey," Ramón said, shaking his head, coming back to himself with a start. "You're the one who put this fucking thing in my neck! Don't blame *me.*"

Maneck blinked its strange orange eyes and seemed to settle back, subtly defeated. "You are correct," Maneck said after a long pause. "Your language allows for deception, but your participation in my flow was not willed. The failure is mine. I am sick and injured, or I would not have lost control of the *sahael.* Still, the fault is mine."

Its voice surprised and confused Ramón. It was still deep and sorrowful, but there was something else in it—a sense of regret and dread that couldn't have come entirely from Ramón's imagination. He wondered whether the *sahael* was still leaking some signal from the alien's mind into his own. Ramón felt as if he'd walked in on a weeping man. In his own discomfort, he shrugged.

"Don't let it bother you," he said. "It wasn't something you meant to have happen either."

"You must not diverge any further," Maneck said, almost

pleadingly. "Your mind is twisted and alien. And that is as it *should* be. You will cease to diverge from the man. You will not integrate with me any further. We will wait here and hunt him. If he does not reach his hive, there will be no *gaesu*. You *must not* diverge any further."

"I won't, then. Don't worry. I'm still plenty twisted and alien."

Maneck didn't reply.

Around them, the sounds of night slowly began to come back as the animals and insects frightened by their raised voices began tentatively to return to their songs and court-ships and hunts. It occurred to Ramón to wonder whether the other Ramón had heard, if he was close enough to know now that the coring charges hadn't finished off his pursu-ers. But for that to be true, he would have to be very close, yet Ramón and Maneck had slept through most of the night unmolested by anything other than *jabali* and ugly dreams. The other Ramón would not have missed a chance to attack them in their sleep—*he* would not have—and so he must not be that close. He was still out there in the forest somewhere, and the job of hunting him down was still ahead of them. But, as he now knew, theirs was not the only hunt.

"The Silver Enye," Ramón said tentatively. "The big, ugly, boulder-shaped things."

"The eaters-of-the-young," Maneck said.

"They're what you're hiding from."

"It is better if this does not affect your function," Maneck said. "It must not inform your action."

"Don't fucking diverge, I got it. But I'm the guy who can tell you about being a man, and I say that if you tell me, it'll help."

"There has been too much participation already," Maneck began, but Ramón cut it off.

"I know enough that I'll be spending all my time guess-ing. Men, they make sense of the universe. They make sto-ries about it and then see if they are right. It's what we do. Like I thought there was something interesting about that mountain, and I was fucking right, wasn't I? So if you tell me, I can stop wondering. If you don't, it's all I'll do."

Maneck's quills fluttered in a pattern that Ramón recognized as akin to resignation.

"They came to us, to the planet that spawned the first of us. For many generations, they appeared to be *siyanae;* their proper function appeared to flow in channels compatible with our own. We were not aware of the divergence until . . ."

"Until they started killing you," Ramón said.

"Their *tatecreude* expressed in crushing the hatchlings. Of the ten billion of our *kii,* fewer than a hundred thousand survived. The eaters-of-the-young would enact rituals with the bodies. It seemed to offer them pleasure. We saw no function in it. It is necessary to our function that we exist, and so those that remained followed the channels which did not include the eaters-of-the-young. Of the six hundred ships, we are aware of three hundred and sixty-two that failed to isolate themselves from the flow of the enemy. Four came here and engaged in stillness. The others we cannot speak to. Their function has entered a place of *nietudoi.* If it is part of their *tatecreude,* it will be made clear once we have achieved conjugation. If it is not, then the illusion of their existence will not be acknowledged."

Ramón sat on the ground at Maneck's feet. Tiny leaves tickled the palms of his hands as he leaned back. The soup of alien thought and terminology had been less disturbing when he had been able to comprehend none of it. Now, with every idea half making sense, every untranslatable word on the verge of familiarity, it was worse than a headache.

"They'll kill you if they find you," Ramón said. "The Enye. They'll kill you."

"It would be consistent," Maneck said.

"You know they're coming. The galley ships. They're coming here ahead of schedule."

"This is known. They have no need for stillness. Their flow is . . . compelling."

"So that's why you have to stop the man. Ramón. The *other* Ramón. If he goes to Fiddler's Jump, he tells everyone where you are, and the Enye . . . fuck! Those *pendejos* will come down and eat you!"

"It would be consistent," Maneck said again.

A thousand questions swarmed in Ramón's mind. Were the human colonies sponsored by the Enye all secretly hunting missions designed to flush out hives like Maneck's? Were the Silver Enye going to turn on humanity one day, as they had with these poor alien sons of bitches? If the hive were discovered, would the São Paulo colony have accomplished its mission—fulfilled its function—and if it had, would the Enye suffer it to continue? And what had the *sahael* done to him that these things were even thinkable, these feelings possible? Where did Maneck end and he, Ramón, begin? In his turmoil, he grabbed at a single question, clinging to it as if everything hinged on its answer.

"Why did they do it?" he asked. "Why did they turn on you?"

"The nature of their function is complex. Their flow has properties unknown to us. They were like us until they were not. It had been our hope that you would reveal this to us."

"Me?" Ramón coughed. "I didn't know it had happened until just now. How would I be able to tell you what those mad *pendejos* were thinking?"

"The man is of them," Maneck said. "He participates in their function. You possess an understanding of killing and of purpose. You kill as they kill. Understanding what drives your killing would explicate the drive of theirs. The freedom of hard drink."

"We aren't like that. I'm not part of their *fucking* holocaust! I'm a prospector. I look for minerals."

"But you kill," Maneck insisted.

"I do, but—"

"You kill your own kind. You kill those who are most like you in function."

"That's different," Ramón said.

"In what manner does the difference come?"

"It wasn't about being drunk. That lets it get out of hand, maybe. It was something between the other guy and me. But I didn't eat his fucking *kids*."

"If we were to understand the nature of the eaters-of-the-young and the expression of their *tatecreude*, we might channel their flow back to its previous path," Maneck said, and Ramón heard desperation in its tone. Even despair. "It might be possible to find a new method of fulfilling their function. But I cannot find a plausible reason."

Ramón sighed.

"Don't try," he said. "You'll only make yourself crazy. There's no way to understand them. They're fucking aliens."

Chapter 14

Ramón surprised himself by going back to sleep, and was even more surprised in the morning when he woke up and actually found himself leaning against Maneck, who had sat stoically, unmoving, throughout the rest of the night.

Before then, though, three times before the sun rose, Ramón was assaulted in his dreams by memories. One was a card game he'd played on the Enye ship during his flight out, away from Earth. Palenki had been having a good day—there were fewer and fewer of those—and had insisted that his crew come together and play poker. Ramón felt the strangely soft, limp cards in his hands again. He smelled the high, acidic reek of the Enye's huge bodies and the ever-present undertone of overheated ceramic, like a pan left empty in a heated stove. He'd beaten Palenki's full house with a straight flush. He remembered seeing the sick man's delight falter and fail when the cards came down, disappointment filling the old prospector's eyes like dry tears. Ramón regretted that he hadn't folded without showing.

That was the only memory that seemed related to his strange interaction with the alien's mind. The other two were mundane moments—first, bathing in a hotel in Mexico City before going off to a brothel, and second, a meal of river fish encrusted in black pepper he'd eaten shortly after his arrival on São Paulo. In each case, the memory was so vivid that it was as if he had momentarily stopped living in the present and begun to live again in the past, as if he was actually *there* rather than here, sitting on his butt on the grass in the middle of a chilly night next to an alien monstrosity. Each time he woke for a second to see Maneck sitting next to him, as still as a statue, and he got the impression that it knew what was happening to him, but it offered no advice on how best to accommodate this intrusive blooming of the past. Ramón didn't ask. It was his mind coming back to the way it should be, and that was all. Still, he wondered how many years it had been since the other Ramón had thought of that card game.

The daymartins were singing their low, throbbing song as the eastern sky lightened from star-filled blackness to a dimmer charcoal, and then at last to the cool light of morning. Something squawked and fled when Ramón rose to go for water. Whatever it was, it had snuck in and gnawed silently on the corpse of the *jabali rojo* in the night. Tenfin birds and whirlygigs flew through the trees, shouting at one another and fighting over places for their nests, food, mates to bear their children. The same petty struggles of all life, everywhere. Larger beasts, hoppers and fatheads, came to the stream's edge, glanced incuriously at him, and drank from the water. Fish leaped and fell back. He felt himself relax as he watched it all, able to forget for a moment what he was, what his forced mission was, and how bleak were his hopes.

Then back to the camp, to eat more sug beetles, make the usual review of his biological functions for the alien, and prepare himself for the hunt. Maneck's skin was still ashy, but the oil-swirls were beginning to reappear. Its stance remained low to the ground, its movements careful and pained. Ramón wished he knew enough to judge how serious the alien's injuries were—if it was just going to keel over at some point, there was no need to make elaborate plans to escape. On the other hand, suppose he found he couldn't free himself from the *sahael* after Maneck was dead? How horrible, to be shackled to the alien's rotting corpse until he starved to death himself! Or perhaps if Maneck died, *he* would die—they shared physical impulses through the *sahael,* after all. He'd never thought of that before, and it was unsettling. Still, given the opportunity, he'd take his chances . . .

When it had grown light enough, Ramón and Maneck rose without consulting each other and set off again, moving downstream. The other Ramón's path tracked toward the north, though Fiddler's Jump was far to the south. Perhaps he hoped to throw off the pursuit by taking the less likely route. Or perhaps he expected to find better wood for a raft there. Or perhaps there was some other reason that Ramón had not yet fathomed.

They walked in silence, only the crackling of old leaves and needles under their feet to compete with the whooping calls of *anaranjada,* the scolding of flatfurs, the chittering chorus of vinegar crickets. It was midmorning before they came to a game path running through the trees. The soft, fibrous spoor of the kyi-kyi told Ramón that the antelope-like beast had been by within the last day, and likely the last few hours. These would have been good hunting grounds, he thought, and felt a stir of unease, the source of which he couldn't quite identify.

Ramón guessed that they would reach the river itself before nightfall. The other Ramón was bound to be close. He guessed that it would have taken him three days to make a decent raft, if he had the right tools: ax, wood, rope. And all his fingers, of course. The other Ramón was going to be working at a disadvantage, but . . .

But the smart thing would be to slap together something third-rate—a raft barely strong enough to float—and use it to flee farther downriver. Once he had more distance, the man could afford to spend the time to make something sturdy. It would be a balancing act: speed against the danger of trusting himself to something so flimsy that it could come apart in the water. Ramón walked, trying to remain silent, and wondered what risks *he* would have taken in the other man's place. It was a tug deep in the flesh of his neck that brought his mind back to Maneck.

The alien had stopped. Its hot orange eye looked dull.

The red, swollen eye had darkened like congealing blood. Its skin, neither ashen nor displaying the slick dancing patterns it had first had, was the matte texture of drawing paper and the color of charcoal.

"We must pause," Maneck said. "We must regain our strength."

Ramón felt a stab of annoyance. There wasn't time for this. But it was also a sign that Maneck was weak. The devil wasn't shrugging off the injuries from the other Ramón's trap. That, at least, was a good sign. Maneck might still be armed, but it wasn't invulnerable. If the other Ramón could only find a way to break the alien's hold on *him,* then together they could destroy it.

Ramón pursed his lips. There was a tightening in his chest that he didn't like. Not illness, but regret. The memory of the *kii* crushed beneath the powerful Enye returned to him. As the hours passed, the memory of the dream he'd had the night before was fading, the sadness becoming not an emotion but the memory of one. The conviction he had felt that *any* price would be justified if it turned aside the horror of *gaesu* also faded, but did not vanish. It was *Maneck's* thought, not his, and he knew it. That didn't stop him from feeling the urgency of it, though.

"All right, monster," Ramón said. "We rest. But only for a few minutes. We don't have much time."

The alien considered Ramón, its quills stirring in a way that made Ramón think it was both amused and exhausted, then trudged to the wide, thick trunk of a fire-oak with leaves as wide as Ramón's two hands together and bark that collapsed with a sound like packing foam when Maneck leaned against it. Ramón hunkered down beside the game path, rubbing his chin and staring out into the forest. It was strange to have gone so long without a shave. Normally by now his whiskers would have been getting almost long enough to go from prickly to nearly soft. Instead, his neck and chin sprouted a kind of weak fuzz, like he was twelve years old again. He opened his robe and considered the scar where Martín Casaus had sliced him with the sheet metal hook. The pale line was wider now than it had been, but still not the ropy, puckered scar that it had been before the aliens got hold of him. The machete scar on his elbow was still hardly more than a lump under the skin. It was growing, though. He was becoming the man that he remembered being. And at least he could still grow whiskers. The *pinche* aliens hadn't turned him into a woman.

I'm still going to kill you fuckers for this, Ramón thought. But even though he had the intent and the focus, his rage seemed more distant; like something he had *chosen* to feel rather than something that actually possessed him. It felt like being in love with Elena. Familiar but hollow.

"What are you going to do with me?" Ramón asked. "When this is over. When you kill the man, what happens to *me*?"

"Your *tatecreude* will be complete," Maneck said.

"So what happens to someone when their *tatecreude* is complete?"

"Your language is flawed. To have completed *tatecreude* is to return to the flow."

"I don't know what that means," Ramón said.

"Once our function is fulfilled, we will return to the flow," it said.

Suddenly, with a flash of insight intense enough that he wondered if it partook of the two-way flow through the *sahael,* he knew what would happen to them both: they would die. They would be reabsorbed into the "flow," whatever that was. Once they had fulfilled their *tatecreude,* they would have no reason for existing anymore, like tools that were disposed of once the job they were needed for was done.

Perhaps Maneck was content to submit to that fate, perhaps the alien even welcomed it, but, as far as Ramón was concerned, that was another good reason to escape as soon as possible. "Whatever you say," he said wearily.

Ramón found that resting was more pleasant than he'd expected. He was more tired than he thought he'd be. But then, he had marched all the previous day after nearly being killed in an explosion. He'd slept poorly. And perhaps Maneck's distress was carried over in some alien fashion through the still-bruise-colored *sahael.*

The connection between Maneck's people and the Enye haunted him, but he found it difficult to wrap his mind around it in any meaningful way. A war that crossed stars, that lasted through centuries, possibly millennia. A vendetta against Maneck's kind, which had no discernible reason, which employed the human race as a tool.

They had always been hunting dogs for demons. Mikel Ibrahim, Martín Casaus, Ramón himself. Everyone, always. Dogs sent into the bush to flush out Maneck and beings like it. It was as deep a change of his view of the world as the curious fact of his twinning, but this time he didn't have the alien injunction not to diverge. He was free to think anything of this that he saw fit, and discovered that a small-time independent prospector fleeing from the governor's constabulary wasn't the right man to make sense of it all. It only made his head ache.

Instead, he wondered what Elena was doing now. It had to be near noon, and . . . how many days since he'd snuck out of her apartment before dawn? A week? More than that? He wasn't even certain of the day anymore. He wasn't religious. Sunday mostly meant that the bars were closed. So perhaps this was a weekday, and she'd risen with the sun, showered, pulled on her dress, and gone to work.

He noticed with detachment that he had never fucked around on Elena. He'd killed men, he'd lied, he'd stolen. He'd beaten Elena and been attacked by her, but he hadn't frequented the whores down by the port when they were together. Even when they'd had a fight, he hadn't taken up with other women.

Elena would have killed him *and* any woman he slept with, for one thing. And also, the prospect of finding a woman who would think Ramón worthy of her attention, much less of her body, filled him with either a sick dread that came from years of rejections or the quiet aloofness that sprang from the anticipation of refusal. But besides all that, and to his surprise, Ramón found that it was simply not something that a real man did. Fuck women who were for hire, yes. Tempt your friend's woman away from him, certainly. See more than one woman, yes—if you were the kind of lucky sonofabitch who could juggle girlfriends that way. But cheat on your woman once she'd become your woman? That, somehow, was crossing the line. Even when the woman was a crazed weasel in human skin like Elena. Even when you didn't love her, or even like her very much, it wasn't something a real man did.

Ramón coughed out a laugh. Maneck's turtle head rose and swung toward him, but apparently there wasn't enough mirth in Ramón's laugh to bring the wrath of the *sahael*.

"Turns out I've got morals," Ramón said. "I wouldn't have thought so."

"And this sound. It was an expression of surprise?"

"Yeah," Ramón said. "Something like that."

"And what is the reason for displaying the food in a tree branch? Would it not be better to consume it?"

Ramón frowned his confusion, and Maneck gestured toward the crotch of the tree under which they sat. There, wrapped in leaves that almost obscured the blood, was the skinned body of a flatfur. Ramón shifted the *sahael* over one shoulder and climbed up to look at the corpse. It was like the one he had found by the lake. Hidden, but hidden poorly. He was a little disconcerted that he hadn't noticed it himself. Scavengers would find it by its scent, the way they had found the *jabali rojo* that Maneck had killed. Ramón's twin was doing something. But . . .

With a feeling of connection that was almost physical, he understood. He remembered Martín Casaus, back in the early days when they'd been friends. The drunken stories he'd told of trapping *chupacabras,* using fresh meat as bait to lure them into a pit . . .

"That cocksucking son of a whore," Ramón said under his breath, and then dropped back down to the ground. "That *pendejo*'s fucking *insane*!"

"What do these words mean?" Maneck demanded. "The display of the food is *aubre*?"

"No, it's got a function. That bastard is leading us into a *chupacabra*'s range, and these things are meant to draw it toward us."

"This *chupacabra*. It is dangerous?"

"Fuck yes. It'll kill him if it finds him."

"This would undermine his function," Maneck said. "His actions lack meaning."

"No, they don't. He knows we lived through the blast. He's seen us, and he knows we're close enough that he won't have time to build a raft. He's tired, he's hurt, and he knows we're going to catch him. So he's trying to put us in the same place as the *chupacabra,* and hope that it kills us before it kills him. It's a crazy risk to take, but it's better than giving up," Ramón said, and shook his head in admiration. "That's one tough *cabrón* we're up against!"

For a moment, Maneck's shoulders rose in confusion, but then it seemed to understand what Ramón was saying and feeling. Perhaps the *sahael* had given the alien some insight into human perversity.

"We will find the man before this happens," Maneck said, rising to its full height.

"We'd fucking *better,*" Ramón said.

Chapter 15

For two more days, Ramón and Maneck trekked through the forest, the man leading the way and the alien at his heels. They paused for Ramón to eat and drink, and to piss and shit, but rested only at night. The other Ramón had made perfunctory camps, sleeping in the hollow of a lightning-struck milkpine one night and in a poorly constructed lean-to the next. The fire pit and well-built shelter of the earlier campsites were gone, and Ramón understood why. His twin was truly on the run. They were down to the final sprint.

They found three more flatfurs along the path, and Ramón was fairly sure they had overlooked several others. The path they traveled would reek of blood to the creatures of São Paulo. And more and more often, Ramón saw signs of *chupacabra:* evil-smelling spoor on the path, trees gouged by sharpened claws, and, once, a distant call that was equal parts solitude and murder.

Maneck remained distant and reserved, but more comprehensible than it had been at first. With every night's rest, the alien seemed to gain strength and focus. None of the strange dreams had troubled Ramón again, and the issues of *tatecreude* and killing, Enye and genocide had come up in their conversation no more often than before. Memories still flooded Ramón from time to time—moments from his childhood, trivial events from his time in the Enye ship, and arriving on São Paulo. He found that he was better able to ignore them if he intentionally kept his mind on the path before him.

It was the middle morning of the third day when the game path they had been following reached the river. The great Río Embudo. The river was almost too wide to see across—what had been a thin ribbon seen from afar had stretched into a clear expanse of glacier-cold water, fast and smooth. Trees pressed up to the banks, exposed roots trailing into the flow like thick fingers. No human footprints marred the muddy bank, but Ramón didn't doubt that the other one had been at this place, seeing this same landscape. But how long before? And where would he have gone from here to construct his escape raft? Ramón considered the sunlight glittering on the water's surface and let his mind turn the problem over. If he had been here, and free, fleeing the alien and dodging the *chupacabra,* what would he have done?

Scratching his wispy beard, he turned south and began plodding along the riverbank. Maneck followed without a word, the *sahael* bobbing between them like a length of rope. The water murmured softly. On another day, with some other errand, Ramón would have stopped, perhaps dipped his bare feet into the river water, and enjoyed the beauty of the place. As it was, his mind buzzed with a hundred different questions; had his twin already finished some small raft and floated away to the south, and what would Maneck do if they found the other Ramón, and how large was a *chupacabra*'s territory anyway? He spoke about none of it, only judging where best to place his feet and what angle to take around the trees in order to keep the *sahael* from catching on a branch and tugging at his throat.

There were fewer signs of his twin now—no footprints, few small branches broken at the correct height for a man to have done the damage. It wasn't that the other Ramón had become more careful, but the river drew forest animals to its banks to obscure any more human traces. There would be more kyi-kyi here. More salt rats and *alces negros.* The mud banks they passed showed the marks of thin hooves, wide-slung soft toes, the tiny birdlike cuneiform of *tapanos* and stone kites. The river at their side was teeming with life. The planet was alive around them. They were two aliens marching through a world they didn't belong to. Three aliens, if he counted the other Ramón.

The river bent lazily to the east, offering Ramón a majestic view of the water and the distant forest on the far bank but restricting what he could see of the path up ahead. He paused, squatted beside a fallen iceroot, and spat. Maneck came looming up beside him and stopped.

"The man is not here," Maneck said. Its voice likely carried across the water like a distant landslide.

"He's here. Somewhere."

"He may have gone against the flow of the river," Maneck said. "If we are searching in the wrong direction, then we will be unable to find him."

"Then he'll be floating on by, won't he? That's why I'm holding close to the bank. So we can see him if he passes."

The alien was silent.

"You hadn't thought of that," Ramón said.

"I am not an apt tool for this purpose," Maneck said. The quills on his head shifted in something akin to despair.

"You're doing fine," Ramón said. "But if we don't find this *pendejo* before sundown, we're going to have a problem. He'll have the chance to—"

The sound was like something falling; the rattle of leaves, the faintest hush of moving air. The beast burst from the trees in near silence. It wasn't until Maneck turned toward it that the *chupacabra* bared its teeth and shrieked.

Ramón had seen pictures of *chupacabras* before—even once held the scaled pelt of what must have been a young member of the species. Nothing he had seen had prepared him for the reality of the creature that faced him now. As tall as a man, and perhaps twelve feet long, its limbs were engines of power and speed. Black claws tipped its almost handlike paws, and the wide mouth—lips drawn back to reveal the deep-red gums—seemed too small for the doubled rows of teeth. Its eyes were not the red glow of the parade float, but pure black. The predator stink of it—rotten meat, animal musk, and old blood—rushed on ahead of it like a wave.

Maneck's arm shifted, and energy exploded on the *chupacabra*'s breast. The screaming cry rose to a higher register, and the air suddenly filled with the stink of burning hair and flesh, but the shot wasn't enough to stop the beast, and its attack didn't falter. The *chupacabra* crashed into the alien, and, for the first time, Maneck seemed small. Ramón backed instinctively into the water until the *sahael* tugged at his neck, unable to take his eyes from the whirling tangle that was alien clashing with alien. His mind was empty with fear, his own high voice squeaking out the Paternoster without realizing it.

Through the *sahael,* he could *feel* Maneck's body grappling with the *chupacabra,* exerting every last bit of strength it possessed. It was not as hopelessly uneven a struggle as it would have been had Maneck been human—the *chupacabra* was stronger and heavier, but not so much so that Maneck was completely without a chance. Both Maneck and Ramón screamed in agony when the thing raked its claws down Maneck's side. But then Maneck's long arms found some purchase. The *chupacabra*'s battle calls shifted, becoming at first alarmed and then agonized as Maneck hugged it close, its cablelike arms squeezing the air from the predator's lungs. Ramón could hear the *chupacabra*'s ribs crack, hear it gasp in pain, and, for a moment, he felt a surge of amazed hope that they would win.

But then the *chupacabra* writhed and twisted, its legs flailing. A claw pierced Maneck's wounded eye, and unbearable pain radiated down the *sahael* into Ramón's flesh. He and the alien cried out as one. The *chupacabra* bounded back and landed on all fours, already bunched to spring again. Ramón felt Maneck's distress echoing his own. The *chupacabra* leaped, and Maneck fired another blast of energy. The bolt went wide, and the impact of the *chupacabra*'s hurtling body knocked Maneck back. Now it was the *chupacabra* with its arms locked around Maneck, its thick hind legs digging at the alien's legs and belly with long, saber-sharp claws. Ramón screamed in agony, pulling at the flesh of the *sahael,* as if he could rip the leash free.

And, to his astonishment, Ramón felt movement in his throat—a loosening, like tendrils of metal withdrawing from his bones and nerves. His experience of Maneck's pain lessened, his doubled consciousness faded. With a disturbing slithering sound, the *sahael* pulled away from him and turned, snakelike, to whip at the *chupacabra.* The flickering exposed wires at the *sahael*'s end arced with energy as it struck at the *chupacabra,* and the beast screamed in pain, but Maneck seemed to be weakening, and nothing that had happened so far had significantly slowed the *chupacabra*'s relentless attack. Ramón, standing thigh-deep in the icy river water, bent to find some stones to throw at the beast— then came to his senses.

He was free, and once the *chupacabra* had killed Maneck, *he* would be next. This was no time to fight. This was the time to flee.

He took a great breath and dove, kicking as hard as he ever had, moving with the current. The sounds of battle vanished as his ears filled with water. Beneath the river's glittering surface, bright green fish swam, unconcerned with the violence on the shore. Fine golden filaments rose from the muck at the bottom and were bent by the water as if they pointed the way to the sea. Ramón was careful to swim well above the golden threads; they could sting as bad as jellyfish. When he came up for air, he had already covered at least a hundred meters, and the howls of the *chupacabra* were fading behind him. He took a fresh lungful and dove again.

His first impulse was to set out for the opposite bank, but seconds after he'd had the thought, he abandoned it. The water was hardly warmer than the ice that had spawned it, and adrenaline would do little to stave off hypothermia. Crossing the river would be suicide. Ramón angled back for the near shore and realized as his arms flailed and clawed at the current that he was in trouble. The fast river flow had pulled him around the bend, but it had also taken him farther from the bank than his own efforts could have. He rose again, treading water and borne along like a cork. He could hear no sound of the struggle. Either the fight had ended or he was far enough away that the sound of it was drowned out by his splashing. He turned his head, blinking hard to clear his eyes, and found the shore. His heart sank.

Come on, Ramón, he told himself. *You're a tough* pendejo. *You can do this thing.*

He turned himself toward the riverbank and started swimming as hard as he could perpendicular to the flow. The river plants and streamers of moss below him were his guides as he pushed himself toward the uncertain safety of land. His feet and hands stung and soon went numb. His earlobes ached. His face and chest grew thick-fleshed and rubbery, but he pushed on. He couldn't die out here. He had to reach the shore. It was his goddamn *tatecreude*.

He focused on moving his body—legs kicking, arms and hands scooping at the water. Time lost its meaning. He might have been swimming for three minutes or an hour or his whole life. The chill was deadly, and he could feel it knifing into him. He faltered once, seduced into thinking he needed a moment's rest.

He was dead. The only reason to keep trying was stubbornness, and Ramón Espejo was a very stubborn man. Even when he was hardly doing more than floating, he pushed his mouth free of the water and gulped one more breath. And then one more. And then one more. His mind began to fade, and he recalled his dream of being one with the river, of becoming the flow itself. Perhaps that would not be so bad after all. Just one more breath so he could think about it. Then one more.

It was a sandbar that saved him. The river widened, its eastern half becoming shallow as it broadened. Driftwood rose from the sand like the antlers of some nightmare beast. Ramón found an ancient log standing at an angle from the water. He crawled up its black, slimy side and held it like it was a lover. He was too cold to shiver. That wasn't good. He had to get out of the water. The river still lapped at his knees, and his feet were numb. Ramón bit down on his lip until he tasted blood, the pain focusing his mind.

He had to reach the shore. Then get dry, and then hope that the sun would warm his flesh. There was enough debris on the sandbar that he could move from one support to another; it seemed as if anything that went into the water upstream ended up caught here. The danger was that he might slip, fall into the water, and lack the will to rise again. He had to be careful.

With a deep breath, Ramón pushed his blackwood lover away and stumbled to a small dam of branches that had been laced together with ivy and strips of bark. Then from that to a low stone. Then another slime-slick log. And then the water was no higher than his ankles. Ramón trudged slowly to dry land. He collapsed on the ground, laughed weakly, and vomited up what seemed like several liters of river water. His alien garments were sodden and heavy, the shoes kicked off somewhere in the river. Fingers clumsy as sausages, he pulled the clothing from his skin and lay back naked, trying with the last of his conscious will to angle himself toward the sun.

It wasn't sleep that took him, but neither was it death, because sometime later his mind re-formed and he struggled to sit up. The sun had moved the width of three hands together, lowering toward the western sky. His teeth were chattering like a badly tuned lift tube. His hands and feet were blue, but not black. The alien robe he had cast aside was dry and sun-warmed. He pulled it on awkwardly and sat, arms around his knees, laughing and weeping. His neck, where the *sahael* had entered him, felt unnaturally hot. The skin there was smooth as river stone and numb as a witch's mark. Ramón rubbed his fingertips over the insertion point and let the reality of his situation sink into him. He had made it. He was free. He looked out over the water with a sense of glee and disbelief. He'd done it!

It didn't occur to him that the mesh of branches tied together on the sandbar was odd until he heard the sharp intake of breath behind him and turned to see a surreal and familiar sight. The other Ramón stood at the tree line. His chest was bare, his pants ripped into rough shorts. Dark hair rose crazily from his head. His right hand was wrapped in a bandage black with dried blood and his left gripped the old field knife, Ramón's field pack slung over one sunburned shoulder. Of course. He'd made a raft; the branches out there hadn't wrapped themselves with bark. And now the flow of the river and the cruel irony of the gods had brought both Ramóns to the same place at the same time, caught up on the same sandbar.

He rose slowly, unsteadily, trying not to startle his twin. He raised a hand in greeting, fear closing his throat. His twin took a step back, eyeing him balefully.

"Who the fuck are you?" the man said.

Part Three

Chapter 16

Ramón's mind was slow to react. He had to answer, but none of the things that came to his lips was the right thing. *I'm Ramón Espejo* and *I'm you* and *Why should I tell you who I am,* pendejo? He felt his mouth open and close, and saw the shock in his twin's eyes shift to something else, something more dangerous. The other man's grip on his knife tensed.

"Aliens!" Ramón spat out. "There's fucking aliens out there! They took me prisoner. You've got to help me!"

It was the key. The other man's tension eased a little. His head turned and he looked at Ramón, measuring him, his eyes still radiating mistrust but no longer on the edge of violence. Ramón leaned forward, moving slowly and being careful to do nothing that might startle the other man.

Ramón looked at him closely for the first time, feeling an odd fascination. After all, in spite of his memories to the contrary, this was the first human being he'd ever actually met! His twin was filthy and unkempt—the light stubble that often darkened his chin was already a moth-eaten beard. Distrust shone in his black eyes. His right hand was wrapped in bloody cloth, and Ramón realized, with a profound sense of vertigo, that in that mess of soiled bandages, a finger was missing. A finger from which he had been born.

But the other Ramón also looked *wrong* somehow. He had expected it to be like looking into a mirror, but it was not.

The face he was accustomed to seeing reflected back was different than this. It was more like seeing a video recording of himself. Perhaps, he thought, his features were not so symmetrical as he'd liked to believe. Also, the voice was higher than he believed his own to be and slightly whiny. The voice he heard and hated when he heard himself recorded. The other Ramón's bearded chin jutted aggressively.

What did *he* look like in his twin's eyes? Finer hair. Fewer lines and creases in his skin. No scars, and thin whiskers. He would appear to be a younger man. And if the other Ramón didn't already feel that he was seeing himself, there was no reason for him to suspect what the aliens had done. Ramón's advantage was that he knew what had happened, who he was, and all that the other man knew. The other man's advantage was that he hadn't half drowned. And he had a knife.

"Please," Ramón said, searching for things he could say that would make him seem more plausible. "I've got to get back to Fiddler's Jump. You got a van?"

"I look like I have a fucking van?" the other man said, raising his arms out at his sides like Christ crucified. "I've been running from those fucking things for a week. How is it you came to get loose from them just here and now, eh?"

It was a good question. They weren't near the alien hive, and the timing was too convenient. Ramón licked his lips.

"It's the first time they took me out," Ramón said, deciding to keep as near the truth as he could. "They were holding me in a tank. Under a mountain up north of here. They told me there was someone they were hunting. I think they were using me. Seeing what I could eat and like that. I think maybe they didn't know much. You know. About people."

The other man considered this. Ramón kept his gaze away from the knife. Better that neither of them think of it. He heard himself going on, his voice thin and shrill. He sounded afraid.

"I tried to fight against them, but they had this thing. In my neck. Right here, you can see where it went in. If I did anything they didn't like, they shocked me. I've been walking for days. Please, man, you can't leave me here."

"I'm not going to leave you here," the other man said.

There was disgust in his voice. Disgust and perhaps superiority. "I've been running from them too. They blew up my van, but I had a few tricks. Fucked them up pretty good!"

"That was you?" Ramón said, trying to make his voice sound admiring instead of false. "You're the one that blew up the *yunea*?"

"The what?"

You only get one slip like that, Ramón told himself. Hold it together, *cabrón*. At least until *you* have the knife.

"The flying box thing. That's what they called it."

"Uh," the other man said. "Yeah. I'm the one. I saw you, too. I was watching."

"So you saw the thing they put in my neck."

The other man seemed reluctantly to agree that Ramón's story had some truth to it. Ramón could see it in the man's stance when he decided not to kill him.

"How'd you get away?" the other man asked.

"*Chupacabra* killed the alien. Came out of nowhere. The leash came free while they were fighting, and I got out of there."

The other man smiled to himself. Ramón decided to let him think they hadn't seen through his plan with the flatfurs. Better that the other Ramón spend his time thinking how clever he was, and how stupid everyone else could be.

"What's your name, anyway?" the other man asked.

"David," Ramón said, pulling a name out of the air. "David Penasco. I live down in Amadora. I'm a banker with Union Trust. I was camping by myself, maybe a month ago. They took me when I was sleeping."

"Union Trust's got a branch in Amadora?" the other man asked.

"Yeah," Ramón said. He didn't know if it was true, didn't know if there was some other memory that hadn't grown back yet that would rip his story apart, so he plain barefaced lied it through and prayed. "Has been for about six months."

"Sonofabitch," the other man said. "Well, get off your ass, David. We got work to do if we're going to get out of here. I got maybe a third of a raft finished. If there's gonna be two of us, you better get to work. Maybe later you can tell me what you know about those *pinche* motherfuckers."

The other man turned and started walking back into the forest. Ramón followed.

The clearing was twenty meters or so into the woods, and the man hadn't bothered to make a shelter or a fire pit. This wasn't a place to live, it was a construction site. Four sheaves of bamboolike cane lay bound with strips of iceroot bark, the red skin of the cane glittering as it died as if it had been lacquered. Pontoons, Ramón thought. Laced together with thin branches and saplings young enough to be hewn with the serrated back edge of the field knife, they would float. It wouldn't be anything near watertight—the river would be splashing onto their legs and asses the whole way down if they didn't have something to cover the raft floor. And the sheaves were too small and too loosely bound. It was damn impressive for some crazed *pendejo* out by himself with a wounded hand and a demon out of Hell trotting after him, but it wouldn't get one of them to Fiddler's Jump, much less two.

"What?" the man said.

"Just looking," Ramón replied. "We're going to need more cane. You want me to cut it? Just show me where you found it. . . ."

The man considered the offer with a pinched, sour face. Ramón knew the calculation going on behind those dark eyes. Ramón—or David, whatever his name was now—was going to harvest faster than the injured man himself, but it meant giving him the knife.

"I'll do it," the man said, nodding toward the deeper forest farther from the river. "You go see if you can find some good branches to put between them. And some food, maybe. Be back here before sundown. We'll try to get this sonofabitch ready to haul down to the water in the morning."

"Yeah, okay," Ramón said. The man spat and stalked off to the south, leaving him alone. Ramón scratched at his elbow where the knot of scar tissue was growing back and turned to walk into the gloom beneath the trees. He realized he'd never asked the man his name. Of course he hadn't; he already knew. The dread grew in him that the other Ramón would think the omission strange. He had to be more careful.

The rest of the day was spent dragging fallen branches and wide iceroot leaves back to the campsite and making up the story he could tell his twin. He stopped once to crack open some sug beetles and eat the raw flesh. Uncooked, they were saltier and the meat slick and unpleasant. There wasn't time, though, for anything more. He tried not to wonder what had happened between Maneck and the *chupacabra,* which of the two had lost and which was still under the roof of branches, hunting him. It didn't change what needed doing, so there was no point spending valuable time on the question.

By sundown, he and his twin had gathered another six sheaves and perhaps a third of the branches that they would need to make the raft floor. The man seemed pleased by Ramón's wide, soft pile of iceroot leaves as well, though he didn't go so far as to say it. Ramón boiled a double handful of sug beetles and his twin roasted a cooper's dragon—one of the small, birdlike lizards that inhabited the low branches. The dragon had an unnerving way of writhing as it cooked, as if the flesh were still living even though both brains had been cut out and the thin, pale blood drained from the body.

They made small conversation, Ramón careful to ask the man's name and background. Then they planned for the next day—how to carry the branches and sheaves to the water for assembly, how much more would need to be harvested, whether they needed to strip more bark to use for rope.

"You've done this before," the man said, and Ramón felt a pang of distress. Maybe he'd come across as knowing too much.

"I explore a little. When I can. Most of the time, I'm stuck behind a desk," Ramón said, trying to seem flattered. "Banking. You know. But the money's good."

"You ever do any prospecting?"

"No," Ramón said. "Just go out, camp. Look around. You know. Get away from people for a while."

The man's expression softened a little, as Ramón had known it would. He felt a twinge of guilt at playing on the man's feelings that way.

"What about you?" Ramón asked, and his twin shrugged.

"I spend a lot of time in the field," he said. "Not much point staying in town. It's a pretty good living, if you know what you're doing. A good season, I can pull in six, maybe seven thousand chits."

That was a gross exaggeration. Ramón had never taken in more than four thousand, even at the best of times. Two and a half was nearer the average, and there had been several seasons he hadn't managed more than a thousand. The man's dark eyes seemed to challenge him, so he shook his head, feigning amazement.

"That's really good," Ramón said.

"It ain't hard, you know what you're doing," the man said, settling back.

"What happened to your hand?" Ramón asked.

"Fucking aliens," the man said, and started to unwrap the blood-stiffened cloth. "I was shooting at them, and my gun blew up. Fucked me up pretty good."

Ramón leaned close. In the firelight, it was hard to see how much of the redness was the swollen flesh itself and how much was reflected flames. The skin of the palm looked like taco meat that had been left out overnight. Where the index finger had been was a rough stump, the flesh burned and scarred to an oddly beautiful opalescent silver.

"You cauterized it," he said. His mind went back to the camp where he'd found his cigarette case, where Maneck had revealed to him the story of his doubling. This was why the man had spent so long there. He'd been recovering from the self-treatment of his wound.

"Yeah," the man said, and his voice was casual and drawling in a way that Ramón knew meant that he was proud of having done it. "I heated up the knife until it glowed and then used that. Had to. I was bleeding all over the place. There was some bone I had to cut out too."

Ramón suppressed a smile. They were tough sons of bitches, him and his twin. He couldn't help feeling a little proud of himself too, for what the other man had done.

"Fever?" he asked.

"On and off," the man admitted. "No streaks up my arm, though. So it looks like no blood poisoning. Or else I'd be dead by now anyway, eh? So tell me about how you got caught by those devils."

Ramón launched into his tale. A little over a month ago, he'd been out camping by himself in the far north. His lover, Carmina, had left him, and he'd wanted to spend some time alone where she couldn't find him and his friends couldn't offer sympathy. He'd seen a flying box, gone to investigate, and the aliens had done something—knocked him out, drugged him. He didn't remember much about that part. Then he'd been imprisoned in a tank until they pulled him out and told him to go hunting. It was a simple enough story to remember, and not so far from the truth that he'd be likely to get caught flat-footed. And the other Ramón would likely sympathize. He talked about the explosion that had ruined the *yunea,* the forced march, the attack by the *chupacabra,* and his own escape. He pretended to be amazed when the man explained the strategy behind the flatfur corpses. The delight the other took in his own cleverness started to become annoying. If Ramón didn't nod or make appreciative noises at the right moment, his twin glared at him.

The whole thing was a manipulation from start to finish. And it seemed to work. When Ramón explained how he needed to be away from civilization, that the comfort offered by friends was as painful and humiliating as being mocked, the man nodded to himself. And when the tale was finished, he didn't comment on it. He wouldn't. It wasn't the sort of thing men did.

"Sleep in shifts?" the man asked.

"Sure," Ramón said. "Probably better that way. I'll take first. I'm not tired."

It was a lie. He was deeply weary, but he'd had the period of unconsciousness that was almost like sleep after he'd pulled himself from the river. The other Ramón hadn't even had that. And anyway, it was best to do the sorts of things that a banker from Amadora would do to ingratiate himself to his rescuer.

The man shrugged and held out his field knife. Ramón

hesitated for a moment, then took it. The slightly sticky feel of the leather grip, the balanced weight. It was familiar, and yet different than he remembered it. A moment's consideration told him that it was his body that had changed; he'd never held it without calluses on his hands. The other man misread his expression.

"It's not much," the man said. "It's all that we've got. Won't fight off a *chupacabra* or redjackets, but . . ."

"No trouble," Ramón said. "Thanks."

The man grunted, lay down, and turned his back to the fire. Ramón tested the heft of the knife again, growing used to it in his new hands. These unlikely companions he traveled with—men and aliens—seemed to be pretty comfortable handing him knives. Maneck had done it because it knew it was safe. The man had done it because he assumed Ramón was an ally. It was a mistake he would have made himself. Obviously.

Ramón peered into the darkness, careful not to let the light of their modest cook fire blind him to the shadows, and considered his options. The man had accepted him, for the time being. But it was a long way to Fiddler's Jump, and if what Maneck had said was true, Ramón would grow to more closely resemble his old self before they got there. Sooner or later, the man would figure out that something was wrong. And even if he didn't, Ramón didn't know what he'd do when they got back to the colony. A judge would be hard-pressed to accept that he was the real, legal Ramón Espejo. And the Enye might well decide that he should die along with Maneck's people. Nothing good would come from two Ramóns walking out of the bush together.

The smart thing to do would be to kill the man. He had a knife, his twin was snoring and wounded. One quick slice to the neck, and the problem would be gone. He'd make his way south, resume his life, and the other man's bones would never be found. It was what needed to happen.

And yet, he couldn't do it.

Under what circumstances do you kill? Maneck's question echoed in his memory. Ramón settled down for the long, slow hours of his watch and found himself less and less able to answer the question.

At first light, they went back to the work of building the raft. Ramón retied the cane floats, his two hands cinching them tighter than his twin could manage. They considered how many branches they'd need to finish the structure. It was a quick, easy negotiation. Ramón and the other man approached the problem the same way, came to the same conclusions. The only real difference was in his twin's refusal to give over a larger share of the work. It made sense that the uninjured man should bear the heavier load, but his twin was bent on putting the soft-handed Amadora banker in his place, and Ramón recognized the impulse clearly enough to know there was no point arguing.

By noon, they had enough raw materials to put the raft together. Ramón fashioned a rough harness from two cut branches and a length of bright blue panama ivy and used it to haul the cane and the branches down the short path to the water. The man allowed him that much, bringing the armful of stripped bark and iceroot leaves instead. Ramón figured it meant his twin was feeling tired.

The sandbar was smaller than Ramón remembered it, but just as cluttered with debris. Without consulting the man walking behind him, he pulled the load to the bank just downstream. The bar created a still place in the waters. The eddy was a good place to test their raft before they launched themselves out into the unforgiving flow.

Ramón shrugged off the harness and squatted on the bank. In the still water, he could see himself reflected, and his twin standing behind him. Two men, similar, but not yet identical. Ramón's growing beard was softer and lighter. His hair hung closer to his head than it had before, changing the shape of his face a little. Still, they might have been brothers. Since he knew to look for it, he could see where the moles on his twin's cheek and neck were echoed by minute discolorations on his own. The scar on his belly twinged.

"Not bad," the man said, and spat thoughtfully into the water, the ripples disturbing its soft mirror. The raft was going to be big. The lower gravity of São Paulo lent itself to fast-growing trees, and rather than take the time to cut the long saplings twice, they'd used them all at their full height. It wasn't luxury, but there would be easy room for them both. "We should put some shelter on it, though."

"Like a cabin?" Ramón asked, looking at the collection of sticks before him.

"A lean-to. Something to sleep in, get out of the weather. And if we got enough wood, we can add a fire grate, too. Line the bottom with iceroot leaves, fill it a couple hands high with good sand, and we can keep warm on the river."

Ramón squinted at the man, then upriver, back toward where Maneck and the *chupacabra* had done battle. He tried to guess how long he'd been in the water, how far he'd swum. He couldn't be sure. It had felt like a long time, a huge distance. But he'd been on the verge of death, so his impressions probably weren't all that good.

"Let's put those on farther down the river," he said. "I want to get away from here first."

"You scared?" the man jeered. His tone was taunting, and Ramón felt anger and embarrassment surge through him. Ramón could see the frustration in the other man, the anger always simmering under the skin, ready to be fanned awake, the desire to strike out and make himself feel better by hurting someone, and felt its twin in his own breast. He'd have to tread carefully here, or they'd end up in a fight neither could afford.

"Scared to face down a pissed-off *chupacabra* with a field knife and a stick?" he said. "Anyone isn't scared of that's stupid or crazy."

The man's expression hardened at the insult, but he shrugged casually.

"There's two of us," he said, turning half away from Ramón. "We could take him."

"Maybe," Ramón said, letting the obvious lie stand. They could no more take down a *chupacabra* than flap their arms and fly to Fiddler's Jump. If he pressed it, though, they'd end up fighting about it. "Thing is, what if the *alien* won?"

"Against a *chupacabra*?" the man asked, incredulous. It was easy to summon up the bravado to say they could kill the beast, but hard to stretch the imagination far enough to think that Maneck might win against the same odds. Ramón kept his expression somber.

"It was looking pretty even when I got out of there," he said. "The alien had a gun of some kind, and it shot the *chupacabra* at least twice; maybe that weakened it. I wasn't going to hang around to find out how it ended, you know? Besides, if the fucking alien is still alive and still has that gun, we don't want it catching up with us."

"Fine," the man said. "If it makes you feel better, we'll head downstream for a day or two. We can pull in somewhere, add a lean-to and a fire pit. Maybe check the cane, make sure it's still tied tight enough."

That was a dig. The man was still smarting over Ramón insisting that he could tie the floats better with two hands than his twin could with one.

Once Ramón would have risen to the bait, taken offense, maybe pushed it into a fight, but not now. *Fine,* pendejo, Ramón thought. *Dig at me all you want. I know how scared you are too.*

"Good plan" was all he said.

Lashing the branches together and binding them to the cane floats was long work, but not difficult. Ramón found himself falling into a rhythm—setting the wood in place, tying it on one side, then the other, then in the center where it crossed another branch. One, two, three, four, then start again. He fell into the work, abandoning himself to the sheer physicality of it. His hands and feet, unprotected by calluses, hurt and blistered. He ignored the pain; it was just part of the package. If the other man could cut away his own stump of a finger bone, Ramón could sure as shit stand scraping up his palms a little.

His twin kept pace as best he could, but the crippled hand slowed him badly. Ramón could feel the frustration rising in the man as he struggled not to be shown up by a *pinche* banker. As the sun dipped toward the treetops on the opposite shore, Ramón noticed, with some satisfaction, that the other man's bandage showed the bright red tinge of new blood.

At the end, they laid the iceroot leaves over the branches, tacking the broad, leathery fronds together until they were like a carpet. Not wholly waterproof, but enough that they wouldn't be getting their asses wet with river water all the way south. The raft wasn't much to look at. There was no rudder, and only an improvised paddle to steer with at the stern. It wasn't more than two and a half meters square; it was a decent size for a wrestling match, but as a way to travel, it would be pretty damn close quarters. Still, all it had to do was stay on top of the big river long enough for them to float down to Fiddler's Jump. And when they dragged it out into the lagoon, it floated high off the water, and when they both clambered on, it felt solid and secure.

"Not fucking bad, David," his twin said. "You did a man's job of it, eh?"

"We did all right," he agreed. "You want to get out of here?"

And as the words left his mouth, they heard a sound— the distant, gurgling cry of a *chupacabra*. It sounded as if it were in pain. Ramón's belly went tight, and the other man's face was pale.

"Yeah," his twin said. "We might as well get going."

Ramón paddled them out from behind the sandbar and nearer the center of the river where the current was fastest. The other man squatted at the raft's edge, looking back. Neither the beast nor Maneck emerged from the forest, and the screaming call didn't come again. Ramón, settling back to steer, couldn't help feeling they'd had a near miss. Another night on shore would have ended badly for them. Maybe even another hour. It was a good fucking thing that his twin had tried so hard to keep up. A good thing that Ramón hadn't been able to bring himself to kill the man in the night. One man would never have been able to finish the raft alone in time.

But the sound of the predator—even if it was in pain— also filled him with a strange melancholy. If the *chupacabra* lived, then Maneck was dead. The *athanai* of his cohort had been killed attempting to protect his people from the violence that had tracked them across stars and centuries. And the creature who had frustrated Maneck's *tatecreude*? A jumped-up little monkey from the badlands of Mexico who'd stumbled on the hive while running from the law, and who even now didn't have any idea what the consequences of his discovery would be. At least Maneck had died trying. Died fighting. There was some honor in that, even if it had failed its people. In an odd way that surprised and disquieted him, he found he almost missed Maneck, now that it was over, now that he was free. And in spite of all the pain it had visited upon him, in spite of the hatred he'd felt for the alien at times, Ramón couldn't help but feel a pang of regret and sorrow at the thought of its terrible death.

"Still, better you than me, monster," Ramón said under his breath. "Better you than me!"

Chapter 17

The first night was the worst. The river was placid so far north, so the only dangers were logs and debris floating invisibly in the dark water, aquatic predators like bloody mormons and *carracao,* and the cold. They were under no power, so unless the rocks or debris were stuck in the bed of the river itself, chances of a damaging collision were slim, and they were too far north to be in the range of most river predators. That left the cold.

Once the sun slipped behind the western trees, the river seemed to suck all the warmth from the air. Ramón was wearing the alien robe; warm enough, but too small to cover his legs and arms both at the same time. The other man, however, had sacrificed his shirt and the lower legs of his trousers to bandages and traps, so they'd agreed that the man should take the one-piece alien garment. He was curled on the iceroot leaves, wrapped tight and still shivering. There was no call to sleep in shifts. The light of a near-full moon was too bright and the chill too uncomfortable to allow for anything like sleep. Ramón considered pulling in to shore for the night, but he didn't suggest it. His twin would only take it as a slight, and the man never made the suggestion himself. Besides, Ramón knew they were both anxious to put as much distance as they could between themselves and the *chupacabra*. Ramón wondered how far a *chupacabra*'s range was. Fifty kilometers came to mind, but he didn't know where he got the figure from. By morning, it would be safe to pull to the side. But perhaps they could move to the western shore, just to be sure.

"Hey, David," the other man said. Ramón blinked back to full consciousness, only now aware how near he'd come to dozing.

"Yeah?" he said, and coughed. He hoped he wasn't getting a cold. That would be just his luck.

"You ever spend time in Diegotown?" the man asked.

Ramón fought to focus his mind, looking over at the man. His twin was sitting up now, legs hugged to his chest. His frown cut deep lines in his face. He looked both brutish and desperately uncomfortable, but it was clear enough he'd been watching Ramón for a while.

"A little," he said. "Why?"

"I think I've seen you someplace before. What kind of things do you do in Diegotown?"

"Business, mostly," Ramón said. "You might have seen me around the governor's palace. You spend any time there?" He knew damn well he didn't, so the other man's shrug was expected. Ramón felt the urge to echo the movement—it was the natural thing; the motion most familiar to his flesh. It took an effort to shake his head and smile instead. "There was a bar I went to a few times," Ramón said, not knowing why he was choosing the embellishment until he'd already begun. "The El Rey. It was down by the river. You ever go there?"

"No," the other man said harshly. "I've never heard of that one."

"Huh," Ramón said. "Maybe I got the name wrong. It had wood floors. And the guy who ran it was named Michael or Miko or something like that. I got sick in the alley out back. There was one of those shifting LED lights. I remember that."

"Don't know the place. Maybe you're thinking of a bar in some other town."

His tone made it clear that the conversation was over, but in case Ramón hadn't taken the hint, his twin shifted, turning his back. Ramón permitted himself a smile and a shrug. He wasn't surprised the man had lied. If he'd met a stranger in the wild, he'd have been wary of the subject too. It was a good conversation stopper.

And yet there was also regret. His mind kept returning to the time before the fight, like a tongue exploring the hole left by a missing tooth. Killing the European, he had that like he was seeing it on a screen. But how exactly had things gone that far? He remembered a pachinko machine. There had been a woman, her hair straightened to make her look Asian, at the European's side. He knew that the woman hadn't been there because she knew or liked the man; being with him had been some kind of work thing. But he didn't know how he knew that. He remembered her laugh—tight, short, frightened.

How would he have explained to Maneck that laughter could be more than what was funny? The alien wouldn't have understood that the same thing that people did when something was funny could also be a way to express fear. To cry for help.

Ramón grabbed the thought, trying to follow it back to some more solid recollection, but it swam away, just out of his reach. Only his twin knew it, and Ramón had no way to ask.

They didn't speak again until shortly after dawn. Ramón and his twin agreed to move the raft across the river and hug the western shore until they saw a good stand of cane. They could make the pit out of anything thick enough to hold the dirt and sand that kept the fire from burning the raft itself, but using cane would be the easiest way to make a lean-to. And judging from the stars, the cane might start getting scarce if they went much farther south.

They found a decent spot by the middle morning, and Ramón gently paddled them to a landing. The impact of the bank caused the other man to stumble slightly, but the raft held together just fine. Ramón checked all the cane floats, to be sure, but none of his knots had come loose.

The other man cut cane for the rest of the morning while Ramón rounded up food. It would have been easier with a pistol, but there were a few sug beetles to be found and he managed to trap three fat, mud-colored things that looked like a cross between crayfish and eels. He didn't know what they were, but the rule of thumb was that the poisonous animals were brighter colored, so the eel-things were more likely to be edible than not. Still, he might let the other man try them first.

When he found his twin, the man was squatting on the ground, his head hung low. The field knife was in his hand and pinked by the cane juice; it looked less like blood than some sort of cherry sauce. The pile of cane on the shore was smaller than Ramón had expected. Ramón cleared his throat hard enough to be heard over the water, and the man's head rose. The black eyes squinted at Ramón for a moment before his twin lifted his chin in greeting.

"Hey," Ramón said. "I got some things. They're probably good to eat. You seen these before?"

His twin shifted his focus to the eel-things.

"No," the man said. "But they're dead. So let's cook them, eh?"

"Right," Ramón said. "You okay, man? You look tired."

"Didn't sleep," his twin spat. "And before that, I was running for my fucking life with nothing but what I had on for a few days. And before that, I had my hand fucking blown up."

"Maybe we should take a day," Ramón said, dropping the dead creatures and holding his hand out for the field knife. "Rest up, you know. Get our strength back."

"Fuck that," the twin said. He shifted his gaze to Ramón's outstretched hand.

"I can't gut these things with my fucking fingernails," Ramón said. His twin shrugged, tossed the knife in the air, catching it by the blade, and held it out grip-first for Ramón to take. He was fucked up, no question, but Ramón's twin still had reflexes.

The eel-things had a simple enough gut. Ramón cleaned out everything that didn't look like muscle, on the theory that any weird digestive enzymes or venom sacs weren't likely to be in that tissue. He roasted them on a spit, and, while cooking, they smelled like roast beef and hot mud. The sug beetles, he boiled in the tin drinking cup from the field kit. The other man sat at the riverside, looking out over the bright water, his gaze empty. Ramón decided he'd try the eel-things first after all. He carved off a sliver, placed it on his tongue, gagged, and threw the eel-things still on their spit out into the river.

"Sug beetles," he said. "We're having sug beetles."

The other man looked up at him, shading his eyes with his wrapped hand.

"They're here," his twin said.

"Who?" Ramón asked, but the man didn't answer. When Ramón followed his gaze, it was clear enough. Like hawks riding the thermals in the high air. The great black galley ships.

The Silver Enye had returned to São Paulo.

Chapter 18

After they ate, the man curled in a ball and fell into a profound sleep. There were still a couple hours of daylight left, so Ramón took the knife and harvested cane. The stalks were green as grass before he cut them, and turned red within a minute or two of being severed. It wasn't hard work, and by the time the sunset filled the western sky—distant clouds glowing gold and orange and gaudy pink—he'd almost doubled the pile that his twin had made. He washed his hands and the blade in the river, then rooted through the field pack until he found the rough, gray sharpening stone. His twin hadn't been doing much of a job keeping the knife sharp. But, then, the poor fucker only had one working hand. It was a pretty good excuse.

He sat at the water's edge, listening to the sharp, dangerous hiss of steel against stone, and looking up. Even after the trees and the river had fallen into a deep gray twilight, the Enye ships in their high orbit glowed with the light of the sun. Brighter than stars. He watched as they fell into São Paulo's shadow, dimming like someone had flipped a switch until they were only visible by the violet and orange running lights—less obvious, but present just the same. It was like God had come and hung a skull in the sky to stare down and remind Ramón of the slaughter that he'd seen in

Maneck's mind. And the slaughter that was likely to come once he and his twin returned to the city.

As the prisoner of Maneck and the aliens, he had spent relatively little time concerning himself with his return from the wild. It had, he supposed, been so unlikely a prospect that more immediate problems had kept his attention. But now that he was free and traveling toward home with his twin, the question loomed large. He brushed his hand over his arm, where there was now a thin white line, jagged and half-formed. The machete scar slowly welling up. What had Maneck said? That he'd "continue to approximate the source form." He touched the thin line of knotting flesh with his fingertips. His beard was also thickening, his hands becoming rougher. He was becoming more and more like the other man. He closed his eyes, torn between relief at seeing his own flesh coming back again and anxiety about what would come—no one would mistake them for different men. No one would even think they were twins—they were too close for that. By the time they reached another human being, they would have the same scars, the same calluses, the same faces and bodies and hair.

He couldn't very well march in and announce himself to be Ramón Espejo, with the other man at his side. Even if there was no way to tell them apart—and who could say what traces Maneck's technology would leave?—the governor would hardly ignore it. And Ramón knew himself well enough to know what his twin would think of him.

It would be better to go quickly, and arrive at Fiddler's Jump while they still looked similar but not yet identical. Ramón could engineer some excuse to slip away. Then south, maybe even to Amadora. He'd need to find someone who could give him fake papers. Not that he had the money to pay for forged documents, but again, there couldn't be *two* Ramón Espejos. . . .

He let the knife falter, the whetting stone heavy in his hand.

No. He needed money to start again. He knew all of his banking codes, could pass any authentication tests the banks required. The thing was to go back to Diegotown while his twin was still recuperating, clean out the accounts, maybe borrow some on credit, and then make his way south. It would leave the other man saddled with debts, but at least people would know him. He could start over. They both could. And it wasn't even stealing, really. He was Ramón Espejo, and that was his own money he was taking.

And if the police were looking for the man who'd killed the European, well, then perhaps his twin wouldn't mind the missing cash so much after all. Ramón chuckled. It wasn't as if they could hang him twice for the same crime. He imagined himself setting up in Amadora, maybe a simple beach house on the south coast. Once he had papers, he could rent a new van. At least until he found enough work to buy his own. He imagined waking to the sound of the surf, the cool light of morning. He imagined waking alone, on a cot too small for two bodies to share. Elena, after all, would have the other man. And he would have her. Ramón could start again. Like a snake shedding its skin, he could leave his old, gray life behind. Maybe he'd stop drinking so much. Stop going to bars and picking fights. Killing men or having them try to kill him. He could be someone *new*. How many men had dreamed of that, and how few had the chance?

It all depended on getting south quickly, before the recapitulation had thickened his scars and coarsened his hair. Before the wrinkles in his face matched the other man's, before the moles they shared became dark enough to be obvious on casual inspection. Ramón didn't know how long that would be, but he couldn't imagine it would take long. Not so many days ago, he'd just been a severed finger, and now he was nearly back to normal.

Far above, one of the Enye ships blinked out of existence and then back as the jump drives cooled. Ramón's gut tightened, remembering how it felt to be aboard those ships when they stuttered like that. The first time had been with old Palenki and his work gang. The ship had launched from its orbit, rising like a transport van and never leveling out. Ramón remembered the press of acceleration when the rockets fired. It had been like letting the water out of the tub after a hot bath, or like the torpor after sex. The muscles themselves had felt heavy on his bones. He'd smiled and looked over at Fat Enrique—he hadn't thought about Fat Enrique for years—and grinned. The boy had grinned back. They were leaving everything behind, and by the time their journey ended, everyone they'd known or spoken to or been bullied by or fucked or fucked over or been fucked over by would have died from old age. There were stories about the conquistadors burning their boats when they'd reached the new world. Ramón and Palenki and Fat Enrique and all the rest were doing the same. Earth was dead for them. Only the future mattered.

Ramón shook his head, but his mind refused to leave its track. This was another memory growing back. This time, though, he could think as well—observe the river, the Enye ships, the stars, the full moon hardly risen in the east. It was less like experiencing the thing again, and more like a powerful and autonomous daydream.

When they'd stepped onto the Enye ship, his first thought had been of how odd the place smelled—acid and salt and something reminiscent of patchouli. Palenki had bitched that it was giving him a headache, though that had probably been the cancer. They'd unloaded and stowed the equipment, found their way to their quarters by following the painted lines on the walls, eaten a small meal in the pleasant weight of the rocket acceleration, and taken to their couches when the klaxon sounded and the jump drives were set to warm up.

It had been the way Ramón had always imagined a stroke would feel. The world narrowed to a point, peripheral vision dimming, sounds growing distant, and then the discontinuity. He'd never been able to say what changed during a jump; everything could be in precisely the same place, a wrench he'd just dropped still partway to the floor, and still he knew—*knew*—that time had gone by. Quite a lot of time. That something had happened while he was unaware. He'd hated the feeling.

It was a week after that that he saw his first Enye. Ramón remembered Palenki's smile; knowing and smug and pleased with himself, as he'd gathered the work gang and instructed them on the etiquette their hosts expected. And then the thing had lumbered through the hatchway . . .

Ramón screamed. Then the memory was gone, nothing there but the river and the forest. His heart was tripping over fast, his grip on the field knife so hard that his knuckles ached. He scanned the tree line and the surface of the water, ready to attack or flee as if the Devil himself had risen up with a whip in one hand and a flaying knife in the other. The image of the Enye—huge, boulder-shaped body; wet, oysterlike, inscrutable eyes; squirming fringes of cilia; incongruously tiny and delicate hands, like doll's hands, sprouting from its middle; barely visible pucker where its beak was hidden within its flesh—faded slowly from his mind and the electric fear abated. Ramón forced himself to laugh, but it came out thin and tinny. He sounded like a coward. He stopped and spat instead, anger filling his breast.

Maneck and that pale alien fuck in the hive had made a weakling of him. Just remembering the eaters-of-the-young was enough to make him squeak like a little girl!

"Fuck that," he said. There was a low growl in his voice that pleased him. "I'm not afraid of a goddamn thing!"

He was still in a foul mood when he got back to the campsite, which meant, he knew, that he'd have to be even more careful to avoid getting into a fight with his even more short-tempered and irritable twin. The fire was down to the embers, the other man still asleep on the ground nearby. With a flash of anger, Ramón realized that he'd have to take the first watch again. He threw a handful of leaves and tinder on the coals and slowly rebuilt a small fire. The flames hissed green and popped, but they cast light and warmth. Ramón knew that the fire was as likely to draw danger as to drive it away. He knew that the brighter it got, the harder it was to see beyond it, but he didn't care. He wanted some *pinche* light.

One of the moons rose, sailing slowly past the stationary Enye ships—that was Big Girl, to be followed before dawn by the smaller, closer-orbiting Little Girl. Ramón waited, brooding over how little cane had been cut and how many hours of work lay ahead, until the great pale disk was directly above them before he tried to wake the other man. Calling his name didn't work, and the effect of calling his twin "Ramón" was unsettling enough to keep him from trying it again. He went over and shook the man's shoulder. His twin groaned and pulled away.

"Hey," Ramón said. "I've been up half the fucking night. It's your watch."

The other man rolled onto his back, frowning like a judge.

"What the fuck are you talking about?" he demanded, his voice thick and sleep-drunk.

"Keeping watch," Ramón said. "I did the first watch. Now you get up and I'll sleep."

The other man lifted his ruined right hand as if to rub his eyes, snarled, and used his left instead. Ramón took a step back, waiting with growing impatience as the man failed to rise. When his twin spoke, his voice was clearer but thick with disdain.

"You're telling me you haven't gone to sleep? Are you fucking stupid? You think the fucking *chupacabra* is swimming across the river to get us? That's a candy-ass banker talking, all right. What a pussy! You want to watch, go ahead and watch. *I'm* sleeping."

And the man rolled back over, tucking his arm under his head like a pillow, his back to the fire. Rage hummed in Ramón's ears like wasps swarming. The impulse to roll the little shit back over and poke the knife into his neck until he saw reason warred with the desire to kick his kidney until he was pissing blood all the way back to Fiddler's Jump.

But if he did either one, he'd then have to follow up with handing the knife over and going to sleep vulnerable and defenseless a few feet from a pissed-off *cabrón*. Ramón growled low in the back of his throat, wrapped his robe closer around him, and went to find a place to sleep where any predators that happened on them would be likely to eat the other man first.

Morning came. Ramón groaned and rolled onto his back, his arm thrown over his eyes to keep the sunlight out for another minute more. His back ached. His mind was foggy and reluctant. The smell of the cook fire roused him. The other man had scrounged a handful of white-fleshed nuts and caught a fish, which he'd wrapped in monk ivy leaves and set in among the coals. It was an old trick for cooking when there was nothing to cook with. He'd forgotten it, or else not yet remembered.

"Smells good," he said. The other man shrugged and flipped the packet of ivy leaves onto its other side. Ramón could see his twin start to say something and then stop. It occurred to him that the meal hadn't been meant for two, but the other man was too embarrassed now to refuse to share. Ramón rubbed his hands together, squatted close to the fire, and grinned.

"Lot of work to do," the other man said. "Looks like we got enough cane, though."

"I cut some last night," Ramón said. "Some iceroot leaves for bedding and to make the roof. Then a few good branches for the fire pit. I figure we can get the sand from down on the river. Find a sandbar. That'll be better than just mud from the bank. And firewood."

"Yeah," the other man said. He plucked the ivy leaves out of the coals with his left hand, tossing the bundle up and down a little to keep his fingers from burning until it cooled. A few moments later, he cut it in half with the field knife—Ramón realized that the man had taken it from him while he slept—and sliced the packet in two. He handed Ramón the one with the fish's head.

The nuts were oily and soft. The fish's skin had hardened and cracked, thin as paper and salty. Its flesh was dark and flaky. Ramón sighed. It was good to eat something he hadn't had to prepare himself. He was glad the other man had been too chickenshit to refuse to share.

"How do you want to split this up?" the other man asked, gesturing at the pile of reddened cane with the knife. "You want to make the lean-to, and I'll go find the leaves? Maybe some good branches?"

"Sure," Ramón said, wondering as he did whether there was an angle he was overlooking. Gathering leaves and sticks was easier than construction, but he was the one with both hands to work with. And his twin had gotten up early to make the food. It almost made up for not taking the second watch. Without discussion, they both went to the river and washed their hands. The other man's hand looked worse than Ramón remembered it, but his twin didn't complain.

"I want you to know something," the other man said as he rewrapped his palm and the remaining fingers.

"Yeah?"

"I know we're in this together, you and me. And the work you do—getting the sug beetles, building the raft, all that shit? It's better with the two of us than just one, you know? But if you go through my pack one more time without asking, I'll kill you in your fucking sleep. Okay, partner?"

His twin locked eyes with him—irises so dark Ramón couldn't make out the pupils, the whites bloodshot and yellow as old soap. He didn't think for a second that the man was joking. Now that he thought about it, he knew what he'd think of some half-assed banker pawing through *his* stuff. He wondered if this was what it was going to be like, going back. Maybe he'd resent his twin having all his things. His knife, his pack. Even Elena, maybe.

"Okay," Ramón said. "I just didn't want to leave the knife dull, you know. It won't happen twice."

The other man nodded.

"I do need it, though," Ramón said. "The knife. I've got to strip bark to tie the cane with. And if I need to cut more . . ."

He shrugged. The other man growled without making a sound, and Ramón braced himself for violence. But the other man only spat into the water and handed the blade over, handle-first.

"Thanks," Ramón said, and tried for a placating smile. The other man didn't answer. Ramón went back to their little camp, the other man tramping off into the forest, presumably to gather the leaves and wood. Ramón waited until he was sure he was out of earshot before he muttered, "And fuck you too, *ese*."

Ramón began working after the other man left. He got enough ivy and stripped bark to complete the design he thought would work best for the lean-to, then hauled the cane to the raft and the river. He saw at once that his first thoughts on how best to connect the shelter to the body of the raft had been optimistic. He had to spend an hour redesigning the thing. Giving his mind over to the task, losing himself in the physicality of his work, was like taking a drink of good whiskey. He hadn't realized that the knot had formed in his gut again until it released a little. Being with his twin was totally unlike being alone. Even being with Maneck and having that fucking *sahael* stuck in his neck hadn't wound his guts up this way. It was being around another human—any other human. And in particular *this* prickly sonofabitch!

At the same time, he understood that he was also setting his twin's teeth on edge. How could he not? Better to worry about which knots best bound the cane to the branches of the raft. He was already quite aware of his own failings as a man. No reason to stew in them.

By afternoon, Ramón was satisfied with his new design, and it still took him hours to lash the cane onto the raft, build the framework, and then lace the remaining lengths together as a support structure. He set aside four long poles to tie down over the layer of leaves that would actually serve to slough off the rain. Providing, of course, that the other man ever got his lazy ass back. Ramón had been working all day. How long did it take to pull down some leaves and find a few *pinche* branches? They were in a forest; wood shouldn't be that hard to find.

As it happened, his twin emerged from the forest an hour or so before nightfall. He had what looked like half a bushel of iceroot leaves bound to his back with ivy and an improvised stretcher of branches trailing behind him, loaded with sticks the right size for burning. Ramón had to admit it wasn't a bad load for a man with a broken hand and no knife. The other man dropped his burden at the riverside, squatted, and cupped handful after handful of water up to his lips. High above, the Enye ships hung in the sky.

"Looks good," Ramón said.

"Yeah," the other man said, weariness in his voice. "It's okay. May need a way to keep the firewood from rolling off, though."

"We can do that."

The other man looked at the raft and rubbed his cheeks with his palm. Ramón came to stand at his side.

"Solid," the man said. "Good design. Kind of small, though, eh?"

"Didn't figure we'd both be in it at once," Ramón said. "One of us is going to be steering. Sleep in shifts. That kind of thing."

"What if it rains?"

"Then whoever's steering gets wet," Ramón said. "Or else we both crawl out of the rain like we're humping each other."

"We get wet, then. Right. You got the knife?"

He held out his hand. Ramón dropped the leather grip into the man's palm.

"Thanks," his twin said, then spun and brought the tip of the blade to Ramón's throat. The man's eyes were narrow and furious, his mouth in a wide grin that had nothing to do with pleasure. It was the expression the European had seen; Ramón was sure of it.

"Now," the man said through clenched teeth. "How about you tell me what the fuck you really are?"

Chapter 19

"I don't . . . I don't know what you're talking about, man," Ramón said.

The other man dug the knifepoint into Ramón's neck. Ramón felt the urge to step back, away from the blade, but he fought it. Showing weakness now would be an invitation. He forced himself to stay calm, or as calm as he could.

"You're no fucking banker," the man said, spitting the words out. "You build like that. You know how to sharpen my knife. What kind of banker knows that?"

"I told you," Ramón said. "I spend a lot of time—"

"Out at the ass end of nowhere? Yeah, because that makes a fucking lot of sense. And you just happen to come up here. A month ago. And no one gives a shit that you're gone? No one sends out a search party? That sound likely to you? And your beard. You telling me that's a month's growth on your chin? Or did the aliens give you a razor to clean up with while you were there? Your hands. You've got calluses on your fingers. That from data entry?"

Ramón looked at his hands. The hard, yellowed flesh was starting to come back a little. He balled his fists. The man's grip on the knife got stronger, the pressure against Ramón's skin hurt a little.

"You're paranoid, *ese*," Ramón said. His voice was steady and strong. He tried to gauge his chances of wrestling the knife away. If he threw himself back, out of the man's reach, he could get a few seconds. And the man was going to be fighting off-hand. But Ramón's twin was scared and angry and crazy as a shithouse rat from what he'd been through these last days. Ramón gave himself a-little-worse-than-even odds.

For a half second, he wondered what the man would do if Ramón told him the truth. Kill him? Run away? Accept him as a brother and move on? Only the last one seemed laughable.

"And then you asked about the El Rey!" the man shouted. "What the *fuck* do you know about the El Rey? What the fuck are you?"

"I'm a cop," Ramón said, surprised as soon as he heard his own words. But it was clear. It was the story he had already spent days telling himself. All he had to do was turn it around. "My name really is David. The European ambassador got killed. There were some people in the crowd who said you were there. And the knife man, he matched your description."

His twin nodded, encouraging Ramón on as if he were confirming his suspicions. Which he probably was, if only because he was making it all up. Ramón swallowed, loosening the knot in his throat. As soon as he could, he went on.

"Then you take off. Skip town. The constabulary think it's a little weird, so they send me out to track you. I have spent a lot of time up north. It's why they picked me. So I find your van blown up like you had a bomb in there or some shit. I start poking around, looking for maybe your arm or something. The next thing I know, there's this flying box thing. It's just hanging there. I go to take a look, and then bam! These big-ass things with quills on their heads take my clothes, they take my badge and my pistol, put me in this fucking baby-shit outfit and start marching me around telling me I was supposed to find you."

"And so you did it," the man said, stepping an inch closer, the metal of the blade digging into Ramón's flesh, stinging like the *sahael*. "You followed their orders like a dog!"

"I tried to go slow at first," Ramón said. "I thought maybe

I could buy you time. You know. You get back to the city, you can tell people what's happened, send help. But then we found that camp. We were too close on you. The only thing I could do was wait and hope you were smarter than the *pinche* aliens. And you were. So here we are." And then, because he couldn't help himself, "You would have done the same thing in my position, man. Seriously."

"I didn't kill the asshole European," the man said through clenched teeth. "It was someone else. I didn't fucking do it."

"Ramón," Ramón said, and shook off a moment of vertigo at using his own name in this way. "Ramón, you saved my ass from those demon *pendejos*. As far as I'm concerned, you were at my house the night the ambassador got himself cut up. The whole time."

In the silence between them, Ramón heard the distant chimes of a flock of flapjacks, like church bells. The blade wavered, but Ramón didn't move. A thin flow of blood tickled his collarbone. The knife had broken the skin. A confused, distrustful expression came over the man's dark eyes.

"What are you talking about?"

"I owe you," Ramón said, putting as much sincerity into his voice as he could without sounding weak.

"Guy got killed," his twin said. It was an objection.

Ramón shrugged. If he was lying, he might as well lie big.

"You know Johnny Joe? You know who he is?"

"Johnny Joe Cardenas?"

"Yeah. You know why he gets away with so much?"

"Why?"

"Because we let him. You think we don't know how many people he's killed? Thing is, he works for us."

The man rocked back an inch. The blade was no longer touching Ramón's neck. Maybe sixty-forty in his favor now. Ramón kept talking. That was the thing; keep the two of them speaking.

He had to make it a *talking* fight.

"Johnny Joe's a snitch?" the man asked. He sounded stunned.

"For the past six years," Ramón said, trying to remember how long Johnny Joe had been in Diegotown. The man didn't seem to think the number implausible. "Keeps us informed on what's going down. And no one suspects him because who the fuck would believe it? He's a thug. Everyone knows the governor wants him hanged. No one thinks it's all bullshit and he's calling us every Sunday like he's our fucking girlfriend."

"I'm not a snitch."

"Not saying you are," Ramón said. "What I'm saying is this: São Paulo? It doesn't have laws. It has cops. I'm one of them, and you helped me. Whatever happened at the El Rey, it was someone else. That way we're square."

"How do you know I'm not innocent? What if I really didn't do it?"

"If you didn't do it, then I'm gypping you big-time," Ramón said, and grinned. His twin wavered for a moment, then a smile plucked at his mouth too. The knife blade lowered. The man stepped back.

"It's my knife. I'm keeping it. It's mine."

"You want to hold on to it, that's cool," Ramón said, trying to sound reassuring, the way cops did when they were talking you down. He'd heard the tone a few times, and it wasn't hard to fake. "I understand you'd want to keep the weapon. That's not a problem. After all, we're just two guys on the run from a bunch of goddamn aliens, right? Doesn't matter which one of us has the knife, because we're on the same side."

"If you fuck me over . . ." the man said, and left the threat hanging. Because, Ramón thought, really, a cop decides to break his word to you, exactly what could you do? Take him to a judge and see who got believed?

"If I start fucking people over, Johnny Joe and all the other *pendejos* like him will lose their shit," Ramón said. Grave. Authoritative. Like a cop. "It ain't worth it. I tell you you're clean, man. That makes you clean. But any reward we get for turning in those alien fucks, we split it. You and me. Right down the middle."

"Fuck that," the man said. "*I* saved your ass. You were walking bait. I get three quarters."

Ramón felt his belly loosen. He was clear. The crisis was gone, and nothing left but a little posing and haggling. "Sixty-forty," he said. "And you didn't kill anyone. Ever."

"I'm getting gyppcd," the man said.

"So's everyone. We're the cops, remember?" Ramón said, then smiled. The other man coughed out an incredulous laugh, then smiled himself. "You want to start getting these leaves in place, so we can get out of here and back to someplace they've got plumbing?"

"Fucking cops," the man said, but now it was a joke. The man was half-drunk with relief. And why shouldn't he be? Ramón had just forgiven him his sins.

They worked until the light failed. The little lean-to was half-ready; a bed of leaves made and the covering laid down with the leaves arranged in overlapping rows so that any rain would run down the top and into the water instead of dripping through. Ramón called the halt; his twin would have kept going all night, he guessed, just to prove something. And yet, as they walked the short path back to their little camp, he could tell that the relationship had changed. Clueless banker lost in the wild was one thing. Policeman and granter of pardons was another beast entirely. Ramón built a small fire and the other man unloaded a double handful of sug beetles, suicide nuts, and the bright green berries that Ramón had never found named in the planet's taxonomies and that tasted like cheap white wine and pears. It wasn't a feast, but it tasted good. Afterward, Ramón drank water until his belly felt full. He'd have to piss in the middle of the night, but for the moment, it fooled his body into feeling sated.

His twin lay back beside the fire. Ramón saw the man's fingers twitching, and knew he was wishing he had a cigarette. The thought immediately made him want one too. How long, he wondered, before the nicotine stains grew back, yellowing his fingers and teeth? How long before the teasing fan dance of identities he was doing for the other man stopped working and the truth came out? Maybe the right thing was to leave now, go into the wild and avoid his twin, the governor, the police, and the Enye entirely.

He'd thought about living off the land many times before.

The idea of fading away into the forest had seemed more plausible when it was a fantasy, or else something he could do with a good, solid van that he could lock up at night. Or if he at least had his *pinche* knife back.

There had been stories from the first wave of colonists of men who had gone feral; moved out into the forests and steppes, deserts and tide pools of the planet and never came back to civilization. Some of them might even be true. Colonies didn't tend to pull people who loved their old lives on Earth. There would be a percentage who hated life here too; men and women who'd hauled their sorry personal failings all the way from Earth. Ramón wondered if he was one of those. Except that he wanted to get back now. So he wasn't feral yet. And as long as his fingers kept twitching toward a cigarette case that was days behind him and across a river, he would never wholly abandon the cities.

"Why'd you become a cop?" the man asked, his voice already slurred by exhaustion and impending sleep.

"I don't know," Ramón said. "It seemed like the right thing at the time. Why'd you become a prospector?"

"It was better than being on a work gang," the man said. "I'm pretty good at it. And there was a time I needed to get out of town, you know? Get kind of lost for a while."

"Yeah?" Ramón said. He was tired as well. It had been a long day in a series of very long days. His body felt heavy and comfortable.

"There was this guy," the other man said. "Martín Casaus. We were friends for a while, you know. When I first got here. He was one of those guys hangs out by the orientation centers and tries to make friends with new people since no one who knows him here likes him." The other man spat. "He called himself a trapper. I guess he even killed things sometimes. Anyway, he got this idea I was after his woman. I wasn't either. She was a fucking dog. But he got it in his head that I was trying to cut him out."

Lianna. Ramón remembered her, the night at the bar. The deep red wallpaper, like drying blood. He'd gone to her, sat at her side. She'd still smelled of the kitchen—frying oil and herbs, hot metal and chili. He had offered to buy her a drink. She'd accepted. She'd taken his hand. She'd been gentle about it. Tentative. He'd had enough to drink that he was a little fuzzy in the head. Martín's fantasies of her—of opening her blouse, of whispering filthy, exciting things into her ears, of waking in her bed—had intoxicated him as much as the drink.

"I didn't give a shit about her," the man said, chuckling. "She was a cook. Kind of dumpy, you know. Ate too much of her own stuff. Martín, though. Fuck. He was crazy about her."

Lianna's room had been in the back—a separate building grown from cheap chitin out behind the cantina with a little bathroom, a shower, but no place to cook. The LEDs spelling out LOS RANCHEROS had filled the room with dim, harsh light. He'd undressed her to the sound of Portuguese *fado* music on the music feed, the singer crooning about love and loss and death, a song whose words he heard again now. It had been a beautiful song. In spite of the mild night air, Lianna had had goose bumps. He remembered the gooseflesh on her arms. Her thighs. Her breasts. She'd been shy at first. Feeling guilty about having him there. And then less so. And then not shy at all.

"So Martín gets it into his head that I fucked this girl. Now, he wasn't seeing her. Hadn't spoken more than maybe a dozen words to her his whole life. But he thinks he's in love. So he gets crazy. Jumps me with a sheet metal hook. Almost kills me."

Afterward, he'd run his fingers through her hair as she slept. He'd wanted to cry, but hadn't been able to. Even now, the memory growing in like a vine in his brain, he couldn't say why he'd wanted to do that, what mixture of lust and sorrow, loneliness and guilt had moved him so much. Part of it was that he'd betrayed Martín. Only part of it, though. Lianna.

"So I figure, you know, as soon as I'm healed up, maybe I should get scarce. I put a down payment on a van from this place I'd been working that was about to go tits-up. I got some old surveying software from the widow of a guy I knew that died. Took off. It just went on from there. You know how that goes."

"I do," Ramón agreed. "You ever see her again?"

"The dumpy cook girl? No, man. Why bother, you know?"

She'd snored a little, just a wheeze in and then out. She had a cheap poster of the Virgin of Despegando Station over her bed, the bright blue eyes and robes glowing in the near dark. Ramón had thought he was in love with her. He'd written her letters but deleted them before he hit SEND. He couldn't conjure up what he had put in them. He wondered if the other man remembered what they said. If not, the words were gone forever.

He hadn't told that story in years. If he had, he would have talked about her exactly the way his twin had, just now. Some things you just don't say to people.

"You got quiet," the man said. "You thinking about that Carmina? She had you whipped, *mi amigo*. I could hear it when you talked about her."

A sneering tone had crept into the other's voice, and Ramón knew he was on dangerous ground, but he couldn't keep himself from asking, "How about you? You got a girl now?"

"I got someone I fuck," the other said. "She's got a mouth on her sometimes, but she's okay. I don't mind fucking her. She's pretty good in bed."

Time to take a chance, push it a little. "You love her?"

The other man froze. "That's none of your business, *cabrón*," he said in a hard voice.

Ramón allowed himself to lock eyes with the other man for a heartbeat, then said gruffly, "You're right. Sorry." Not rising to the insult. Backing down, but in a way consistent with his tough-cop persona. Not craven enough to arouse the other's ire.

After a moment of silence, Ramón said, "Let's get some sleep, eh? Long day tomorrow."

"Yeah," the man said, his tone sour. "Sure."

But, as Ramón had hoped, the subject of who he loved didn't come up again.

Chapter 20

They launched the raft around noon the next day, the morning spent in final preparations and unsuccessful hunting. It was more cramped. The fire pit sat at the back, where one of them could both tend it and steer with the oar. The lean-to ran lengthwise along one side. It unbalanced the raft a little, but if Ramón had put it in the midline, he wouldn't have been able to see ahead and steer. Of course it blocked part of his view no matter where it sat. And as a counterbalance, he'd put a pile of wood for the fire on the other side, not so near the edge that it was likely to get soaked.

Ramón steered them out into the river where the flow was swiftest, then spent the afternoon holding steady. The man sat at the side, a fishing line in his hand. And here it was, the grand escape plan brought to its perfect end. Two unwashed and unshaven guys on a grungy raft, fishing to eat and taking turns steering down the middle of the river. Ramón scratched his belly. The scar was growing, and the one on his arm. His hair was slightly coarser too; he could feel it. No doubt he was starting to get the creases in his face back as well.

He wished he'd kept the cigarette case. Or anything he could use for a mirror. How long would it be before the other man realized what was happening? Every time his twin glanced back at him, Ramón felt his belly growing tighter.

As they moved south, the forests changed. Needle-leaved iceroot gave way to lacy sponge oak. Twice, Ramón caught sight of the great pyramids of *dorado* colonies, their sides swarming with the crawling black spiders. The sounds also changed. The chirr and squawk of the thousand varieties of half lizard, half bird, as they threatened one another and fought for food and mates. Deeper calls, like the voices of women singing in some beautiful African tongue, from kyi-kyi preparing to shed their summer skins. And once, the soft, whistling sound of a redjacket cutting through the underbrush. Ramón didn't see the animal, though, and since it didn't attack, apparently it hadn't seen them either.

Above them, the sky-lilies were being blown south and east by some high-atmosphere wind. Their distant bodies looked like points of deep green against the blue arcing sky, strewn like dark stars against the daylight. One precocious colony had bloomed, sending out streamers of yellow and red that were likely miles long, though from so far away, Ramón could cover them with his thumb. When the others joined it, it would look like a flower garden swimming up into space.

But it was the hovering black Enye ships that kept drawing his attention. Six of them hung in the air. It struck him for the first time how much the ships were shaped like ticks, and once the image was in his head, he couldn't get rid of it. He had ridden from his home, his world, his past in the belly of a great tick, and been puked out onto this beautiful planet. None of them belonged here—not the Enye, not Maneck and its people, not humanity. And yet São Paulo suffered them.

Maybe he could ship out again. Get back on the Enye ship, move to some other colony. Or cast his fate to the sky and come down wherever God put him. São Paulo wasn't so big he could be assured of never running into his twin again. The universe, on the other hand, *was* that big. Bigger. For a moment—as strong as a memory reawakening—Ramón felt again the gaping abyss from his dream. He shuddered and looked back at the river's edge.

Shipping out would mean getting a false identity, but *anything* meant that now. The real problem was going on the ship. Smelling the skins of the Enye, hearing their voices. Knowing what they had done, and what they were doing, and the real purpose of these colonies. Before, he might have been able to do it. His twin, sitting on the edge of the raft with his head resting on his good hand, *he* might be able to do it. But Ramón had felt the flow, had become the abyss, and heard the cries of dying *kii*. Of dying babies. He couldn't do it. Not anymore.

The easiest thing would still be to kill the man. If his twin were dead, all this would go away. He could step back into his own life, call in the little insurance policy he had on the van, and try to start over. It had been hit in a rockslide. Why not? The policy was cheap enough that no one would bother with more than a cursory investigation, and they wouldn't find any pieces chopped and sold secondhand. He could have his life back instead of ceding it to this *cabrón*. And if the cops were looking for someone to pin the European's death on, they'd have found someone else by the time he got back.

It wouldn't even be that hard to do. He cooked. He kept watch while the man slept. Even if he didn't have the knife, there were other ways. Shit, he could just push the bastard off the side of the raft. Ramón had damn near died in the river before, and he'd been nearer shore then. Trapped out in the middle of the river, where the current was strongest, the other man would almost certainly drown. And if by some miracle he did reach land, there were redjackets out there. And hundreds of miles to Fiddler's Jump. It was the safest thing. It was the *sane* thing.

He let himself imagine it. Standing up, pulling in the oar. Two steps, three. Then bringing the oar down fast and hard. He could almost hear the man's cry, the splash, the gurgling scream. It would fix everything. And would it really be killing? Would it really be murder? After all, one Ramón went into the wild, and one Ramón came out. Where was murder in that?

Under what circumstances do you kill?

Ramón blew out his breath and looked away. *Shut up, Maneck! You're dead!* The man jerked his head back toward Ramón, distrust in the dark eyes.

"Nothing," Ramón said, raising a hand. "Just caught myself dozing off."

"Yeah, well. Don't," the man said. "We don't have another oar, and I don't want to have to push this sonofabitch to shore so we can look for one."

"Yeah. Thanks," Ramón said. And then, "Hey. *Ese*. You mind if I ask you something?"

"You gonna tape it? Tell it to the judge?"

"No," Ramón said. "It's just something I was wondering."

The man shrugged and didn't bother to look back.

"Ask if you want. I don't like the question, I'll tell you to go fuck yourself."

"That guy you didn't kill. The European?"

"The one I never saw and don't know shit about?"

"Him," Ramón agreed. "If you had done it—you didn't, but if you *had*. Why? He wasn't fucking your wife. He wasn't after your job. He didn't go for you."

"Didn't he? How do you know?"

"He didn't," Ramón said. "I saw the report. It wasn't self-defense. So why?"

The man was silent. He tugged at his fishing line, let it play back out, and tugged it in again. Ramón thought that he wasn't going to answer at all. When he did, his voice was dismissive and conversational.

"We were drunk. He pissed me off. It got out of hand," the man said, dropping the pretense. "Just something that happened."

He had tried to back down, Ramón thought. The European had tried to get back to just name-calling. Ramón had been the one who set the terms of the fight. Something about the straight-haired girl's laughter. That and the moment after the European went down, when the crowd stepped back. It was in there. Why could he kill a man whose death brought him nothing, and yet *not* be able to kill somebody when he had everything in the world to gain from it? When his very life might depend on it?

Ramón's twin caught four fish: two silver flatfish with blunt noses and permanently surprised mouths, one black-scaled river roach, and then something Ramón had never seen before, which looked to be equal parts eyes and teeth. That one they threw back. The man roasted the three edible fish while Ramón used the oar to keep the raft near the river's center. Birds or creatures near enough like them to take the name called from the tops of the trees, flew overhead, skimmed down across the river for a drink.

"You know," his twin said, "I always thought it would be good to go out for a while. Live off the land. When I came out, I was thinking I'd stay out here three, four months. Now I just want to get back to Diegotown and sleep in a real bed. With a roof."

"Amen," Ramón said.

The man cut a hunk of pale flesh from the flatfish, tossed it in his hand for a moment to let it cool, and popped it in his mouth. Ramón watched the tiny smile on the man's lips and realized how hungry he was.

"It's good?"

"Doesn't suck," the man agreed, then paused, his head tilting a degree. And then Ramón heard it too—a distant low rumble, constant as a radio link tuned to an empty channel. They realized what they were hearing at the same moment. Water, an unthinkable volume of it, falling.

"East," the man said. "The east bank's closer."

"That's where the *chupacabra* was."

"That fucking thing's days behind us. Come on. East!"

Ramón grabbed the oar and angled the raft as best he could toward the eastern shore. The man pulled their meal free of the coals and then went forward to look at the river. The sound rose from a bare whisper, something hardly noticeable, to a roar that almost drowned out the man's words.

"Hurry the fuck up," he said. "I can see it."

Ramón could too by now. A slight haze where the cataract threw mist into the air. Rapids, perhaps. A waterfall. But their raft wouldn't survive even a small insult. He had to reach land.

"Come on!" the man yelled, then dropped to his knees and started paddling with his good hand, scooping water as if he could swim the raft to safety. Ramón's shoulders were sore; his hands gripped the oar until his joints ached. The muddy bank inched nearer. The roar increased. The haze grew higher.

They were close, but they weren't going to make it. The flow of the river was too fast, and the raft had no purchase on the water. Boulders were beginning to slide past them, the water breaking white over the stone. The roar was near deafening. The shore was four meters away. Three and a half.

Something in the water caught Ramón's attention; a shifting. An eddy that meant something the back of his mind knew. Without thinking, Ramón switched his grip, pushing the raft away from the bank, aiming for the point on the river where the flow was . . . *right*. The bank edged away.

"What the fuck are you doing?" the man shrieked. "What the fuck are you—"

In the same instant, a sick, grinding sound overcame the cataract's voice, the forward float shattered, and the raft lurched, throwing Ramón forward beside the fire pit. The other man nearly tipped into the water. The flow of water arced at the raft's sides, an icy wave running over the back edge and draining between the loose branches. Ramón slid forward slowly, careful not to dislodge the raft from whatever had stopped their rush. A boulder just below the surface and sharp as the prow of a kayak had nearly split the front float. The stone still penetrated the bent and broken cane. A half meter toward the bank, and they would have missed it. Ten meters on, Ramón saw the streaks in the water where it gained speed as it prepared to fall. His twin's amazed and joyous whoop barely reached his ears, but the man's pounding congratulatory slaps on his shoulders conveyed the meaning clearly enough.

He'd saved them. Precarious as their position was, at least they hadn't died. Yet. Four meters of fast water still divided them from the land, but the raft was stationary.

"Rope!" his twin shouted in his ear. "We've got to get some rope to haul this *pinche* motherfucker onto the shore! You wait here!"

"What are you . . . Hey! Don't—"

But the other man had already taken two long, fast strides

and leaped out over the water. The raft shifted one way and then the other, the ruined cane float twisting. For a sick moment, Ramón was sure the other man had freed him from the rock, but the raft steadied. Ramón sat, waiting, with his back and belly aching with fear. Was the other man going to be able to get to shore, or would he be swept over the brink? And if he was, where the fuck did that leave Ramón? And the raft itself, pressed up against the boulder by the constant push of the river, was like a coin balancing on its edge. If the float gave way or the river rose, he was dead. And rope? Where was his twin going to find rope, anyway? They were in the middle of the wilderness. By the time he'd thought all these things, he saw the slick shape of his twin pulling himself from the water.

As Ramón watched, the man hauled himself up the bank, paused for a moment, head hung low, and then vanished among the trees. Ramón squatted at the front of the raft, adding his weight to the raft's in hopes of keeping the float stuck where it was, and also crouching down, ready to leap for the shore if it did come loose. But as time passed, the sun pressing down on his back and shoulders, warming his skin and the cloth of his robe, his urgency and fear mixed with a strange kind of peace.

It was like one of those meaningless Zen stories Palenki liked to tell when he was drunk. He was trapped at the edge of a waterfall, on a raft that might come loose from its stone at any second, waiting for a man who was also in a sense himself to return from the wilderness with some scrounged tool that would save him—a man who would probably try to kill him if he knew the whole situation. And if he did make it out of here, it was a race to get to a city where his future was totally uncertain, where the law might, after all, still be after him, while genocidal aliens floated overhead. And what was he thinking about?

How good the sun felt.

Hours passed. When Ramón's legs began to ache from squatting, he took the risk of sitting. The raft still shifted to the side sometimes, but never enough to alarm him. His mind wandered. He remembered lazy, empty afternoons under the blazing Mexican sun, nothing to do but pray that rain would fill the cistern before it ran dry. It didn't have the immediacy of a newly returned memory. It was just something that had happened to him once, when he'd been a boy on another planet. A school of fish sped past him, scales flashing green and gold under the skin of rushing water. Ramón didn't know if they were all speeding to their own deaths at the falls ahead or if there was some trick they knew that would preserve them. There had to be some way that the inhabitants of the deep, fast flow of the river coped with accidents of geography like this. Perhaps it was only that when enough bodies were thrown out into the void, some few would survive; like seeds strewn over rocks, a handful might find a soil-filled niche. It didn't matter if a thousand died so long as a hundred lived. That must have been what Maneck and its people had felt, throwing themselves at the sky.

Fish putting their faith in the river.

When at last his twin reappeared at the river's edge, he had to shout and wave his arms to wake Ramón from his half drowse. He carried a coil of vine wound over one shoulder, thick as his thigh. Ramón didn't know if this was some plant the man had known of, the knowledge of which simply hadn't returned to his own mind yet, or if it was a lucky discovery—and he didn't care deeply. After a long series of gestures, Ramón understood the man's intentions: he would cast the vine out to Ramón, tied around a small branch. Ramón was then to haul enough of the vine onto the raft to throw the original branch back. When they'd made the double-strand fast to the raft and a tree near the shore, Ramón was to dislodge the raft and let the force of the river work against the constraint of the vines to swing the injured craft to shore. An ideal plan, so long as the vines were strong enough. It occurred to Ramón that the man's standards for the risk might be more forgiving than his own, but there was no better plan.

It took three tries to get the vine across to Ramón and five more to return it to his twin on the riverbank. The man was grinning as he made their improvised rope fast to a tree.

Ramón was less sure. But even if the plan only got him nearer the shore, he'd be able to swim the shorter distance. When the man gave the high sign, Ramón began rocking the raft from one side to the other, catching the flowing water from one direction, then another, searching for the combination that would dislodge the float. For long minutes, it seemed the raft was stuck faster than he'd imagined, and then, with a lurch, it came free. Ramón lost his footing as the vine pulled taut, the raft shuddering and tipping. The pile of firewood broke free, branches and twigs spilling into the river and bobbing away into the mist. On his knees, Ramón waited as the raft swung slowly in an arc, the lashed wood groaning and creaking under the unfamiliar strain. The man whooped as the raft touched the muddy ground. Ramón leaped off the side, and together they hauled it up and out of the water.

"Good fucking work, *pendejo*!" the man said, clapping Ramón's shoulder with his uninjured hand and grinning like an idiot. The roar of the cataract was so loud the man had to shout to be heard. Ramón, half against his will, found himself grinning back.

"I thought there weren't any falls on this river," Ramón shouted.

"There aren't supposed to be," the man agreed. "But this far north, who checks the mapping programs? They missed one."

"Hope they didn't miss any others," Ramón said. "Did you get to scout it out? How bad does it look?"

The man had. The roar and the mist were the products of two drop-offs, one a little more than three meters, the second not quite half again as much. The raft would have been torn to kindling. But after the cataract, the river seemed to be smooth and relatively placid again. The trick would be to carry the raft to the lower river and launch it again from there.

They took the vine and cinched the raft to a tree nearer where it had come to rest, hoping to keep it safe in case of an unexpected rise in the river. Then, together, Ramón and his twin set out into the bush. There were game paths where animals had pushed through to the fresh water, but none of the animals had been hauling a two-man raft. Ramón began to regret they'd made the thing as large as they had. Night fell before they'd discovered a good path, and they set up a makeshift camp.

"It's going to be a real sonofabitch getting that thing down," the man said.

"Yeah," Ramón agreed. "Better than trying to make another one, though. Not much cane this far south."

"Think we can do it? Move the fucking thing?"

In the distance, something howled. It was a fluting, lovely sound that reminded Ramón of coyotes and wind chimes. He sighed and spat into the fire.

"Between us, we'll do it," he said. "We're tough bastards."

"Probably couldn't do it, just one of us, though."

"I don't think so."

"Good thing I didn't kill you back there, eh?" the man said. His tone was joking, but Ramón knew it was a joke with teeth. Remember, the man meant, that I had you at knifepoint. You live because I let you. It was the sort of thing he'd have said himself, to remind the constable who owed what to whom. Only now, seeing it from outside, did he understand how alienating and stupid it was.

"Good thing, yeah," he said, and smiled.

◄ Chapter 21 ►

Morning found Ramón aching and tired. Through the boughs above him, the sky was gray. The breeze smelled heavy with rain. The other man had risen before him and was boiling a handful of honey grass. Ramón yawned mightily, then rubbed his eyes. His elbow itched, so he scratched, feeling the hard knot of scar where the machete had bitten. It was almost its familiar size and hardness. He plucked the sleeve of his robe down to cover it.

"Storm coming on," the other man said. "Gonna be pretty wet by tonight."

"Better get moving, then," Ramón said.

"I was thinking we could hole up. Find someplace dry to wait it out."

"Good idea. How 'bout Fiddler's Jump? Dry enough there."

"We got days before we can even think of seeing people."

"We've got more of them if we screw around like a couple of schoolgirls trying not to get our hair wet," Ramón said. The other man's gaze hardened.

"Fine," the man said. "That's the way you want it, we'll do that."

After they ate breakfast, the honey grass tasting rich and heavy as wheat after the boiling had burst the grains, Ramón and his twin mapped out the path that made the best sense.

Unsurprisingly, they shared the same basic idea. The other man objected to a few of Ramón's suggestions, but that was more for the sake of the objection itself.

"We'll have to clear some of the brush. Maybe a sapling or two," Ramón said. "You want to give me the knife, we can share the shit work."

"I can do it," the man said.

"Your choice."

When they reached the raft again, Ramón used the vines with which they'd pulled it from the river to make a simple yoke. When pulled from the side, the floats acted more like runners, and dragging it was easier than lifting the full weight. The man walked ahead, clearing what he could, or went back to the raft itself to lift it over the rocks and bushes with which it became entangled. The sun sloped unseen toward the top of its arc. The Enye ships peeked through the rare break in the cloud cover. The work was backbreaking, but Ramón pushed through the pain. His spine was screaming, his feet felt on the verge of bleeding, his shoulders were rubbing raw where the yoke rested, but it wasn't like he was cauterizing the stump of his own lost finger. If he was capable of that—and, judging by the man, he was—pulling a raft through the woods shouldn't be worth thinking about.

And as the hours passed, he found the burden growing more bearable. The endless ache in his muscles became less a sensation and more an environment. The other man darted back and forth, clearing the path ahead, lifting the raft and pushing it past the tighter spots when he went behind. Ramón didn't speak much, just leaned into his task. He sensed that his twin was coming to respect him. He knew how much that would gall the man, and it put an extra strength in his back. He thought of Christ bearing his cross while the Romans beat him and the crowd jeered. The raft had to be lighter than that, and it wasn't his own death waiting when he reached the water, but instead his salvation. He had no room for complaint.

The third time he stumbled, he barked his shin on a rock. The gash didn't hurt, but blood slicked his skin. He cursed mildly and started to rise to his feet. A hand on his shoulder stopped him.

"Take a break, *ese*," the man said. "You've been busting your hump all day. It's time for lunch."

"I can keep going," Ramón said. "No trouble."

"Yeah, okay, you're a badass. Got it. Put your fucking leg up and I'll go find us some food."

Ramón chuckled, then shrugged off the yoke and rolled onto his back. The sky was darker now, closer than a cathedral's ceiling. He heard what might have been distant thunder or only a heightened awareness of the blood in his own ears. The man shook his head and turned away. Ramón smiled.

It was strange, not knowing whether or not he liked the man who was himself. He'd never seen how he was from the outside. Smart, resourceful, tough as old leather, but wound tight around his fears and ready to blame everyone but himself. All that insecurity and rage fizzing inside him, ready to explode at the slightest provocation, strutting around like a bantam cock, staring down whoever was nearby. This was what he had always been. Only it took becoming an alien monstrosity to see it.

But there was a dignity to the man, in spite of his flaws. And a surprising strength of will. He'd engineered Maneck's death. He'd sealed the stump of his missing finger when most men would have tried to live with the open wound, and the fact that he wasn't dying of fever right now was a testament to his wisdom. He was even capable of a kind of weird compassion. Keeping Ramón from pushing on now. Lying about Lianna so he wouldn't sound weak. What was he really like? All the pieces of the man's personality seemed at odds with each other, and they also seemed to fit.

The only thing that didn't make sense to him, even now, was staying with Elena. He couldn't see why his twin would do that. He understood why *he* would have, but this other self could surely do better. Even if they were the same man.

He didn't remember dozing off, only waking when the man shook his arm. Ramón slapped a hand over the scar at his elbow almost before he opened his eyes. The man was squatting beside him, two fat *jabali* cubs in his hand. Ramón sat up, his body protesting.

"Where did you get those?" he asked.

"I got lucky," the man said. "Come on, I've got a fire started. You can talk with me while I clean these poor *pendejos*."

Ramón levered himself up to sitting, and then stood.

"Tomorrow, I'll cook," he said. "You did breakfast and lunch both."

"Go ahead," the man said. "You want to make some food, I'm not going to stop you."

Ramón sat close to the fire, watching the man gut and skin the little animals. The wood hissed and popped, the flame fluttered with a sound like wings when a gust of air blew through it. It would take them another couple of hours to reach the lower riverbank. He wondered if it would be raining by then, and which of them would spend the night in the lean-to. Pushing himself as hard as he had would win the man's respect, but probably not so much as that.

"You from Mexico?" the man asked.

"What?"

"Mexico. On Earth. That where you from?"

"Yeah," Ramón said. "Oaxaca. Why?"

"Just thinking. You look like a *mejicano*. You've got that kind of face."

Ramón stared at the fire, willing the man to talk about anything but how he looked. Either the man picked up on it, or he hadn't been that concerned with the subject to start.

"What's it like, being a cop?" he asked instead. "You like it?"

"Yeah," Ramón said. "I like it. It's a good job, you know?"

"Looks shitty to me," the man said. "No offense. But all the time, you have to take guys who are just trying to get along, and bust their balls. And why? Because the governor tells you to? So what? I mean, who's the governor? You take away his power and his money, and you think he's going to act any different than the folks he's coming down on?"

"Yeah, well," Ramón said, trying to think how a cop would answer. "The governor's a snooty Portugee prick. That's true. But it's not all like that. Yeah, part of it's colonial bullshit. Checking licenses and permits and shit. But it's not just about that."

"No?"

"No," Ramón said. "There's also the real bad *pendejos*.

The guys who sneak into church, piss all over the altar. The ones who mess with children. I deal with those assholes too."

"Guys who stab ambassadors, you mean?" the man said, his voice cool.

"Fuck that. I mean *bad* ones. The kind that *need* killing. You know what I mean."

The man looked up. There was blood on his hands, red and darkening. Ramón saw something in the man's face—something unexpected. Pain. Embarrassment. Regret. Pride. Something.

"There's all kinds of crazy bastards out there," Ramón said, still pretending to be a policeman. "Most of the time, we don't care about people just getting on with their lives. But there's rapists. There's the guys who just want to kill people for no reason. And there's nothing worse than someone who hurts *kii*."

"Kii?"

"Children," Ramón said, surprised at himself for the slip. "Kids who are too small to defend themselves. Or even know what's going on. There's nothing fucking lower than that. That's why I'm a cop. And people know it, you know? People know that on one side, there's them, and then on the other side, there's me."

Ramón broke off. He didn't know what he was saying anymore. The words, the thoughts. They were all jumbled in his head. The Enye crushing tiny alien things; the European; Mikel Ibrahim taking his knife; the feeling of being Maneck and watching its people die. Maneck was right. They shouldn't laugh. There was nothing to laugh about. If she just hadn't *laughed*.

"You okay?" the man asked.

"Yeah," Ramón said. "I'm fine. I just . . . I'm fine."

The man nodded and turned back to the carcasses, holding them over the fire. Letting the fat liquefy, the muscle tissues sear. The scent of rain was growing stronger. They both ignored it.

"I could have been a cop," the man said at last. "I'd have been good."

"You would have," Ramón agreed, wrapping his arms around his drawn-up knees. "You'd have been great."

They were silent, the only sounds the hissing of grease as it dripped into the fire and the constant rustling of leaves. The man turned the carcasses, setting the other sides to brown.

"That was a good call, back there. When we were trying to get to shore. I didn't even see that *pinche* rock. But you, *ese*. You headed right for it. We'd have gone over for sure if you hadn't."

He was giving Ramón an out; a way to change the subject. Even without knowing what it was that was bothering him, the man knew it was a kindness to steer away from it, and Ramón clutched at the chance.

"It's all about flow," he said. "Knowing how it looks when there's something disrupting it. It just feels different, you know."

"Whatever it was, you did a fucking man's job of it," the man said. "I couldn't have."

Ramón waved the compliment away. If this went on too long, they'd cross the line into patronizing. He didn't want that. Right now, for this moment, he liked the man. He wanted very much to like his twin, and the *cabrón* wasn't often very likable.

"You'd have done the same if you'd been steering," Ramón said.

"Nah, man. I really wouldn't."

And it struck Ramón that that might be true. Being inside Maneck's head might have taught him something about being a river. About *flow*. Just because he and the other man had started off the same, these last few days had been different for both of them. There was no reason they should be identical now. They'd had different experiences, learned different lessons from the world. He hadn't lost a finger. His twin hadn't had the *sahael* digging into his throat.

You are not to diverge from the man, Maneck's voice rumbled in the back of his mind. But how could he help it? The world looked different, depending on where you sat.

They ate, digging into the cooked flesh with their fingers. The meat was hot; it burned his fingers a little. But it tasted like the finest meal he'd ever had. Hunger did that. The other man seemed to feel the same. He was grinning as he stripped the still-pink flesh from the bones. They talked about other things, safer ones. When the time came to start again, the man picked up the yoke.

"You go on ahead, clear the path," he said, shrugging the vine into place on his shoulders. "I'll haul this piece of crap the rest of the way."

"You don't have to do that," Ramón said, but his twin waved the objection away. Ramón was secretly relieved. His body felt beaten half to death the way he'd been abusing it. But still, there was a problem. "I can't do it, man. You've still got the knife."

His twin scowled, pulled the blade from his field pack, and held it out, handle-first. Ramón nodded when he took it. They didn't say anything more about it.

Clearing brush turned out to be almost as arduous as hauling the raft. Every step seemed to require hacking away some bush or sapling. And the knife was growing dull with use. Twice, sudden sheets of rain descended, pattering on the leaves and Ramón's shoulders, but the little squalls didn't last. When the storm did hit—if it hit—it promised to be rough. But perhaps the runoff would speed the river.

It was just before dark when they reached the water's edge. Ramón tried for a low whoop, but it came out sounding sarcastic. The man grinned wearily. They surveyed the damage their transit had caused. One of the floats had lost a few ties and needed rebinding. The structure of branches that made up the bulk of the raft had suffered, but not so badly that Ramón felt moved to repair it.

"Give me the knife," his twin said. "I'll strip a little bark, tie that cane back together. You get a little firewood, and we can launch this motherfucker again. Leave tonight, maybe outrun this weather."

"Good idea," Ramón said. "But you sure you don't want to get the firewood? It's easier than stripping bark."

"I don't want to take another fucking step," the man said. "You do it."

Ramón handed back the knife in answer. His twin smiled as if some tacit agreement had just been made with the weapon's return. Ramón pulled himself back into the trees to the sound of the other man scraping steel against the whetstone. It was a fast-growth forest here, soft wood that rose quickly and collapsed. No centuries-old copperwood here. Just black-barked idiotrail and the spiral-trunked godsarm oaks. It would be easy to find fallen branches and double handfuls of moss analogs to use for tinder. The question was how many trips back to the raft he wanted to make before they set out.

If it was raining upstream—and it was clearly raining upstream—the runoff could raise the level of the river anytime. It might already be running high. If they were lucky, the extra runoff might cut over some of the bends and give them a straighter path to the south.

Lost in his calculations, Ramón didn't realize what he was looking at until he felt the fear start his heart beating hard and fast. There, in the soft ground, were fresh prints as wide as his two hands together. A four-lobed paw with deep-dug claw marks. *Chupacabra.* Somewhere nearby was a fucking *chupacabra*!

He dropped the branches held in his arms, and turned to run back to the river, but he hadn't made it halfway before he skidded around a stand of close-knit godsarm oaks and found the beast itself, glaring at him with what seemed like equal parts hunger and hatred. The mouth hung open, the thick, split tongue lolling out of it. Its teeth were yellowed and sharp as daggers. Ramón froze, and the black, rage-filled eyes met his. He braced himself for death, but the thing didn't attack. Even then, knowing something was wrong, it took the space of five fast breaths together before he noticed the flattening in the animal's neck ruff, the fleshy, ropelike thing buried in the *chupacabra*'s neck. A *sahael*.

He let his gaze move past the *chupacabra* to the form looming behind it. Beaten, battered, slashed across its chest and legs, Maneck still stood at its full, towering height. Its wounded eye had gone black and oozed a noxious ichor, but the uninjured one remained the hot orange Ramón remembered. The alien's arms waved for a moment, gently as kelp under the sea. When it spoke, its deep, half-sorrowful voice was perfectly familiar.

"You have done well," it said.

Chapter 22

"What the fuck?" Ramón said through a tight throat. "You're dead! You died!"

The alien shifted its head. The quills rose slightly and fell again.

"What you say is *aubre*. I am not dead, as you can see," Maneck said. "Your task was to engage in flow as the man would. You have done so in accordance with your *tate-creude*. My own function was compromised for a time, but has now returned to its proper channel."

"How did you find me?"

"The river flows south. You are constrained by the river," Maneck said. "This is a strange question."

"But we were traveling faster than you. We could have been on the other bank of the river. You couldn't know we'd be here."

"I could not reach you farther down the river than I could go. I could not reach you on the river's opposite bank. Therefore I went where I could go that you could as well. You suggest things that are not the case. This is *aubre*. You must cease to express *aubre*."

The *chupacabra* emitted a low growl, its body shifting and restless, but constrained. There were scorch marks along the beast's side where Maneck had shot it; the fur had burned away and left wide streaks of reddened, blistered flesh. Maneck had given, it seemed, as good as it got. The *sahael* pulsed twice, the bruised flesh engorging like a worm's. Ramón felt a passing ghost of sympathy for the *chupacabra*. At least when he had suffered the thing in his neck, he'd understood what was happening. He wondered how many times Maneck had punished the *chupacabra* before it had understood that it was no longer its own master. And how many tricks the alien had been able to teach it.

"So," he said, with a bravado he didn't feel. "What've you got planned now? You can't just kill the poor fucker."

Maneck paused again.

"You are not accurate," it said. "The man must not know of us. The illusion of his knowledge will be corrected. You have proved yourself an apt tool. That will be expressed. The man is by the water now? We must approach him quickly."

"They're here," Ramón said. "The eaters-of-the-young. Those are their ships overhead. What if they're watching? What if they *see* you?"

Maneck seemed to hesitate, but it might only have been Ramón's overwhelming desire that made it seem so. The alien head bobbed.

"They do that, you know," Ramón went on. "They have sensors. Eyes. Last time they came through, the governor asked them to help find a kid that got lost out on the *tierra hueso*. And they did it. Took them a couple hours, and they told us exactly where the little *pendejo* was. How do you know they're not watching me right now? Tracking me because of that man I killed? You go out there where they can see you and kill him, they'll see the energy blast. And you think they'll mistake that for a tree falling or something? They'll *know*."

It was the purest line of bullshit Ramón had ever spun. Maneck wouldn't need to fire an energy blast to kill the other man, not with a fucking attack *chupacabra* on a leash, ready to do whatever it was told. For that matter, Maneck was strong enough to wring the man's neck like a chicken's with its bare hands without any other help at all. But he didn't have the leash in his neck to tell Maneck what his intentions were anymore, or help it judge when he was lying.

If the alien didn't believe him, the worst it could do was kill him. He waited, chest thrust out like he was spoiling for a fight. Maneck shifted its body from side to side. The *chupacabra* whined.

"What better course do you recommend?" Maneck asked.

"You let me go back to him," Ramón said. "You stay right here. You get it? Right here. I'll think of a reason for him to come back with me here. Under the trees where they won't see you, get it? Then you can correct whatever fucking illusion you want."

Because, he didn't say, we'll be on that raft again and out of here while you're still standing around like the ugly girl at a dance. Maneck was quiet and still as stone for the length of three slow breaths.

"Why would you do this?" the alien asked at last.

"It's my *tatecreude,* monster. I'm supposed to help you track him down, right? Well here I am. Helping."

"No," Maneck said, and its voice seemed almost relieved. "Your function was to behave as the man would. You are attempting deceit."

"So what do you think the *man* would do then?" Ramón demanded, the despair blooming in his chest, expressing itself in rage. "I'm trying to save my own skin. You think he wouldn't give up fucking anyone to help himself out?"

"No," the alien said. "He would not. You have performed your function, I must now—"

The shriek was high and squeaked at the end, like a little girl's cry of alarm or delight. All eyes—Ramón's, Maneck's, the *chupacabra*'s—shifted. The man stood in the path behind Ramón. His face was pale and bloodless as marble.

"This is in accordance," Maneck said. "The flow brings him down the specific path. You are sometimes excellent creatures. I suspect it is your ignorance that . . . the man? Where is he going? You will restrain him! You will do so immediately!"

"Stay there! Stay there! Stay there!" Ramón shouted over his shoulder as he bolted off after the other man. The alien likely wouldn't remain where it was, but even if it only

paused for a moment, it was a moment more than they'd
had. As soon as he thought Maneck could no longer hear
him, he turned all his energy and attention to just running.
If they could get to the raft, get out onto the river, they could
still outpace the bastard. They could still get away. If only
Ramón hadn't built a lean-to. If the *pinche* river could have
kept its waterfalls to itself. If anything that had made them
pause in the journey hadn't happened, Ramón wouldn't have
been crashing through the forest, lifting his legs high to
clear brush and roots and stones, the alien and its new pet
chupacabra close behind. He found himself calling out to
the man, his twin, who was already so far ahead that Ramón
couldn't see him.

"Go!" he shouted. "Run! Go, you bastard!"

If he could just reach the river . . .

Ramón reached the river. The water was fierce and the
roar of the cataract louder than he remembered it. The other
man was nowhere Ramón could see, and where the raft had
been, deep muddy furrows angled down the bank. It took a
moment for him to believe it. Powered by mortal fear, desperation, and panic, the other man had somehow managed to
launch the raft by himself, something Ramón wouldn't have
believed possible. He ran out, his feet sinking into the mud,
cold water soaking his knees and thighs. There, five meters
out from the bank and ten or more from where he stood, the
raft bobbed on the rushing water, his twin crouched at the
helm. Ramón could see his wide, fear-rounded eyes.

"Stop!" he shouted. "Get back here! Stop!"

The man on the raft waved; a wide, frantic gesture that
carried no meaning. Ramón spat out a stream of invective,
wading uncertainly out into the water. When he looked over
his shoulder, Maneck and the *chupacabra* were just coming
into sight, slowed only slightly by the cumbersome leash
and Maneck's wounds. Ramón lifted a hand to the alien, his
palm out; a gesture that was intended to mean "It's okay, I've
got it." And then, before waiting for the alien's response, he
took a deep breath and dove. His robe soaked through in an
instant, but he didn't stop to shed it. Under the water's surface, the river seemed misty—tiny bubbles from the cataract

and floating silt conspired to hide anything at more than a meter's distance. Arms and legs flailing, Ramón struck out for where he thought the raft would be.

The man, like him, was at the mercy of the water, Ramón told himself. They'd be pulled along at the same rate. All he had to do was make up the distance. The turbulence was hard, though, and Ramón felt the water buffeting him as he fought to rise up for air.

"Motherfucker!" he shouted as his head broke the surface, and his mouth filled with water before he could say more. The raft was closer, but not as near as Ramón had hoped. A blast of energy lit the air; Maneck firing from the shore. The man yelped and started working the oar as Ramón took another breath and dove again. Maybe Maneck would hit the sonofabitch and solve Ramón's problems for him.

The cold here was unpleasant, but not the vicious, deadly chill it had been farther upriver. Maybe they were farther south than Ramón had thought. Or maybe there was warmer water from rain swelling the flow, as he'd expected. The water above him glowed twice more as Maneck fired. So at least the raft was still that close. A swirl in the gloom warned him a moment before he struck a wave of powerful turbulence, the water hitting him in the gut with the power of a fist. He lost his air, the bubbles rising awkwardly as he clawed his way after them.

The river was definitely faster. Already, Maneck seemed like a tiny figure on the distant shore. Inexplicably, the *chupacabra* was loping down the bank, free of the *sahael* and running like all the demons of hell were after it. Ramón spat and bobbed, trying to find his twin and the raft. The other man had drawn farther out into the river and was yelling something, his face flushed almost purple and his mouth gaping wide. Ramón couldn't tell if the asshole was yelling at him or at Maneck or at God. Maneck seemed to have given up the shooting match, so Ramón didn't dive again. He broke into a crawl, kicking at the waves, lifted by them. Tossed. Slowly, the raft drew near, and then the river drove them apart and brought them near again. The other man was on his knees now, the oar extended out into the water. He was still shouting. Ramón couldn't yet make out words, but the man's expression was more nearly one of encouragement now.

Too little, too late, cabrón, he thought, but reached for the oar all the same. His fingers grazed it, the coarse grain of the wood feeling improbably solid after struggling in the water. He pushed again, surging forward, catching it in both hands and pulling it close to his body. He felt the tug as the man pulled him in toward the raft, but Ramón let himself hang limp, his arms and legs tingling with exhaustion. Let the little coward sonofabitch do some of the work.

It was less than a minute before the man's hand touched Ramón's shoulder. The raft was right before him. Ramón raised his arm, throwing it onto the laced branches. He pulled, and the other man helped, dragging him up. Ramón lay on the raft's leafy deck, his sodden robe heavy as lead, his lungs working like bellows.

"Fuck!" the other man said. "I thought you weren't going to make it there, *ese.*"

Thanks, Ramón thought but didn't spend the energy to say.

"Bastard sonofabitch tracked us," the man said, returning to the oar and the river. "I thought you said the *chupacabra* killed him."

"I thought it did," Ramón said, sitting up. He belched. It tasted of silt. "Maneck used the *sahael* on the poor fucker. He enslaved it. Never thought I'd feel sorry for a *chupacabra*. Did we get any firewood at all before—"

He looked up at the man, his twin, and saw horror on the familiar face. Ramón blinked, looking back over his shoulder. He expected anything: Maneck walking on the water like some alien Christ, another wall of cataract mist, even the European back from Hell with the Devil at his side. There was nothing. Gray river, stormy sky. Waves with tiny touches of white. He looked back at the man. The oar was forgotten in his hand; his face a mask of fear.

"What?" Ramón said, then looked down. His robe had fallen open. His belly was in the light, the thick, ropy scar livid against the brown of his skin. "Oh. That."

"Jesus Christ," the other whispered. "You're *me*!" He was staring at him in frozen horror.

"Calm down," Ramón said. "I can explain—"

"What are you?" the man shouted. "What the fuck *are* you?"

The man had drawn the knife. Lightning lit the world, flashing from the naked blade. A crackling detonation of thunder. Ramón rose to his feet, unsteady on the tilting raft.

"What the fuck are you?" There was hysteria in the man's voice now. He'd dropped the oar. It was floating away, a prisoner of the river.

"Listen to me! Would you stop being such a little pissant and fucking *listen* to me?" Ramón said. Then, looking at the man's eyes—eyes he'd seen in the mirror his whole life—he sighed. "Fuck it. Never mind."

There was no point. This wasn't a talking fight anymore.

Chapter 23

Two and a half meters by two and a half meters, the space complicated by the fire pit, the lean-to. This was the kind of fight that didn't last long. Ramón pulled off the sodden robe and wound it around one arm, scuttling to get the lean-to between them. Going into a knife fight naked didn't make him happy, but with the full robe wrapped around his forearm, he had something he could block with. And his twin had to hold the blade in his left hand, where Ramón could use his right. They weren't evenly matched. Not close. Ramón was going to lose.

The other man went into a low crouch, the knife at the ready. There was nothing. If there had been some firewood, he might have been able to grab a branch and use it as a club. If the oar hadn't floated off into the darkening gray, he might have used it like a staff.

"You led them here!" the other man shouted.

"I didn't!"

"Lying sack of shit!" the man yelled. "You're one of them. You're a monster!"

"Yes. Yes, I am. And I'm *still* a better man than you."

"Monster!"

Ramón didn't bother to answer. The man had made up his mind. Just the way Ramón would have in his place. The one thing he understood was that there was no reason, no

explanation, no perspective he could bring to this that would
make the ending any different from what it was going to
be.

"You're a fucking coward, you know that?" Ramón said,
hoping to enrage his twin into making a mistake. "You're a
pussy. Elena's a waste of air, and you know it."

"Don't fucking talk about her!"

"You were in *love* with that cook, Lianna. The one you
stole from Martín Casaus. And you don't even have the
fucking balls to say so! You hang on to Elena because you're
scared not to. Because, without her, you know you aren't
part of anything or anyone. You're just some *pendejo* with a
third-class van and some prospecting tools."

Rage flushed the other man's face. Ramón bent his knees,
center of gravity low, ready to dodge in whatever direction
he needed to. Except back. There was no raft left behind
him.

"You don't know shit!"

"I know *everything*. Come on, bitch," Ramón said. "You
want to dance? Fine. Come on. I'll fuck you up and shit you
out."

The man swung wild, the raft rocking with his shifting
weight. Ramón sidestepped and turned, throwing a kick that
connected with empty air. The man swung around in a lower
stance now. They'd done little more than trade places. The
knife was held sideways before him in a defensive block.
The anger had drained out of the other man; his eyes were
slitted and cold. That wasn't good. If he'd been possessed
by fear and blind rage, Ramón would have had a chance. If
the bastard was *thinking,* then Ramón had just become the
European.

The man feinted left and then right, his eyes locked on
Ramón's. Testing him. Ramón danced back, his feet finding
the rough edge of the raft. The man swung, and Ramón dove
into the attack, getting under and past the knife before it
could score him. The raft creaked and bucked, making them
both stumble, but the man was the first to regain his feet.
Another stroke of lightning flashed. Thunder came almost
before the glow had faded. Ramón grinned. His twin did as

well. Whatever else, however bad this was, there was still a certain joy in it.

Under what circumstances do you kill?

When the motherfucker needs to die.

Ramón took a careful swing with his unarmored hand, then dodged quickly when the knife flickered up to block him. The other man thrust low, leaving a shallow cut on Ramón's leg, just above the knee. It was nothing. He forgot about it. They circled awkwardly, Ramón bouncing gently on the balls of his feet. A light rain began, making the ice-root leaves beneath them slick. The other man gathered himself for a rush, the subtle bunching of his shoulders giving his intentions away. Ramón jumped, making the raft shift crazily. The man slipped to one knee, and then rose again immediately.

"You killed him because you thought it would make them like you!" Ramón shouted.

"What?"

"You killed the *pinche* European because you thought all those people in the El Rey would think you were a fucking hero! You're pathetic!"

"Fuck you, monster!" the other man said, and swung. It was what had to happen. Ramón didn't give himself time to think; he jumped forward, letting the blade skate across his ribs, pinning the man's arm against his side. Pain shrieked as the knife touched bone, but the man couldn't pull back to stab again. Ramón used his free hand to grab the man's injured hand and squeeze. His twin grunted with pain and tried to pull back. They wrestled together in a drunken embrace. This close, he could *smell* the other man, a rank, musky, unwashed reek that he found amazingly unpleasant. His breath huffed into Ramón's face like a blast of foul air, stinking of dead meat. Ramón kept the blade arm pinned against his side, but the other man lost his footing, and they slid to the deck together. Rain and river water splashed over them. Something struck the raft, and it spun crazily; there was no oar to stabilize them and no oarsman.

"You shouldn't be alive, you fucking abomination," the man hissed. *"You shouldn't be alive!"*

"The thing is, you don't understand flow," Ramón said, in a strangely conversational tone, as if they were having a beer together in a bar somewhere. "You don't understand what it is to be part of something bigger. And, Ramón, you poor bastard, you aren't ever going to know, either." Then he butted his head into the bridge of his twin's nose. He could feel the bone give way, and the man yelped and pulled back. Ramón stuck with him, and they rolled. The little lean-to dug into Ramón's back and then gave way with a snap. They turned once, both trying to regain their feet; the man refusing to release the knife, Ramón refusing to release his twin. Together, they fell in the water.

Ramón gasped despite himself and earned a throatful of river water. The other thrashed and twisted, and then they were apart, floating. Floating in a bright, flowing river. Ramón noticed the red bloom that came from his side, his blood mixing with the water, becoming a part of it. He was becoming the river.

It would have been easy to let it happen. The living sea called to him, and part of him wanted very much to join it, to become the river completely. But the part of him that was alien remembered the threatened sorrow of *gaesu* and the human part of him refused to be beaten, and together the two parts of himself forced him on. He shifted, and kicked against the flow with all his strength, the heat and blood pouring out of him.

In the raging flow of the river, the one who lived would be the one who found the raft first. He kicked, spiraling in the flow. The water around him was like a veil of pink. His blood. The thought flickered through his mind—*How bad did he get me?*—and was gone. There wasn't time.

He found the raft, a darkness on the water, and swam toward it. In the corner of his eye, he saw the other man flailing. A thick length of vine had come loose from the raft and was snaking its way across the surface. Ramón gritted his teeth and pushed. Now. He could make it there *now*.

He shot up from the water, his arms slamming down on the top of the raft. The other man was to his left, also crawling up, his breath a plume of water and spit. A branch caught on something; Ramón thought it was his robe until he remembered that the cloth was all wrapped around his arm. The wood had caught a flap of his own torn skin. The other man was almost on the raft. Ramón pulled his leg up, his ankle on the top, and pulled, desperately hauling himself up. The loose vine slid past his back, bumping him like a water snake. The rain felt like a thousand tiny blows. And he was up. He was on the raft again. He rolled over, and the man dropped a foot heavily onto Ramón's chest, pinning him.

His twin was breathing like he'd just run a four-minute mile; his hair clung to his scalp like lichen on a stone, and his mouth was a pale grin surrounded by blood from his broken nose. Teeth like yellowed bone. Ramón tried to catch his breath, but the pressure from the man's foot prevented him. He felt the grin on his own face.

"You got something to say before you die, monster?" his twin demanded.

"Sure," Ramón said, then fought to inhale. "You know what? Ramón?"

"What?"

Ramón wheezed out a laugh.

"You don't like yourself very much."

Time took the strangely powerless and dreamlike slowness that accompanies moments of horror and trauma. Ramón took pleasure in tracking the reactions as they made their way across the man's face; surprise followed by confusion, confusion by embarrassment, embarrassment by a rage that towered over Ramón like summer thunderheads dwarfed the mountains, and all of it in less than two beats of his racing heart. The blade drew back, prepared for the strike that would open Ramón's throat. As he raised his arms against it, Ramón thought of the marks on bones and skin that came from dying men's attempts to fend off steel with flesh; this was how those marks were made and there was nothing more he could do now than show whatever imagined coroner ever looked over his mortal remains that he'd put up Hell's own fight.

Ramón was screaming, pure animal rage drowning out fear and the hopelessness of his effort, when the loose vine reared up from the water like a pale serpent; wires sparking and hissing in the place where its head would have been.

The man jumped back. The killing stroke became an awkward parry as the *sahael* lungcd at him. Ramón rolled until he was almost at the raft's edge, then looked up.

The *sahael* had wrapped itself twice around his twin's leg, once around his belly, and was pressing its maw toward the man's neck. Ramón's twin had both hands gripping the *sahael*, struggling to hold it away from himself. The muscles in the man's arms were bulging and quivering; Ramón half expected to hear the bones snap under the strain. It only took a moment to realize that if the man had both hands on his new attacker, he must have dropped the knife.

Yes, there. In the ruins of the lean-to, the blade caught the flash of lightning, and before the thunder could crackle and detonate, Ramón was scrambling forward, hand outstretched. The worn leather grip felt warm in his palm.

The man was shrieking something, the same syllables over and over. It took Ramón a moment to realize that he was saying *kill it kill it kill it kill it*. He didn't pause to think, he simply moved, his body knowing what it intended. He lunged forward, the knife in his right hand, and punched it hard into the man's belly. Then twice more, to be sure. They were pushed together like lovers before Ramón pulled himself away, the man's bearded cheek rasping against his own, the man's breath panting against his face, rich with the earthy smell of decay. For a second, he could feel the man's heart hammering against his own breast. Then he stepped back. The man's face had gone white, his eyes as round as coins. That same look of surprise on his face, the look he'd seen on the European's face; *this can't be happening to me, not to* me. The *sahael*, as if repelled by the blood, dropped from Ramón's twin to land in a coil at their feet.

"*Pinche puto,*" the man said and dropped to his knees. The raft shuddered. Sheeting rain mixed with the blood pouring down the man's face, belly, and legs. Ramón stepped back and squatted. The *sahael* shifted, as if considering each of them in turn, but it made no move to attack. "You're not me," the man gasped. "You're never going to be me! You're a fucking *monster*."

Ramón shrugged, not arguing. "You got anything else you want to say? Talk quick."

His twin blinked as if he was crying, but who could see tears in all the rain?

"I don't want to die!" the other whispered. "Please Jesus, I don't want to die!"

"No one does," Ramón said gently.

His twin's face shifted, hardened. He gathered himself, raised himself up a bit, and spat full in Ramón's face.

"Fuck you, asshole!" the other rasped. "Tell them I died like a man!"

"Better you than me, *cabrón*," Ramón said, ignoring the spittle running down his face.

Chapter 24

Ramón's twin sank down, his eyes focused on the angels, or on whatever it was dying men saw; something Ramón couldn't see, anyway. His mouth went slack, and blood rushed through his lips and down over his chin.

Was there the faintest of tugs as the other died, as whatever bond was between them broke? Or was it just his imagination? It was impossible to say.

Ramón rolled the body to the edge of the raft and pushed it into the water. His twin's corpse bobbed once, twice, and then slid beneath the water. He wiped the dead man's spit from his face with the back of his palm.

The storm was pushing the little raft one way and then another, and Ramón couldn't say how much of his nausea was from the unpredictable spinning and shudders of the craft, how much from the death of his other self, and how much from the loss of his own blood. The *sahael* snaked across the raft, its pale flesh reminding Ramón of a worm now more than a snake. Its wires sparked, but did not turn to him.

"We got a problem, you and me?" he asked, but the alien thing didn't respond. He hadn't known that Maneck could send the *sahael* out to operate on its own; or perhaps Maneck was controlling it from a distance somehow. Either way, it was more versatile than he'd thought. Maneck must have launched it after them as soon as he'd freed the *chupa-cabra* from it.

Ramón let out a long sigh and considered his wounds. The cut across his side was serious, but it hadn't gone so deep that he had to worry about a collapsed lung. That was good. His leg, he discovered, had also been pierced at some point. He remembered something from the beginning of the fight. It was a little hard to recall the details. The wound bled freely, but it was superficial. He'd be fine.

He could feel the adrenaline dissipating. His hands were shaking, the nausea growing worse. He was surprised to find himself weeping, and more surprised than that to find the tears had their source not in exhaustion or fear or even the release that came after a bad fight. The sorrow that possessed him was profound. He mourned his twin; the man he had once been. His brother and more than brother was gone, and gone because he himself had killed him.

Perhaps it had been fated to end this way; the colony had room for only one of them. And so either he or his twin had had to die. His dreams of slipping away, becoming a new man had been just that. Dreams. And now, like the body of the man he'd killed, they slipped away. He was Ramón Espejo. He had always been Ramón Espejo. He had never had a real hope of being anyone else.

He unwrapped the sodden robe from his arm slowly. His awareness of the pain was growing. His pierced side was the most pressing issue. He could hold the robe against it, maybe stanch the bleeding. He wondered whether it would help if he wrung the cloth out first. He tried to guess how far he was from Fiddler's Jump and medical help. And what, he asked himself, would they find when they looked at him? Had Maneck and his people left any surprises for the doctors?

Even awash in his grief and uncertainty and pain, some part of Ramón's mind must have anticipated the attack. It was no more than a flicker in the corner of his vision; the *sahael* lashed out at him, thrusting spearlike. He didn't think. The blade was simply where it needed to be at the instant it needed to be there, the human-made steel impaling the alien flesh just inches below the wires at the thing's head.

Ramón's heart didn't race. He didn't even flinch. He was too tired for that.

The *sahael* let out a long, high whine. A spark blackened the tip of the knife where it protruded through the thing's thin body. Snakelike, the *sahael* thrashed, pulling Ramón one way and then the other with its throes. He drove the blade's tip into a branch, pinning the *sahael* to the wood. The flesh below the blade was pale and thrashing violently. The wires and mucous membrane that had once burrowed into Ramón's neck were lolling like a dead thing.

"If you get back," Ramón said, then forgot what he was doing. His flesh felt as heavy as waterlogged timber. A few breaths later, he remembered. "I did Maneck's job for him, but I'm Ramón Espejo, not someone's goddamn dog. You get back, you tell them that. You and all the rest of them can go fuck yourselves."

If the *sahael* understood him, it gave no sign. Ramón nodded and muttered a string of perfunctory obscenities as he jerked the knife free and shoved the snakelike body off the raft. It sank into the water; only the head was visible as it bobbed away through the rain, first dim, then grayed, then gone. Ramón sat for a moment, the raindrops tapping his back and shoulders. A roll of thunder roused him.

"Sorry, monster," he said to the river. "It's just . . . what it is."

There was too much to do. He had to pull himself together. He was cold. He was seriously injured and losing blood. He'd lost the oar and with it what little steering power he'd had. They'd never gotten any firewood onto the raft and he didn't have anything left to light a fire with anyway, although he'd need to dry off and warm up once the storm passed. His mind whirled back to the cataract and the queer peace that had settled over him when he'd been stuck on the rock. The thought related somehow to the dream of being Maneck and his trip from Earth with the Enye. He had a sense of something profound coming clear, like recognizing a face once known and then forgotten. When he realized he'd fallen asleep and forced his eyes to open again, the rain had stopped, and a wide gold-and-green sunset was lighting the clouds from below. He heard the chiming call of a flock of flapjacks somewhere far above him.

He had to get an oar. Something to steer with in case there was another waterfall or rapids. But he'd hear the roar of it if there was one, and his twin owed him a watch anyway. Let the *pendejo* stay up and keep them safe. Serve the bastard right after he'd blown Ramón off back in the forest. He had wrapped himself in the ruins of the iceroot leaves, the wide fronds reflecting his own body's heat back against him, before he noticed the flaw in that plan, and by then he was too comfortable to care whether he died.

Days passed in fever. Reality and dream, past and future, knotted together. Ramón found himself possessed by the memory of things that could never have happened—flying like a sparrow over the rooftops of Mexico City with a slat of the alien *yunea* in his teeth, Elena weeping like a baby about his death and then fucking Martín Casaus on his grave, trekking through the bush with the raft strapped to his forehead, Maneck and the pale alien in the pit applauding and throwing a celebratory party for him—all hail Ramón Espejo, hero of monsters!—both of them wearing silly cone-shaped party hats and blowing noisemakers. His consciousness vibrated, split, and reformed like a bubble rising through turbulent water. In his rare moments of lucidity, he drank the fresh, clear water of the river and tended as best he could to his wounds. The cut on his ribs was scabbing over, but his leg had the hot, angry look of infection. He would have considered reopening the wound in case there was some foreign body—wood or cloth or Christ alone knew what—that was keeping him from healing, but sometime during his fever dreams, he'd lost the knife—maybe it had washed over the side—and he no longer had anything he could use to operate. One time, when he woke in mid-afternoon, he felt so strong and well, he imagined he might be able to catch a fish to eat. But just going to the raft's edge to drink had exhausted him.

One night Little Girl sailed overhead, but the moon had Elena's face, peering down at him disapprovingly. *I told you a* chupacabra *would get you!* the moon said.

On another night—or was it later the same night?—he saw *La Llorona*, the Crying Woman, walking the riverbank, luminescent in the darkness, wringing her hands and wailing over all the children who had been lost, her grief endless and inconsolable.

Another time, he had caught up on a sandbar and spent the better part of a day wondering how he might get the raft loose in his weakened state before realizing that he was wearing clothes—his shirt, his field jacket—and was therefore still asleep and dreaming. He woke to find the raft still well in the middle of the wide, now placid river.

Most unnerving, though, were the voices in the water. Maneck, his twin, the European, Lianna. Even when he was fully awake, he could hear them in the clicking and murmuring of the water, like a conversation in a nearby room, whose words he could almost make out. Once he thought his twin was screaming, *Madre de Dios,* help me! Help me! Please Jesus, I don't want to die!

The worst was when he heard Maneck laughing.

The small, still part of his mind that could sometimes watch the rest and evaluate it understood all of this. The hallucinations, the burning thirst strong enough to motivate even a man lost in the ruin of his own mind, the swelling and reddening leg. Ramón was in trouble, and there was nothing he could do to save himself. He was too disorganized in his thoughts to manage even the simplest of prayers.

Twice, he felt himself drifting off into a strange twilight sleep. Both times he managed to will himself back to awareness, death retreating perhaps halfway to shore. After all, Ramón Espejo was a tough sonofabitch, and he was Ramón Espejo. Still, when the third time came—as it inevitably would—he didn't think he could pull himself back again.

The Enye ships remained his only companions. No longer hawks. Carrion crows and vultures, they hung in the sky, watching him. Waiting for him to die.

When he heard unfamiliar voices gabbling—high-pitched and excited as monkeys—he thought at first that this was some new phase of his deterioration. It wasn't enough that he imagined voices he knew; now the whole São Paulo colony would escort him down to Hell, babbling in tongues. The fishing boat cutting through the water, moving slow to keep its wake from swamping his raft, was a new dream. The rustproof paint, white and gray but decorated with a rough image of the Virgin, was a nice touch. He wouldn't have thought his mind capable of such lovely detail. He was trying to make the Virgin wink at him when the raft tilted beneath him. A man knelt at his side, his skin as black as tar, his eyes wide with concern.

A Yaqui was too much to hope for, Ramón thought, *but I always thought Jesus would at least look like a* Mexican.

"He's alive!" the man shouted; Spanish had not been his first language, and whoever taught it to him had had a distinct Jamaican accent. "Call Esteban! Hurry! And get me a line!"

Ramón blinked, tried to sit up, and failed. There was a hand on his shoulder, gently pushing him down.

"It's okay, *muchacho,*" the black man said. "It's okay. We've got you. Esteban's the best doctor on the river. We'll get you taken care of. Just don't try to move."

The raft thudded again, shifting on the breast of the water. Something else happened, time skipping like he'd dropped acid, and he was on a stretcher with his robe lying over him like a blanket, rising up the side of the boat. The painted Virgin at his right winked as he went past.

The deck stank of fish guts and hot copper. Ramón craned his head, trying to make out something, anything, that could tell him for certain that this was real and not another artifact of a dying brain. He wet his lips with a sluggish tongue. A woman—fiftyish, gray-haired, with an expression that said nothing could surprise her—sat on the deck beside him. She took him by the wrist and he tried to grasp her. She turned his wooden fingers aside, holding him firmly still as she took his pulse. Overhead, the Enye ships blinked in and out of existence. The woman made a disapproving sound and leaned forward.

It occurred to him for the first time that he'd reached Fiddler's Jump. His first reaction was relief so profound it approached religious awe. His second was an unfocused, suspicious anger that they might steal his raft.

"Hey!" the woman said again. He didn't know how often she'd said it, only that this wasn't the first. "Do you know where you are?"

He opened his mouth, frowning. He had known. Just a moment ago. But it was gone.

"Do you know *who* you are?"

That, at least, was worth a chuckle. She seemed pleased by his reaction.

"I am Ramón Espejo," he said. "And, hand to God, that's all I can tell you."

Part four

Chapter 25

Ramón Espejo awoke floating in a sea of darkness.

The tiny lights—green and orange, red and gold—that blinked or flickered around him illuminated nothing. Ramón tried to sit up, but his body rebelled. Slowly, he became aware of the machines around him, the pain in his flesh. For a muzzy, half-sleeping moment, he was certain that he was back in the strange caverns beneath the mountain, back in the vat where he'd been born, swimming again in that measureless midnight ocean. He must have cried out, because he heard the soft, fast sound of human footsteps, and a cheap white LED light blinked on. He tried to lift his arm against the sudden brightness, but he found himself tangled in the thin tubes that were penetrating his flesh like a half-dozen *sahaels*. And then there were hands on his wrists—human hands—guiding him back down to the bed.

"It's okay, Señor Espejo. It's all right."

The man had to be near fifty, short gray hair in tight curls and a smile that looked like the aftermath of sorrow. He wore a nurse's smock. Ramón squinted, trying to see him better. Trying to see the room better.

"You know where you are, sir?"

"Fiddler's Jump," Ramón said, surprised by the gravel in his voice.

"Good guess," the nurse said. "They brought you down

from there about a week ago. You want another try? You know what this building is?"

"Hospital," Ramón said.

The nurse turned to look at him more directly. It was as if he'd said something interesting.

"You know why you're here?"

"I got fucked up," Ramón said. "I was on a raft. I was prospecting up north. Things went bad on me."

"That's pretty good. Up to now you've been saying that you were swimming under water, hiding from baby killers. You keep this up, I'm telling the doctors that you're oriented."

"Diegotown. I'm in Diegotown?"

"Have been for days," the nurse said. Ramón shook his head, vaguely surprised to find an oxygen tube stuck under his nose and hissing softly. He reached up and started to pull it off.

"Señor Espejo, don't . . . you shouldn't take that off, sir."

"I gotta get out of here," Ramón said. "I can't stay in here."

The man took his wrist, his grip at the friction point between reassuring and painful. His gaze locked with Ramón's. He was beautiful, just for being a real person and not some kind of alien, he was beautiful.

"There's no point, Señor Espejo. The constabulary's already been by here twice. If you try to go, I have to call security. And you can't outrun them."

"You don't know that," Ramón said. "I'm a tough sonofabitch."

The man smiled, maybe a little sadly.

"We got a catheter running up your cock, Señor Espejo. It's what you've been peeing out of. I've seen men try to pull it out. You'd wind up with a piss tube about as wide as your little finger. You know, until it scars over."

Ramón looked down. The nurse nodded.

"You're gonna be here awhile, Ramón. Try to relax and heal up. I'll bring you some fruit gel. You should try to eat a little. Okay?"

Ramón rubbed a hand over his face. His beard was thick and wiry, the way it had always been.

"Yeah," he said. "Okay."

The nurse patted his leg sympathetically. He'd probably known a lot of men in his care who had been visited by the constabulary. He might know what was coming better than Ramón did.

Ramón lay back against the thin hospital pillow, prepared for a long, anxious night, and fell asleep again before he knew he was fading. He woke to the cool light of morning pressing at the windows. He tried to watch a newsfeed, but the cheerful nattering voice of the anchor annoyed him. He made do with the quiet hum of the machines, the distant chiming alarms. He cataloged the aches in his body and wondered what he was going to do.

At the start, it had been simple—get out of town until the Enye came and went and the whole thing with the European had blown over. And then get free, get back, and raise hell over Maneck and its hive in the north. Then get back and remake himself, maybe leave his twin to figure out the whole problem with the police. And now here he was, back in Diegotown, tied down by his penis, and waiting for the constabulary to arrive. Made the *sahael* seem dignified.

Outside, the city was alive with morning traffic. Vans and transport flyers filled the air, catching the light of the rising sun and reflecting it back into Ramón's eyes like waves flashing on water. The low throb of a shuttle's lift drive announced some traffic sliding up through the thin air to the ships hovering above. Ramón couldn't see the spaceport from his window, but he knew the sound the way men in ages past had known the wail of trains.

The knock on his doorframe was soft and polite. It said *I don't have to intimidate you. I don't give a shit if you're scared of me or not. That's how much I own your sad ass.* Ramón looked over. The man wore the dark uniform of the governor's constabulary. Ramón lifted a hand in greeting, trailing the IV tube like seaweed.

The man who came in was young and strong. Wide through the shoulders, strong jaw freshly shaved, with still just a shadow of stubble. He was the man Ramón had imagined chasing him up in the north before he'd known about his twin, the man Ramón had pretended to be when he was on the river. He was a convenient fiction made flesh.

"You look a lot better, Señor Espejo," the constable said. "Do you remember speaking with me before?"

Ramón plucked at the plastic weave of his hospital gown. Whatever he'd said before didn't count. He'd been out of his *pinche* mind. If his story didn't match, he could say he'd been dreaming or something, so nothing before counted.

"Sorry, *ese*. I've been a little fucked up, you know?"

"Yes," the constable said. "That's why I wanted to speak with you. Do you mind?"

Like the fucker would go away if he refused. Ramón shrugged, added another little pain to his list of injuries, and gestured toward the small plastic chair beside the hospital bed. The constable nodded his imitation of thanks and sat on the foot of the bed instead, his weight pulling the mattress toward him.

"I was wondering what exactly happened."

"You mean?" Ramón gestured at his ruin of a body. The constable nodded.

"I got fucked up," Ramón said. "I went out surveying up north. That's what I do."

"I know."

"Yeah. Well. Anyway, I was up there, and I landed my van at the river, right by this overhang. I figured it was like shelter, right? So, middle of the night, the fucking thing gives out. Must have been three, four tons of rock. Knocks my van right into the river."

Ramón slapped his palms together, the needle in his arm tugging at his flesh in a way that was disconcertingly familiar.

"I was lucky to get out alive," he said. The constable smiled coolly.

"You got in a fight?"

Ramón felt his chest tighten. The heart monitor to his left betrayed him, the blue LED numbers jumping to something just shy of a hundred. The constable almost suppressed a smile.

"I don't know what you're talking about," Ramón said. "I thought you were here about the accident."

"The 'accident' left knife wounds in your side and your leg," the constable said. "Why don't you tell me about that."

"Oh, shit. That?" Ramón said and laughed. "No, man. That's my own dumb fault. I had my knife, out of the field kit. Used to make the raft. Anyway, I was trying to cut some vines, and I slipped. Fell right on it. I thought I was dead, you know?"

"So. No fighting?"

"Who's out there to fight with?" Ramón said. The blue numbers were slipping back down. The constable seemed unfazed.

"I notice that the field pack wasn't among the things recovered with you."

"Maybe it fell off the raft. I'm not so clear on those last couple days out there."

"Can you tell me where your van was when this landslide took it?"

"Nah. It was all logged on the computer. It wasn't the main river though. It was one of the tributaries." There might be a hundred places that would match the description. Proving Ramón was full of shit just got a whole lot harder. The constable looked peeved.

You could tell him the truth, a small voice in the back of Ramón's mind murmured. Tell him about Maneck and the *yunea,* the *sahael,* and the other Ramón. You could even give him proof. You could lead them all right up to that *pinche* mountain and everything under it. They took you prisoner, tortured you, almost got you killed. You don't owe them shit. You've got no reason to lie.

Except that the man was a cop, and Ramón was a killer.

And besides which, fuck him.

The constable coughed, rubbed his chin. The subject was about to change. Ramón took a breath, trying not to do anything that would change the readings on his monitors. No wonder they wanted to question him here and not wait until he could get out.

"Do you know a woman named Justina Montoya?" the constable asked.

Ramón frowned, looking for the trap in the question. He shook his head.

"Don't think so," Ramón said.

"Calls herself Keiko. Maybe you know her by that name. She's the governor's secretary. She was showing the ambassador around. Tour guide."

Ramón thought of the woman at the El Rey, the European's date. The laughing woman. She'd straightened her hair to look Asian. Maybe she would give herself a stupid name too.

"Don't think so, man," Ramón said.

"How about Johnny Joe Cardenas?"

"Shit, man. Everyone knows Johnny Joe."

"He's a friend of yours?"

"He's not anybody's friend. I respect him. Like you respect a redjacket, you know?"

"He doesn't have a very good reputation, does he? I thought it was strange, then, when I heard that he'd gotten in a fight defending Justina Montoya. He's not the sort of man to do something . . . chivalrous like that."

The stink of danger made Ramón's skin crawl.

"Defend her from what?" Ramón asked. "Someone try to rape her?"

"Maybe," the cop said. "Maybe he would have defended her from that, even Johnny Joe. There were a lot of people there who said that the guy she was with was pushing it with her pretty hard. A big shot. Made some remarks. Twisted her arm when she tried to leave or something. And then Johnny Joe got into it. Maybe saved her."

The silence hung between them, pressing. Ramón's neck throbbed where the *sahael* had bound him. The monitors chirped and hummed. He knows, Ramón thought. They grabbed Johnny Joe so they can show the Enye that they're on top of it, and this *pendejo* fucking well *knows* it's a frame. He's waiting for me to fuck up so they can grab me for it instead.

"Weird, all right."

"Why do you think he'd do something like that?" the constable asked. "Put himself in harm's way to protect a woman he didn't even know?"

Come on. Tell me what a hero he was. Tell me how he

defended the weak. Tell yourself what a good man you are,
and maybe in the end, you can even let slip that the big man
was really you and not Johnny Joe. Ramón grinned. There
was a time he might even have fallen for it.

"Man, you can't figure someone like Johnny Joe! You
might as well not try, you know? He's like a whole different
species."

The constable shifted his weight, annoyance flashing in
his eyes.

"Sorry I couldn't help you out," Ramón said. "I sure wish
I knew old Johnny Joe better. You know, so I could help.
But we just didn't hang out together much. Maybe the guy
just pissed him off, you know? Which was never hard to do.
Maybe Johnny Joe just did a good thing for once in his life.
Even a badass like him might not like to see some little girl
getting slapped around, eh? Especially if maybe he had his
eye on her himself." He exchanged level glances with the
cop, who was looking sour. "There anything else? 'Cause
I'm getting kinda tired."

"Maybe later," the constable said. "You were lucky, getting back to Fiddler's Jump. All that happened out there—
the van getting destroyed, hurting yourself with the knife
like that. It's really unbelievable."

Meaning that you don't believe me, Ramón thought. *Well,*
prove *something, and then come see me. Asshole.*

"I'm blessed," Ramón said, nodding like a pious idiot
drunk on incense and communion wine. "Truly blessed.
God ain't done with me yet, you know?"

"No, He's not. You take care, Señor Espejo. I'll be in
touch if there's anything more I need to ask you."

"Anything I can do to help," Ramón said, almost sorry
that the constable was rising from the bed. Ramón liked the
feel of winning. There were a few more insincere pleasant-
ries exchanged, and then the constable was gone. Ramón lay
back against his pillow and thought his way through it all.

They knew that Johnny Joe, for all his failings as a good
citizen and an upright human being, hadn't killed the European. He was just the convenient bastard to hang, the scape-
goat—and if he was the wrong man, well, shit, at least he

deserved it for some *other* time when he'd killed and gotten away with it. The constable knew it was shit. Hell, the whole colony probably knew it was shit. But what were they gonna do? Tell the Enye that they'd screwed up? That they couldn't even catch the right man? That they'd *lied*? That would be suicide. The investigation was closed. If Ramón didn't open it again for them, and he wasn't about to do that, it would stay closed.

Not that the eaters-of-the-young would care, one way or the other. What humans did among themselves didn't matter, because humanity wasn't a species that the Enye cared about, except where they were useful. Impressing them with the colony's sense of law and justice and righteousness was like a pack of dogs trying to impress their catcher by howling in harmony. But the governor didn't know that, and so, perversely, the way that they all failed to understand the aliens around them was going to save Ramón's ass. He might be the next one strung up when a convenient perpetrator was needed to take the fall for something, but *this* time, for *this* murder, the government of the colony was going to give him a pass. What else could they do?

A weight lifted from him, and he laughed with the relief. His initial plan had worked. He'd been in the wilderness long enough that the problem had solved itself. He was safe now. He could feel it.

It was almost two weeks before Ramón found out what he'd overlooked.

Chapter 26

Ramón walked out of the hospital eight days later, unsteady on atrophied legs. He wore one of his white shirts and a pair of canvas pants that Elena had brought by one afternoon when he was asleep. The shirt was too big; wide across the shoulders and through the chest, a measure of how badly he had been reduced by his time in the wild and on the river. His new scars ached sometimes if he turned wrong. The Enye ships still hovered high above the planet, but here among the street vendors and the gypsy boats, the rheumy-eyed buskers with almost-tuned guitars and the truant children smoking cigarettes on the corners, the alien ships seemed less of a threat.

He'd intended at first to make his way to Manuel Griego's shop. Ramón was going to need a new van. He didn't have the money to buy one outright, and there wasn't a bank on the colony or off that would front him a loan big enough to cover the expense. That left making deals, and Manuel was the one to start with. But his shop was far from the center of the city, at the edge of neighboring Nuevo Janeiro, where most of the Portuguese lived, and Ramón found himself growing tired more quickly than he'd expected. He had no money and only a temporary emergency identification chit from the hospital. More trivia that he'd have to address in the days ahead. At the moment, it meant that when he sat on the bench at the edge of the park, he could smell the sausages, onions, and peppers cooking on the cart's grill but couldn't buy any.

In a sense, this was the first time he'd seen his adopted hometown. This particular pair of eyes had never looked down these narrow brown streets or at the faded yellow grass of the park. These particular ears hadn't heard the demanding blatting of the urban flatfurs, or the *tapanos* scolding from the tree branches on the edge of the canal like amphibious squirrels. Ramón tried to concentrate on how he felt about that, examining his own soul for unease or some sense of dislocation greater than usual. But what he really felt was tired, impatient, and pissed off that he was too weak to walk to where he wanted to, and too broke to take a fucking pedicab or bus.

The obvious place to go was Elena's. He didn't have any place else to sleep, and she'd brought him clothes, so the fight they'd been having when he left was probably forgotten. And she'd have food and maybe sex if he was up for it.

He was half tempted to go to the El Rey first, thank Mikel Ibrahim for keeping that knife away from the police. But then he remembered again that he had no money, and trying to hustle a free beer seemed like a piss-poor way to express gratitude. Ramón took a long, deep breath—nostrils filling with the ozone stench of city air—and heaved himself back up from his bench. Elena's place it was. And with that, Elena.

It wasn't a long walk, but it felt that way. When he reached the butcher's shop that squatted below her apartment, Ramón felt like he'd tracked a full day through the underbrush, Maneck at his side. He wondered, as he made his way up the dingy, dank-smelling stairs, what Maneck would think of this wide, flat human hive that lay open to the sky. He thought the alien would think it naive, like kyi-kyi grazing in a meadow where a *chupacabra* was sunning itself. The Enye ships stuttered in and out of existence high above, vanishing only for a moment before returning.

At the top of the stairs, Ramón punched in the code, hoping that Elena hadn't changed it in a fit of pique when he'd slipped out on her. Or if she had, that she'd changed it back. And when the last number shifted the status light to green, the bolt clicking audibly and the hinges hissing as the door swung open, Ramón knew he'd been forgiven.

Elena wasn't home, but the cabinets were stocked with food. Ramón opened a can of black bean soup—one of the self-heating kind—and ate it with a beer. It tasted of the heating element, but not so much that he didn't enjoy the meal. The couch smelled of old smoke and cheap incense. The afternoon light showed all the dirt on the windows; skitterlings scurried across the ceiling, the charnel stink of the butcher's shop tainted the air. Ramón lay back on the couch, his limbs heavy. He let his eyes close for a moment and opened them again in panic. Something had him, strangling him, pulling him off the ground. Ramón had cocked back a fist, ready to kill the alien or his twin or the *sahael* or the *chupacabra* or the cop before his muzzy brain recognized the shrill squealing. Not an alarm. Not a battle shriek. Elena, delighted.

"Fuck," he breathed, but softly enough that even with her head pressed against his she didn't seem to hear him. The threat of violence passed. Elena pulled back from him, her eyes wide, her mouth in a little knot like she was trying to make her lips look like a baby doll's. She wasn't bad-looking.

"You didn't tell me you were getting out," she said, half accusing, half pleased and surprised.

"They didn't tell me for sure until today," Ramón lied. "Besides, what were you gonna do? Miss work?"

"I would have. Or I could have got someone to come get you. Fly you home."

"I can walk," Ramón said with a shrug. "It's not far."

She put her hand around his chin, jiggling his head like he was a baby. Her eyes were merry. It was an expression he knew, and his poor abused penis stirred slightly.

"Big macho guy like you doesn't need any help, eh? I know you, Ramón Espejo. I know you better than you do! You're not so tough."

I cut off my own finger stump, he didn't say, in part because it hadn't exactly been *him* and in part because there wasn't any point in telling her anything. It was *Elena,* after all. Batshit-crazy, even if she was in her good place right now. He couldn't trust her, not any more than she could trust him. Whatever meaning she attributed to his silence, it wasn't what he was thinking. She smiled, shifting her body from side to side.

"I missed you," she said, looking up at him through her eyelashes. Ramón felt a twinge of pain in his groin and stepped back.

"Jesus Christ," he said. "They only took that thing out of my cock a few days ago, woman. I'm not healed up down there yet."

"Yeah?" she said. "That hurts? What about this?"

She did something very pleasant, and it did hurt, only not enough to tell her to stop.

The next few days were better than Ramón had expected them to be. Elena was away at work most of the day, leaving him to sleep and catch the news. At night, they screwed and listened to music and watched the half-assed *telenovelas* they made down in Nuevo Janeiro. He made himself walk as long as he could, never straying too far from the apartment, in case the weakness came on quickly.

His strength came back faster than he expected. His weight was still down; he looked like a fucking twig. But he was coming back. He was getting better. He told Elena the story—the one he'd made up—over and over. It wasn't long before he half believed it himself. He remembered the roar of the stone as it came down, the shuddering of the van. He remembered racing out into the cool northern night and watching his ride washed into the river. If it hadn't happened, so what? The past was what you made it.

The only thing that marred the time was the small voice in his head reminding him of what had really happened, and what he had heard and thought. In the early hours of the morning, when Elena was still fast asleep, Ramón found himself waking and unable to fall back into slumber. His mind returned to the realization that his twin could have done better with Elena, that even that sad sack of shit he'd dropped into the river had been a better man than he made himself out to be. He had meant to break things off with her when he came back, but here he was. Drinking her beer, smoking her cigarettes, spreading her legs.

When things got bad again, he told himself. *No point ending things when they were still good.*

And, like a ghost, there was Lianna. He remembered the way his twin had told the story—all bravado and bluster, none of the real pain. The loss. He was coming to understand better now why it came out the way it had. It hadn't only been to avoid the appearance of weakness before another man. He needed to tell it to *himself* that way too. And that was harder for Ramón to do now that he had seen all that he'd seen. He kept meaning to go see Griego, but he never quite got around to it.

Almost a week after Ramón had left the hospital, he woke before dawn, haunted by dreams he couldn't remember. He slipped out of bed, pulled on a robe, and, as quietly as he could, took Elena's good whiskey from its hiding place behind the kitchen cabinet. It took him three drinks and almost an hour to get the courage to open a link to the city directory and search for her. But there she was. Lianna Delgado. Still a cook, but at a new place now. Her address was down by the river. He'd probably walked past it a hundred times, stumbling back from the bars. He wondered if she'd ever seen him, and if she had, what she'd thought. Elena mumbled something and shifted in her sleep. Ramón killed the link, but the idea that had taken root out there in the wilderness was growing again in the city.

He had wanted to be someone new, had been ready to be someone new. Start again. So why not now? All the things he had done and suffered could pass away from him just as easily now with his old name and face and self as they might have had his twin lived. It only meant doing the things that needed to be done: leave Elena, find a new place for himself, a new van to work with, some other way of being himself. Himself like he'd always been, only better. And then, when he was cleaned up and solid, when he had something in the bank and didn't have to beg off a woman just to keep from sleeping in the *pinche* park, Lianna was in the directory. He could call her or, if he had the balls, go to her house like a schoolboy singing at his lover's window. He was Ramón Espejo, after all. He was a tough sonofabitch. The worst that would happen was that Lianna would turn him away, and if it broke his heart, so what? He was strong enough to make a new one. A better one.

In the next room, Elena yawned and stretched. Ramón took one last clandestine pull at the whiskey bottle and silently returned it to its place, rinsing the glass out before slipping into the bathroom to brush the scent from his breath. If Elena found out he'd been breaking into the good stuff without her, there'd be hell to pay.

"Hey, baby," he said as she shambled into the kitchen. Her hair was in disarray and her jaw set a little forward.

"You couldn't make some fucking coffee?" she replied. "I feel like shit."

"You should stay home," he said. "Take a day off."

"It's Sunday, asshole."

"Sit," Ramón said, gesturing to the cheap plastic-and-chitin chair at her kitchen table. "I'll make you some food, eh?"

She managed a smile at that, her black mood thinning a little. Ramón surveyed the contents of her pantry carefully, consulting the freshness readouts on the sides of the cans and boxes and having a little trouble with them. He might have had a little too much of the whiskey. He just needed to seem sober long enough for a little of the alcohol to burn off.

He got a can of black beans, a couple of tortillas, some eggs from the back of the refrigerator, and a hunk of cheese. A little green chili, and it would be *huevos rancheros*. It was a good meal because with a little practice it could be made in a single pan. Ramón had enough practice cooking it in his van that he could probably do it even a little drunk.

"So you gonna get a job in town now?" Elena asked.

"No," Ramón said. The beans dropped from their can to one side of the heating skillet, hissing and popping as the juice started to boil. He reached for the eggs. "I figure I'll go talk to Griego about renting a van. I figure if I promise him a part of the cut, it'll only take me three or four good runs to pay the thing off."

"Three or four good runs," Elena said, as if he'd said *shit gold and piss rosewater.* "When was the last time you had three or four good runs in a row? Did you ever?"

"I got some ideas," Ramón said, realizing as he did so that it was true. There was the struggling precursor of a plan at the back of his head. Maybe it had been there since the first time he'd had the dream of the Enye and understood what Maneck and its people were fleeing. He smiled to himself.

He knew what he was going to do.

"You should get a real job," Elena said. "Something steady."

"I don't need that. I'm a good prospector."

Elena raised her hand like a schoolgirl asking to speak. "Last time you went out, you came back three-quarters dead without any of your shit."

"It was bad luck. It won't happen again."

"Oh. You control luck now, eh?"

"It's the European," Ramón said, flipping the eggs. "He was after my ass. It was like a curse. It's gonna be fine next time."

"Sounds like you found God out there," Elena said, and then paused. When she spoke again, her voice was less surly. "Did you find God, *mi hijo*?"

"No," Ramón said. He crumbled a handful of cheese over the beans, then slid the tortillas onto plates. Coffee. He needed to heat up some water. He knew he'd forgotten something. "I figured some other stuff out though."

"Like what?" Elena asked.

Ramón was silent as he served up the eggs, spooned the beans and cheese over the top, got the coffee brewing. He could feel her gaze on him, neither accusing nor sympathetic. He wondered what was going on behind her eyes; what the world meant to her. She was more predictable, more familiar, but in some ways she'd always been as alien to him as Maneck. He didn't trust her because he wasn't stupid, and yet there was something, some other impulse, that prompted him to speak.

"Like why I killed the European in the first place," he said.

He explained to her as best he could, his memory still a thing of shadows and dream, something he remembered knowing more than something he had participated in first-hand. A reconstruction.

They'd been drunk, yes. Things got out of hand, yes. But it had happened for a reason. Ramón walked through it all again. He could explain what the cop had said; the woman, the laughter. He could guess from what his twin had and hadn't said, from what he knew about himself, about the sense of the whole bar turning against the European, and Ramón himself on the top of the swell.

He could tell with certainty what it had been like when, in the alleyway, they had all pulled back, all the people who'd been shouting him on. The sense of loss and betrayal. He'd been what they wanted him to be, and then they'd dropped him for it.

The European, the girl, the laughter. It hadn't really been about them at all. Ramón hadn't killed the man because the fucker needed to die or because the woman was one of their own and the man an outsider, or to protect her from getting mauled. Ramón had done it so that the other people in the bar would think well of him. He'd killed out of a need to be part of something.

Ramón shook his head, smiling. Elena hadn't touched her food. The coffee was warm, the beans cold as the table. Her eyes were locked on his, her expression unreadable. Ramón shrugged, waiting for her to speak.

"You were fighting over a fucking woman?" Elena breathed.

"No," Ramón said. "It wasn't like that. There was this lady he was with but—"

"And you didn't like how he was treating her, so you picked a fight. You drunk, selfish sonofabitch! And what the fuck was wrong with the woman you had *waiting* for you here? You had to go risk getting your ass killed for some *puta* because of what?"

Ramón felt the rage swelling up in his breast. He'd told

her, he'd bared his soul to Elena, and all she could do was turn it into some kind of bullshit jealous fight. He'd been really talking to her, talking like real lovers are supposed to, and this was what he got for it. Another fucking bunch of accusations. Another load of shit. His face flushed, his fists clenched.

But then it faded, the bottom dropping out of the rage. Elena threw her plate at him, the food splattering against the wall, immediately gathering a swarm of skitterlings. Ramón watched it like it was all happening someplace else, to someone else. He'd known, hadn't he? He'd known she wouldn't be able to hear him. That even if he explained himself the best way he could, she wouldn't understand. *If lions could speak,* he remembered Ibrahim saying.

"It's not happening," Ramón said, his voice gentle and matter-of-fact. His calm seemed to startle Elena out of her rage. He saw her trying to get it back, and rose to his feet. "You're not a bad person, Elena. You're a little crazy, but I don't see how anyone lives in this fucking city all the time without getting a little crazy. But this . . ."

He gestured at the food dripping down the wall, Elena's small hands curled tightly into fists, the apartment. He gestured at their life together.

"This isn't going to happen anymore," he said.

Elena tried. She baited him, she screamed. She shouted obscenities at him and taunted him about his sexual inadequacies, all the things she had done before, the familiar, habitual sickness. When it was clear that he was going to leave, she wept and then grew quiet as if she were thinking through a puzzle. She barely raised her head as he closed the door behind him. An hour later, Ramón was walking down the riverside, listening to the music coming off the boats. He had a satchel packed with two changes of clothes, a toothbrush, a few documents that he'd left at her apartment. Everything he owned. The sun shone on the water, and the air was cool with the first bite of autumn. It was like being born again. He had nothing—and yet he couldn't stop smiling. And somewhere nearby, in one of the small apartments with their weedy courtyards and leaking roofs, Lianna was making her life. She wouldn't be that hard to find. And he was a free man.

First, though, there was Manuel Griego and the problem of the van. There was a future to create. And now, he had a plan to do it.

"Ramón Espejo?"

Ramón stopped, looking back over his shoulder. The man looked familiar, but it took the two uniformed brutes coming from the van behind him to give the face and voice context. The man from the constabulary. The cop. Ramón considered running. It was only a few yards to the river; he could dive in before they caught him. But then they could also get boats out and haul him up like the world's ugliest fish. Ramón raised his chin in greeting.

"You're that cop," Ramón said. His mind was racing. Elena. It had to be Elena. She'd called the cops and passed on all he'd told her about the European. Johnny Joe Cardenas had just gotten his prayers answered.

"Ramón Espejo, I have a warrant from the governor for your detainment for questioning. You can come with us of your own free will, or I can put you in restraints. Any way you want."

There was a glitter in the cop's eye, a lilt in his voice. He was having a very good day.

"I didn't do anything," Ramón said.

"You aren't accused, Señor Espejo. We just need to talk to you about something."

The station house was one of the oldest in Diegotown, grown when the first colonists had arrived, and not updated since. Where the chitin superstructure showed, it had become gray with time. The plaster and paint had been freshened for the Enye, but the building still seemed old and sad and brooding, ominous.

The interrogation room wasn't entirely unfamiliar territory for Ramón. Dirty white tiles lined the walls, marred by unidentifiable stains and threatening dents and cracks. A long table set just a little too high, a metal chair bolted to the floor and set just a little too low, so you felt like a kid. The light was too bright, and blued to make anyone look dead.

The air was stale and close and still as the grave; Ramón felt like he'd been breathing the same four lungfuls since he'd entered. There was no clock, no window. Nothing to tell him how far the hours had stretched. His only company had been the uniformed guard who'd told him he couldn't smoke, and the old flat-black surveillance camera set into the wall at the corner of the ceiling. The design was intended to make a man feel small, insignificant, and doomed. It worked pretty well, and Ramón found his resentment of it fueling his anger.

Anger at Elena and the constabulary, the European and the alien hive and his dead twin. It wasn't rational, it wasn't even coherent, but it was what he had to carry him through this, and so he cultivated it. He didn't have money for a lawyer. There would be no one to defend him besides himself. And what defense could he give? That he was so drunk he didn't remember doing it? Elena would be more than happy to flirt with the judge, say what she knew, and sink that story forever. That it was in his own defense? The defense of the straight-haired woman? He couldn't even remember what had happened, not in any real detail. He'd be better off claiming he hadn't been at the El Rey when it happened, no matter what all the witnesses said or the fingerprints on the gravity knife showed.

No, as far as he could tell, he was well and rightly fucked. By the time the door opened and the sound of voices at last cut the thick air, Ramón had just about decided that he might as well assault whatever poor *pendejo* they sent in to talk to him. At least he could do some damage going down. And he might have done it if a human had come into the room.

The Enye was like a boulder; its green-black skin the texture of lichen, oyster-silver eyes set in pale, fleshy, wet gouges. A tiny pucker of a mouth—lipless and round— marked where its beak lay concealed. The stink of acid and soil filled the room as the thing lumbered into the corner below the surveillance camera and hunkered down, its eyes on Ramón. The constable who'd visited him in the hospital and collared him on the street came in behind it. The man was less pleased with himself now, his mouth set in a professional scowl, his shirt freshly starched and ironed and looking uncomfortable. He carried a black cloth case in one hand and a cigarette in the other. A second man followed him; older and better dressed. The poor fucker's boss. Ramón looked up into the black mechanical eye of the camera and wondered who else was watching him.

"Ramón Espejo?" the constable said.

"Better be," Ramón said, then gestured at the alien with his chin. "The fuck is this?"

"We're going to ask you some questions," the constable said. "You are under warrant from the governor to answer completely and honestly. If you fail to do so, you will be charged and punished. Do you understand what I've just said?"

"I been arrested before, *ese*. I know how this works."

"Good," the constable said. "Then we can get straight to business."

He lifted the cloth case to the table, unzipped it, and pulled something out. With a flourish that the *cabrón* must have practiced for an hour, he unrolled something.

Dirty rags, colorless where they weren't bloodstained, cut almost to ribbons in places. They might have once been leather or a thick cloth. It was his robe. The one he'd worn tracking through the northern wilderness, the one he'd wrapped around his arm in the final knife fight with his twin. The one Maneck's aliens had given him. He looked up into the Enye's glistening eyes and saw nothing he could understand. The alien hissed and whistled to itself.

"Señor Espejo," the constable said. "Would you please tell us exactly where you got this?"

Chapter 27

They began God only knew how far away, how many hundreds or thousands—or, with time dilation, shit, maybe millions—of years ago. They came up from some alien sludge under some forgotten star; struggling and fighting and evolving just like humanity rose from small, unlikely mammals dodging the dinosaurs. And then the Silver Enye came, killed their children, and scattered them to the stars. Centuries in the darkness, fleeing blind. One group carried this way, another that. So many lost. And then here, to São Paulo, far to the north where they pulled the mountains up over them like a child with a blanket. Don't let the monsters see me.

So long, and so far, and then to have everything rest on some selfish fuck more than half in trouble with the law. Ramón almost felt sorry for them.

I will kill you all, Ramón had thought, back on that first day, the *sahael* newly dug into his flesh. *Somehow, I will cut this thing out of my throat, and then I will come back and kill you all.*

And now here was his chance. He scratched his arm even though it didn't itch.

"Can I have a cigarette?" he asked.

"Why don't you answer my question first," the constable said, his jaw tense.

He wasn't going to gain anything by lying. Maneck and the aliens had used him. Had created him as a tool, for their own selfish purposes. Turning them over to the Enye would settle his score with them and make him a hero in the governor's eyes, all at the same time. He had every reason to tell them everything. Just the way he'd had every reason to keep to himself in the El Rey. But on the other side of the balance were the *kii,* the young. Killed for no reason that Ramón or Maneck could fathom.

That and the fact he didn't like the idea of dancing to some *pinche* alien's tune, no matter if it was Maneck or the Enye.

"Maybe you could tell me," Ramón said, "what the fuck business it is of yours?"

The constable's boss glanced at the Enye and then the surveillance camera and back. Just a flicker, like a poker player's tell.

"We'd like to know," the constable said.

"The governor wants to know about my fucking bathrobe?" Ramón said. "He gonna have you sniff my panties too? Fuck off."

The Enye spoke. Its voice was high and piping and awkward; a being speaking a language not merely foreign to it but nearly unthinkable.

"Why do you refuse?"

Ramón gestured to the constable with his chin.

"I don't like this motherfucker," Ramón said.

The Enye considered this, its long tongue flickering out to cover its body in saliva. The constable flushed nearly purple with rage, but said nothing. The alien was running the show now, the power shifting visibly. Ramón tried to keep his body relaxed while his thoughts darted and spun. Part of his mind was bright with panic, another part defiant and amused. It was like being in a fight.

He enjoyed it.

"You," the Enye said. "The one called Paul."

The constable took on an attitude of respect just short of clicking his heels. Ramón shook his head in disgust.

"You are removed. Leave. Do not return."

The constable blinked, his mouth gaping for a moment, then audibly closing. He looked at his supervisor, who shrugged and nodded to the door. The constable—Paul—walked out of the interrogation room, stiff as a man with a broom up his ass. Ramón lifted a finger to the remaining human.

"Hey, *ese*," he said. "I get that cigarette now?"

The supervisor was an older man, and his anger had room for amusement at the corners of his eyes. He took a cheap self-lighting cigarette from his pocket, struck it on the floor and rolled it, burning, across the table to Ramón. It smelled like old cardboard and tasted like somebody's ass. Ramón sucked the smoke in deep and let it float out as he spoke.

"It's my bathrobe," Ramón said, pointing with his left hand. "Had it for years. There was this accident with my van. I was sleeping. That's all I got out in. Fucking pain not having shoes, too. I still got blisters."

"Where did it come from?" the Enye fluted.

By now, Ramón had come up with his lie. For short notice, he was proud of it.

"From you," he said.

In the ensuing silence, the supervisor leaned forward a centimeter. His voice was equal parts warm avuncular joking and cold steel threat.

"Don't push it, *hijo*."

The Enye shifted back and forth, its eyes rolling slowly. Its tongue, thankfully, had retreated inside its hidden beak. Ramón knew from his time, years before, that when an Enye stopped licking itself, it was pissed off.

"I got it on the trip over," Ramón said. "From Earth. On an Enye ship. There were a couple of you people wanted to learn how to play poker. We had a game going, so we let them in on it. They sucked. One time I was drunk, I let this one big *pendejo* put this fucking bathrobe in instead of whiskey. He said it was a battle souvenir or some such shit. I didn't catch it all. Anyway, he loses fours and sevens to my three queens, and I got me a bathrobe. It was bigger then. I had to make him cut it down to fit me, but it held up pretty good until now." He paused to take another drag. "So you want to tell me what's so important about it?"

A stench like rotting eggs and boiling turnips filled the room, intense enough to make his eyes water. "This one will be isolated," the Enye said. Its eyes were still on Ramón, but it was clear enough that it was speaking to the supervisor. "There will be no communication."

"We'll see to that, sir," the supervisor said. The Enye turned, and Ramón could see the supervisor brace himself as the alien's tongue emerged and licked the man in farewell. He took it pretty well, Ramón thought. Some trace of Ramón's amusement must have shown through, though. When the Enye lumbered out of the room, the supervisor raised an eyebrow and smiled mirthlessly. Ramón shrugged and finished his cigarette. He had a feeling it would be his last for some time.

Two uniformed cops came in to escort him to his new quarters. The cells under the station house were also not entirely new to Ramón, but this was the first time he'd walked down the gray concrete hallways sober. He caught sight of the supervisor still wiping his neck with a bandana and talking to a tall, intense man whom it took Ramón a moment to recognize as the governor. A third person glanced up as Ramón stepped out of sight—a woman with dark, straight hair. Ramón was sorry, as he descended the stairs, that he hadn't gotten a chance to wave at her. He hadn't seen her since the night at the El Rey.

Down in the cells, the constable was waiting. Ramón could feel the anger coming off the man like heat. His gut went tight, his mouth dry. Ramón's guards stopped him, and the constable stalked forward like a hunting cat.

"I know you're lying," the constable said. "You think you can fool them with some bullshit story about your van going missing? I can smell the shit coming off of you."

"So what the fuck do you think I'm hiding?" Ramón said. "You think it's all part of some big *pinche* plan? I go out, lose everything I own, almost die, and it's all about a *bathrobe*? What have you been huffing, *ese*?"

The constable stepped closer, gaze locked on Ramón. His breath felt unpleasantly warm on Ramón's face. It smelled of peppers and tequila. He was five or six centimeters taller than Ramón, and drew himself up to make the fact clear. Ramón had to fight the instinct to step back, away from the big man's anger.

"I don't know what you're hiding," the cop said. "I don't know why those fucking rock-lickers care. But I do know Johnny Joe Cardenas wasn't the one who killed that ambassador. So how about you tell me what's really going on here?"

"Don't have a clue, man. So how about you get out of my way?"

Something half sneer, half smile twisted the constable's mouth, but he stepped aside. Nodding to one of the guards, he said, "Put him in twelve."

The guard nodded as he pushed Ramón forward. It was like going into a heavy-weather shelter; reinforced concrete and unpainted composite doors and hinges. Ramón let himself be steered to an intersection of corridors, and then down a short hallway. The air was thick and stale. In one of the cells, some poor bastard was crying loud enough for the sound to carry. Ramón tried to shrug it all off, but tension in his gut was cinching tighter and tighter. How long would they hold him here? Who would come to his defense?

He didn't have anyone.

The door to cell twelve swung open silently and Ramón stepped in. It was a small room, but not tiny. Four bunks stood on each side wall, an open hole in the middle of the room serving as the toilet. The light was white LED recessed behind security glass in the ceiling. Someone had scored words into the glass, but it was too bright for Ramón to read it. The door shut, the magnetic bolt closing with a deep clank. A man in one of the lower bunks rolled over to look at him; he was huge. Broad across the shoulders, his scalp covered by cheap tattoos and a thin stubble of black hair going gray at the temples. His eyes were like a dog's. Ramón's balls tried to crawl up into his belly.

"Hey, Johnny Joe," Ramón said.

They took him out before Johnny Joe could quite manage to kill him, half carrying him to another cell. Ramón lay on the concrete floor, feeling himself breathe. His mouth tasted of blood. His ribs ached, and his left eye wouldn't open. He thought a couple of his teeth were loose. The LED in this cell was off, so it was a lot like being in a grave. Or the aliens' tank. He chuckled at the idea, and then at the arcing pain that came from chuckling. There was another thing that laughter could be. Despair. Pain.

To have come so far, to have endured so much, just to wind up rotting in a cell under the station house of the governor's constabulary. And for who? The aliens who'd humiliated and used him? He didn't owe them shit. Maneck and all the motherfuckers like it. Ramón owed them nothing. He didn't remember now why he thought he did. The *kii*, slaughtered by the Enye: they weren't human babies. They didn't matter. If he just *told* them, he could go. He could find Lianna. Maybe send old Martín Casaus a message saying how sorry he was, and that he understood why Martín had tried to kill him. He could sit beside the river and listen to the water slap the stones of the quay. He could get a van again, and go out where there were no people or aliens or jails. All he had to do was tell them.

He levered himself up to his elbows.

"I'll tell," he croaked. "Come on, you *pendejos*. You want to know what's out there, I'll fucking tell you. I'll fucking tell. Just let me go!"

No one heard him. The door didn't open.

"Just let me go."

He fell into an exhausted sleep there on the floor and dreamed that his twin was in the cell with him, smoking a cigarette and bragging about sexual conquests Ramón didn't remember. He tried to yell to the other man that they were in danger, that he had to get away, before recalling that the man was dead. His twin, who had also become Maneck and Palenki, had launched into a lascivious description of fucking the European's companion when Ramón managed to break in, protesting in thought more than words that it had never happened.

"How do you know?" his twin asked. "You weren't there. Who the fuck are you?"

"I'm Ramón Espejo," Ramón shouted, waking himself with the words.

In the darkness, the prison floor harder than mere stone under his back, Ramón shook his head until the last tendrils of nightmare were gone. He forced himself to sit up and take stock of his injuries. They were, he decided, more painful than dangerous. Disgust washed over him—for his weakness, for his willingness to help the police even after they'd done this to him. Maneck and the aliens had collared him like a dog, but they hadn't locked him in with a psychopath just for fun. It took a *human* to do that.

"I'll kill you fuckers," he said to an imagined constable, his supervisor, the governor. "Somehow, I will get free of this, and will kill each one of you sorry *pendejos*!"

Even he wasn't convinced. When the door swung open, he realized he'd fallen asleep again. The supervisor walked in, light from the hall making a halo around him. As Ramón's eyes adjusted to the brightness, he saw resignation and amusement on the man's face.

"You don't look so good, Señor Espejo."

"Yeah. Well, you go ten rounds with Johnny Joe Cardenas, see how you do."

The LED in the ceiling flickered on as the door closed, leaving the two of them alone.

"I'd do fine," the supervisor said. "Hung him this morning. You want a cigarette?"

"Nah," Ramón said. "I'm quitting." Then, a moment later, held out his hand. The supervisor squatted beside Ramón, struck a cigarette against the floor and handed it over.

"Got some food coming too," the man said. "And I'm sorry about Paul. He doesn't do so good when someone embarrasses him. The Enye taking your side with the governor watching? Well, he overreacted."

"That's what you call this, eh?"

The supervisor shrugged like a man who'd spent too many years looking at the world.

"Got to call it something," he said. "They're gonna take your story apart. I'm just saying, Ramón. It's going to happen."

"Why would I lie about my van getting—"

"No one gives a shit about your van. The Enye have been going crazy about this robe. It's some kind of alien artifact."

"That's what I fucking said it was!"

The supervisor let that pass.

"If there's something you're hiding, we're going to find out. The governor's not going to watch out for you. He knows you killed the European ambassador, even if he doesn't want to admit it. The cops . . . well, we can't back you if the governor doesn't. The Enye are hot about this thing, whatever the fuck it is. They'll want us to turn you over to them."

Ramón sucked the smoke deep into his lungs. When he exhaled, he could see where a little draft from the hallway caught the air and spun it. The smoke made the flow visible.

"You're negotiating for them?"

"I'm saying it's gonna be better if you tell them what they want to know. They're the ones who've got all the power."

Ramón rested his head on his knees. A memory assaulted him, the first flashback of its kind in many days—the last, it turned out, he would ever have. It began with laughter. A woman's laughter, fighting its way past the clink and clatter of the pachinko machine. Ramón was in the El Rey. The memory was clear now. The reek of the smoke, the smooth blackness of the bar. He remembered the glass in his hand, the way it clinked when he plunked it with his fingernail. The way the back mirror looked gray from the low lights and the accumulated film of old cigarettes. Music played, but softly. No one had paid to have the speakers turned up loud enough to dance to.

"It's about power," the European said. His voice was too loud. He was drunk, but not as drunk as he pretended. His accent was broad and nasal. "You know what I mean? Not like violence. Not *physical* violence."

The woman beside him glanced around the bar. There were maybe twenty people in the place, and they could all hear the conversation she and her European companion were having. She caught Ramón's eyes reflected in the mirror for a fraction of a second, then looked away and laughed. She neither agreed with the European nor disagreed. He went on as if she had spoken; that her opinion didn't matter proved his point.

"I mean, take *you*," he said, his hand on her arm as if he was pointing it out to her. "You came out with me because you had to. No, no. Don't disagree, it's okay. I'm a man of the world, right. I understand. I'm the traveling big shot, and your boss wants to make sure I'm happy. That gives me power, you see? You came out to this bar with me, didn't you?"

The woman said something, her voice too low to hear, her mouth in a tight smile. It didn't work.

"No, seriously," the man said. "What would you do if I told you to come back to my room with me right now and fuck me? I mean, are you really in a position to say no? You could, right? You could say you didn't want to. But then I'd have you fired. Just like that." He snapped his fingers and grinned coldly.

Ramón sipped his drink. The whiskey seemed watery. But he'd been listening to the European talk for a while now, and the ice in the glass had melted down to ovals like little fingernails.

"Or not even my room," the European said. "The alley, out back. I could take you out there and tell you to take off that little dress, and spread your legs, and, seriously, what could you do about it? Just hypothetically, you know. I'm just saying what if? That's what I mean about power. I have power over you. It's not because I'm a good person and you're a bad one. It's not about morality at all."

His hand dropped from her arm. From where he sat, Ramón guessed that it had found its way to her thigh or maybe even beyond. She was sitting very still now. Still smiling, but the smile was brittle. The pachinko machine had gone quiet. No one else in the bar was talking, but the European didn't take notice. Or maybe he did, and this was the point: that everyone should hear and know. Ramón met Mikel Ibrahim's eyes and tapped the rim of his glass. The barkeeper didn't speak, only poured more liquor in.

"Power is what it's all about." His voice was lower now. There was a bass roll in the words. The woman laughed and pushed back her hair. A nervous gesture. "You understand what I'm saying to you?"

"I do," she said. Her voice was higher. "I really do. But I think it's time that I—"

"Don't get up," the European said. He wasn't asking.

This is shit, someone whispered. Ramón drank his whiskey. It was his fourth. Maybe his fifth. Mikel had his credit information. If he'd been out of money, Mikel would have kicked him out. Ramón placed the empty glass on the bar and deliberately put both hands palm-down and stared at them. If he was too drunk, they wouldn't seem like his own. They seemed like his own. Mostly. He was sober enough. He looked forward and saw himself in the haze of the mirror; he watched himself smile a little. The woman laughed. There was no mirth in the sound. There was fear.

"I want you to say that you understand," the European said, his voice low. "And then I want you to come with me, and show me how much you agree with me."

"Hey, *pendejo,*" Ramón said. "You want power? How about you come outside, and I'll kick your *pinche* ass."

The European looked over, surprised. There was a moment of utter silence, and then the bar was shouting, on its feet, cheering. Ramón saw the moment of fear in the European's eyes, the rage that followed. Ramón adjusted the knife in his sleeve and grinned.

"What have you got to smile about, *hijo*?" the supervisor said.

"I was just thinking about something," Ramón said.

There was a long pause. The supervisor hunched over like they were both prisoners in the same cell.

"You gonna change your story?" he asked.

Ramón took a long draw on his cigarette and sighed slowly, releasing a long, gray plume of smoke. A half-dozen smart-ass comments came to mind. Things he could say to show them he wasn't scared of them or of the aliens for whom they'd made themselves into hunting dogs. In the end, he said simply, "No."

"Your call," the supervisor said.

"I still get the food?"

"Sure. And do yourself a favor. Reconsider. And do it fast. Paul's got an idea how he's going to show the Enye you're full of shit. And if they ask to take you back to their ship, you're gone. And then you're doomed."

"Thanks for the warning," Ramón said.

"De nada," the supervisor said, making it clear by his tone that it really *was* nothing to him. One way or the other.

Chapter 28

Time was a strange thing in the cell. The darkness had left him feeling discarded and forgotten. Now that the LED was on, Ramón had the sense of being scrutinized. The light was unforgiving; it made every squalid stain and scratch and chip in the cell perfectly clear. Ramón considered his wounds and came to the conclusion that while he would ache and piss blood for days, he wouldn't be the last man Johnny Joe Cardenas had killed. He would recover—if the Enye let him.

There were stories, all officially denied, about what happened to men who transgressed against the crews of the transport ships. Ramón had heard his share and believed them—or not, depending on who told them and when and where. Once he'd reached the colony, they had the same status as ghost stories. They were pleasantly frightening and grotesque, but nothing to spend time thinking about. Now, though, he wondered. If they took him, would he hold out?

There wasn't any advantage to him in keeping Maneck's secret if the Enye would wrench it out of him anyway. The slaughter that followed would be the same whether Ramón offered up the information or had it taken from him. Except, of course, to Ramón.

On the other hand, he was a tough sonofabitch. So maybe

he could stand it, even if they tried to break him. No way to know without trying.

Instead of obsessing about it, Ramón attempted to pinpoint the moment when he'd stopped thinking of Maneck and the aliens beneath the mountain as his enemies. It had to have happened. He had dedicated himself to killing them for the indignities they'd heaped upon him, and now here he was, wondering if he would be strong enough to die to protect them if the need arose. It wasn't a small change of heart, and yet he couldn't say when it had happened. Or why it felt so much like the moment he'd spoken up for the woman in the bar. Or why the prospect of his own torture and death didn't fill him with some greater dread.

But there had been no promise of survival with the European either. He could have died in that alley as easily as he had killed. The result wasn't the point. It was all about being the kind of man who would do the sort of thing he was doing. It was a reason to be, a reason to die a good death, if that's what it meant. And maybe he had a thing for lost causes. Like that guy in the *telenovela*.

And then there were also long stretches when Ramón knew that if anyone had asked at that particular moment, he'd have told them anything. Everything. Just as long as they'd let him *go*. As the hours passed, he came to fix Maneck's chances at maybe sixty-forty against. Depending on what part of its cycle of heroism and cowardice his mind was in when they came, and whether they pissed him off enough that he'd be willing to sacrifice himself out of spite.

When the door opened and the guards stepped in, the supervisor was with them. He'd changed his suit, so Ramón figured at least a day had passed since he'd been hauled into the cell. That seemed plausible.

Once he was shackled, the guards marched him—one before, two behind, and all of them with electric batons out and charged—to a small meeting chamber. It was nicely appointed. None of the slaughterhouse feel that the rest of the station maintained. The Enye from before, or else one enough like it to fool Ramón, stood against one wall, its slick tongue darting contentedly over its body. The governor was there, and, to Ramón's surprise, the woman from the bar. The supervisor had the guards lead Ramón to a chair bolted to the floor and chain him to it. The governor looked at him with a mixture of disgust and shrewd evaluation. The woman glanced at him once, her expression profoundly bored, and turned back to her datapad.

This is all your fucking fault. He projected the thought toward the woman. *If you had stood up for yourself instead of counting on us to do your fighting for you, I wouldn't be in this fucked-up situation.*

"Okay," the governor said, sounding annoyed. "Can we get this over with?"

"They're just getting her into the interrogation room now, sir," the supervisor said.

"Who?" Ramón asked. "What the fuck's going on?"

"What I told you, *hijo,*" the supervisor said. "End of the line."

A wall screen popped once and then hummed to life. The hellish little interrogation room came into being, canted at a disturbing angle. He could see the back of the constable's head and the place where the man was just starting to bald. Across from him, Elena was looking annoyed and fidgeting with a cigarette. Ramón coughed.

"Hey! Hey, wait. No fucking way. No way! I just broke it off with her. She's fucking *loca*! You can't believe a thing she says!"

The governor shot a glance at the supervisor. The Enye's wet oyster eyes seemed to flicker as it considered Ramón. The woman pretended she hadn't heard him.

"Señor Espejo," the supervisor said. "Extradition hearing needs the governor, a representative of the foreign power, a representative of the police, and the accused. That's you. Doesn't say a goddamn thing about the accused getting to talk. With all due respect for your rights as a citizen, this is your chance to shut the fuck up before I gag you. Okay?"

On the screen, the constable and Elena were going through the motions—stating her name and address, whether she knew Ramón Espejo.

"But she's a liar!" Ramón said, embarrassed to hear the whine in his voice.

"I known that ass-wipe for seven years," Elena said from the screen. "Whenever he comes to town, he stays with me. Eats my food, leaves his crap on my floor. I even washed his *pinche* clothes, you believe that? I got a good job, and I'm spending my time off-shift making sure that slack-ass *cabrón* has clean socks!"

"So you would call your relationship with Señor Espejo an intimate one?"

Elena glanced at the constable, then down at the floor, shrugging.

"I guess," she said. "I mean. Yeah. We were intimate."

"In your time with Señor Espejo—seven years, you said? You washed his laundry often?"

"Sure," Elena said.

"She never—" Ramón began. The supervisor shook his head once—left, right, stop—with a sense of threat that made Ramón go quiet.

"And in that time," the constable said, "did you ever come across this garment?"

With a flourish, he produced the robe. Ramón looked over at the Enye. Its gaze was on the screen, its tongue moving restlessly, darting in and out of its mouth, the fringe of chartreuse cilia that lined its body squirming like worms.

I've got to tell them, Ramón thought. *For fuck's sake, I got to tell them now before they give me to that thing.* Secondhand visions danced through his mind—the Silver Enye on their path of slaughter. What methods would they devise to wring information from a human? All he had to do was talk, say a few words, and condemn Maneck's people to death. How fucking hard could that be?

"That rag? All the time," Elena said. "Leaves it on the floor of the fucking bathroom whenever he takes a shower. And you know why? Because he thinks I'm his goddamn maid! *Pendejo.* I'll tell you what, I'm way better off without him. Kicking his ass out was the best thing I ever did!"

Ramón's panic had deafened him, so it took a moment before the meaning of her words came to him. He turned to the screen, his jaw slack. In the interrogation room, silence stretched. The constable's mouth moved as if he were speaking, but no words escaped. Elena scratched herself indelicately. Ramón's head spun. It was bullshit. Elena *couldn't* have seen this robe, not even after he'd come back from the hospital. She was lying, and lying in just the right way to save his sorry ass. He couldn't understand it.

"Are you *sure* of that?" the constable asked. His voice sounded a little strangled. "Please take a very close look at this. You're sure you've seen this particular piece of clothing?"

"Yeah," Elena said.

"But in your deposition, you said that Señor Espejo doesn't own a robe."

"That's not a robe," Elena said. "Robe is like, down-to-your-ankles long. That would only go to just under his knee. It's more like a smock."

"And this smock . . ." the constable said, then trailed off. Ramón almost felt sorry for the little shit. What was there left for him to say?

"He's had it since I met him," Elena said. "I kept telling him to throw the fucking shabby thing out, but did he ever listen to me? Never. Never once, about anything. *Pinche* motherfucker."

"Ah," the constable said. And then, hopelessly, "You're sure?"

"Do I *look* stupid?" Elena asked, frowning.

A sense of unreality washed over him. Someone had gotten to her. Someone had gotten to Elena between the time she gave her deposition and now, and coached her on how to pull Ramón's sorry balls out of the fire. He wondered how much it had cost. Knowing Elena, probably a fair amount. He didn't let himself laugh, but the relief was like taking a drink of the best whiskey he'd ever had. Better, maybe.

Standing beside the governor, the straight-haired woman looked over at him, her face empty of any expression.

The problem with aliens, Ramón realized, was that they could never truly understand all the subtle ways that humans could communicate with humans. A hundred years of talking, and Ramón would never have been able to explain to anyone else how exactly the woman raising her chin a few millimeters meant "you're welcome" and "thank you" and "we're even" all at the same time. Ramón imagined the European's soul, trapped somewhere in Hell, keening his anger as Ramón escaped.

On screen, the constable limped through a few more pointless questions and then closed the interrogation. The governor tapped at his datapad once, and the wall-screen image faded. Ramón rubbed his hand against his thigh, trying to hide his elation by feigning impatience and rage.

"So you still want to gag me, *pendejo*?" Ramón asked. "I don't mean to be, you know, unreasonable or anything. But now that you fuckers have locked me up, kicked the shit out of me, and tried to hand me over to that great glob of snot over there, can someone unlock these fucking shackles so I can go talk to a lawyer about how much I can sue you for?"

"His account is consistent," the Enye piped. "He is of no interest."

Never in his life had Ramón been so thoroughly pleased to be of no interest. The governor, his assistant, and the Enye all left while Ramón was being processed out. The supervisor went through the forms and procedures with a bored efficiency; only his continued presence indicated that he wanted to be sure nothing else about all this went wrong. Within an hour, Ramón stepped onto the street, worse for wear but grinning all the same. He paused to spit on the ground at the base of the station-house stairs, then strode out into the city, making it almost half a block before he realized that he had nowhere to go.

He had been on his way to find Lianna and create some kind of new life for himself. He was maybe two hours' walk from there now, still with the wristband identification they used when he was in custody, bruised and beaten from his time with Johnny Joe, and not feeling up to a long walk anyway. He kept moving until he found a public square— a sad little plot of dirt in the shadow of an administrative complex. He sat on a bench; just for a few minutes, though. He didn't want the police to hassle him, and he figured he looked like a bum.

A bum. Without a place of his own. Without a job. He had nothing, only a half-baked plan to rebuild himself and

a secret he couldn't tell anyone. High above, the Enye ships
flickered, their forms dimmed by the haze of smoke that
squatted over the city. The sun would set soon, and the few
stars that could struggle against the city lights would come
out. Ramón shoved his hands in his pockets.

Lianna seemed like a dream now. An idea he'd had when
he was drunk only to find it nonsense when sobriety returned. He tried to imagine what he would say to her, how
he would explain that the beaten-up, penniless prospector
without a van or even a place to sleep was someone who had
worth. Never mind that he'd just gotten out of the station-
house jail and probably smelled like it. Never mind that he'd
just become the new Johnny Joe, first on the list of usual
suspects to be rounded up the next time the governor needed
someone to take the fall for some inconveniently unsolvable
crime. He knew what Lianna would see when she looked at
him.

She'd see Ramón Espejo.

It was still twilight when he reached the butcher's shop. It
had been closed for hours, metal bars hugging the door and
windows. He took the side stairs up. There were lights on in
Elena's apartment. He stood in the gloom at the top of the
stairs for a long time. There were cats in the alley—another
species imported from Earth. Lizards skittered up the wall
and took wing. The scent of old blood rotting in the alley
mixed with the wood smoke and van exhaust; the odor of
Diegotown was acrid and familiar. The tension in his shoulders and gut was also familiar. Up in the night sky, Big Girl
was peeking out from behind the high clouds. The boom and
blare of distant music.

He knocked.

When she opened the door, he could see the question in
her eyes. There were any number of reasons he might have
come. To say thank you. To get some of the shit he'd forgotten and leave again. To stay. Each one had a different greeting to match it, and she wasn't sure which to use. He wasn't
either.

"Hey," he said.

"You look like shit," she said. "The cops do that?"

"Get their fucking hands dirty? No, they had a guy do it for them."

Elena crossed her arms over her breasts. She hadn't stood aside—afraid, he guessed, that he wouldn't accept the invitation.

"You give as good as you got?" she asked.

"He's dead," Ramón said. "I didn't kill him, so I'm not in trouble or any shit like that. But he was there because of me, and they killed him. I figure that means I won."

"Tough *cabrón,*" Elena said, half mocking, but only half. "Dangerous to cross."

An orbital shuttle throbbed up into the night. Ramón smiled; it hurt a little, around his eye. Elena looked down, smiled shyly at his knees, and stepped back. He went inside, closing the door behind him. She'd made rice gumbo. It was the kind of dish she could tell herself she made so she could eat the leftovers through the week. Or it could be meant to feed two. Ramón sat at the table and let her serve him a bowl.

"You were good," he said. "With the cops, I mean. That thing about how it's a smock?"

"You liked that?" Elena asked. "That was my idea."

"It was good," Ramón said. "Only thing was, with the camera like that, I couldn't see his face."

Elena grinned, made a bowl for herself and sat down. The atmosphere surrounding them seemed as fragile as blown glass. Ramón cleared his throat, but didn't have any words to follow up with, so he took a mouthful of gumbo. It wasn't very good.

"That rich lady," Elena said. "The one who came and talked to me? She was the one at the El Rey?"

"Yeah," Ramón said. "That was her."

"She seemed okay."

"I don't know. I never talked to her."

Elena's eyes narrowed, her lips thinned. Ramón felt the distrust emanating from her like heat. He shook his head.

"No shit," he said. "She never said a fucking word to me. I only ever heard her name because one of the cops said it."

"You got in a knife fight with a guy over some woman

you never even talked to?" Elena's voice was incredulous but not angry.

"Well. *He* didn't know it was a knife fight," Ramón said.

"You're fucking crazy," she said.

Ramón laughed. Elena laughed with him. The fragile moment passed; the fight they'd had was just another fight now. One of a thousand before and a thousand still to come, too insignificant to remember. He reached out and took her hand.

"I'm glad you came back," she said.

"I fit here," he said. "I thought for a while I was someone else, but this is where I am, you know? To be Ramón and not Ramón is *aubre*."

"What's that mean?"

"Damned if I know," Ramón said through a grin. "It's just something a friend of mine used to say."

Chapter 29

It was a crisp clear day in Octember. The van's lift tubes whined, and one of the rear pair lost power sometimes. If Ramón didn't keep an eye on it, he'd wind up flying in a long, slow circle, the *terreno cimarrón* below him going on until his fuel cells ran down. It was especially a pain in the ass because the winter night fell early this far north, and he would have liked to put the van on autopilot and get a little sleep. Instead, he stayed humped over the bullshit instrument panel running diagnostics and telling himself that his days of fifth-rate rented vans were going to end. Just four or five good trips in a row. And after this trip, four or five good runs should be easy.

The Enye had remained parked above São Paulo for two months, shuttles rising into the sky and dropping back down, sometimes as often as a dozen times a day. As the weeks went by, Ramón had found it harder and harder to stay in the city. Once his latest set of wounds had more or less healed, the impulse to get out of the city and into the wild returned. His patience with the people around him grew shorter and shorter. And to make things worse, he didn't dare get drunk.

The police were making it quite clear that they had their eyes on Ramón. He couldn't go to the store without seeing someone in a uniform lurking nearby. On the few occasions

he did go into a bar, a constable always seemed to material-
ize a few minutes later. Twice, he got pulled in for questioning over some petty crime he'd had nothing to do with. Both
times he'd had alibis that even the police couldn't deny. But
it was clear enough. They wanted him out, and he wanted to
oblige them. He would have, if he had any money.

Instead, he stayed at home and drank a little of Elena's
whiskey. When he got a little buzzed, he'd get on her link
and snoop through the records and boards for answers to
idle questions. It was how he learned that Martín Casaus
had died three years before in a wreck, that Lianna was mar-
ried and had a kid. It was where he discovered that the European's name had been Dorian Andres, and that the trade
agreements he'd been working to broker—agreements that
wouldn't be signed in this generation or the next—were
being sent back to Europa in hopes that the process wouldn't
have to be postponed for another hundred or thousand years,
followed up by the children of children whose parents hadn't
yet been born. Space was too large for these things to mean
as much as the politicians wanted them to.

And it was where he discovered that the Silver Enye were
moving on. The eaters-of-the-young had finished trading,
and they were heading out to the next colony. Searching for
their prey, though no woman or man on the planet knew that
besides himself. The afternoon they were scheduled to go,
there was another big carnival downtown in their honor, but
instead of attending, Ramón got a couple beers, crawled up
onto the roof of Elena's apartment by himself, and watched
the ships go. When the last light of their drives had faded
from the deep blue sky, Ramón flipped them off. Fucking
pendejos!

Elena kicked him out about the time of the first snow, but
even that was strange. The way it used to be, he would have
done something, she would have got pissed, and they'd have
ended throwing punches and plates. Instead, one morning
Elena looked at him, shook her head, and told him it was
time for him to go before he did something stupid. It had
been like that ever since she'd saved his ass with the police.
They still fought, they still yelled, but when it was something important, it was just a statement. *The beans are cold.*

That shirt's not clean. It's time for you to go before you do something stupid. The plan Ramón had been working on was as close to ready as it was ever going to be, and the call of the open sky was getting louder in his heart every day. She was right. He needed to get out for a while. And then, when the city and the people and the lingering threat of the Enye were out of his system, he would need to come back.

Griego had been a hardass about the whole thing, pressing Ramón about why he didn't have better insurance on his last van. Pointing out that Ramón was asking him to trust equipment to a crazy fuck who'd gone out last time with a perfectly good machine and come back naked and three-quarters dead with nothing to show for it. The negotiation had gone on over cans of Griego's beer until they were both drunk off their asses and singing old songs. In the morning, they both remembered they'd made an agreement, but the contract they'd drawn up was half gibberish. It had their signatures on it, though, so Griego had agreed to loan Ramón a van on the understanding that the rental fee would be half of any income that resulted from the run plus depreciation on the van. He was fucking Ramón over, but Ramón didn't care. He wasn't making shit off this run anyway. This was just the first part of the plan. Getting rich came later.

The moons were both out, Big Girl high in the sky while Little Girl was just starting to peek over the horizon. Their cool blue light allowed glimpses of the terrain below. The Océano Tétrico was black as coffee in the darkness, but Ramón knew that the daylight, when it came, would reveal water a deep, lush green. Winter was growing time in the ocean, just the reverse of the land. Something to do with oxygenation levels, but what it meant to him was an endless plain of tiny green waves, the bite of winter air, and the scent of salt and turning tides. He conjured it all now, constructing the world in his mind. His belly had lost that sick feeling since he'd left Diegotown. His mind felt calmer, slower, less like a dog caged in a kennel. It was moments like this that made the difference. The van chimed, and he turned his attention back to the next of the near-infinite small manual corrections flying the thing required.

In a real van and not this half-dead lump of tin, he would

have gone on to the Sierra Hueso in a single jump, but he knew that if he left the panel and tried to bed down, his distrust of the van would keep him awake anyway. Near midnight, he overflew Fiddler's Jump, aimed the van east to the unlogged forests, and circled until he found a little clearing to set down in. The snow was deep enough that it would have been hard work to get the door open, had he intended to go out. But inside the small box, its heating system online and keeping the air warm, it felt like being wrapped in a good wool blanket on a cold night. He curled up on his cot and fell asleep wondering what the difference was between blackmail and extortion.

The plan, once it had finally coalesced, was a simple one. Maneck and its people had been squatting hidden on this planet since long before the colony had begun. They'd chosen the place to hide their hive. They might even have other hives scattered around the planet. He would offer them the trade—share the information they had about the planet's mineral resources, and once he was making enough money to keep it from seeming weird, he'd put stop claims on the land they inhabited, make sure those sites weren't developed, that no other prospectors blundered upon them. In order for that to work, he'd have to be making a lot of stop claims. So he'd have to be making a lot of money. In fact, he'd have to be one of the richest men in the colony, so it was pretty important for Maneck and the others to make sure Ramón got a lot of very rich claims.

The trick, of course, was that he had to tell all this to the aliens so that they'd understand what the deal was, and what the consequences to them would be if they just killed him on the spot rather than listen. He'd recorded it all—times, coordinates, descriptions of the aliens and their relationship to the Enye—then encrypted the file and given it to Mikel Ibrahim to keep in whatever drawer held Ramón's old gravity knife. The man had proven himself capable of keeping a secret. Maybe, when Ramón got rich, he'd hire him as an overseer or something. Regardless, the agreement was that Ramón would come get the data when he was done with this run. If spring came without him, Mikel would hand it over to the cops. Ramón knew intellectually that trusting the aliens'

fate to Griego's fifth-rate van was a shitty thing to do; if
the lift tubes failed or the power cell blew, the aliens would
suffer the same fate as if they'd killed him. But Ramón
hadn't seen any other way to go about it. Plus, if it came
down that way, he'd be dead himself and wouldn't care.

It was a risk, of course. Maybe a big one. There was no
knowing what these bastards would think or do. Stranger
than a *norteamericano,* or even the Japanese. If he couldn't
make them understand about the insurance policy he'd left
behind, they'd probably kill him. Hell, maybe they'd kill him
anyway, even if they did understand. Who could know? But
life was a risk. That was how you knew you were living.

The morning came late that far north, and Ramón had
to cycle through startup three times before the lift tubes all
de-iced the way they were supposed to. It was just shy of
noon before he took to the sky again, skimming over the
snow-laden treetops, watching the ice clouds high over
the mountains, and humming to himself. Off to the west
was the thin silver-white band that was the Río Embudo,
where he'd almost died. Somewhere in that flow—eaten by
fish, his bones washed out to sea—the other Ramón had by
now become part of the world in a way that could never be
undone. Ramón touched his brow in a sign of respect for the
dead. "Better you than me, *cabrón,*" he said again.

He had been afraid that the change of seasons would
have made the discontinuity in the land's face hard to find.
He'd budgeted three days to poke through the mountains,
but he didn't need them. He put the van down in the same
upland meadow where he'd landed so long ago, in another
life, wrapped himself in warm, waterproof clothes, and took
up his new field kit. It took him less than an hour to divine
the shape of the stone beneath the snow, to recognize where
exactly he was and where he wanted to go.

As he trudged through the snow, he pulled the caver's
spike from his pack. It was as long as his forearm with a
tempered, sharp point and a small blasting cap on the end.
Ramón had also brought coring charges, but he didn't want
to take down the whole rock face again if he didn't have
to. When he reached the cliff, he dusted it with his hands,
looking for a likely spot, paused to judge the overhanging

snow—dying in an avalanche would be a stupid way to go, at this point—and set the caver's spike.

It fired off with a sharp, dry report. White-feathered lace crows unfolded themselves awkwardly from the trees, squawking in complaint, and tenfin birds flew up along the slope, crying like grieving women. Hopefully the tip of the spike had driven into the silvery metal of the hive. Ramón remembered what he'd felt like, walking up to that imperfect mirror, seeing his own foggy reflection stumbling toward him out of it.

For a long time, nothing happened. Ramón began to wonder if he'd gotten the wrong place. Or if the spike hadn't gone in far enough. Or if the aliens had abandoned the hive, fleeing to some even more distant corner of the world, or maybe burrowing deeper into it. That would have been just his luck. What if they'd decided that his own escape had constituted *gaesu* after all, and all committed suicide? What if inside the mountain there was nothing but the dead?

But as he began to turn back to the van to get the coring charges, to try again, the snow far above him and off to the left shifted. Great sheets of it crumbled and fell as the stone beneath it irised open. A hole appeared, blacker from being set in the white of winter. And then, with a high-pitched whine like a centrifuge spinning up, a *yunea* emerged, its pale, ropy sides shining the yellow of old ivory. The box hovered for a moment as if considering him.

Ramón waved his arms, trying to catch the thing's attention and also show that he wasn't afraid of it. He'd come there intentionally. The alien craft hovered, shifted one way and then another, as if trying to make sense of him. Ramón, reassured by the alien's hesitation, lit a cigarette and grinned into the cold wind. The slats of the *yunea*'s side thinned, and Ramón saw the alien form within. It was perhaps two meters tall, its skin yellowish with a swirling pattern of black and silver that was scarred in places from old wounds. One of the hot orange eyes had darkened permanently. Ramón smiled at his old friend and captor.

"Hey, monster!" he shouted, his hands cupped around his mouth. "Come on down! Another monster wants to talk to you!"

◀ Afterword ▶

How the story told in *Hunter's Run* arrived at its final form as a novel is itself an epic tale. It relates how a good idea demands its due. The complete process took thirty years.

The birth of the story was an image in the mind of Gardner Dozois: of a man floating in darkness. In thrall to this idea, Gardner needed to know how the man had got there, where he was, what had happened to him. He knew instantly that the man's name was Ramón Espejo and he was mixed-race Hispanic. Before even putting pen to paper (this was 1976) he had worked out many of the plot strands and the extraordinary circumstances of Ramón's existence. So far, so good. A few thousand words later, however typed without margins and single spaced, he stalled. The brief manuscript then spent a year in a drawer, the first but by no means the last or the longest spell it was to spend in limbo.

In 1977, George R. R. Martin invited Gardner to be guest instructor at a summer SF writing workshop in Dubuque, Iowa, at a small Catholic women's college where George was then teaching journalism. The staff room was full of nuns. Worse, they were Secret Nuns—they did not wear their habits—profanity was met by blanching faces and hurried signs of the cross. There was plenty of profanity in the story Gardner took for the workshops: the nascent but very embryonic story of Ramón.

As Gardner recalls, everyone pretty much hated the Ramón story, but George liked it. After another three years in the drawer, Gardner took it out again and asked George to collaborate on it. George retyped the unnumbered, margin-free, single-spaced pages on his fancy Smith Corona electric. Gardner had got Ramón out of the mountain where he was "born" and now George was moving the story down to the river, with Ramón the Clone and Maneck hunting Ramón the Original. This took until the summer of 1981.

As he worked on the story it occurred to George that this could well become a novel: there was a whole alien world, an ecosystem, to discover. The questions of loyalty and identity that formed the thematic heart of the story deserved to be examined in depth, and the river journey was the perfect vehicle for that. He thought of Huck and Tom on the Mississippi and how the epic journey had revealed and defined their characters. He wanted Maneck and Ramón the Clone to experience each other this way, and be transformed, before they caught up with Ramón the Original. Before the Ramóns came face to face. By now, George had come up with the title the story would appear under as a novella: *Shadow Twin*.

George suggested to Gardner that they should between them grow the forty-three-page fragment into a five-hundred-page novel, each taking turns at moving the story forward until they stalled, each revising the work done by the other as they went . . . George sent the fragment back to Gardner in 1982 with a note, "the ball is now in your court."

Shadow Twin lay essentially untouched in a drawer in Gardner's study from 1982 until 2002. It was mentioned in passing, from time to time. It would not be forgotten. Gardner had stalled, true, and stayed stalled for two decades, but then it came to him: if he couldn't move the story on, as he had to before handing it back to George, why not get someone young, dynamic, prolific and very good to galvanize the Ramóns to the next stage. Enter Daniel Abraham.

It was George who explained the situation to the young and enthusiastic Daniel. Daniel entered the typed manuscript on his word processor. George's work on the story had brought it up to 20,000 words. It went up to that point at which Ramón the Clone fell asleep and entered the flow. Daniel reminded himself that his coauthors were barely older than he when they last worked on the story, and so it was a collaboration of three young writers across time, not two venerable and successful authors and one young Turk.

Daniel developed the story of Ramón in Diegotown, bringing him into contact with other people, so that the changes in him are revealed when he returns to the city. He worked on suggestions from George, and a finished novella was in sight. However, being the young Turk, Daniel cut as many words as he added. These Gardner put back in, adding and polishing, newly inspired at last, preserving the color and landscaping of the original.

Author Q & A

Gardner Dozois

1. The alien species in the book are very powerfully imagined and brought to life. Can you talk about how you went about creating their distinctive appearances and how you chose to portray both their physical appearances and their internal lives?

Well, I think the hardest thing to do—the thing that was important—was to make aliens that were as different from humans as possible without being impossible for a humanoid to talk and communicate with it. The Enye, for example, are essentially big boulders, but they still eat and drink, so just biologically, there is some level of similarity.

I suspect if we ever did find alien life, it would be so totally unlike us, there would be no way to communicate meaningfully at all. That's not much use when you want to write about something, though, so there was some compromise about that. A way to make them things we could interact with but not just make them guys with unlikely bumps on their foreheads.

As for Maneck and his aliens, their appearance really comes from a trip to the zoo. There were some African birds—I don't remember the species—but the description of the eyes and the crest on the top of his head came from that. Observation of animals really helps set a basis for that kind of thing.

2. The protagonist Ramón was also your creation. When you started writing the story in the 1970s, how common was it to have a protagonist of explicitly Mexican descent, and how do you think it has changed now that it's being published thirty years later?

One of the big differences is that I made Ramón in the 1970s very stereotypical. I mean, he didn't wear a big sombrero or ride a mule, but he talked like the Cisco Kid. *We* needed to move away from that.

The original idea of the story was that it would be easier to hunt someone if you had their clone. If you knew what someone's psychology was, you could anticipate their moves. Of course that wouldn't work with an actual clone, and we explain in the book that he isn't an actual clone. But I wanted to do something rather unusual with that.

There was an essay by Damon Knight complaining that almost all heroes in science fiction are middle-class white Americans whereas almost no one on Earth is. Or the percentage is so vanishingly small. Damon wrote in that essay "Where is the space hero who is Mexican?" I thought that was a fair question. The only one I could think of offhand who had addressed that was G. C. Edmondson (Jose Mario Garry Ordoex Edmondson y Cotton), who was actually from that cultural background. I didn't know very much about Mexican culture, but it seemed like something close enough that we could write a story without having to do years and years of research. And of course with George living in the southwest, and then later Daniel too, it seemed like an interesting thing to do.

So I started to wonder what a colony would be like if it sprang from South and Central American culture? There would be some similarity, certainly, but there would also be other points.

Since the 1970s, I've gotten a little more direct experience of those cultures. I've spent some time in Barbados and the Caribbean and that gave me a better feel for what a colony that comes from Hispanic culture might be like, especially with the Indian admixture.

3. As both the first and last writer on the project, you saw the story grow from a tiny idea to first a novella and now a full novel. What are the differences you see in this final form as compared to the earlier novella? How did the story itself change?

When we expanded into a novel, we got to get into things that we regretted not having done. We had wanted more interaction—more of a relationship—between Ramón and Manuel. And between Ramón and the other Ramón. In this version, we even get a moment with all three of them. That was missing in the earlier story.

Also in the novella, the ending doesn't leave you sure how he's really going to get out of trouble. We got to deal with the implications of his journey in a much more sophisticated way than we could have in the shorter form, especially since we were coming up on the limit of how long you could write a novella and really have it be commercially viable.

In an ideal world, we could have done even more, but we don't want this to be a six-volume story.

4. Despite, or maybe because of, his failings, Ramón is an Everyman figure: to what extent did you mean for the story to work as a moral tale?

Well, primarily, it's meant to be a good rip-roaring adventure tale. But it's like *Treasures of the Sierra Madre;* anytime you have complex, motivated creatures interacting with each other, there will perforce be a moral you can point to.

Ramón at the beginning of the story is both not as good as he thinks he is and not as bad as he thinks he is. By the end, he's gotten a more realistic appraisal of what his obligations and his abilities are. The Ramón at the end of the story

is a better one—not in a goody-goody way—than the one at
the start.

George R. R. Martin

*1. Speaking as the first person Gardner brought onto the
project, there must have been something in that very early
draft that caught your attention. Could you talk a little about
what attracted you to the idea of collaborating on it? Was it
the particular project or the idea of collaboration itself?*

I read the story several years before I got involved with
writing it. The first time I saw it was in 1977 in the context of
a writer's workshop, and I liked it at the time. I mean, I had
some quibbles and things I wanted to change, but basically
I responded to it well. It drew me in. I wanted to know how
it ended. By the time Gardner came to me—I think it was
1981—it was pretty clear that if I wanted to know, I'd have
to write it myself.

And I also liked the idea of working with Gardner. This
was going back decades, you know. Before he was editor of
Asimov's and before he was doing the *Year's Best* antholo-
gies, Gardner was one of the most interesting new writers of
the 1970s and early 80s. He did some very interesting work.
I'd done a number of other collaborations. With Howard
Waldrop and Lisa Tuttle, for example.

There's a stage in a career where it's useful to collaborate.
Even if you yourself are fairly accomplished, other writers
have other techniques and strategies. You can discuss what
exactly a scene is going to be, but when they go off and actually write it, there are going to be differences in the way you
would have approached it. By working closely, you can see
those techniques, and it makes you a better writer.

*2. From the beginning, you were the one who had the stron-
gest sense that the story deserved to be a novel. Can you
talk about what potential you saw even in the early stages
that gave you that faith?*

In the novella, we had this whole alien world that was hardly explored. Ramón thinks back to the colony and his girlfriend and things like that, but we never really get to see things. The planet wasn't explored in any depth. I wanted to travel through the place more. I thought there was something there.

The river journey was something I brought to the story. I'd just finished writing *Fevre Dream*, and I had been reading a lot of Mark Twain, particularly Huckleberry Finn. And the sense of this journey that the two characters took together and of that travel as a changing event . . . I saw that there was a lot of depth and possibility in that.

The story also evolved a lot of echoes of Ursula Le Guin's *Left Hand of Darkness*. That was another story of two people together on a journey and the kind of exploration that happens there. With Estraven and Genly Ai trapped on the ice, there was a serious exploration of sex and gender, which is one part of being human. With Ramón and Maneck—and then with Ramón and the original Ramón—there were other questions about what it means to be human. I saw the chance to do something similar.

3. It sounds as if you had a pretty clear vision of how the novel would grow out of the earlier versions of the story, but you were also working with two collaborators who no doubt had their own visions and opinions. How closely did the final result come to the potential novel that you imagined?

Well, hindsight colors perceptions. It seems to me now that the outcome is quite similar to what I'd pictured. It's these three characters and all the questions of identity and humanity and what defines them. To go back for a minute to Huck Finn, that was a story about two people on a river where one of them—Nigger Jim—wasn't even defined as human. He was a slave, and the book was, among other things, about Huck's struggling to decide what helping Jim said about him. Could you be a good person and also help an escaped slave? What does it mean to say Jim isn't really human? I think those kinds of questions were what drove the novella first and then the novel.

I mean, all the contributors added certain things, but no one took any hard left turns. We didn't put a bunch of dragons in or anything. I think we all had very similar ends in mind. So I think this is very much the structure I envisioned. I'm very pleased with it.

Putting it into Gardner's universe was actually something that came late in the process, but I think it worked. I think if someone picked up Gardner's novel *Strangers*, they wouldn't see any conflicts with the universe we show in this novel. It was pretty much seamless.

4. In my interview with Gardner, I asked how much he thought Ramón was an Everyman figure, and he said that the story is primarily meant as a rip-roaring adventure. Would you agree with that assessment?

Well, I hope it works as an adventure story, but I think it's more than that. There are a lot of questions that the story asks. What is the protagonist?? Is he an alien? Is he Ramón Espejo? Is he superior to the original Ramón? Does he have the right to kill this other man and take over his life?

The original title of the story was *Shadow Twin*, and I always thought that spoke to the issues in the story. Identical twins have the same genetics, but they're different people. There's the old good twin/evil twin cliché.

The protagonist has human DNA, but he was born in a vat. Maneck and the aliens are his father and mother. And then Gardner had the *sahael* which, I thought, had really creepy umbilical cord overtones. So was the protagonist the human's twin? The alien's?

The book had a lot to say about these deeper issues of what identity is, about what humanity is. I don't see Ramón—the protagonist Ramón, I mean—as an Everyman. He's a particular man. To say Everyman loses something. He's there to stand in for humanity, but he's a very particular human being. People don't like reading about Everyman. They want Raskolnikov or Gully Foyle.

Daniel Abraham

1. You were the last of the writers to come in on the project. How much of the story was in place when you first saw it, and how much influence did you have on the final form of the story?

Well, in a lot of ways, I felt like this was a collaboration with three beginning writers over the course of thirty years. Of the three beginning writers, I was the lucky one, though. I got to consult with older, more experienced folks. They didn't have that resource.

By the time I put hands to it, there were a lot of things already set. The characters, the setting, the plot arc. And even though it hadn't been written, the ending was kind of there. With a good plot, the ending is already being set up at the very start, and I could see as soon as we knew that our guy wasn't really Ramón where this was all going to end.

But that said, I think I had a lot of influence over how we got there. And when the time came to expand into a novel, I was the one who pushed for throwing out the novella and starting again. I thought it would make for a better book; a real, unified piece of work instead of a novella that got padded up. They gave me that, and it was a real concession. I appreciate it.

2. In the novel, Ramón's relationship with other people is very ambiguous, especially with the women in his life. How do those relationships fit in with the character's journey through the wilderness?

Part of the sort of symbolic underpinning of the story is that Ramón when we meet him is about the most alienated man you can picture. Alienated, get it? He hates being around other people. We don't hear about family or close relationships apart from this really dysfunctional lover. The closest thing he has to parents is a rough mentor-figure who died on the journey over from Earth.

The first part of the story—the part that's set in the city

before he goes out and everything falls apart—has a lot to do with seeing Ramón as a violent, unstable, unreliable guy. There's this whole sort of James M. Cain plot about killing a guy and being on the run. As we learn more about the murder and more about Ramón's romantic past, he becomes more human to us as readers. There's a scene on the river when he listens to the original Ramón doing the traditional masculine bluster about a woman Ramón used to be in love with. The way the original man minimizes that story is really sad. It's one of the things that really make the new Ramón who comes back a different person from the one that went out. The heartbreaking thing about Ramón is how much he wants to be a hero, and just can't quite swing it. It's not him.

3. The setting of the novel is, of course, very exotic. How did you come up with an alien world and make it plausible and interesting?

A lot of the credit for that goes to Gardner. He's very into the kind of big, lush, weirdness that makes the wilderness in the novel what it is. I admire it, but it's not something that comes naturally to me. Gardner says I'm more interested in characters and their internal psychological lives. He calls me a modernist, and I think he means it as a compliment about half the time.

To answer the question, though, I think the real power is in the details. The way the flat bird-like things—flapjacks—chime like church bells. The little monkey-lizards jumping from branch to branch with high, frightened voices. Or mundane things like how cold the river is. Even if you don't remember them once you're done reading, it's the kind of thing that puts you in the moment. And I think that's true of any story. I've never been to Victorian England or an FBI crime lab either, but a good writer will use the same techniques to put me there.

4. In my previous interviews, George and Gardner have taken slightly different views of Ramón as an Everyman

*figure. Gardner holds that the book is primarily meant as
an adventure story. George thinks there are deeper philo-
sophical issues. Which perspective do you have?*

Well, I'm a modernist, right? So I think it's a psychological allegory. We've got a guy who has this encounter with
something that's just barely explicable, and it changes him
by making him more authentically himself.

This is the real joy of science fiction and fantasy writing. Or horror. Maybe especially horror. It's all about literal-
ized metaphors. It isn't as if Ramón is driven by forces he
can't understand; he's driven by Maneck and the *sahael*, and
he can't understand them. It isn't as if he meets himself; he
meets himself. It isn't as if he kills his old self. He does. He
kills his old self.

The thing that I think really sets the novel version of
this story above the novella is the ending. In the novella,
Ramón breaks up with Elena and starts making himself
into a good, respectable citizen. In the novel, it's much more
psychologically realistic. He was an alienated, violent monster in the first chapter, and then he went on this journey of
self-discovery. At the end, he's an alienated, violent monster
who's more at peace with that identity. I find that profoundly
satisfying in a way that having him become a traditional
hero figure wouldn't have been.

THE BATTLE FOR
THE FUTURE BEGINS—IN
IAN DOUGLAS's
EXPLOSIVE
HERITAGE TRILOGY

SEMPER MARS
978-0-380-78828-6

LUNA MARINE
978-0-380-78829-3

EUROPA STRIKE
978-0-380-78830-9

AND DON'T MISS
THE LEGACY TRILOGY

STAR CORPS
978-0-380-81824-2

In the future, Earth's warriors have conquered the heavens. But on a distant world, humanity is in chains . . .

BATTLESPACE
978-0-380-81825-9

Whatever waits on the other side of a wormhole must be confronted with stealth, with force, and without fear.

STAR MARINES
978-0-380-81826-6

Planet Earth is lost . . .
but the marines have just begun to fight.